W9-CCZ-694

THE EAGLE & THE NIGHTINGALE

BARDIC VOICES

BOOK III

THE EAGLE & THE NIGHTINGALES

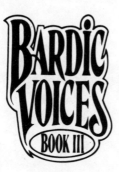

BARDIC VOICES

BOOK III

MERCEDES LACKEY

BAEN

THE EAGLE AND THE NIGHTINGALES

This is a work of fiction. All the characters and events portrayed in this book are fictional, and any resemblance to real people or incidents is purely coincidental.

A Baen Books Original

Baen Publishing Enterprises
P.O. Box 1403
Riverdale, NY 10471

ISBN: 0-671-87636-8

Printed in the United States of America

***Dedicated to**
Gail Gallano,
Mother of all Tulsa wildlife rehabbers!*

CHAPTER ONE

*All the world comes to Kingsford Faire, the Midsummer Faire of
Kings. . . .*

A Gypsy known only as Nightingale sat on a riverside rock on the edge
of the Faire grounds, with the tune of "Faire of the Kings" running
through her head. Not that she liked that particular piece of doggerel, but
it did have one of those annoying tunes that would stick in one's mind for
hours or days.

A light mist hung over the Kanar River, and a meadowlark nearby
added his song to the growing chorus of birds singing from every tree and
bush along the riverbank. The morning air was still, cool, and smelled of
river water with a faint addition of smoke. Sunlight touched the pounded
earth that lately had held a small city made of tents and temporary booths,
then gilded the grey stone of the Cathedral and Cloister walls behind the
area that had been home to the Kingsford Faire for the past several weeks.
Nightingale didn't particularly admire the fortress-like cloister, but examining it was better than looking across the river. She kept her eyes pur-
posefully averted from the ruins of Kingsford on the opposite bank, although she was still painfully aware of the devastation that ended only
where the river itself began. There was no avoiding the fact that Kingsford, as she had known it, was no more. That inescapable fact had lent a
heaviness to her heart that was equally inescapable.

This had been a peculiar year for the annual Kingsford Faire, with
something like half of the city of Kingsford itself in ruins and the rest
heavily damaged by fire.

I am glad that I was not here, but the suffering lingers.

Perhaps other people could forget the suffering of those who had been
robbed of homes, livings and loved ones by that fire, but Nightingale
couldn't, not even with the wooden palisade surrounding the Faire and
row after row of tents between her and the wreckage on the other side of
the river. The pain called out to her, even in the midst of each brightly

dawning midsummer day; it had permeated everything she did since she had arrived and crept into her dreams at night. She would never have used the Sight here, even if she had needed to—she knew she would only see far too many unquiet ghosts, with no means at her disposal to settle them.

She had dreams of the fire that had swept through the city last fall, although she had no way of knowing if her dreams were a true vision of the past or only nightmares reflective of the stories she heard. She'd had one last night, in fact, a dream of waking to find herself surrounded by flames that reached for her with a lifelike hunger.

Such a complete disaster as the fire could not be erased over the course of weeks or months. Even now, with the fire a year past, there were blackened chimneys and beams standing starkly in the midst of ashes, and a taint of smoke still hung in the air.

The Faire *had* been profitable for just about everyone who came this year, herself included. Knowing that the folk of Kingsford would be needing every possible article of daily living, even so many months after the fire, merchants had flocked to the Faire-site across the river with their wagons piled high, their pack-beasts loaded to the groaning point. They had prospered, and they had been generous to those who came to entertain. The Bardic Guild, bane and scourge of the Free Bards for as long as that loosely organized group had existed, had been remarkable for its reticence during the Faire.

Her polite encounters with Guild Bards had been odd enough that they still stuck in her mind. Time after time, she had gotten a distant nod of acknowledgement from Bard and Guild hireling alike, and not the harassment and insults of previous years. *One might have thought that the Guild did not particularly want attention drawn to it,* she mused. The Guild simply held its auditions and performances quietly and gave no opposition to anything that the Free Bards did. There were rumors, never verified, that the Bardic Guild had a hand in the burning of Kingsford, and that the Church, in the person of a Justiciar Mage and Priest called Ardis, as a consequence had its eye on them. Nightingale discarded both rumors; there was no reason to believe the former, and the Church and the Guild had always operated hand-in-glove in the past and it was unlikely that situation would change any time in the future. Never mind that Ardis was reputedly the cousin of the head of the Free Bards, Talaysen, also called Master Wren; there was only so much a single Priest could do. And one could not change attitudes by fiat.

The meadowlark flitted off, his yellow breast with the black "V" at his throat vivid in the morning sun. *Well, I endured; nightmares, sorrow hanging like a heavy mist over the Faire, and all. It will take more than old sorrows and nightmares to keep me from my music.* Nightingale had suffered too many lean seasons in her short life to allow personal discomfort to get in the way of her performances. She was, after all, a professional, however much the poseurs of the Guild might deny that. So she, too, had passed a profitable term at the Faire, and now at the close of it found herself prosperous enough to afford a donkey to carry her burdens for her for the first time in her life as a musician. Heretofore when she traveled she had been forced to rely on the kindness of fellow Free Bards or Gypsies, who would grant her a corner of their wagons to stow her goods in. And while the company was welcome, this arrangement forced her to depend on others, and constrained her to whatever itinerary they chose and not one of her own choosing. When given the option, she preferred to avoid cities, towns, even larger villages altogether. Unfortunately, such destinations were usually where her traveling companions preferred to go.

She closed her eyes and pressed her hands against her temples for a moment; not because she had a headache, but to remind herself to stay calm and bulwarked against the outside world. She could not help but wish she had chosen not to come to the Faire this year, but to stay in one of the lands held by those who were not human, or even pass a season or two in the halls of an Elven king, perilous as that was for mortals. The Faire had posed a trial for her ability to keep herself isolated from her own kind, and more than once she had been tempted to give over her ambitions for a wider reputation as a musician and simply walk away.

But all that was in the past now; there was a sweet-tempered little donkey tethered beside her, his panniers loaded with her gear and her two harps strapped over the top of it all. She had a tent as well, if a small one, and with the donkey she could carry provisions to see her through to better lodgings instead of being at the mercy of greedy or stingy innkeepers.

She was all packed up and ready to go, and eager to be on the road and away from the all-pervasive aura of tragedy that hovered over the city across the river. Only one thing kept her here, an appointment that she had made last night, and she wished *he* would just show up so that—

"Thank you for waiting, my friend." Talaysen's speaking voice was as pleasant as his singing voice, and Nightingale gratefully turned her back to the river and the Church's stronghold to catch his hands in hers in the traditional greeting between Gypsies of the same clan. Talaysen smiled at her, his grey-green eyes warming, and gave her hands a firm squeeze before releasing them. Free Bard Talaysen looked prosperous, too, in his fine leather jerkin, good linen trews, and silk shirt with the knots of many-colored ribbons on the sleeves that denoted a Free Bard. *He* did not owe his prosperity to the Faire, however. Talaysen shared the post of Laurel Bard to the King of Birnam with his wife, Bard Rune, and his clothing reflected his importance. They were the only Free Bards with any kind of position in all of the Twenty Kingdoms.

Not that he has ever let rank go to his head, Nightingale reflected, allowing his pleasure at seeing her to ease the distant ache of Kingsford's sorrow within her. *He has made Birnam a haven of freedom for all of us.*

"I would wait until the snow fell for your sake, Master Wren," she told him truthfully, scanning his honest, triangular face for signs of stress and his red hair for more strands of grey than there had been the last time she saw him. She saw neither, and felt nothing untoward from him, which eased her worries a little. He had been so adamant in asking her not to leave after the Faire closed—at least until he had a chance to speak with her—that she had been afraid there was something wrong with him personally. They were old friends, though only once, briefly, had they ever been lovers.

"Well, it is lucky for us both that you won't have to do that," he replied, and his eye fell on her little donkey. "So, the rumors of your prosperity were not exaggerated! Congratulations!"

She raised her eyebrow at that, for there was something more in his voice than simple pleasure in her good fortune. There was some reason why he was particularly pleased that she had done well, a reason that had nothing to do with friendship or his unofficial rank as head of the Free Bards.

"This simplifies matters," he continued. "I have a request to make of you, but it would have been difficult if you had already arranged to travel with anyone else this winter."

A blackbird winged by, trilling to find them standing in his territory, so near to his nest. Her other eyebrow rose. "A request?" she said cautiously, a certain sense of foreboding coming to her. "Of what nature?"

Wren can charm birds out of the trees and honesty out of Elves, and I'd better remember that if he's asking favors of me. It was mortally hard to refuse Wren anything.

But I can hold my own with the Elves; it will take more than charm to win me.

Talaysen sighed, and shifted his weight from one foot to the other, like a naughty little boy who had been caught in the midst of a prank —which further hardened her suspicions. "There is something I would like for you to do for me—or rather, not for me, but for the Free Bards. Unfortunately, it will involve a rather longer journey than you normally make; I expect it will take you from now until the first Harvest Faires to reach your goal even if you travel without stopping on the way."

She pulled in a quick breath with surprise. "From now until Harvest

Faire?" she repeated, incredulously. "Where in the world do you want me to go? Lyonarie?"

She had thrown out the name of the High King's capital quite by accident, it being the farthest place from here that *she* could think of, but the widening of his eyes showed her that her arrow had hit the mark out of all expectation.

A pocket of sudden stillness held them both, and it seemed to her that the air grew faintly colder around her.

"You want me to go to *Lyonarie?*" she asked, incredulously. "But—why? What possible business have the Free Bards there? And of all people, why me? I am no Court Bard, I know nothing of Lyonarie, and—"

And I hate cities, you know *that,* she thought, numbly. *And you know why!*

"Because we need information, not rumor. Because of all people, you are the one I know that is most likely to learn what we need to know without getting yourself into trouble over it—or inflaming half the city." He nodded at the ruins of Kingsford behind her, and she winced; there were also rumors that enemies of the Free Bards had set that fire and that it had gotten out of hand. "You're clever, you're discreet, and we both know that you are a master of Bardic and—other magics."

"Perhaps not a master," she demurred, "and my talents are as much a hazard as a benefit—" But he wasn't about to be deflected.

"I know I can trust you, and that I can trust you to be sensible," he continued. "Those are traits this task will need as much as mastery of magic."

"Which is why you are not entrusting this to Peregrine?" she asked. "You could trust him, but he is not always sensible, especially when he sees an injustice."

"He does not do well in cities, any more than you do," Talaysen pointed out. "And he won't abide in them unless he must under direct threat to himself or his clan."

And because I have a large sense of duty, I will endure them if I must, she thought with misgiving. *I had better have a very good reason—other than that Wren wants me to, however.*

"What could possibly be so pressing as to send me across half the Twenty Kingdoms?" she replied, favoring him with a frown. "And there, of all places. Peregrine may not like cities, but neither do I, and I have better reason than he to avoid them." Her frown deepened. "I'm not minded to risk another witch-hunt because I seem to know a little too much for someone's comfort—or just because I am a Gypsy."

"Not in Lyonarie—" he began, but she interrupted him.

"So you *say,* but no one had word of what was chancing in Gradford until Robin stirred the nest and the wasps came flying out to sting," she retorted. Talaysen did not wince this time; instead he looked ever more determined. "And I ask again, what is so pressing as to send me there?"

Now Talaysen's changeable eyes grew troubled, and the signs of stress that had not been there before appeared, faintly etched into his brow and the corners of his generous mouth. "King Rolend is concerned, and as Laurel Bard and leader of the Free Bards he often asks me for *my* opinion. High King Theovere has been—neglectful."

Now Nightingale snorted. "This is hardly news; his neglect has been growing since before Lady Lark joined us. And so just what is it that I am supposed to do? March up to the High King and charge him with neglecting his duty?"

Talaysen smiled, faintly. "Scarcely, though I suspect *you* could and would do just that if it suited you. No, what Rolend and I both want is the reason why Theovere has become this way. He wasn't always like this—he *was* a very good ruler and kept the power neatly balanced among the Twenty Kings, the Guilds and the Church. He's mature, but not all *that* old, and there has been no suggestion that he has become senile, and he hasn't been ill—and besides, his father lived thirty years more than he has already, and *he* was vigorous and alert to the last."

She shook her head, though, rather than agreeing to take on Talaysen's little wild-goose hunt with no more prompting than that. "I won't promise," she said, as the dim sense of foreboding only increased with Talaysen's explanations. "I will think about it, but I won't promise. All I *will* say is that I will take my travels in the direction of Lyonarie." As Master Wren's face reflected his disappointment, she hardened her heart. "I won't promise because I have no way of knowing if I can actually reach Lyonarie," she pointed out. "I'm afoot, remember? You and Rune came here in a fine wagon with a pair of horses to pull you and the baby—travel is harder when you walk, not ride. *You* ought to remember that. A hundred things could delay me, and I won't promise what I am not sure I can deliver."

"But if you reach Lyonarie?" Talaysen persisted, and she wondered at his insistence. Surely he—and the King of Birnam—had more and better sources of information than one lone Gypsy!

"If I decide to go that far and if I reach Lyonarie any time before the next Kingsford Faire, I will reconsider," she said at last. "I will see what I can do. More, I won't promise."

He wasn't satisfied, but he accepted that, she saw it in his face.

"You still haven't answered the other question," she continued, suspiciously. "Why choose me?"

His answer was not one calculated to quell her growing unease, nor warm the prickle of chill prescience that threaded her back.

"Much as I hate to admit this," said Talaysen, wielder of Bardic Magics and friend to the High King of the Elves, "I was warned that this situation was more hazardous than we knew, and told to send you and only you, in a dream."

Three weeks from the day she had left Talaysen beside the river, Nightingale guided her little donkey in among the sheltering branches of a black pine as twilight thickened and the crickets and frogs of early evening started up their songs. Black pines were often called "shelter-pines," for their trunks were bare to a height of many feet, and their huge, heavy branches bent down to touch the ground around them like the sides of a tent. The ground beneath those branches was bare except for a thick carpet of dead needles. Nightingale held a heavy, resin-scented branch aside with one hand, while she led the donkey beneath it; her hair was wet, for she had bathed in a stream earlier that afternoon, and the still, cool darkness beneath the branches made her shiver.

It wasn't just the cool air or the dark that made her shiver. Not all the warm sunlight on the road nor the cheerful greetings of her fellow travelers had been able to ease the chill Talaysen's words had placed within her heart.

He was warned to send me to Lyonarie in a dream, she thought, for the hundredth time that day, as she unloaded her donkey and placed the panniers and wrapped bundles on the ground beside him. *What kind of a dream—and who else was in it? Wren can be the most maddening person in the world when it comes to magic—he hates to use it, and he hates to rely on it, and most of all he is the last person to ever depend on a dream to set a course for him. So why does he suddenly choose to follow the dictates of a dream now?*

There had been a great deal that Talaysen had not told her, she *knew* that, as well as she knew the fingerings of her harp or the lies of a faithless lover, but he had simply shut his secrets inside himself when she tried to ask him more. Perhaps if she had agreed to his scheme, he might have told her—or perhaps not. Talaysen was good at keeping his own council.

She went outside the barren circle of needle-strewn ground within the arms of the black pine and found a patch of long, sweet grass to pull up for the donkey. She hadn't named him yet; Talaysen had driven all thoughts of such trivial matters out of her head.

Infuriating man. She hadn't even been able to enjoy the feeling of freedom that picking and choosing her own road had given her.

Once the donkey had been fed and hobbled, she made a sketchy camp

in the gloom of dusk with the economy of someone who has performed
such tasks too many times to count. She scraped dead, dry needles away
from a patch of bare earth, laid a tiny fire ready to light, rigged a tripod
out of green branches over it, and hung her small kettle full of the sweet
water she had drawn at the last stream from the apex of the tripod. She
took the tent and her bedding out of one of the panniers and dropped
them both nearest to the trunk of the tree. Then she lit the fire and laid
her bedding out atop the still-folded tent. Her weather-sense gave her no
hint of a storm tonight, so there was no point in putting the tent up, and
screen-mesh was not needed since this wasn't the territory for blood-
suckers. She preferred to sleep out under the open sky when she could;
she would sprinkle certain herbs over the smoldering remains of her fire to
keep biting insects away as she slept. Sometimes the touch of the moon
gave her dreams of her own, and it would be useful for one such to come
to her tonight.

The water in the kettle was soon boiling, and she poured half of it over
tea leaves in her mug. She threw a handful of meal and dried berries into
what remained; porridge was a perfectly good dinner, and she had feasted
every night of the Faire. It would do her no harm to dine frugally tonight,
and there were honey-cakes to break her fast on in the morning, an
indulgence she had not been able to resist when she passed through the
last village this afternoon.

The moon rose, serene as always. Its silver light filtered through the
branches of the tree she sheltered beneath. The donkey dozed, standing
hip-shot with his head hanging, the firelight flickering over him but not
waking him. Somewhere in the further distance, an owl called.

Nightingale strained her ears for the notes of her namesake bird, but
there was no sweet, sad song wafting on the warm air tonight. It was the
wrong season for a nightingale to be singing, but she never drifted off to
sleep without listening for one, no matter where she was or what time of
year it might be. Nearby crickets sang cheerfully enough that she didn't
miss the absence of that song too much.

Although it was very lonely out here. . . .

Abruptly, a whistle joined the cricket chorus, and Nightingale sat bolt
upright on her sleeping-pad. That was no night-bird song, that was the first
few bars of "Lonely Road"! There was someone out there—someone near
enough to see the light of her tiny fire, even through the masking
branches!

"Might a friend come in to your fire, Bird of the Night?" asked a voice
out of the darkness. It was a clear voice, a silvery tenor, a voice of a *kind*
that a trained musician would recognize, although she did not recognize

who the speaker was. It held that peculiar lack of passion that only Elves projected.

An Elf? First Master Wren, and now one of the Elvenkin? The chill that had threaded Nightingale's spine since her meeting with Master Wren deepened.

Elves did not often call themselves the "friend" of a mortal, not even a Gypsy. Though Nightingale could boast of such a distinction if she cared to, she was very far from the hills and halls of those few of the Elvenkin who normally called her "friend."

"Any friend is welcome to share my fire," she replied cautiously. "But an unfriend in the guise of a friend—"

"—should be aware that the fierce Horned Owl is as much a bird of the night as the Nightingale," the voice replied, with a hollow chuckle. "Your reputation as a hunter in the dark also precedes you." The branches parted, with no hand to part them, as if servants held two halves of a curtain apart, and the speaker stepped through them as into a hall of state.

It was, quite unmistakably, one of the Elven lords, though the circlet of silver he wore betokened him a lord only, and of no higher estate than that. Amber cat-eyes regarded her with a remote amusement from beneath a pair of upswept brows; the unadorned circlet confined hair as golden as the true metal, cut to fall precisely just below his shoulders. His thin face, pale as marble, was as lovely as a statue carved of marble and quite as expressionless. Prominent cheekbones, tapering chin, and thin lips all combined to enhance the impression of "not-human." The tips of his pointed ears, peeking through the liquid fall of his hair, only reinforced that impression.

He was ill-dressed for walking through a forest in the dead of night, though that never seemed to bother the Elvenkin much. He wore black, from his collar to the tips of his soft leather boots, black velvet with a pattern of silver spiderwebs, velvet as soft as a caress and fragile as the wings of a moth. Nightingale had worn cloth like that herself, when she spent time beneath the Hills.

"Call me a friend of a friend, Bird of the Night," the Elven lord continued, as the branches closed behind him without even snagging so much as a sleeve. Nightingale sighed; the Elves always made such a performance out of the simplest of things—but that was their nature. "And in token of this, I have been asked to gift you with another such as the gift you already bear, the maker of which sends his greetings—"

He held out his hand, and in it was a bracelet, a slender ring of silver hardly thicker than a thread.

It had a liquid sheen that no other such metal had—it was the true

Elven-forged silver, silver that no mortal could duplicate, more valuable than gold.

She opened herself cautiously, and "touched" it with a purely mental hand. She *did* know that bracelet; she wore its twin on her right wrist. The maker could be trusted, insofar as any Elf could be trusted. She relaxed, just a trifle.

"In the name of friendship, then, I accept the gift and welcome the bearer," she replied, holding out her hand. The Elf dropped the silver bracelet into her open palm without a word; the bracelet *writhed* in a strange, half-alive fashion and slipped across her palm and ringed itself onto her hand, then moved over her hand and onto her wrist, joining to the one already there. As it did so, she heard a strange, wild melody—but only in her mind. This was the music of Magic, true Magic, the magic that the Gypsies, the Elves, and some few—very few—of the Free Bards shared.

If she had not already had this experience with the quasi-life of Elven silver more than once, she would probably have been petrified with fear—but that first bracelet had been set on her wrist when she was scarcely more than a child, and too inexperienced to be frightened. She had not known then that Elves could be as cruel as they were beautiful and that very few of them were worthy of trust by human standards.

For a moment, a fleeting moment, she felt very tired, very much alone, and a little frightened.

When she pulled her hand back to examine her wrist, she could not tell where the first bracelet began and the second ended—only that the circle of silver on her wrist was now twice as wide as it had been. She did not try to remove it; she knew from past experience that it would not come off unless she sang it off.

The Elven lord dropped bonelessly and gracefully down on the other side of her fire, and caught her eyes in his amber gaze. "I come with a message, as well as a gift," he said abruptly, with that lack of inflection that gave her no clue to his intentions. "The message is this: *The High King of the mortals serves his people ill. The High King of those who dwell beneath the Hills would know the reason why, for when mortals are restless, the Hill-folk often suffer. If Nightingale can sing and learn, her friends would be grateful.*"

The chill spread to Nightingale's heart, and she shivered involuntarily at this echo of Master Wren's words.

First Talaysen speaking for one king, now an Elven messenger speaking for another—This was so unreal that if someone had written it as a story-song she would have laughed at it as being too ridiculous to be believed. *Why is this happening to me?*

"Is there no further word from my friend?" she asked, hoping for some kind of explanation.

But the Elf shook his head, his hair rippling with the movement. "No further word, only the message. Have you an answer?"

It wasn't a wise thing to anger the Elves; while their magic was strongest in their Hills, they could still reach out of their strongholds from time to time with powerful effect. Songs had been made about those times, and few of them had happy endings.

"I—I don't know," she said, finally, as silence grew between them, punctuated by the chirps of crickets. Firelight flickered on his face to be caught and held in those eyes. "I am not certain I *can* send him an answer. I am only one poor, limited mortal—"

But the Elven lord smiled thinly. "You are more than you think, mortal. You have the gift of making friends in strange places. This is why the High King asks this question of you, why the runestones spelled out your name when he asked them why the mortals grew more troublesome with every passing month, and who could remedy the wrongness."

Nightingale grew colder still. The Elves lived outside time as humans knew it, and as a consequence had a greater insight into past and future than humans did. Elven runestones were the medium through which they sought answers, and if the runestones really *had* named her—

But I have only his word for that, and the word of the one who sent him. Elves lie as readily as they speak the truth; it is in their nature.

"I will do what I can," she said finally, giving him a little more of a promise than she had given Talaysen. "I cannot pledge what is not in my power to give. The seat of the High King of the mortals is far from here, and I am alone and afoot."

She waited for his response, acutely aware of every breath of breeze, every rustling leaf, every cricket chirp. He *could* choose to take offense; that Elves were unpredictable was a truism.

The Elven messenger regarded her with one winglike eyebrow raised for a moment, then grudgingly acknowledged that she had a point. She breathed a little easier.

"I will take him your answer," he said as he nodded, and rose fluidly to his feet. Before she had blinked twice, the branches of the tree she sheltered beneath had parted once again, and he was gone.

There was nothing else to do then but finish her porridge, strip off her leather bodice and skirt, and lie down in her bedding. But although she was weary, she stared up into the interlacing branches overhead, listening to the crickets and the breeze in the boughs, tense as an ill-strung harp. This was two: Wren and the Elves. Gypsy lore held that when something came in a repetition of three, it was magical, a geas, meant to bind a person to an unanticipated fate.

Whether or not that person wanted it.

It was a long time before she was able to sleep.

She made better time than she had thought she would; she had assumed she would be walking at the same pace unburdened as carrying her own packs, but she found that she could make a mile or two more every day than she had anticipated, with no difficulty whatsoever. She reached the crossroads and the small town of Highlevee three days sooner than she had expected to—

Which only increased the tension she felt. If she went south or north, she would be traveling out of the Kingdom of Rayden and away from the road that would take her to Lyonarie. If, however, she traveled eastward, she would soon strike the King's Highway, which led to Lyonarie, and there would be no turning back. She'd hoped to have more time to think the problem through.

Though the height of summer was past, the heat had not abated in the least. The sun burned down on her with a power she felt even through her wide-brimmed, pale straw hat; dust hung in the air as a haze, undisturbed by even a hint of breeze. The grasses of the verge were burned brown and lifeless, and would remain that way until the rains of autumn. She had kilted up her skirts to her knees and pushed her sleeves up over her elbows for coolness, but she still felt the heat as heavy as a pack of weights on her back.

Summer would linger in Lyonarie, long past the time when it would be gone here—or so she had heard. At the moment, that did not seem particularly pleasant.

As she led the donkey down the dusty main street of Highlevee, a little after noon, she found herself dragging her feet in the dust, as if by walking slower she could put off her decision longer.

It was with a decidedly sinking feeling that she spotted someone she knew sitting at a table outside the Royal Oak Tavern, just inside the bounds of the town. It wasn't just any acquaintance, either.

Omens come in threes. So do portents. And so do the bindings of a geas set by Fate and the Lady. If ever there was an omen, this must surely be it—for there was no reason, no reason at all, for *this* man to be here at *this* time.

Unless, rather than a geas, this is a conspiracy set up among my dear friends. . . .

For sitting at his ease, quite as if he belonged there, was a man called "Leverance" by those who knew him well. The trouble was, most of those who knew him well lived within the walls of the fabulous Fortress-City that the Deliambrens called home.

He should not have been here. He *should,* by all rights, have been back there, amid the wonders of Deliambren "technology," as they called it. Few of the odd half-human folk ever left those comforts—why should they? There they had lighting that did not depend on candles, as bright as the brightest sunlight on a dark winter night. They had heat in the winter and cool in the summer, and a thousand other comforts even the wealthiest human could only dream of. He should not have been sitting calmly at a wooden table, with a wooden mug in one hand, nibbling at a meat pasty and watching the road, his strange features shadowed by a wide hat of something that was *not* straw.

He should definitely not have been watching the road as if he was watching for *her.*

She knew that he was going to hail her as soon as she saw him; the scene had that feeling of inevitability about it. She thought about trying to ignore him—but what was the use? If Leverance was not the next person to request her to go to Lyonarie, someone else surely would be.

Omen or conspiracy, it seems that I am caught.

So she led her donkey toward him, feeling weary to the bone, and wondering if for once she might get a real answer to her question of, "why me?" After all, the Deliambrens didn't believe in portents and omens. Their faith was placed on machinery, on curiosity, on discovery, on something they called "science."

"Don't tell me," she said, before he could open his mouth even to greet her. "You want me to go to Lyonarie to find out why the High King has been neglecting his duties."

Deliambrens resembled humans for the most part, far more than did, say, a Mintak. Leverance wore ordinary enough human garb: a jerkin, trews and boots of leather, and a shirt of what appeared to be silk. She knew better than to assume that the garments were as ordinary as they seemed, however, for nothing about a Deliambren was ever ordinary. Like all Deliambrens, the long, pale hair growing along the line of his cheekbones was immaculately groomed and blended invisibly into the identical shoulder-length hair of his head. His eyebrows were similar to those of an Elf in the way they rose toward his temples, but were thicker and as long as a man's thumb. Leverance fancied himself as something of an adventurer, so his hair was simply cut off straight rather than being styled into some fantastic shape as many Deliambrens sported. Nightingale sighed, but only to herself, knowing that Leverance was certain he was "blending in" with his surroundings. It would be quite impossible to convince him otherwise.

He stared at her with a flash of surprise, quickly covered. "Whyever do you say that?" he asked innocently. Too innocently.

"Because every other person I know seems to want me to go there," she replied tartly, and sat down on the wooden bench across from him. The wood of the table was smooth and bleached to grey by sun and rain, and another time she would have been quite pleased for a chance to sit here in the shade on such a broiling day. She had lost what patience she had and decided it was time to show it. "You may order me something to eat and drink, and you may pay for it. If you are going to try to get me to go to Lyonarie, you might as well begin with a bribe." She kept the tone of her voice tart, to show him she was not going to tolerate any evasions, no matter how clever.

Both of Leverance's eyebrows twitched, but he summoned the serving girl with a single lifted finger and placed an order for wine, cheese, and sausage pastries. The serving girl, dressed far more neatly than Nightingale in her buff linen skirt, bodice, and white blouse, glanced covertly at the Gypsy, her contemptuous expression saying all too clearly that she could not imagine why this exotic Deliambren would be ordering luncheon for such a scruffy stranger, and a Gypsy to boot.

Nightingale straightened abruptly, gathering all her dignity about her, then caught the girl's glance and held it, just long enough that the girl flushed, then paled, then hurried off. Now, at least, there would be no more covert looks and poorly veiled contempt.

"I wish I knew how you did that," Leverance said with interest and admiration.

Nightingale shrugged. There was no explaining it to him; he simply wouldn't understand why spending most of her time with Elves and other nonhumans made Nightingale seem strange and fey to those of her own kind. Most people, if asked why they avoided her after one direct confrontation, would stammer something about her expression—how they were *sure* she saw things that "normal folk" couldn't, and wouldn't want to.

Well, and I do, but that is not why I unnerve them.

As long as the impression she left with them caused them to leave her alone, she planned to cultivate the effect. If she had reasons to be fonder of her own company, and of nonhumans, than of her own kind, it was none of their business.

"Well," Leverance said, when the girl returned with the food and vanished again with unseemly haste, "as it happens, I *was* sent to find you, and to ask you to go to Lyonarie."

He laid the food out before her; wine in a pottery bottle, beaded with moisture, a thick slice of cheese and crusty rolls, beautifully brown pastries, a small pottery firkin of butter. She took her time; selecting a roll and buttering it, then pouring herself a cup of wine.

"Why?" she asked, then amended her question. "No, never mind. Why *me?*" She bit into the roll; it might just as well have been straw, for she could not taste it.

Now I discover if this is simple mortal conspiracy, or something I cannot escape.

Leverance stroked the hair on his cheekbones thoughtfully. "Several reasons, actually, although you are not the only person being asked to go there. And you *can* refuse."

Not the only person? That's new. Or does he mean that it is only his people who are sending more than one person to gather their information?

She snorted delicately. "You still haven't answered the question."

He held up a finger. "You are very observant, and yet you are very adept at making yourself unobserved." He held up a second finger. "You have served as a willing collector of information for your people, for the Elves and for mine in the past." A third finger joined the other two. "For some reason that my people are unable to fathom, things happen around you, and you are able to influence things through no medium that *we* recognize, and which other people refer to as 'magic.' We don't believe in magic, but we do believe you have some kind of power that acts in a way we can't measure. We think that will help keep you safe and sane where other investigators have failed."

Other investigators? This was the first time Nightingale had heard about others—and the chill now filled her, body, soul and heart. She put down the roll, all appetite gone. The still, hot air could not reach that chill to warm her.

"How, failed?" she asked in a small voice.

He correctly interpreted her frozen expression. "Nothing serious—no one *died,* for Hadron's sake! They were just found out, somehow, and they were discredited in ways that forced them to leave the city. We think we failed by choosing someone too high in rank. *You* know how to extract information of all kinds—Harperus says that you have the ability to sieve gold out of the gutters. That is why you." He scratched his head, then added, "Besides, the roads north and south of here are closed. North the bridge is out, and south Sire Yori has put up a roadblock and he's taking all beasts of burden as 'army-taxes.' You could only go on to the King's Highway or retrace your steps."

Nightingale flushed, and mentally levied a few choice Gypsy curses on the Deliambren for choosing the precise words guaranteed to make her go on. Gypsy lore held that to retrace one's steps was to unmake part of one's

life—and you had better be very sure that was something you wanted and
needed to do before you tried it.

Leverance blinked benignly at her as she muttered imprecations, just as
if he didn't know the implications of his words. "Well," he asked. "Can
you go? Will you help?"

*Signs and portents, omens and forebodings. I do not want to go, but it
seems I have no choice.*

But she was not going to *tell* him that. For one thing, if they had sent
others on this path, others who had been found out, that argued for
someone *knowing* in advance that they had been sent. She trusted those
Deliambrens that she personally knew, but within very strict limits—just as
she trusted, within limits, those Elves she knew. But there were Gypsies
that she would *not* trust, so why should every Elf, every Deliambren, or
even every Free Bard be entirely trustworthy?

*Talaysen probably didn't know about the others. The Elves might not have
thought it worth stooping to ask help of mere mortals until now. Only the
Deliambrens know the whole of this; but if there was someone acting as an
informant against their agents, there is no reason why it could not have been
an Elf, a Deliambren, or even one of us. Everyone has a price; it is only that
most honest folk have prices that could never be met.*

"I will think about it," she temporized, giving him the same answer she
had given Master Wren. "My road goes in that direction; I cannot promise
that I will end up there."

*If there is an informant, damned if I will give you the assurance that I will
be the next one to play victim! It is too easy for a lone woman, Gypsy or no, to
simply disappear.*

She smiled sweetly and ate a bite of tasteless roll, as if she had not a
care in the world. "I am alone and afoot, and who knows what could
happen between here and there? I make no promises I cannot keep."

Leverance made a sour face. "You'll think about it, though?" he persisted. "At least keep the option open?"

She frowned; she really did not want to give him even that much, but—
she had a certain debt to his people. "Did I not say that I would?"

Leverance only shrugged. "You hedge your promises as carefully as if
you were dealing with Elves," he told her sourly, as she packed up the rest
of the uneaten lunch in a napkin to take with her. "Don't you know by now
that you can trust us?"

The sun's heat faded again, although no clouds passed before it, and she
took in a sharp breath as she steadied herself, looking down at the rough
wood of the table, grey and lifeless, unlike the silver of her bracelet.

Trust them. He wants me to trust them, the Elves want me to trust them, and Talaysen, damn his eyes, trusts me. *There is too much asking and giving of trust in this.*

Her right hand clenched on the knot of the napkin; her left made a sign against ill-wishing, hidden in her lap.

"I only pay heed to what my own eyes and ears tell me," she said lightly, forcing herself to ignore her chill. "You should know that by now, since it is probably one of the *other* reasons why you picked me. Thank you for the meal."

She rose from the bench and untied her donkey from the handrail beside the road without a backward glance for him.

"Are you sure you won't—" Leverance began plaintively.

Now she leveled a severe look at him, one that even he could read. "I gave you what I could promise, Deliambren. A nightingale cannot sing in a cage, or tethered by a foot to a perch. You would do well to remember that."

And with that, she led her donkey back out into the road. It was, after all, a long way to Lyonarie, and the road wasn't growing any shorter while she sat.

She only wished that she could feel happier about going there.

CHAPTER TWO

From the vantage of a low hill, at the top of the last crest of the King's Highway, Lyonarie was a city guaranteed to make a person feel very small, entirely insignificant.

That was Nightingale's first impression of the metropolis, anyway. There was no end to it from where she stood; seated in the midst of a wide valley, it sprawled across the entire valley and more.

It did not look inviting to her; like something carved of old, grey, sun-bleached wood, or built out of dry, ancient bones, it seemed lifeless from here, and stifling. In a way, she wished that she could feel the same excitement that was reflected in the faces of the travelers walking beside her. Instead, her spirit was heavy; she hunched her shoulders against the blow to her heart coming from that grey blotch, and she wanted only to be away from the place. Heat-haze danced and shimmered, making distant buildings ripple unsettlingly. As she approached, one small traveler in a stream of hundreds of others, she had the strangest feeling that *they* were not going to the city, it was calling them in and devouring them.

It devours everything: life, dreams, hope. . . .

The great, hulking city-beast was unlike any other major population center she had ever been in. There were no walls, at least not around the entire city, though there were suggestions of walled enclaves in the middle distance. That was not unusual in itself; many cities spilled beyond their original walls. It would have been very difficult to maintain such walls in any kind of state of repair, much less to man them. The city simply *was;* it existed, just as any living, growing thing existed, imbued with a fierce life of its own that required it to swallow anyone that entered and make him part of it, never to escape again.

Was this the reason why I felt such foreboding? That was reason enough; for someone of Nightingale's nature, the possibility of losing her own identity, of being literally devoured, was always a real danger.

It was not just the heat that made her feel faint. *Thousands of silent voices, dunning into my mind—thousands of people needing a little piece of me—thousands of hearts crying out for the healing I have. . . . I could be lost in no time at all, here.* She would have to guard herself every moment, waking and sleeping, against that danger.

She took off her hat and wiped her forehead with her kerchief, wishing that she had never heard of Lyonarie.

The shaggy brown donkey walked beside her, his tiny hooves clicking on the hard roadbed, with no signs that the heavy traffic on the road bothered him. Traffic traveled away from the city as well as toward it, right-hand side going in, left-hand side leaving, with heavy vehicles taking the center, ridden horses and other beasts coming next, and foot traffic walking along the shoulder. The road was so hard that Nightingale's feet ached, especially in the arches, and her boots felt much too tight.

She'd had a general description of the city last night from the innkeeper at the tavern she'd stayed in. From this direction, the King's Highway first brought a traveler through what was always the most crowded, noisy, and dirty section of any city, the quarter reserved for trade.

Oh, I am quite looking forward to that. Stench, heat, and angry people, what a lovely combination.

About six or seven leagues from the city itself, the road had changed from hard-packed gravel to black, cracked pavement, a change that had given both Nightingale and her beast relief from the dust, but which gave no kind of cushioning for the feet. She knew by the set of the donkey's ears that his feet hurt him, too. This grey-black stuff was worse than a dirt road for heat, on top of that; waves of heat radiated up from the pavement, and both she and the donkey were damp with sweat.

I do wish I'd worn something other than this heavy linen skirt—and I wish I'd left off the leather bodice. I should have chosen a lighter set of colors than dark-green and black. This is too much to suffer in the name of looking respectable. I think I could bake bread under this skirt! She dared not kilt it up, either, not and still look like an honest musician and not a lady whose virtue was negotiable.

The road up the valley toward Lyonarie led across flat fields, every inch cultivated and growing a variety of crops, until suddenly, with no warning, the fields were gone and buildings on small plots of land had taken their place.

As if they had grown there, as well, like some unsavory fungus.

These were small, mean houses, a short step up from the hovels of the very poor, crowded so closely together that a rat could not have passed between them. Made of wood with an occasional facing of brick or stonework, they were all a uniform, grimy grey, patched with anything that came to hand, and the few plants that had been encouraged to take root in the excuses for yards had to struggle to stay alive under the trampling feet of those forced off the roadway by more important or more massive traffic.

The sight made her sick. *How can anyone live like this? Why would anyone want to? What could possibly tempt anyone to stay here who didn't have to? No amount of money would be worth living without trees, grass, space to breathe!*

The houses gave way just as abruptly a few moments later to warehouses two and three stories tall, and this was where the true city began.

Those who ruled the city now showed their authority. A token gate across the road, a mere board painted in red and white stripes, was manned by a token guard in a stiff brown uniform. He paid no attention to her whatsoever as she passed beneath the bar of the gate. His attention was for anyone who brought more into the city than his own personal belongings. Those who drove carts waved a stiff piece of blue paper at him as they passed—or if they didn't have that piece of paper, pulled their wagons over to a paved area at the side of the road where one of a half-dozen clerks would march upon them with a grimly determined frown. No one cared about a single Gypsy with a donkey, assuming they recognized her as a Gypsy at all. She passed close by the guard, fanning herself with her hat in her free hand, as he lounged against the gate-post, picking his teeth with a splinter. She was near enough to smell the onions he had eaten for lunch and the beer he had washed them down with, and to see the bored indifference in his eyes.

She was just one of a hundred people much like her who would pass this man today, and she knew it. There was virtue and safety in anonymity right now, and suddenly she was glad of the sober colors of her clothing. Better to bake than to be memorable.

How could I have forgotten? I wanted to be sure that no one would remember me; there might be someone waiting and watching to see if I show up! It must be the heat, or all this emotion-babble. . . .

But the press of minds around her was a more oppressive burden than the heat. *This* was why she hated cities, and Lyonarie was everything she disliked most about a city, but constructed on a more massive scale than anything she had previously encountered. There were too many people here, all packed too closely together, all of them unconsciously suffering the effects of being so crowded. Most of them were unhappy and had no idea how to remedy their condition—other than pursuing wealth, which brought its own set of problems whether the pursuit succeeded or failed. Their strident emotions scratched at her nerves no matter how well she warded them out.

Never mind that. I'm here, so now I need a plan, however sketchy. She hadn't actually formulated a plan until now; she'd been hoping, perhaps, for some unavoidable reason *not* to go on to Lyonarie. Geas or fate—or not—here she was, and it was time to make some kind of a plan.

Something simple; the simpler, the less likely it will be that I'll have to change it.

Once past the guard, Nightingale pulled the donkey off to the side of the road, taking a moment to stand in the shade of one of the warehouses. She fanned herself with her hat, pretended to watch the traffic, and considered her next move on this little gameboard.

It is a game, too—and I can only hope I've made myself less of a pawn than I would have been if I'd jumped into it without care and thought.

People streamed by her as she stood on the baking pavement with her patient little beast; as she watched, she saw everything from farmers hauling wagonloads of cabbage to the carriages of prosperous merchants— from footsore travelers like herself to the occasional creature more alien than a Deliambren. They all apparently had places to go, and they were all in a dreadful hurry to get there. They paid no attention to her; their eyes were on the road and the traffic ahead of them.

The buildings on either side of the road trapped the rays of the sun; the pavement beneath absorbed the heat and radiated it up again. Sweat ran down her face and back, and not even the most vigorous fanning helped cool her even a little. She licked her lips and tasted salt, wishing for the cooler clothing she'd worn at Kingsford Faire—the light skirt made of hundreds of multi-colored ribbons sewn together from knee to waist, but left to flutter from knee to ankle, the wide laced belt of doeskin, the shirt of fabric just this side of see-through, and the sandals. . . . The leather of her bodice and boots was hot, stifling hot. The soles of her boots were far too thin to cushion her feet in any way or deflect the heat of the pavement.

What she really wanted right now was a cool place to sit, a cool drink, and a moment in semi-darkness to build up her mental defenses.

Well, the sooner I join in this game, the sooner I can leave. If I'm both lucky and clever, I might even be able to get out of here before winter. At least I didn't lose any time on the road.

In fact, she had made such good time getting here that it was not quite Harvest Faire season. She had met with no obstacles, and her earlier good start had been typical of the whole journey. She'd been able to stop before dark every night, and hadn't even been forced to spend much of her hard-earned Faire money.

In fact, her purse was now a bit heavier than it had been when she had left Kingsford. She had made such good time that it had been possible to trade performances in the kind of small country inns she preferred in return for food, a bed, and whatever came into her hat. If she had just been making her rounds of the Faire-circuit, she would have been pleased but not particularly surprised by this. She was a *good* harpist, a fine musician, and there was no reason why innkeepers should turn her away. Her hat usually had a few coppers in it at the end of the night, no matter how poor the audience.

But the very smoothness of her travel had made her suspicious, or rather, apprehensive. It felt as if someone or something was making quite sure she would get to Lyonarie, and seeing to it that she would be ready for just about anything when she arrived there.

A geas? The hand of God or the Gypsy's Lady of the Night?

Or just a string of unprecedented good luck? And did it matter?

Not really. What did matter was coming up with a course of immediate action that would keep her inconspicuous. *If I were truly in the "service" of any of my so-needful friends, what would I do first?* she asked herself. The answer seemed obvious: find a tavern or an inn at the heart of the city and take up lodging there. If she was expected to gather information, that would be *all* that she would do; there would be no time for anything like taking on a regular job as a musician. And that *would* make her conspicuous—someone who carried musical instruments, yet did not try to find a position; someone who spent money but did nothing to earn more. It would be "logical" to devote all of her time and energy into collecting information, but it would not be wise.

So, since that is what is predictable and logical, it is what I will not do.

She considered her options further as she also pondered the question of High King Theovere. The two were inextricably linked. How to gain information on the High and Exalted without venturing out of her persona as Low and Insignificant?

At least, now that she wasn't moving, she didn't seem to be quite as warm.

As Talaysen had pointed out, the King should have been overseeing the business of his twenty vassals—but they had been left, more and more, at loose ends, without a guide or an overseer. As often as not, though the King of Birnam was an exception, they had been making use of this laxness to enrich themselves, or simply to amuse themselves.

The King of Birnam thought more of his people and their lands than himself; he was a good ruler, and as a result, his kingdom prospered in good times and survived the bad in reasonable shape. But those lands whose rulers were not out of Rolend's mold were showing all the signs of a careless hand on the reins. The signs were everywhere, and touching everything. In Rayden, for instance, there was little or no upkeep on the public roads: bridges were out, roads were rutted and full of potholes, signs were missing or illegible. In some remoter parts of Rayden and in other lands, the neglect was far more serious, as rivalry between Sires and even Dukes had been permitted to escalate into armed feuding.

The High King was supposed to represent the central unifying power in the Twenty Kingdoms. Now the Church was well on the way to taking over that function.

As if her thought of the Church had summoned a further reminder of its power, the tolling of bells rang out over the rumble of cart wheels on pavement and the babble of thousands of voices. Nightingale lifted her eyes from the road to see the spire of the Chapel housing those bells rising above the warehouse roofs.

And that represented another interest in the dance. There were perhaps hundreds of Chapels in Lyonarie, ranging in size from a single room to huge Cathedrals. The Church was an all-pervasive presence here, and there was no way to escape it. The Church might also have an interest in keeping Theovere weak and ineffectual.

She swallowed in sour distaste. There was no love lost between herself and most representatives of the Church. Too often of late she had been the subject of attempts by Churchmen to lay the blame for perfectly ordinary accidents at her door, because she was a Gypsy, a Free Bard, and presumably a wielder of arcane and darksome powers. In some places, at least, it seemed that the Church was trying to incite people against Gypsies, nonconformists, nonhumans—indeed, against anything that did not obviously and directly benefit the Church itself as much as a flock of sheep would benefit the herdsman.

Well, one advantage of being in a large city was that there were too many people for the Church to play at the kinds of games some Churchmen were able to foment in less populous places. It was harder to find an individual to use as a target and a scapegoat—harder to incite people against a stranger in a town when so *many* people were strangers, and in fact, people living on the same street might not even know or recognize each other.

Still it behooved her to find a venue that was not too near a Chapel, if she could. *Not near the prosperous, either; they have the leisure to notice things.* All things considered, although this was probably the worst part of town, *this* district would be a good one to try to find a tavern that might have need of a musician.

Another good thing about a city this large—not all the Guild Bards in the world could take all the positions available here. Really, most of them are going to be positions no Guild Bard in his right mind would ever want!

Now that she had gotten her mind moving, and had managed a little rest, she felt ready to rejoin the mob. She pulled the donkey into the stream of traffic again, and scanned the fronts of the buildings she passed for tavern signs. *I'll look for information from two sources,* she decided as she walked, letting the traffic carry her along rather than trying to force a faster pace. *Once I get established, I'll build myself a little army of street-children and pay them to go listen for me. No one ever pays attention to them, and they can get into the most amazing places. . . .*

This would not be the first time she had built herself such a network. Children were never regarded as threatening by adults, but street-brats were wise beyond their years and knew how to listen for anything that might be of value. The nice thing about children was that they tended to stay loyal to the person who hired them. They might be wise beyond their years, but they lacked the experience that taught them double-dealing. Children still believed, in their heart of hearts, in playing fair.

Servants, too—they're the other invisibles. I'll show up at the kitchen doors, clean but very shabby. I'll ask to play in return for food. The Courts of Kings might boast the cream of entertainers, but the servants never saw it, and any chance for a little entertainment of their own usually was snatched at. Kitchen gossip often reflected the doings of the great and powerful long before many of their masters knew about it. So long as she pretended not to notice, she would probably get an earful.

Raven never did learn that lesson, silly boy. He would always *start asking questions rather than letting servants babble to each other.*

She would be just as invisible as a servant or a street urchin; just another common tavern-musician. There weren't many Free Bards who traveled all the way to Lyonarie; it was a long way from Rayden, where the group first came to be organized, and Free Bards had their routines like anyone else. Likely no one would even recognize the knot of multicolored ribbons on her sleeves as anything other than decoration. Even if they did know her for what she was, well, the Guild had made it difficult for a Free Bard to work in Rayden, and the Church had done the same in Gradford, so it made sense for someone to come this far afield for work.

I look like a Gypsy and there is no disguising that, but that might work for me rather than against me. People like things that are a bit exotic; it gives them a taste of places they'll never see, a kind of life they'll never lead.

Gypsies didn't like cities much, which also might mean she would *not* be recognized as one. Ah, well. It was always a case of playing odds being a Gypsy.

And if she was recognized, and it caused her trouble—well, she would deal with that when she saw what cards were in her hand.

The donkey suddenly gave a frightened bray and reared back against the lead-rope, trying to dig all four hooves into the pavement. The rope scraped her palm and she tightened her grip automatically as she looked around for what danger might have alarmed him—but a sudden whiff of powerful odor told her that he had simply reacted to another aspect of a city that she hated. There was no mistaking that charnel reek as it wafted into her face: blood and feces, urine and fear.

She put her hat back on her head and soothed him with her free hand as she continued to pull his lead, gently but firmly, until he started walking again. His eyes rolled, but he obeyed her. She couldn't blame him for balking; she'd have done the same in his place. He might even have scented a relative in that reek.

Or rather, an ex-relative.

The warehouses gave place to something else, and now she knew why she had seen so many carts laden with smaller beasts on this road. This was the district of slaughterhouses and all that depended on them.

She held the donkey's halter firmly under his chin as he fought to escape, shivered and rolled his eyes. There wasn't anywhere he could go, and the press of traffic on all sides was enough to keep him moving. Nightingale wished she had taken thought to cover her mouth and nose with a neckcloth as so many around her were doing—she needed both hands to control the donkey, and her kerchief was in her pocket.

The reek of the slaughterhouses and holding pens was not all that came drifting by on the breeze. There were other, equally unsavory smells—the stench of the leather-workers' vats, the effluvium of the glue-makers' pots, the pong of garbage- and dung-collectors' heaps. Fortunately there was something of a real current of moving air here, and it ran crossways to the road; as soon as they were out of the immediate area, the worst of the smell faded, diluted by distance.

But now the slaughterhouse odor gave way to new odors, or rather, older ones. Nightingale winced and tried to barricade herself against a stench that was both physical and mental. Her stomach heaved, and she tasted bile in the back of her throat.

Mighty God. Even animals wouldn't live like this. Even flies wouldn't live like this! And why does the Church allow this? There is a question for you!

Only the poorest would live here, so near the slaughterhouses and the dreadful stench, the flies, and the disease—and the tenement houses lining the road bore ample testament to the poverty, both monetary and spiritual, of those living within. The houses themselves leaned against each other, dilapidated constructions that a good wind would surely send tumbling to the street. Drunken men and women both, wrapped in so many layers of rags and dirt it was hard to tell what sex they were, lay in the alleys and leaned against the houses. Filthy children crowded the front stoops, big bellies scarcely covered by the rags they wore, scrawny limbs showing that those bellies were the sign of malnourishment and not of overeating. They, too, lay about listlessly on the steps, or sat and watched

the passing traffic, too tired from lack of food to play. The scream of
hungry babies joined the sound of commerce on the road; Nightingale
resolutely closed her ears to other sounds, of quarrels and blows, of weep-
ing and hopelessness. *This* was new; poverty was always part of a city, but
never starvation, not like this. It was one more evidence of King Theovere's neglect, even here, in the heart of his own land and city.

*I can't do anything about this—at least, I can't do more than I'm already
planning to do. I can recruit some of my children from these—I can feed as
many as my purse will permit.* She salved her conscience with that; there
was too much here for even every Gypsy of every clan to correct.

She sighed with relief as more and sturdier buildings took the place of
the tenements. More warehouses, mills for cloth, flour and lumber—and
something that Nightingale had never seen at firsthand among humans
before, although she was familiar enough with the Deliambren version,
which they called "manufactories."

Here, in enormous buildings, people made things—but not in the way
they were accustomed to make them in villages and towns elsewhere.
People made things *together;* each person performed a single task in the
many stages of building something, then passed the object on to the next
person, who performed another task, and so on until the object was com-
pleted. Every example was like every other example; every chair looked
like every other chair, for instance, and every pair of trews like every other
pair of trews. The system worked very well for the Deliambrens, but
Nightingale was of two minds about it. It *did* mean made-goods were
much cheaper; no one needed to be an expert in everything, and almost
anyone could afford well-made trews or chairs or tea-mugs. But it felt like
there was no heart in such goods, and nothing to show that a tea-mug was
special. . . .

*Ah, what do I know? I am a crafter of music, not of mugs—and I am sure
there is still a demand for trews and chairs and mugs made by individuals.*
The system did the Deliambrens no harm; they took as much pleasure in
life and crafting as any other being. Still—

*I would not like to work in such a place, but that does not mean that other
folk would feel the same. Stop making judgments for others, Nightingale.*

The donkey relaxed as they entered this district; she let go her tight hold
on his lead-rope, and let him have his head again. The shape of this area
was determined by the river that ran through it; there was scarcely a bit of
bank that did not have a mill wheel on it to make use of the swiftly-flowing
current. The buildings here were old—and Nightingale suspected that few
of the people traveling beside her had any idea how *very* old they were.
The mill wheels and millraces were recent additions to buildings that had
been standing beside this river since before the Cataclysm.

The buildings were not pretty; they were simple, brute boxes with square window-holes where there might, once, have been glass. Now they were covered with whatever might let in light and exclude weather; glass in some places, oiled paper or sheets of parchment in others, but mostly sheets of white opaque stuff the Deliambrens used for packing crates and padding. The base color of these dull boxes was an equally dull grey; where in the past people had tried to apply paint, either to cover the entire building or as crude advertisements, the paint remained only in patches, as if the buildings had some kind of scabrous disease. But the irony was that these places were solid still; they had stood for centuries and likely would stand for centuries more. Nightingale had been inside the Deliambren Fortress-City; she had seen buildings like these being erected. One actually *poured* the walls, using wood to make the molds to give the walls their form, as if they were huge ceramics. Once the grey stuff set, it was stronger than granite and less likely to age due to weathering.

So the irony, lost to those beside the Gypsy, was that these buildings which seemed relatively new were actually much, much older than the tenements that had been falling down.

The road crossed the river on a bridge that also dated back to the Cataclysm; Nightingale privately doubted that anyone could bridge the Lyon River in these days—except, perhaps, Deliambrens. It was a narrow and fierce stream, with a current so swift and deep that "to swim the Lyon" was a common euphemism for suicide.

For a moment, there was relief from the heat; the waters of the Lyon were as cold as they were swift, and a second river flowed above it—a river of fresh, cool air. Nightingale moved as slowly on the bridge as she could, stretching out her moment of relief.

On the other side, the manufactories gave way again to housing, but fortunately for Nightingale's peace of mind the people here lived in better conditions than those near the slaughterhouses.

There were more of those pre-Cataclysm buildings, in fact, given over to living quarters rather than manufactories. These had more windows, and from the look of things, the ceilings were not as high, granting more levels in the same amount of space. In between these older buildings, newer ones rose, not quite as dilapidated as the tenements on the other side of the river, but by no means in excellent repair. These newer buildings huddled around the old as if for support, as if without those grey bulwarks they could not stand against wind and weather.

Nightingale tried to imagine what this area might have looked like before the wooden tenements were built, but had to give up. She just could not picture it in her mind. Why would people have put so much open space between the buildings, then build the buildings so very tall?

Wouldn't it have made more sense to lay everything out flat, the way a small village was built? That way everyone could have his own separate dwelling, and one would not be forced to hear one's neighbors through walls that were never thick enough for privacy. . . .

Ask anyone who has ever spent the night in an inn with newlyweds in the next room.

Well, there was no telling what the ancestors had been thinking; their world was as alien to the Twenty Kingdoms now as that of any of the nonhumans. Nightingale certainly was not going to try to second-guess them.

However, this area would be a good one in which to start her search. However much she disliked the crowding, she could hide herself better in a crowd than in more exclusive surroundings.

At the first sign of a tiny cross street, she pulled the donkey out of the stream of traffic and into the valley between two buildings, looking for a child of about nine or ten, one who was not playing with others, but clearly looking for someone for whom he could run an errand. Such a child would know where every inn and tavern was in his neighborhood, and would probably know which ones needed an entertainer.

And people think that children know nothing. . . .

Nightingale kept her back quite stiff with indignation as she pulled her donkey away from the door of the Muleteer. Her guide—a girl-child with dirty hair that might have been blond if one could hold her under a stream of water long enough to find out—sighed with vexation. It was an unconscious imitation of Nightingale's own sigh, and was close enough to bring a reluctant smile to the Gypsy's lips.

"Honest, mum, if I'd'a thunk he was gonna ast ye pony up more'n music, I'd'a not hev brung ye here," the girl said apologetically.

Nightingale patted the girl on one thin shoulder, and resolved to add the remains of her travel-rations to the child's copper penny. "You couldn't have known," she told the little girl, who only shook her head stubbornly and led Nightingale to a little alcove holding only a door that had been bricked up ages ago. There they paused out of the traffic, while the girl bit her lip and knitted her brows in thought.

"Ye set me a job, mum, an' I hevn't done it," the child replied, and Nightingale added another mental note—to make this girl the first of her recruits. Her thin face hardened with businesslike determination. "I'll find ye a place, I swear! Jest—was it only wee inns an taverns ye wanted?"

Something about the wistful hope in the girl's eyes made Nightingale wonder if she had phrased her own request poorly. "I thought that only small inns or taverns would want a singer like me," she told the girl. "I'm not a Guild musician, and the harp isn't a very loud instrument—"

"So ye don' mind playin' where there's others playin' too?" the girl persisted. "Ye don' mind sharin' th' take an' th' audience an' all?"

Well, that was an interesting question. She shook her head and waited to reply until after a rickety cart passed by. "Not at all. I'm used to 'sharing'; all of us do at Faires, for instance."

A huge smile crossed the child's face, showing a gap where her two front teeth were missing. "I thunk ye didn' like other players, mum, so I bin takin' ye places where they ain't got but one place. Oh, I got a tavern-place that's like a Faire, 'tis, an' they don' take to no Guildsmen neither. Ye foller me, mum, an' see if ye don' like this place!"

The child scampered off in the opposite direction in which they *had* been going, and Nightingale hauled the donkey along in her wake. The girl all but skipped, she was so pleased to have thought of this "tavern-place," whatever it was, and her enthusiasm was quite infectious. Nightingale found herself hoping that this *would* be a suitable venue, and not just because her feet hurt, she was wilting with the heat, and her shoulders ached from hauling the increasingly tired and stubborn donkey.

She also wanted to be able to reward this child, and not have to thread her way out of the neighborhood the little girl knew and hunt up a new guide. The streets were all in shadow now, although the heat hadn't abated; much longer and it would be twilight. She would *have* to find at least a safe place to spend the night, then; it wasn't wise for a stranger to be out in a neighborhood like this one after dark. In a smaller city she wouldn't have worried so much, but she had heard of the gangs who haunted the back streets of Lyonarie by night; she was a tough fighter, but she couldn't take on a dozen men with knives and clubs.

The child turned to make certain that she was still following, and waved at her to hurry. Nightingale wished powerfully then for that rapport with animals that Peregrine and Lark seemed to share; if only she could convince the donkey that it was in his best interest to pick up his feet a little!

But he was just as tired as she was, and surely he was far more confused. He'd never been inside a city at all, much less had to cope with this kind of foot-traffic, poor thing.

The child slipped back to her side, moving like an eel in the crowd. "Tisn't but three streets up, mum, just t'other side uv where ye met me," she said, looking up into Nightingale's face anxiously. "Oh, I swan, ye'll like the place!"

"I hope so," the Gypsy replied honestly. "I can promise you, at least I won't dislike it as much as I did the last!"

The little girl giggled. "La, mum, ye're furrin, an' the Freehold, it's got more furriners than I ken! Got Mintaks, got Larads, got Kentars, got a couple 'a Ospers, even! Half the folk come there be furrin, too!"

Now that certainly made Nightingale stand up a bit straighter. "Why all the—" She sought for a polite word for the nonhumans.

"Why they got all the Fuzzballs?" the child asked innocently. "Well, 'cause other places, they don' like Fuzzballs, they don' like furriners, they even looks at ye down the nose if ye got yeller skin or sompin. Not Freehold, no, they figger Fuzzball money spends as good nor better'n a Churcher. I *like* Freehold. I'd'a taken ye there fust, but I thunk ye wanted a place where ye wouldn'—ah—"

"Where I wouldn't have any competition?" Nightingale replied, laughing at the child's chagrin. "Oh, my girl, I promise you I am sure enough of my own songs that I don't have anything to fear from other musicians!"

The child grinned her gap-toothed grin again and shrugged. "Ye'll see," she only said. "Ye'll see if I be takin' ye wrong. Freehold—it's a *fine* place! Look—'tis right there, crost the street!"

But the building the girl pointed to was not what Nightingale expected—

The Gypsy blinked, wondering if the child was afflicted with some sort of mental disorder. This wasn't a tavern or an inn building—it was a warehouse!

It was one of the old, pre-Cataclysm buildings, four tall stories high, with a flat roof and black metal stairs running up the side of it from the second story to the rooftop, and more black metal bridges linking it and the buildings nearest it from roof to roof. She narrowed her eyes and tried to see if someone had partitioned off a little corner of it at ground level as a tavern, but there was no sign of any partitioning whatsoever. Whoever owned this building owned the whole thing. Set into the blank face of the wall was a huge sliding door, and a smaller entry-door was inset in it. This was a warehouse!

But there *was* a sign above the entry door, and the sign did say THE FREEHOLD. . . .

The child scampered on ahead and pounded enthusiastically at the door. It opened, and she spoke quickly to someone Nightingale couldn't see. By the time she managed to coax her willfully lagging donkey to the doorway, whoever had been there was gone, and the child was dancing from one foot to the other with impatience.

"He's gone t' git the boss," the child told her. "Ye wait here wit me, an' the boss'll be here in a short bit."

Nightingale looked up at the sign above her head, just to be sure. It did say THE FREEHOLD, that much hadn't changed. But how could anyone ever make any kind of profit running a tavern in a place this size? The cost of fuel and candles alone would eat up all the profits!

She tried to make a quick estimate of just how much it *would* cost to heat this huge cavern of a place in the winter; just as she came to the conclusion that she didn't have the head for such a complicated calculation, the "boss" appeared in the door.

A human of middle years, average in every way from his hair to his clothing, looked her up and down in surprise. "You *are* a Gypsy, aren't you?" he said, before she could say anything to him. "And a Free Bard?"

She nodded cautiously, but he only smiled, showing the same gap at the front of his teeth that the child boasted. "Well! In that case, we might be able to do some business. Will you enter?"

"What about the beast?" she asked dubiously, keeping a tight hold on the donkey's halter. She was not about to leave him outside, not in this neighborhood.

"Bring him in; there's a stable just inside the door," the man replied readily enough. "If you have a big enough building, you can do anything you want, really, and the owner thought it would be nice if people didn't have to go out into the weather to get their riding-beasts."

"Oh." That was all she could say, really. It was all anyone could say. Who would have thought of having a stable *inside* your tavern?

"Trust a Deliambren to think of something like that," the man continued, as an afterthought. "He's almost never here, of course, but he's always coming up with clever notions for the place, and the hearth-gods know a Deliambren has the means to make anything work."

Ah. Now it makes sense! And now it made sense for a tavern to be situated in a warehouse, for only a Deliambren would have the means to heat the place—yes, and probably cool it in the summer, as well!—without going bankrupt.

She turned to the girl, and held out the promised penny, and with the other hand fumbled the bag of travel food off the back of the packs. "Here, take this, too," she said, holding it out as soon as the child accepted her penny with unconcealed glee and greed. "Can I find you in the same place if I need a guide again?"

The child accepted the bag without asking what was in it—hardly surprising, since almost anything she was given would be worth something to her. Even the bag itself. She clutched the bag to her chest and nodded vigorously. "Yes, mum, ye jest ast fer Maddy, an' if I ain't there, I be there soon as I hear!" She grinned again, shyly this time. "I tol' ye that ye'd like this place, mum, didn' I jest?"

"You did, and I don't forget people who are clever enough to guess what I'd like, Maddy," Nightingale told her. "Thank you."

Before she could say anything more, the child bobbed an awkward curtsey and disappeared into the crowd. The "boss" of the tavern was still waiting patiently for her to conclude her business with Maddy.

"Don't you think you ought to look us over and see what we can offer before you make a decision?" the man asked her, although his amused expression and his feelings, as loud as a shout, told her he was certain she would want to stay here. This was quite unlike the proprietor of the Muleteer, whose feelings of lust had run over her body like a pair of oily hands.

She simply raised an eyebrow; he chuckled, and waved her inside.

The doorway opened into a room—or, more correctly, an anteroom—paved like the street outside, furnished with a few wooden benches, with a corridor going off to the right. A Mintak boy appeared in the entrance at the sound of the donkey's hooves on the pavement.

Nightingale had seen many Mintaks in the course of her travels, but never a youngster. Like all the others she had seen, this boy wore only a pair of breeches and an open vest; his hide, exactly like a horse's, was a fine, glossy brown. His head was shaped something like a cross between a horse and a dog, but the eyes were set to the front, so that he could see forward out of both of them, like a human, instead of only one at a time, like a horse. He had a ridge of hair—again, much like a horse's mane—that began between his ears and traveled down his neck, presumably to end between his shoulderblades.

Unlike the adults, who were muscular enough to give any five men pause, this boy was thin, gawky, awkward, exactly like a young colt. Although he had three-fingered hands that were otherwise identical to a human's, with nails that were much thicker and black, his feet presumably ended in hooves, for Nightingale heard them clopping on the pavement.

"This lady is a musician, and she'll be joining us, Kovey," the man said. "Take her little beast and—" He turned back to Nightingale. "I assume that room and board will be part of the arrangement?"

"That's the usual," she replied shortly, unable to be anything but amused herself at the way he had decided that she was going to stay.

"Right then, have her things taken up to the Gallery and put 'em in the first empty room. Then leave word at the desk which it is."

The Mintak boy nodded his hairy head and trotted over to them, extending his hand for the donkey's lead-rope. The donkey stepped up to him eagerly as Nightingale put the rope into his large, square hands. He smiled shyly, showing the blunt teeth of a true herbivore.

Interesting. If I did not have the abilities I do, I would be very suspicious at this point. They have parted me from my transportation and my belongings and gotten me inside a building with no clear escape route. Do they assume that I am naive, or do they assume that as a Gypsy I do *have other senses at my command?*

It could be either. Her clothing marked her as country folk; it could be presumed that she was not familiar with the ways of cities and the hazards therein. On the other hand, the man had not only recognized her as a Gypsy, but as a Free Bard. . . .

Boy and donkey trotted off down the corridor, and Nightingale's escort ushered her past the second doorway and into the "tavern" proper.

The man waited for her reaction, but she was not the country cousin she looked, and she didn't give him the gasp of surprise that he had expected. She had assumed that the "tavern" took up a good portion of the building as estimated from outside, and she had not been mistaken. Maddy had not been mistaken in comparing this place to a Faire. The main portion of the tavern—she couldn't think of a better name for it—had a ceiling that was quite three stories above the rest, and pierced with the most amazing skylights she had ever seen. They were not clear, but made with colored glass, exactly like the windows in the larger Cathedrals. Below the sky-lights hung contrivances that Nightingale guessed were probably lights. Beneath these skylights was an open floor, all of wood, with a raised platform at one end and with benches around it, exactly like a dance floor and stage at a Faire, except that at a Faire the dancing-area would be floored in dirt.

This took up approximately half the floor space. The rest—well, it looked very much as if someone had taken all of the entertainment and eating places at a really huge Faire and proceeded to stack them inside this building.

All around the walls, from the ground floor to the ceiling, there were alcoves for eating and drinking, many with comfortable seating and a small stage for one to three performers. Many of the alcoves had recogniz-able bars in the back; some had doors that could be slid across the front, cutting them off from the main room. Some boasted braziers and what might be odd cooking implements as well. Some had nothing at all but the seating.

Not that this place was as elegant as the skylights indicated; in fact, the opposite was true. The building showed its heritage quite clearly; walls and the ceiling were roughly finished, huge metal beams were exposed, and ropes and wires hung everywhere.

Still it was a monumental undertaking, putting this place together at all, and Nightingale rather liked the unfinished atmosphere. That was the difference—outside, things looked unkempt. In here, they looked unfin-ished. Out there in the rest of the city, there was the feeling of decay and decline, but in here there was unfulfilled potential.

It was then that she realized that she was no longer hot, or even warm; that from the moment she had passed within the front door, she had been cooled by a dry, crisp breeze that came out of nowhere.

Ah, more Deliambren magic, of course. And how better to lure patrons to a place like this, down in a dubious quarter of the city, than to ensure that they will be invisibly cooled in summer and warmed in winter!

There was no one on the main platform, but about half the other small stages had performers on them; not just musicians, but a juggler, a contortionist, a mock-mage, and a storyteller who had his audience of ten in stitches. Savory—though unfamiliar—aromas drifted from three of the tiny kitchens. It was difficult to say precisely where every sound and scent came from in this cavernous place, but Nightingale had the impression that there were similar setups just off the second or third floor balconies. And as Maddy had claimed, a good half of those customers that Nightingale spotted were not human.

"The top floor's lodgings," her escort said diffidently. He waved his hand vaguely at the upper story. "Right side's for customers, left's for staff. You'll be staff, of course—"

"You're assuming I'm going to stay," Nightingale could not resist pointing out dryly. He turned to her with his mouth agape in surprise.

"You—why wouldn't you?" he managed, after a moment during which his mouth worked without any sound emerging.

"You might not want me, for one thing," she said with patient logic. "You don't know anything about me."

"You're a Free Bard, ain't you?" the man retorted. At her nod, he shrugged, as if that was the only answer he needed. ' 'Tyladen—that's the boss, the owner—he's left orders. Free Bards show up looking for work, they got it. *He* says you're all good enough, that's enough for me. He's the one with the cashbox."

The man had a point—but there were still a few things she had to get clear. "Before I agree to anything, I want to know the terms I'll be working under here," she told him severely.

He nodded, his former surprise gone. "You pick the shift—except we got no openings on morning, so it's afternoon, supper to midnight, or midnight to dawn. You can double-shift if you want, but we don't really like it."

Thus far, sounds reasonable. "Go on," she told him, as the sound of a hurdy-gurdy brayed out on her right.

"Terms are pretty simple: room and board, and you pick what kitchen you want your meals out of. We don't go writin' up food, so if you want to stuff yourself sick, that's your problem. You hire on as a musician, that's what you do—no cookin', no waitin' tables, no bartending, no cleanup."

She sensed that he was about to add something else, then he took a look at her and left the words unsaid. She knew what they were, of course—that she was not to offer "extra services" to the customers.

"We don't argue if the customer brings a—a friend here, and wants a room to share for—oh, a couple of hours," he said finally, "but we don't offer him things like that here."

"Oh, please," she said, exasperated. "I've been on the road most of my life. You don't have whores, and you do have an arrangement with the Whores' Guild, I take it, so you don't allow your entertainers to freelance their sexual services?"

He looked just as startled as he had when she had suggested that she might not want to work here, but again, he nodded.

She suppressed a smile. *Well, occasionally clothing does make the person, it appears. I dress like a Churchgoing country girl, he assumes that's what I am! I wonder what he'll think when he sees some of my performing clothing? Perhaps that I am some mental chameleon!*

"That will be fine with me—" she began, but he held up his hand to forestall her.

"There's only one more rule," he told her. "That's the one you might not like. No puttin' out a hat."

She raised one eyebrow as high as it would go. "Just how am I supposed to make a living, may I ask?" she said, more than a bit arrogantly. "No one has *ever* made that part of my arrangements before."

He flushed and looked apologetic. "That's the rule. There's a charge at the door t' get in. You get a salary, an' it depends on how big a draw you are. Lowest is five coppers each shift, highest—well, we only had one person ever get highest, that was a half-royal."

A half-royal? The equivalent of *five gold pieces?* It was Nightingale's turn to stare at him with mouth agape. Very few *Guild* Bards were ever granted that kind of money, and no Free Bard that Nightingale had ever heard of—not even Talaysen, Laurel Bard to a King, was ever paid that much!

"So in other words, I'm on trial until you see what kind of an audience I can collect," she said, finally, after she had gotten over her astonishment. "And I have to take your word for what I'm worth."

He lifted his shoulders, apologetically. "That's the terms; that's what the boss set," he replied.

She considered it for a moment, leaving her own pride out of it. This wasn't entirely a bad thing. She could, if she decided it was worth it, exert herself only enough to pay for her army of children. She had shelter, food, and an excellent venue to hear a great deal. A place like this one would be very popular, not only with working-class folk, but with those with wealth and jaded appetites—or a taste for "uncommon" entertainment. If she had petitioned the Lady of the Night for the perfect place for her information-gathering, she could not have come up with anything better.

Most of all, she would only have to work six hours of every day; that left her at least six to make her own investigations, provided she cared to exert herself that much. She could make herself as conspicuous, or as *inconspicuous* here as she wanted.

In fact, that was not a bad idea. She could play the exotic Gypsy to the hilt here within these four walls—but her persona outside the tavern could be as plain as a little sparrow. No one would connect Nightingale with—whatever she called herself in here.

And if she did that—well, she might not find herself in the "half-royal" category, but she was fairly certain that the five coins she would earn each shift would be silver, not copper.

"I believe I can live with these terms," she said, without bothering to try and strike a better bargain. Not that there would be much point to trying —the price a Deliambren set was not subject to bargaining. One accepted, or one did without.

"Excellent!" The man positively beamed. "I saw that you had harps; we don't have any harp players right now. I can put you up in the Oak Grove, that's on the third floor, far enough away from the dancing that you shouldn't have any trouble with noise. What shift?"

"Supper to midnight," she replied immediately, and he beamed again.

"Perfect! Let's go check the front desk and find out what room you've got—ah—" He looked a little embarrassed. "I didn't catch your name—"

"That's because I didn't give it to you," she replied, softening the words with a faint smile, as she ran a list of possible alternative names in her mind. She would save "Nightingale" for now—just in case *this* Deliambren was already part of her friend's little plot. "My name is Lyrebird."

He nodded with approval. "The lyre's a harp right? Got a nice sound to it—I'm Kyran, by the way, Kyran Horat."

She held out her hand, and he shook it, in the way of Gypsies sealing a bargain. "Welcome to Freehold, Lyrebird," he said heartily. "I think you'll be happy here. You can lighten up now; the bargaining is over."

She chuckled, then looked away from him and out over the expanse of the building and all it contained. There would be enough people here every night that she—or rather, Lyrebird—as flamboyant as that persona would be, would simply be one more flamboyant entertainer among many. She would earn enough to not only get her covert quest done, but quite possibly turn a profit. This place was built by a Deliambren, so she could probably expect some luxuries in her quarters that Kyran hadn't even seen fit to mention—which was a far sight better than anything she'd find in an ordinary inn. All things considered, this had turned out to be luck of the sort that had eased her journey all the way here.

"I think you're right, Kyran," she replied as she suppressed the shiver *that* thought brought her. "Shall we find out about that room?"

Luck this good has to break sometime, she thought as she followed him. *I only pray that when it does, it does not turn as bad as it has been good!*

And if this was the result of that fate, geas, or whatever else had brought her here—well, that turn of good luck to bad, *very* bad, was all too likely.

CHAPTER THREE

Nightingale found nothing to complain about in the room that Kyran assigned to her, except the lack of windows—and on the whole, although it did make her feel a bit closed in, that might have been as much of a benefit as a lack. Certainly there was not going to be much of a view around here, and if the wind happened to come from the wrong direction —well, what traveled on the wind from the direction of the slaughterhouses was nothing she wanted to have to endure.

She surveyed what was likely to be her refuge for the next several weeks, if not months, and on the whole was pleased. There was one light overhead in the main room, a second in the bathroom, both controlled by plates on the wall that one touched—her escort had shown her how to use them, and she had not revealed that she already knew what they were. This was Deliambren light, of course, not an oil lamp or candle; it replicated natural sunlight at about an hour after sunrise; warm, clear, but not too bright. The overall effect with the four walls bare of decoration was of a white box, but that was not altogether bad—Deliambren taste in artwork was not always something she admired, and only the Lady knew who or what had this room before she got it. The one thing this room *did* boast that was quite out of the ordinary was its own tiny bathroom.

It's out of the ordinary, unless you happen to be acquainted with Deliambrens, that is. By their standards, this is all patched together, old and rather tired, the bare minimum for civilization. She considered the closer examination she'd been able to make as she walked up the open staircases and along the balcony to her room. All visible equipment was very shopworn by Deliambren standards—*their* equivalent of secondhand goods. It was all too heavy and too bulky to steal, which made it safe to use here, surrounded by humans who just might try to carry it off otherwise. And those dangling wires and furlongs of conduit—those weren't just afterthoughts, things they hadn't quite tucked out of sight. This equipment was probably reliable, but, to Nightingale's eyes at least, was very clearly cobbled together from several other mismatched pieces of heavy equipment, and likely there was no place else for those wires to go.

The bathroom, stuck off one corner of the main room, was in keeping with the general feeling of "making do." A tiny box, tiled on all surfaces with some shiny white substance that *might* be ceramic, it had a small sink, one of the Deliambren-designed privies, and an oblong object in one corner that she was certain must puzzle the life out of ordinary folk. She had been inside the Fortress-City any number of times; the Deliambrens used these things in places of bathtubs. At a touch, water cascaded from the nozzle in the wall, and although one could not soak in this contrivance, it was the best thing in all the world for washing hair. To her delight, her employers provided soap and towels—probably, she thought cynically, because so few of their new employees had more than a nodding acquaintance with either. That was fine with her; those were two more things she was not going to have to provide.

It isn't a tenth as luxurious as the baths in their guest quarters at home, though, she thought smugly. *And if you look closely, those tiles show some chips and scratch marks, which means they have been reused. Probably all of the fixtures are reused. They probably believe that these rooms are as austere as a Church Cloister, and feel guilty over putting their employees through such hardship!*

A rectangular opening high on the wall with a screen over it allowed warm air—or cool, as now—to flow into the main room, while another on the opposite side removed it. There was a similar arrangement in the bathroom.

All of the furnishings were built into the walls, meaning that they could not be moved—which was a minor annoyance. There was a wardrobe on the same wall as the bathroom, a chest which doubled as a seat, and a bed that folded up into the wall if she needed more floor space. A tiny shelf folded down, next to the bed. It was a very nice bed, though—and typically Deliambren. It bore very little resemblance to the kind of beds that she would find in other inns here. Wide enough for two, the bed was a platform that dropped down on a hinge at the head of it to within an inch or two of the floor and perched on a pair of tiny legs that popped out of the foot. The mattress was made of some soft substance she simply could not identify. The same followed for the sheets, towels and pillows. They weren't woven; that was the only thing she could have said for certain. A single light, small but bright enough to read by, was built into the cavity at the head of the bed; it too was controlled by a palm-plate.

Other than that, the room itself was unremarkable, and as she knew quite well, unlike the kinds of quarters that Deliambrens reserved for their guests.

Oh, I imagine that my good host, knowing that the rooms for staff among humankind are very simple, opted for this as being "typical." Trust a Deliambren never to ask advice on something like this!

The fact was, by most human standards, between the heating and cooling and the bathroom, this place was palatial. Her panniers, covered with road dust and shabby with use as they were, looked as out of place here as a jackdaw's nest in a porcelain vase. Though this "vase" had a few cracks in it, there was no doubt what it was.

She put the bed back up into the wall in order to have more room to work, then set about unpacking her things and putting them away. The harps she left in their cases for the moment, but set beside the cushioned chest-seat. Her costumes were next, and she quietly blessed her instincts as she unpacked them, one by one, and shook them out thoroughly before putting them away in the wardrobe. She *had* been tempted to get rid of the more flamboyant of them, relics of her first days on the road and ill-suited to her current life. There were three of them, all made of ribbons and scarves sewn into skirts; seamed together from the waistband to the knee, then left to flutter in streamers from the knee to the ground. With them went patchwork bodices made to match the skirts, and shirts with a May-dance worth of rainbow-ribbons fluttering from each sleeve. One was made up in shades of green (from forest-green to the pale of new leaves), one in shades of red (a scarlet that was nearly black to a deep rose), and one in shades of blue (from the sky at midnight to the sky at noon).

I was so proud of being a Free Bard, then, that I thought every bit of clothing I owned should shout to the world what I was. They were my flags of defiance, I suppose, and fortunately, at the time, no one who might have taken exception actually recognized them for what they were! Now I hardly ever wear them except at Kingsford Faire.

She hung those at the front of the wardrobe; they would do very nicely for Lyrebird in a casual mood. The majority of her clothing, sensible enough skirts—three of them, of linen and wool—bodices to match of linen, leather and more wool, and six good shirts with only a modest knot of ribbon on each sleeve, she hung in the rear. They were clearly worn and had seen much travel, the wool skirt and bodice were carefully mended, and three of the shirts plainly showed their origin as secondhand clothing to the experienced eye. Those she would use on the street; she could even add a patch or two for effect. She had done so before.

Then came underthings and a nightshift, stockings and a pair of sandals, her winter cloak and a pair of shawls for weather too cold for shirtsleeves but not chill enough for the heavy cloak.

Then, at the bottom of the pannier, the other clothing that would—oh, most definitely!—be suited to the exotic Lyrebird. *These* costumes would virtually guarantee that she was seen and remembered.

The packet she removed from the bottom of the pannier was hardly larger than one of her sensible skirts folded into a square. She had never worn these garments in *human* company before—not that anyone had ever forbidden her to, but she had never felt safe in doing so. Some would have considered them to be a screaming invitation to the kind of activity the proprietor of the Muleteer assumed she would be open to. Others would have considered their mere possession to qualify her for burning at the stake.

She unfolded the outer covering of black, a square of that same, soft black velvet that the Elven messenger had worn, and shook out the garments, one by one.

And as always, she sighed; what woman born could *refrain* from a sigh, presented with these dresses? They were Elven-make, of course, and not even the Deliambrens could replicate them. *Elven silk. Incredible stuff. Now* there *is magic!* The sleeves, the skirts, floated in the air like wisps of mist; they gave the impression that they were as transparent as a bit of cloud, and yet when she wore them, there was not a Cloistered Sister in the Twenty Kingdoms who was as modestly clad as she. There was so much fabric in them that if one took a dress apart and laid the pieces out, they would fully cover every inch of space on the dance floor below, yet each dress packed down into the size of her hand and emerged again unwrinkled, uncrumpled.

One dress was black, with a silver belt, otherwise unadorned, but with its multiple layers of sleeve and skirt cut and layered to resemble a bird's feathers. One was a true emerald-green, embroidered around the neckline, sleeves, and hem with a trailing vine in a deeper green; it had a belt of silk embroidered with the same motif. The third was the russet of a vixen's coat, and the sleeves and hem were dagged and decorated with cutwork embroidery as delicate as lace; the belt that went with this was of goldembroidered leather.

They would suit Lyrebird very well—and because no one save the Elves had ever seen *Nightingale* in this finery, there was very little chance that anyone would recognize her from a description. She would certainly stand out—but no one would know her.

Nor would anyone recognize, in the plain, shabby little mouse who would go out into the streets, the flamboyant harpist of Freehold in her Elven silks.

And since most of my customers and the members of my audience are going to be nonhuman, Lyrebird is going to be perfectly safe from any untoward conduct, even in her Elven silks. Very few nonhumans were going to find her attractive or desirable, which was just fine so far as she was concerned.

She selected the russet for her first performance—what better place for a russet vixen than an Oak Grove?—and gratefully stripped out of her sweat-soaked clothing and headed for the bathroom.

The water-cascade worked just like the one she remembered, and to her great pleasure the soap was delicately scented with jessamine and left a fresh perfume in her hair. She luxuriated in the hot water pouring over her body, washing every last trace of the long journey away. This would be wonderful for easing the aches and strains of long playing, caused by sitting in one position for hours at a time.

She dried and styled her long, waist-length black hair in an arrangement very unlike Nightingale's simple braid; this was an elaborate coil and twist along the back of her head, with the remainder of her hair emerging as a tail from the center of the knot, or allowed to trail as a few delicate tendrils on either side of her face. She slipped the silken dress on over her clean body—it would have been a desecration and a sin to have put it on without a full bath—reveling in the sensuous feel of the silk caressing her hips and legs, slipping sleekly over her arms.

Now she took the cover off the larger of her two harps, the one she could only play while seated, and tuned it. She ignored her stomach as she did so—she could eat later, if need be, but at the moment she had to get the harp ready in good time before her performance. Kyran had told her that he would send one of the servers up to her room, to guide her to the Oak Grove when it was time for her to play—her performance would extend past midnight, just this once, because she would never have had time to bathe and change and ready herself before suppertime.

It was very hard, though, to ignore the savory aromas wafting up from below. Most of them were as strange as they were pleasant—not exactly a surprise, if most of the clientele were not human.

She was going to surprise Kyran, however. He probably expected her to perform human-made music only, but Lyrebird was a bird of a different feather altogether.

Hmm. Perhaps I ought to have worn the black!

She was going to sing and play the music of at least three nonhuman cultures, besides the Elves. Human music would comprise the smallest part of her performance.

And again, since very few people, even among the Gypsies and the Free Bards, knew that she collected the music of nonhumans, this would be utterly unlike Nightingale.

*   *   *

She retired to her room in a glow of triumph, harp cradled in her arms, two hours after midnight; entirely pleased with herself and her new surroundings. Her particular performance room—which was, indeed, decorated to resemble a grove of trees with moss-covered rocks for seats and tables "growing" up out of the floor—was far enough from the dance floor that her own quiet performance could go on undisturbed. She had begun with purely instrumental music, Elven tunes mostly, which attracted a small, mixed crowd. From there she ventured into more and more foreign realms, and before the night was over, there were folk standing in line, waiting for a seat in her alcove. Most of them were not human, which was precisely as she had hoped; word had spread quickly among the patrons of Freehold that there was a musician in the Oak Grove who could play anything and sing "almost" anything. Most of the nonhumans were hungry for songs from home—and most of the time she could oblige them with *something,* if not the exact song they requested.

As she climbed the stairs to her room, oblivious to the cacophony of mixed music and babbling talk, she hardly noticed how tired she was. She was confident now that her salary would be in the three- or four-silver area, if not five. That would be enough; it would purchase the help of quite a number of children at a copper apiece. Kyran had checked on her during one of the busier moments, which was gratifying—he'd had a chance to see with his own eyes how many people were lining the walls, waiting for seats. His eyes had gone wide and round when he'd seen her in costume, too.

He certainly didn't expect that *out of the drab little starling at the front door!*

Finally she reached the top of the stairs, the balcony overlooking the dance floor, and the hallway leading off of it. Though the hall muffled some of the echoing noise from below, she couldn't help but notice that her room was just not far enough from the balcony for it to do much good. She put the harp down to open her door; set it inside and turned on the light, then closed the door behind her. The din outside vanished, cut off completely once the door was closed. She sighed with relief; her one worry had been that she might be kept awake all night by the noise. Evidently the Deliambren had thought of that, as well.

She set the harp safely in the corner, and reached for the plate that released the bed. It swung down, gently as a falling feather, and she fell into it.

And got up immediately at a tapping at her door. She answered it, frowning; had someone followed her up here, expecting the kind of entertainment that Kyran had *sworn* she would not have to provide? If so, he was going to get a rude surprise. Nightingale did not need a knife or a club to defend herself; her Lyncana friends made a fine art of hand-to-hand combat, and while she was a mere novice by their standards, she was confident that there was not a *single* human, no matter how large and muscular, who could force himself upon her. Many had tried in the past, and many had ended up permanently singing in higher keys.

But when she opened the door, there didn't seem to be anyone there— until she dropped her eyes.

"Evenin' snack for ye, mum," said a tow-headed urchin with a pair of ears that could have passed for handles, holding up a covered tray. He had to shout to be heard over the bellows and cheers from the dance floor below. "Boss figgered ye'd be hungered."

She wasn't about to argue; she took the tray from the boy with a smile, and before she could even thank him, he had scampered away down hall to the staircase, nimble as a squirrel and just as lively.

Hmm. My first reward for a job well done? That could be; she wasn't going to press the point. She *was* hungry despite a few bites taken here and there during the breaks in performing. After all, she hadn't eaten since noon, and that was a long time ago!

She took the tray over to her bed, set it down, lifted the cover, and nearly fainted with delight.

There was quite enough there, in that "snack," to have fed her for two days if she'd been husbanding rations. A tall, corked bottle of something cold—water beaded the sides and slid down the dark glass enticingly— stood beside a plate holding a generous portion of rare roast meat, sliced thin and still steaming. Three perfect, crusty rolls, already buttered, shared the plate with the meat. Very few humans would have recognized the next dish, which resembled nothing so much as a purple rose, but she knew a steamed *kanechei* when she saw it, and her mouth watered. To conclude the meal, there was a plate of three nut-studded honeycakes.

Her stomach growled, and she fell to without a second thought. When she finished, there was nothing left but a few crumbs and a blissful memory.

Following Deliambren tradition, she took the tray to the door and left it next to the wall, just outside. As she looked up and down the hallway, she saw another tray or two, which meant that she had done the right thing. The shouting from below had died down somewhat, but it sounded rather as if the drummer for the musical group was having some kind of rhythmic fit, and the audience was clapping and stamping their feet in time. She closed the door again quickly.

Why is it that the drunker people become, the more drumming they want? Maybe the alcohol blunts their ability to enjoy anything subtle—like a melody.

She had intended to read some of her own notebooks of nonhuman songs—but after that wonderful meal, and especially the light, sweet wine that had accompanied it, she could hardly keep her eyes open. So instead, she slipped out of her gown and hung it up with a care for the delicate cutwork; drew her nightshift on over her head, turned off the light and felt her way into bed. She hardly had time to settle herself comfortably, when sleep overtook her.

"Therefore, my friends and brothers," the young Priest said, earnestly, his brown eyes going from one face below him to the next, "Yes, and my sisters, too! You must surely see how all these things only prove the *unity* of everything in the Cosmos—how God has placed the warmth of His light in *every* heart, whether the outer form of that heart walk on two legs or four—be clad in skin, hide, scales, or feathers—whether the being call God by the Name that we know him, or by something else entirely! What matters is this, only: that a being, whatever form he wears, strive to shelter that Light, to make it shine the brighter, and not turn his face to the darkness!"

The homely young Priest signaled his musicians and stepped back with a painfully sincere smile. Nightingale slipped out of St. Brand's Chapel just as the tiny—and obviously musically handicapped—choir began another hymn-song, slipping a coin into the offering box as she passed it. She stepped out into the busy street and blended into the traffic, squinting against the bright noon light.

This was the fourth Chapel she had attended in as many days, and it had her sorely puzzled. In the other three—all of them impressive structures in "good" neighborhoods—she had heard only what she had expected to hear. That only humans had souls; that nonhumans, having no soul to save, had no reason to be "good." That if they had no reason to be good, they must, therefore, be evil.

This wasn't the first time such an argument had been used against nonhumans; obviously one of the things that the Church absolutely *needed* in order to galvanize its followers was an enemy. It was difficult to organize opposition to an abstract evil—and even more difficult to get people to admit that there was evil inside themselves. That meant that the ideal enemy would be something outside the Church and outside the members of the Church, and as unlike the human followers of the Sacrificed God as possible.

Easy enough to point the finger at someone and say, "he doesn't look like you, he doesn't believe in what you believe, he must be evil—and your natural enemy," she thought cynically, as she settled her hat on her head and let the crowd carry her along toward Freehold. She had *expected* this; if the Church was snatching secular power away from the High King, Lyonarie would be the place where it would show its truest hand—and that would be the place where the Church officials would take a stand showing who they had selected to be the "Great Enemy."

What she had not expected was that here the Church was openly divided against itself.

When her patrons first began telling her about this, in discussions she had started during the breaks between her sets, she had at first dismissed it as being a trick of some kind. After all, why in the world would Priests openly preach against what was, supposedly, Church canon? She couldn't come up with a reason behind such a trick, unless it might be to lull the nonhumans into complacency—but what other reason could there be?

She decided to take to the Chapels herself to find out.

Thus far, she had discovered a pattern, at least. Chapels in certain districts—aggressively human-only—*always* held Priests who followed the canonical path. But Chapels elsewhere might just as often harbor Priests like Brother Brion back there; Priests who preached the brotherhood of all beings, and stressed the similarities among the most various of beings rather than their differences. They *could* have been operating the kind of trick she suspected—but they could not hide the feelings behind their words, not to her, not when she chose to follow the music of their emotions.

And the music was of a sweeter harmony than that sadly under-talented choir back there. These Priests truly, deeply, *believed* in what they were saying. And if the stories her patrons told her were true, there were just as many Priests of this radical line as there were who followed canon.

The crowd carried her up to the front door of Freehold, and she slipped out of the stream and onto the doorstep. One or two others followed her there, but she knew after a quick glance that these were patrons, not fellow staff, and she simply granted them a brief smile before opening the door and taking the *other* hallway to the right, the one that led to the back stairs rather than the stable. She really didn't want anyone to know that "Tanager"—her street-name—and "Lyrebird" were one and the same. Especially not customers.

But as she climbed the dimly lit back staircase to the top floor, she couldn't help thinking about the words of that so-earnest young Priest, and all the trouble those words must surely be causing him in certain circles.

And in her brief experience, Priests, no matter how well meaning and sincere, simply did *not* do or say things that would get them in trouble with their own superiors.

Except that here and now, they were.

What, in the name of the Gypsy Lady and the Sacrificed God, was going on here?

T'fyrr tried to concentrate on the music coming out of his friend Harperus' miraculous little machine, but it was of no real use. A black mood was on him today, a black mood that not even music could lift.

He finally waved at the little black cube, which shut itself off, obediently. He turned and stared out the windows of Harperus' self-propelled wagon at the human hive called Lyonarie. *Humans again. Why am I doing this? Surely I shall never interact with humans without something tragic occurring!*

He examined the scaled skin of his wrists, where the marks of his fetters were still faintly visible, at least to his eyes. The invisible fetters, the ones that bound his heart, hurt far more than the physical bonds had.

Why did I agree to come here? How is it that Harperus can charm me into actions I would never take on my own?

Months ago, he had agreed to help Harperus in yet another of his schemes: a partial survey of the human lands. All had been well, right up until the moment that he had been caught on the ground by humans who claimed that he was a demon, a creature of evil, and had fettered and imprisoned him, starving him until he was more than half mad. Their intent had been to kill him in some religious spectacle—

That was what Harperus said. I scarcely recall most of it.

Little had he known he had friends among the crowd assembled to see him die: a pair of Free Bards, who had provided him with a distraction, the means to his escape.

Unfortunately, not everyone had been distracted at the crucial moment. A single human guard had seen that he was about to flee and had tried to stop him.

To a fatal end. . . .

That was the reason for his black depression. It did not *matter* that he had killed in self-defense; the point was that he had *killed*. The man he had eviscerated in his pain and hunger-madness had only been doing his duty.

In fact, no matter what Harperus claims, since he was doing his duty, to the best of his ability, he was as "good" as I—perhaps my spiritual better. Certainly he is—was—not the one with blood on his conscience.

Could this mean, in the end, that the fanatics who had called him a demon, and evil, were actually *right?* The question haunted him, and Harperus, who had found him shivering in a field after his flight, had not helped. Harperus merely shrugged the entire question off, saying that the guard had followed the orders of a superior who was in the wrong. He

further claimed that the man must at some point have *known* that his
superior was in the wrong, and that evened the scales between himself and
the man he had murdered.

*But Harperus is a Deliambren, and they are facile creatures. They can
make white into black and sun into midnight with their so-called logic.*
Harperus simply could not understand why this should torment him so;
after all, it was over and done with, and there was nothing more to be said
or done but to move on.

*Oh, yes. To move on, without a load of guilt upon my soul so heavy that I
cannot fly.*

T'fyrr sighed gustily, and turned away from the window, waving at the
machine again. It started right up obediently. Not that T'fyrr didn't know
this particular human song by heart, but he wanted to have every nuance
that Harperus had recorded. This was a love duet, sung by two of the finest
of the human musicians—at least in T'fyrr's estimation—that Harperus
had ever captured in his little cubes.

*Lark and Wren. Why do so many of these humans bear the names of birds,
I wonder?*

Of course, part of the passion here was simply because the two who
sang this song of love *were* lovers, and they allowed their feelings free
voice. Still, T'fyrr had heard other humans who were their equals since he
had descended from the mountains of his homeland, and not all of those
were represented in Harperus' collection.

The one called Nightingale, for instance. . . .

A Haspur's memory was the equal of any Deliambren storage crystal,
and his meeting with Nightingale was fraught with such power and light
that for a moment it completely overwhelmed his terrible gloom.

He and Harperus had taken a place for the Deliambren's living-wagon
in a park, a place created by Gypsies for travelers to camp together. This
was enlightened altruism; they charged a fee for this, and the intent of the
place was to sell them services they might not otherwise have in the
wilderness between cities.

*Still, they erect and maintain such Waymeets; surely they deserve recom-
pense. I cannot fault them for charging fees.*

T'fyrr had been restless, and Harperus had not seen any reason why he
should have to remain mewed up in the wagon—the Gypsies were very
assiduous about protecting the peace of their patrons. So he had gone for
a walk, out under the trees surrounding the camping-grounds, and after an
interval, he had heard a strange, wild music and followed it to its source.

It had been a woman, a Gypsy, playing her harp beside a stream. He had
known enough about humans even then to recognize how unique she was.
Black-haired, dark-eyed, her featherless skin browned to a honey-gold

from many miles on the open road beneath the sun, she was as slender and graceful as a female of his own race and as ethereal as one of the beings that Harperus called "Elves." With her large, brooding eyes, high cheek-bones, pointed chin and thin lips, she would probably have daunted him in other circumstances, since those features conspired to give her an air of haughty aloofness. But her eyes had been closed with concentration; her lips relaxed and slightly parted—and her music had entwined itself around his heart and soul, and he could not have escaped if he had wanted to.

They had shared a magical afternoon of music, then, once she finished her piece and realized that he was standing there. She had been as eager to hear some of the music of his people as he had been to learn the music of hers. An unspoken, but not unfelt, accord had sprung up between them, and T'fyrr sometimes took that memory out and held it between himself and despair when his guilt and gloom grew too black to bear.

The wagon lurched, and T'fyrr caught himself with an outstretched hand-claw.

Deliambren chairs were not made for a Haspur; the backs were poorly positioned for anyone with wings. Harperus had compromised by having a stool mounted to the floor of the wagon, with a padded ring of leather-covered metal that T'fyrr could clutch with his foot-talons a few *krr* above the floor. It was only a compromise, and T'fyrr found himself jarred out of his memory of that golden afternoon with Nightingale as the wagon lurched and he had to clutch, not only the foot-ring, but the table in front of him, to avoid being pitched to the floor.

Those stabilizer-things must be broken again. Much of the Deliambren's equipment had a tendency to break fairly often; Harperus spent as much time fixing the wagon as he did driving it. Most of the time the things that broke merely meant a little inconvenience; once or twice the Deliambren had actually needed to secure the wagon in a place that could be readily defended at need and call his people for someone to bring him a new part.

Still, this was a marvelous contraption. T'fyrr had, out of purest curios-ity, poked his beak into the wagons of other travelers, and this behemoth was to those little horse-drawn rigs as he was to a scarcely fledged starling.

The wagon was divided into four parts: an eating and sitting part, where he was now; a sleeping part; a bathing and eliminating part; and a mysteri-ous part that the Deliambren would allow no one into but himself. T'fyrr suspected that this final part was where the controls for the wagon were, and where Harperus kept some of the "technical" and "scientific" instru-ments that he used. Not that it mattered. T'fyrr was supremely incurious where all that nonsense was concerned.

The wagon could propel itself down a road without any outside pulling by horses or other draft-beasts. Right at the moment it was doing just that, although up until this point the Deliambren had taken exacting pains to keep humans from knowing it could move of itself. On the hottest days, it remained cool within—on the coldest, it was as warm as the Haspur could have wished. There were mystical compartments where fresh food was kept, remaining fresh until one wished to eat it. There was another kind of seat for elimination of bodily waste, and a tube wherein one could stand to be sluiced clean with fresh water. The whole of the wagon was most marvelously appointed: shiny beige wall and ceiling surfaces, leather-covered seating, rough, heavy rugs fastened down on the floor that one could dig one's talons into to avoid being flung about while the wagon was moving. Even the beds were acceptable, and it had been difficult for T'fyrr to find an acceptable bed—much less a comfortable one—since he had come down out of the mountains.

The very windows of this contrivance were remarkable. *He* could see out, but no one could see in. T'fyrr still did not understand how that was possible.

Unfortunately, the view displayed by those windows at the moment was hardly savory.

And Harperus claims that this is not the vilest part of this city! It is difficult to believe.

The Haspur lived among the tallest mountains on Alanda; while they were not very territorial by nature, they were also not colony-breeders. Each Haspur kept a respectable distance between his aerie and those of his neighbors. No enclave of Haspur ever numbered above a thousand— and there were at least that many humans just in the area visible from the window of the wagon!

They crammed themselves together in dwellings that were two and three stories tall, with the upper floors extended out over the street in such a way that very little sunlight penetrated to the street below. There must have been four or five families in each of the buildings, and each family seemed to have a half dozen children at absolute minimum. T'fyrr could not imagine what it must sound like with all of them meeping and crying at once. And how did their parents manage to feed them all? A young Haspur ate its own weight in food every day during the first six years of its growth; after that, he ate about half his own weight each day until he was full-grown. That was one reason why Haspur tended to limit their families to no more than two—T'fyrr could not even begin to imagine the amount of food consumed by *six* children!

This was not even a good place in which to raise young. In addition to the lack of sun, there was a profound lack of fresh air in this quarter. The buildings restricted breezes most cruelly. T'fyrr did not want to think about how hot it must be, out there in the street; why these people weren't running mad with the heat was a mystery. And the noise must be deafening, a jarring cacophony also likely to drive one mad.

Perhaps they are all mad; perhaps that is why they have so many offspring.

Haspur did not have a particularly good sense of smell, which he suspected was just as well, for he was certain that so many people crowded together—like starlings!—must create an environment as filthy as a starling roost.

The crowds seemed to be thinning, though, and the standard of construction in the residences rising the farther they went. He was not imagining it—there definitely was more room between the buildings; there were even spots of green, though the greenery was imprisoned away behind high walls, as if the owners of the property were disinclined to share even the sight of a tree or a flower with the unworthy.

There were fewer children in the street, too, and those few were not playing; they were with adults, supervised. Some even seemed to be working under adult supervision, sweeping the gutters, scrubbing walls, polishing gates.

They paused for a moment; T'fyrr couldn't see what was going on at the front of the coach, but a moment later they were on the move again and he saw why they had stopped. There was a simple wooden gate meant to bar the road, now pulled aside, and several armed guards to make certain no one passed it without authorization. They watched the coach pass by stoically enough, but T'fyrr noted that they did seem—impressed? puzzled?

Well, Harperus is Deliambren, and he was bent on displaying Deliambren wonders to the court of the High King. . . I suppose he must have decided to begin with everyone in the city.

Harperus had insisted that here in Lyonarie it was of utmost importance to display as much power as one could, conveniently. Abstractly, T'fyrr understood this; the powerful were never impressed by anyone with *less* power than they, after all. But this business of going out of their way to look strange and different, including operating the coach without horses—

Looking different can be hazardous; I have had a crop full of what that hazard can be. Displaying too much power can incite as much envy as anything else, and the envious, when powerful, are often moved to try and help themselves to what has excited that envy, at whatever cost to the current owner.

Still, Harperus claimed that he had "connections" at the court of Theovere, and given the dangerous trends of the past two years, he and his people had felt it was time to employ those "connections."

Theovere was a music lover of the most fanatic vein; apparently this was what had been occupying the time he should have been spending doing his duty as High King. Originally, Harperus was going to offer Theovere one of the music machines and a set of memory-crystals as a blatant bribe for a little more influence in legislation, but since the time that original plan had been conceived, he had evolved a better one—

Better, not just because it means no dangerous "technology" will be in the hands of those who might somehow manage to find an unpleasant use for it, but because it will mean—or so he thinks—that he will have a direct influence instead of an indirect one.

T'fyrr sighed, flipped his wings to position them more comfortably, and drummed his talons on the table. He was not looking forward to this. Harperus' plan was to have T'fyrr appointed as an official Court Musician to the High King himself. Harperus was unshakably certain that once the High King heard T'fyrr sing, the Haspur would become a royal favorite. And once a nonhuman was a royal favorite, it would be much more difficult for other interests to get laws restricting the rights of nonhumans past the High King.

Interests such as the human Church, perhaps . . . though I am not particularly sanguine about one Haspur being able to overcome the interests of the Church, however optimistic Harperus may be. Religion rules the heart, and the heart is the most stubborn of adversaries. Rule the religion, and you rule the heart, and no one can oppose you—unless what you offer is better. Then, you must convince them that what you have is better, and people will die to hold on to what they already believe. . . .

T'fyrr twitched his tail irritably. Harperus was optimistic about a great many things—and T'fyrr did not share his optimism in most of them.

Even if we can get in to see this High King, there is no guarantee he will be impressed with my singing. Even if he is, there is no guarantee that he will actually do anything about it personally; and from what I have seen, if he leaves my disposition up to his underlings, they will find a way to "lose" me. No, Harperus is counting on a great deal of good luck, and good luck seems to have deserted me.

T'fyrr glanced out the windows again and was impressed, though in a negative fashion, by the homes he now passed. *These* dwellings—each a magnificent work of art, each set in its own small park and garden—were clearly owned by those of wealth and high rank. And the guards on that gate they had passed showed just how unlikely it would be for a commoner to get access to these lovely garden-spots.

So the low and poor must crowd together in squalor, while the wealthy and high live in splendor. If I were low and poor—I think I would go elsewhere to live. My home would still be poor, but at least I would have sunlight and fresh air, green things about me and a little peace.

But—perhaps these humans enjoyed living this way. Starlings certainly did. That made them even less understandable.

Not that he had come close to understanding them so far. The humans' own Sacrificed God spoke of fairness and justice and faith in the goodness of others. These things should prevent believers from doing harm to strangers. Why should an underling, clearly seeing his superiors doing vile things to another living being, believe that those things were justified? How could he be convinced that another being, who had done *no* harm, was a monster worth destroying? How could such a man be so convinced that those superiors were correct that he would spend his own life to carry out their will?

Perhaps those superiors *were* right; perhaps T'fyrr was as potentially evil as they claimed. After all, *he* was the one who had killed. Perhaps he misunderstood what the Sacrificed God was all about—after all, if the Deliambrens could make white into black, maybe the humans could, too.

I only hope that Harperus' plan works as well as he thinks it will, T'fyrr thought, depression settling over him again. *I might somehow redeem myself, if only I can be in a position where I can do some real good—or perhaps this helplessness to affect anything for the better is punishment for my evil. . . .*

T'fyrr was not as expert at reading human expressions as he would have liked, but there was no mistaking the look the Court official facing them wore on *his* refined visage.

Disdain.

Not all of Harperus' Deliambren charm *or* magic had been able to remove that look from the face of this so-called "Laurel Herald." He had taken in the splendor of Harperus' costume—a full and elaborate rig that made the Deliambren look to T'fyrr's eyes rather like one of those multi-tiered, flower-bedecked, overdecorated cakes that some races produced at weddings and other festivities. He had watched the coach drive itself off to a designated waiting place with a similarly lifted brow. Of course, he was probably used to seeing similar things every day, and his livery of scarlet and gold, embroidered on the breast with a winged creature so elaborately encrusted with gold bullion that it was impossible to tell what it was supposed to be, was just as ornate in its way as Harperus' costume. He sat behind a huge desk—a desk completely empty so far as T'fyrr could see—in the exact center of an otherwise barren, marble-walled and mosaic-floored chamber. The walls were covered with heroic paintings of stiff-faced humans engaged in conflicts, or stiff-faced humans posing in front of bizarre landscapes. There was a single bench behind the desk, where many young humans in similar livery sat quietly.

Now he waited for Harperus to declare himself, which Harperus was not at all loathe to do. The Deliambren adored being able to make speeches.

"I am Harperus, the Deliambren Ambassador-at-large," he announced airily to the functionary. He went on at length, detailing the importance of his position, the number of dignitaries he had presented his credentials to and the exalted status of the Deliambren Parliament. Finally, he came to the point.

"I have a presentation to make to Theovere," he concluded.

Not "His Majesty High King Theovere," but the simple surname, as if he and the High King were of equal stature. T'fyrr was impressed, by Harperus' audacity if nothing else.

The title Harperus claimed was not precisely a fiction, although very little of what the Deliambren actually did on his extensive trips ever had anything to do with conventional diplomacy. And it was entirely possible he had presented his credentials to every one of the dignitaries he named —they were all wealthy enough to afford Deliambren goods, and Harperus often acted as a courier for such things. The official favored Harperus with a long moment of silence, during which the "Laurel Herald" scrutinized the Deliambren as carefully as an oldster examining her daughter-in-law's aerie for dirt in the corners, unpolished furniture, or a fraction less *klrrrthn* than was proper.

Harperus simply stood there, radiating a cool aplomb. T'fyrr was grateful that no human here could possibly have enough experience with Haspur to read their expressions and body language, or he would have given it all away with his rigid nervousness. He stood as straight and as stiffly as a perching-pole, his wings clamped against his back. Probably the official didn't notice, or if he did, thought it was stiff formality and not nerves.

He didn't seem to notice the Haspur at all; in the simple silk body-wrap, T'fyrr probably looked like a slave.

Finally the "Laurel Herald" elected to take them at face value; he signaled to a boy he referred to as "Page," one of the dozen waiting quietly on the bench behind his desk, and gave them over into the boy's keeping.

"Take them to the Afternoon Court," the Herald said, shortly, and turned his attention to other business on his empty desk.

After an interminable walk down glass-walled corridors that passed through the middle of mathematically precise gardens, the boy led them toward—a structure. If the scale of the Palace had been anything T'fyrr considered normal, it would have been another wing of a central building. But since everything was on such a massive scale, this "wing" was the size of entire Palaces. It was certainly the size of the huge Cathedral in

Gradford, which was one of the largest human buildings T'fyrr had ever seen.

"That's Court, my lords," the boy explained, enunciating carefully. "That's all that goes on in that Palace building, just Court. Morning and Afternoon Court, informal Court, formal Court, Judiciary, Allocation, City—"

The boy rattled on until T'fyrr shook his head in disbelief. How many ways could one entitle the simple function of hearing problems and meeting people? Evidently quite a few. . . .

The bureaucracy here must be enough to stun a thinking being. I feel dizzy.

The doors at the end of the corridor swung open without a hand to open them as they approached; T'fyrr glanced sideways at Harperus, who smirked in smug recognition.

A Deliambren device, of course. Why am I not surprised?

The doors closed behind them, silently, and the Haspur noted larger versions of the Deliambren lighting that Harperus employed in his coach hanging from the ceiling, encased in ornate structures of glass and gold. There were probably hundreds more examples of Deliambren wonders here, but none of them would be of the type that could be taken apart without destroying them.

Well, no matter what the Church says about the "evil magic" of those who are not human, past High Kings have not scrupled to buy and use our devices. T'fyrr grimaced. *No matter what happens, I would place a high wager that they would* continue *to use such things, even in the face of a Church declaration of Anathema. The Church would either look the other way, or the High King would pay the fine and continue to have his lighting and his self-opening doors.*

The High King would be able to *afford* whatever fine the Church levied without even thinking about it; T'fyrr knew, after traveling so long with Harperus, just how much that lighting, those doors, probably cost. Nor was the display of wealth limited to the nonhuman devices so prominently displayed and used. Of course, the money came from somewhere, and T'fyrr's mind played out an image of the human hive they had come through.

They followed down a hallway paved in polished marble with matching marble paneling. Graceful designs had been incised into the marble of the walls and gold wire inlaid in the grooves. At intervals, along the wall and beneath the lighting, where they were displayed at their best advantage, were graceful sculptures of humans and animals, also of marble with details of gold inlay. Between the sculptures stood small marble tables, topped with vases made of semiprecious jade, malachite and carnelian.

The vases were filled with bouquets, not of fresh flowers, but of flowers made of precious stones and gold and silver wire.

T'fyrr could not even begin to calculate the cost of all of this. Surely just one of those flowers would keep a commoner out in Lyonarie fed and clothed for a year!

The page led them to a pair of gold-inlaid, bronze doors, each a work of art in itself, depicting more humans—though for once, these were not in conflict, but gathered for some purpose. The doors swung open, and the boy waved them in.

"They'll have brought your name to the Presiding Herald," the boy whispered as T'fyrr caught sight of a jewel-bedecked throng just inside the door. "He'll add you to the list; just listen for him to announce you, and then present yourself to His Majesty."

"Thank you," Harperus said gravely. The boy bobbed an abrupt little bow, and hurried off; Harperus strode between those open doors as if he had every right to be there, and T'fyrr moved in his wake, like a silent, winged shadow.

He had not donned all of the finery that Harperus had wanted him to put on—a huge, gemmed pectoral collar, ankle-bracelets, armbands and wristbands, a dusting of gold powder for his wings. Now he was glad that he had not. Not only had the wrist and armbands and bracelets felt *far* too much like fetters, but T'fyrr was certain that he would only have looked ridiculous in the borrowed gear, as if he was trying to ape these jeweled and painted humans, who were oh-so-carefully *not* staring at the nonhumans in their midst. There did not appear to be any other nonhuman creatures in this room, although it was difficult to be certain of that. They could have been crammed up against the white marble walls—that, evidently, was the place where those of little importance were relegated. The magic circle of ultimate status was just before the throne, within earshot of everything that went on upon the dais. Harperus strolled toward that hallowed ground quite as if he had a place reserved for him there, and to T'fyrr's amazement, the haughty courtiers gave way before him.

Perhaps they are frightened by his costume!

The nearer they got to the throne, the more annoyed and resentful the glances of those giving way for them became. Just at the point where T'fyrr was quite certain Harperus was about to be challenged, the Deliambren stopped, folded his arms, and stood his ground, his whole attitude one of genial *listening.* T'fyrr did his best to copy his friend.

Harperus was *truly* paying attention to what was going on around the throne, unlike many of the humans here. As T'fyrr watched and listened, following the Deliambren's example, he became aware that there was something very wrong. . . .

The High King—who did not look particularly old, though his short hair was an iron grey, and his face sported a few prominent lines and wrinkles —sat upon a huge, gilded and jeweled throne that was as dreadful an example of bad taste as anything Harperus had ever inflicted on an unsuspecting T'fyrr. The King's entire attitude, however, was not at all business-like, but rather one of absolute boredom.

On both sides of the throne were richly dressed humans in floor-length ornate robes embroidered with large emblems, with enormous chains of office about their necks, like so many dressed up dogs with golden collars. But these dogs were not the ones obeying the command of their master— rather, the prey was in the other claw entirely.

Harperus had been right. Harperus had actually been right. The High King virtually parroted everything these so-called advisors of his told him to say.

Now, T'fyrr was mortally certain that very few of the courtiers were aware of this, for the Advisors bent over their monarch in a most respect-ful and unctuous manner, and whispered in carefully modulated tones what it was they thought he should say. They were taking great care that it appear they were only advising, not giving him orders. But a Haspur's hearing was as sharp as that of any owl, and T'fyrr was positive from the bland expression on Harperus' face that the Deliambren had some device rigged up inside that bizarre head- and neck-piece he sported that gave him the same aural advantage.

During the brief time that they stood there, waiting their turn, King Theovere paid little or no attention to matters that T'fyrr thought impor-tant—given as little acquaintance as he had with governing. There were several petitions from Guildmasters, three or four ambassadors presenting formal communications from their Kings, a report on the progress of the rebuilding at Kingsford—

Well, those might easily be dismissed, as Theovere was doing, by hand-ing them over to his Seneschal. There was nothing there that he really needed to act upon, although his barely hidden yawn was rather rude by T'fyrr's standards. But what of the rest?

There was an alarming number of requests from Dukes, Barons, and even a mere Sire or two from many of the Twenty Kingdoms, asking the High King's intervention with injustices perpetrated by *their* lords and rulers. Wasn't that precisely the kind of thing that the High King was *supposed* to handle? Wasn't he supposed to be the impartial authority to keep the abuse of power to a minimum? That was how T'fyrr understood the structure of things. The High King was the ultimate ruler, and his duty was not only to his own land but to see that all the others were well-governed—enforcing that, even to the point of placing a new King on a throne if need be.

But most of these petitions, like the rest of the work, he delegated to his poor, overburdened Seneschal—everything that he did not dismiss out of hand with a curt "take your petty grievances back to your homeland and address them properly to your own King."

The Seneschal, however overworked he already was, always looked pained when the King used *that* particular little speech, but he said nothing.

Perhaps there isn't a great deal that he can do, T'fyrr thought. The Seneschal's chain was the least gaudy of all of the chains of office—perhaps that meant that, among the Advisors, he had the least power.

The rest of the Advisors however were not so reluctant to voice their opinions—which were universally positive. They actually congratulated the High King every time he dismissed a petition or passed it on to the Seneschal.

They were particularly effusive when he trotted out that little speech.

"A fine decision, Your Majesty," someone would say. Another would add, as predictably as rhyming "death" with "breath," "It is in the interest of your land and people that they see you delegate your authority, so that when you are truly needed, you will be free to grant a problem your full attention." And a third would pipe up with, "You must be firm with these people, otherwise every dirt-farming peasant who resents paying tax and tithe to his overlord and the Church will come whining to you for redress of his so-called wrongs."

And the High King smiled, and nodded, and suppressed another yawn.

T'fyrr flexed his talons silently, easing the tension in his feet by clamping them into fists until they trembled. How in the world did Harperus think he could help with *this* situation? The King was getting all of this bad advice from high-ranking humans who were probably very dangerous and hazardous to cross!

Memories of fetters weighing him down made him shiver with chill in that overly warm room. Hazardous to cross. . . .

But before he could say anything to Harperus, the Presiding Herald announced their names, and it was too late to stop the Deliambren from carrying out his plan.

"My Lord Harperus jin Lothir, Ambassador-at-large from the Deliambrens, and T'fyrr Redwing, envoy of the Haspur—"

A tiny portion of T'fyrr's mind noted the rich tones of the human's voice with admiration; the rest of him was engaged in trying to watch the reactions of anyone of any importance to the announcement.

The King's face lit up the moment Harperus stepped forward; as the Deliambren launched into a flowery speech lauding the greatness of King Theovere, and the vast impact of the High King's reputation across the face of Alanda, the Advisors waited and watched like an unkindness of ravens waiting for something to die. They didn't know what Harperus was up to—if, indeed, he was up to anything. That bothered them, but what clearly bothered them more was the fact that for the first time Theovere was showing some interest and no boredom.

Theovere might not be the man he once was, but he still knows where the "marvels" come from.

Now T'fyrr wondered if the trouble *was* with the King's age; there was a certain illness of the aged where one regressed into childhood. Theovere certainly betrayed some symptoms of childishness. . . .

T'fyrr followed the speech; he knew it by heart, and his cue was just coming up. Without pausing or skipping a beat, Harperus went from the speech to T'fyrr's introduction.

"—and I bring before you one who has heard of your generous patronage of the art of music, the envoy of goodwill from the Haspur of the Skytouching Mountains where no human of the Twenty Kingdoms has ever ventured, here to entertain you and your Court."

Harperus stepped back, and T'fyrr quickly stepped forward. One of the Advisors opened his mouth as if to protest; T'fyrr didn't give him a chance to actually say something.

He had already filled his lungs while he waited for his cue, and now he burst into full-chested song.

Although the Haspur had their own musical styles, they also had the ability to mimic anything so exactly that only another Haspur could tell the mimicry from the genuine sound. T'fyrr had chosen that lovely human duet to repeat—it was ideally suited to his voice, since it was antiphonal, and he could simulate the under- and overtones of an instrumental accompaniment with a minimum of concentration. He did improve on the original recording, however. While Master Wren was a golden tenor, Lady Lark's lovely contralto was not going to impress an audience this sophisticated—so T'fyrr transposed the female reply up into the coloratura range and added the appropriate trills, glissandos and flourishes.

The King sat perfectly still, his eyes actually bulging a little in a way that T'fyrr found personally flattering, though rather unattractive. With his superior peripheral vision, he could keep track of those courtiers nearest him, as well, and many of them were positively slack-jawed with amazement.

His hopes and his spirits began to rise at that point. Perhaps he *was* impressive to this jaded audience! Perhaps he *would* be able to accomplish something here!

The instant that he finished, the staid, etiquette-bound courtiers of High King Theovere broke into wild and completely spontaneous applause.

But the Advisors applauded only politely, their eyes narrowed in a way that T'fyrr did not at all like. They resembled ravens again; this time sizing up the opportunity to snatch a bite.

"So," Harperus muttered under his breath, as T'fyrr took a modest bow or two, "now do you think I'm crazy?"

"I know you are crazy," the Haspur replied in a similarly soft voice, "but you are also clever. That is a bad combination for your enemies."

The Deliambren only chuckled.

CHAPTER FOUR

Ah, T'fyrr thought with resignation, perched uncomfortably upon the tall stool that had been brought for him. *I do enjoy being talked about as if I was not present.*

This was not the first time he had found himself in that position. At least, in this case, the discussion concerned his life and prosperity, not his imminent and painful death.

And at least this time he was seated, and on a relatively appropriate stool—in deference to his wings and tail—rather than standing in an iron cage, fettered at every limb.

Harperus was not part of this discussion, this Council session; the Deliambren had not been invited. This was probably more of an oversight than a deliberate insult, since the subject of this meeting was T'fyrr and not Harperus. T'fyrr wished profoundly for his company, though; as the only nonhuman, as well as the object of discussion, he was alternately being ignored and glared at. It would have been less uncomfortable if Harperus had been there to share the "experience."

By the standards of the Palace so far, this was a modest room, paneled in carved wood, with wooden floors and boasting Deliambren lighting. The Council members, all of the King's Advisors, sat at a rectangular marble-topped table with the King at the head and T'fyrr at the foot. *They* had carved wooden chairs that could have doubled as thrones in many kingdoms; the King had a simpler wooden replica of the monstrosity in the room in which he held Court, gilded as well as carved. Behind the King stood a circle of four silent bodyguards in scarlet and black livery, armed to the teeth, in enameled helms and breastplates, as blank-faced as any Elf.

If they projected the fact that they are dangerous any harder, there would be little puddles of "danger" on the floor around them. Look, it's "danger," don't step in it!

"I want him as my personal Court Musician," King Theovere said, with

a glare across the table at his Seneschal. The King had convened this
Council meeting as soon as Court was over—and he had cut Court embar-
rassingly short in order to arrange the time for the meeting. Evidently
nothing could be done, not even the appointment of a single musician to
the royal household, without at least one Council meeting. But it was
obvious to T'fyrr that no matter what his Advisors thought, this meeting
was going to go the King's way. He wondered if they realized that yet. . . .

Lord Marshal Lupene shrugged his massive shoulders. The Marshal was
an old warrior, now gone to fat to an embarrassing extent, though from
the way he carried himself it was likely he didn't realize it—or didn't want
to. "Your Majesty might consider what the envoys both have to say about
it. They might have other plans."

Theovere did not quite glower, but T'fyrr was as aware as Theovere that
the the Lord Marshal's implying that the King had not already consulted
with T'fyrr and Harperus was cutting dangerously close to insubordina-
tion. This Lord Marshal must have been very sure of himself to chance
such insolence.

"He is willing—even eager!" Theovere said angrily as T'fyrr nodded
slightly, though no one paid any attention to him. "The Deliambren Ambassador says that he can manage without T'fyrr along, that he and T'fyrr
were really no more than convenient traveling companions. I tell you, I
want him in my employ starting from this moment—"

Lord Chamberlain Vidor, who had charge of the King's Court Musicians, pursed his thin lips. The Lord Chamberlain was as cadaverous and
lean as the Lord Marshal was massive. "Your Majesty cannot have considered the impact this will have on his other musicians," Vidor intoned,
keeping his disapproval thinly veiled. "Musicians are delicate creatures
with regards to their sensibilities and morale—appointing this *Haspur*
could wreak great damage among them. After all—he isn't even human,
much less a Guild Bard!"

Theovere turned towards his Chamberlain and raised one bushy eyebrow. "The second follows upon the first, doesn't it?" he asked testily.
"The Guild won't *accept* nonhumans, which makes it altogether impossible for T'fyrr to *be* one. I have, in fact, considered the impact of this
appointment, and I think it will serve as an excellent example to my other
musicians. Having T'fyrr in their midst will keep them on their mettle.
They have been getting lazy; too much repetition and too little original
work. They could use the competition." His tone grew silken as he glanced
aside at Lord Guildmaster Koraen. "Perhaps it might give the Bardic
Guild cause to reconsider their ban on nonhuman members, with so excellent a musician being barred from their ranks."

And from lending the Guild my prestige, my notoriety, T'fyrr added silently, seeing some of the same thoughts occurring to the Guildmaster. Koraen was good at hiding his feelings, but T'fyrr detected the sound of the bulky, balding man grinding his teeth in frustration. *The Guild has just lost a fair amount of prestige thanks to my performance, and might lose some royal preference if I continue to succeed here. This man is going to be my enemy.* He mentally shook his head. *What am I thinking? They are all going to be my enemies! The only question is how dangerous they consider me!*

"The Bardic Guild—" the Guildmaster began.

Theovere slammed his open palm down on the table. "The Bardic Guild had better learn some flexibility!" he all but shouted. "The Bardic Guild had better learn how to move with the times! The Bardic Guild had better come up with something better than elaborations on the same tired themes if they want to continue to enjoy my patronage!"

"But this sets a very bad precedent, Your Majesty," interjected another Council member, a thin and reedy little man who had not been introduced to T'fyrr. He wore a sour expression that seemed to be perpetually fixed on his face.

"My Lord Treasurer is correct," agreed the Lord Judiciar smoothly, an oily fellow of nondescript looks who had been among the first to congratulate the King every time he dismissed a petition. "It sets a very bad precedent indeed. You are the High King of the Twenty *Human* Kingdoms; what need have you to bring in outsiders to fill your household?"

Now, for the first time, T'fyrr saw signs of petulance on the King's face, a childish expression that looked, frankly, quite ridiculous on a man with grey hair. And the royal temper, held barely in check, now broke—but not into shouting.

"I want him in my household, and by God, I will *have* him in my household!" the King grated dangerously, glaring at them all. "In fact—" His expression suddenly grew sly. "I'll appoint him my *Chief* Court Musician! Yes, why not? I have a vacant place for a Chief Musician in my personal household; let T'fyrr fill it! That is a position solely under *my* control, subject to *my* discretion, and the Council can only advise me on it, as you know."

As the expressions of the Council members around the table changed from annoyed to alarmed, he chuckled, like a nasty little boy who has been picking the wings off flies.

"But—but Your Majesty—" the Lord Chamberlain spluttered, obviously blurting the first thing that came into his head. "That is impossible! The—the—Chief Court Musician must be a Knight! All of Your Majesty's household must be of the rank of Sire or better!"

"Oh, well, if that is all there is to it—" Before anyone could stop him, the King rose from his seat and walked to T'fyrr's, pulling out his ornamental short sword as he came. "I can certainly remedy that. I am a Knight as well as a King, and according to the rules of chivalry, I can make other Knights in either capacity as I choose. They need only be worthy, and T'fyrr is certainly far more worthy of this post than any Bardic Guild popinjay you've presented me with thus far!"

Oh, good heavens. He's lost his mind.

T'fyrr was not certain what he should do, so he did nothing, except to rise, turn to face the King, and bow. This did not seem to bother Theovere at all. The King tapped him on each shoulder in a perfunctory manner, then resheathed the sword. The Council members sat numbly in their places, struck dumb by the sudden and abrupt turn of events. Clearly the King was not supposed to take so much initiative.

Obviously they have never tried to balk him before. They have just learned a lesson. I believe they thought the King too much in their control to slip his leash like this.

"There," the King said, casually. "Sire T'fyrr, I now name thee a Knight of the Court, whose duties shall be to serve as my Chief Minstrel in my own Household. Do you accept those duties and swear to that service?"

"I do," T'fyrr rumbled, and *then* a storm of protests arose.

By the time it was all over, the Council had suffered complete defeat. T'fyrr was still Sire T'fyrr—a title which was fundamentally an empty one, since no gift of land went along with the honor. He was still the Chief Court Musician. When the Lord Chamberlain swore that the other Court Musicians would never share quarters with a nonhuman, the King gleefully added a private suite in the royal wing to the rest of T'fyrr's benefits. When the Lord Treasurer protested that the kingdom could not bear the unknown living expenses of so—unusual—a creature, Theovere shrugged and assigned his expenses to the Privy Purse. The only real objection that anyone could make that Theovere could not immediately counter was the objection that "the people will not understand."

Finally Theovere simply glared them all to silence. "The people will *learn* to understand," he said in a threatening tone that brooked no argument. "It is about time that the people became a little more flexible, just as it is about time that the Bardic Guild and the members of my Court and Council became a little more flexible, and the example can be set here and now, in my own household!" He glared once more around the table. "I *am* the King, and I have spoken! *You* work for *me*. Is that understood?"

T'fyrr then saw something he had not expected, as the faces of the Council members grew suddenly pale, and they shut their lips on any further objections.

What? he thought with interest. *What is this? And why? They have been treating him like a child until this moment—now, why do they suddenly act as if they had a lion in their midst? What was it about that phrase, "I am the King and I have spoken," that has sudden changed the entire complexion of this?*

Silence reigned around the table, and Theovere nodded with satisfaction. "Good!" he said. "Now, you may all go attend to your pressing duties. I am sure you have many. You keep telling me that you do."

The Council members rose to a man in a rustling of expensive fabric, bowed, and filed silently out, leaving only T'fyrr and Theovere, and Theovere's ever-present bodyguards. The King chuckled.

"I am not certain, Your Majesty, that I deserve such preferential treatment," T'fyrr said at last, after a moment of thought. *I have had enemies made this day of nearly every important man in this Court. This appointment has just become a most comfortable and luxurious setting in which to be a target!* "Perhaps if you chose to return to your original plan?" he suggested gently. "I am only one poor musician, and there is no reason to make my position in your household into a source of such terrible contention."

Theovere shook his head. "I meant what I said," the High King replied. "They can learn to live with it. There has been too much talk of late about the superiority of humans—and you have just proven that talk to be so much manure, and you have done so in my open Court. It is time and more than time for people to learn better—you will serve as my primary example."

Thus making me a target for every malcontent in the city, if not in the Twenty Kingdoms! Thank you so much, Your Majesty!

"I will call a page to show you to your new quarters, and have your friend, the Deliambren, sent there to meet you," the King continued, rising to his feet. T'fyrr did likewise with some haste, bowing as the King smiled. One of the bodyguards reached for a bellpull, and as the King moved away from the table, a young, dark-haired, snub-nosed boy appeared in the still-open door, clad in the High King's livery of gold and scarlet.

The King acknowledged T'fyrr's bow with an indolent wave of his hand, and walked out of the Council room, trailing all but one of his bodyguards. The one left behind, the one who had summoned the page, gestured to the boy as T'fyrr rose from his bow.

"This gentleman is now the King's Chief Court Musician in his personal household," the bodyguard said to the boy in a voice lacking all expression. He kept his face at an absolute deadpan as well, and T'fyrr could only admire his acting ability. "His name is Sire T'fyrr. You will escort him to the royal wing, see that he is comfortably lodged in the Gryphon Suite, and from here on, see that his needs are attended to. For the immediate future, you will see to his special needs in furnishing his quarters, then, when Sire T'fyrr indicates, find the Deliambren Ambassador and escort him to Sire T'fyrr."

The child bobbed his head in wordless acknowledgement, and the bodyguard left, apparently satisfied that the King's orders had been correctly delivered.

As soon as he was gone, the boy glanced up at T'fyrr, and the Haspur did not have to be an expert in human children to see that the boy was frightened of him. His face was pale, and his fists clenched at his sides. If T'fyrr said or did anything alarming, the poor fledgling would probably faint—or forget his duty and bolt for someplace safe to hide!

"I am a Haspur, young friend," T'fyrr said gently, and chuckled. "We don't eat children. We do eat meat, but we prefer it to be cooked—and we would rather not have had a speaking acquaintance with it before it became our dinner."

The child relaxed marginally. "Would you follow me, Sire T'fyrr?" he said in a trembling soprano. "Do you have any baggage that you will need brought to you?"

"My friend Harperus will see to all that," T'fyrr told him, and added as an afterthought, "He is the Deliambren. You should have no trouble finding him; he is the only being in the Palace who is dressed to look like a saint's palanquin in a Holy Day Festival Parade."

That broke the ice, finally; the little boy giggled, and stifled the laugh behind both hands. But the eyes above the hands were merry, and when he turned a sober face back to T'fyrr, his eyes had a sparkle to them that they had lacked until that moment.

"If you would come with me, then, Sire?" the boy said, gesturing at the door.

T'fyrr nodded. "Certainly—ah, what is your name? It seems rude to call you 'boy,' or 'page.' "

"Regan, Sire," the boy said, skipping to keep up with T'fyrr as the Haspur strode down the hallway. "But my friends call me Nob."

T'fyrr coaxed his beak into something like a human smile. He had learned that the expression made humans feel better around him. "Very well, Nob," he said, projecting good humor and casualness into his voice. "Now, if you were in my place, granted a title and a new home, what would *you* do first?"

"You mean, about the suite and all, Sire?" Nob asked, looking up at T'fyrr with a crooked grin. "Well, I might have some ideas—"

"Then by all means," T'fyrr told him, "let me hear them!"

* * *

Harperus lounged at his ease on one of the damask-covered sofas in the reception room of the suite, watching T'fyrr try out the various pieces of furniture that Nob had suggested he order brought down from storage. Somehow, it all matched—or at least, it coordinated, as the main colors of the suite were warm golds and browns, with gryphons forming the main theme of the carvings. Padded stools proved surprisingly comfortable, as did an odd, backless couch that Nob particularly recommended. And to replace the bed—

When T'fyrr had sketched what a Haspur bed looked like, Nob had studied the sketch for a moment, and then snapped his fingers with a grin of glee. He hadn't said a word to T'fyrr, but he had called another servant —an oddly silent servant—and handed him the sketch with a whispered explanation.

Six husky men appeared about an hour later, just as Harperus arrived with more servants bearing T'fyrr's baggage. The men took the bed out without a single word and returned with something that was the closest thing to a Haspur bed that T'fyrr had *ever* seen in these human realms. He stared at it, mouth agape, while Nob grinned from ear to ear.

He had a suspicion that there was more to this than met the eye, and his suspicion was confirmed when Harperus took one look and nearly choked.

"Very well," he said, mustering up as much dignity as he could. "Obviously this is not the Haspur bed that it appears to be. What *is* it?"

Nob clapped both hands over his mouth, stifling a laugh. *"You* tell him, my lord!" he said to Harperus, gasping. "I—nay, I can't do it!"

He turned around, growing scarlet in the face, obviously having a hard time containing himself. T'fyrr waited, curiosity vying with exasperation, while Harperus struggled to get himself under control.

"It's—it's something no well-bred boy should know about at Nob's tender age," Harperus managed finally. "Let's just say, it isn't meant for sleeping."

Enlightenment dawned. "Ah! A piece of mating furniture!" T'fyrr exclaimed brightly, and clicked his beak in further annoyance when both Nob and Harperus went off into paroxysms of smothered laughter.

I cannot, and never will, understand why the subject of mating should make these humans into sniggering idiots, he thought a little irritably. *It is just as natural as eating, and there are no whispers and giggles about enjoying one's breakfast! So that explains the ever-so-reticent servant that found the thing; in a place like this, there must be a servant in charge of romantic liaisons!*

By the winds, there was probably even a division of labor—one servant for discreet liaisons, one for *very* discreet liaisons, one for indiscreet liaisons, one for the exotic. . . .

Well, at least Nob hadn't been so bound up in this silly human propriety nonsense that he refused to have the object sent for! It might be a piece of mating equipment to these humans, but it made a perfectly *fine* nest-bed, and T'fyrr looked forward to having one of the first completely comfortable nights he'd had in a very long time.

Finally, after many false starts, the page got himself back under control, although he would not or could not look Harperus in the eye. "If you need me any more, Sire," he told T'fyrr with a decent imitation of a sober expression, "just ring for me."

"Ring for you?" T'fyrr asked, puzzled, and Nob walked over to the wood-paneled wall, pulled aside a brown damask curtain, and pointed to a line of gilded brass bellpulls.

"This is the guards—this is the kitchen, if I'm off running an errand—this is the bath servants, if I'm off running an errand—this is the maid, in case you need something cleaned. This is for me—I'm *your* page now, Sire. I'll be sleeping in that little room just next to the bathroom. Unless you want someone older, I'll be your body servant, too. That means I dress you." Nob eyed the simple wrapped garment that T'fyrr wore for the sake of modesty. "Doesn't look as if there's all that much work tending to your wardrobe."

"Not really," T'fyrr agreed. "Do *you* want to be assigned to me?"

"Oh yes, Sire!" Nob replied immediately, and his artless enthusiasm could not be doubted. "There's status in it; I'd be more than just a page— and you'll be a good master, Sire. I can tell," he finished confidently.

T'fyrr sighed. "I hope I can live up to that, young friend," he answered, as much to himself as to the boy. "Well, so what are all these other bells?"

When Nob finished his explanations, Harperus intervened. "I can show him the rest, young one," the Deliambren said easily. "My people built most of the complicated arrangements in this Palace. You go see to getting your own quarters set up."

"Yes, my lord," Nob said obediently, as T'fyrr nodded confirmation of Harperus' suggestion. "Thank you, my lord, I appreciate that—"

As the boy whisked out of the suite, Harperus turned to T'fyrr. "Well, now you're a Sire, and that lad is your entire retinue. The thing to remember is that Nob's duty is always to *you,* first. That means if you keep him doing things for you all the time, he has no right to eat, rest, or even sleep."

T'fyrr's beak fell open as he stared, aghast. Harperus just shrugged.

"It's the way these boys are brought up," he said philosophically. "Chances are, he was hired as a child of four or five, and he doesn't even live with his own family anymore—he probably doesn't see them more than twice or three times a year. His whole life is in Palace service. Just remember that, and if you want the boy to have any time to himself, you'll have to order him to take it."

"I'll keep that in mind," T'fyrr said absently. *Every time I think I have seen the last of subtle human cruelties, another pops up! Can it be that there are masters who would keep their servants so bound as to permit them no time to eat or sleep? Is that why he said he thought I would be a good master?*

"Well, come let me show you the bathing room, old bird," Harperus said, oblivious to T'fyrr's thoughts. "You'll probably like it better than the one in the wagon; since this is a royal suite, there should be a tub big enough for you to splash around the way you do when you find a pond." The Deliambren shook his head with amusement. "Honestly, you look like a wren in a birdbath when you do that!"

"I do *not*," T'fyrr responded automatically, but followed Harperus anyway. This room was bigger than the entire traveling wagon put together, tiled on the walls, floor and ceiling in beige and brown. The bathroom was all Deliambren in its luxury, every fixture sculpted into some strange floral shape, the floor heated, the rack for the towels heated as well. The sink was big enough to bathe an infant in, the tub fully large enough to have a proper Haspur bath, and the "convenience"—convenient, and discreetly placed behind its own little door. The "usual" Deliambren lighting could be made bright or dim as one chose. There was even one of the Deliambren waterfalls that Harperus called a "shower-stall," though it was much more luxurious than the one in the wagon. There were full-length mirrors everywhere, and T'fyrr kept meeting his own eyes wherever he looked. The Deliambren showed him the various controls, then ran water into the basin.

"There," he said under the sound of the running water, "if there's any spies listening, and I'm sure there are, this should cover our conversation."

"Ah." T'fyrr nodded cautiously and pretended to finger another fixture, as if he was asking questions. "Well? Did this proceed as you hoped?"

"I'm overjoyed. You could not have done better," Harperus told him gleefully. "You absolutely exceeded my wildest wishes."

"I didn't do anything—" T'fyrr objected, feeling uncomfortable about taking praise for something he'd had no hand in.

"You kept your beak shut and let the King have his way by not giving his Advisors anything to use against you; that was enough," Harperus said. "Now, I'll have to make my instructions very brief—there is one bag that isn't yours; there are some devices in it that you will recognize. I want you to place them around your rooms; tell Nob that they're statues from your home. Then talk to Nob about everything that happens to you that you think I should know. If there are spies listening, it won't matter; they won't be surprised that you're asking advice from a page, they'll think it shows how stupid you are, and they won't know what those 'statues' are."

T'fyrr made a caw of distaste. "If they are what I think they are—I've seen those little eavesdroppers of yours. They are hideous, and you will make Nob and those spies believe that my people have no artistic talent whatsoever."

Harperus grinned and went on. "You'll need to get directions eventually to a tavern called the Freehold. It's owned by a Deliambren, and he'll be your contact back to us if you need anything else." He correctly interpreted T'fyrr's dubious expression. "Don't worry, before the week is out, people will think it's odd if you *haven't* visited there at least once. It's the center of social activity for every nonhuman of every rank in Lyonarie—and a fair number of humans, as well. It's like Jenthan Square in the Fortress-City. You might even go there just to have a good time."

T'fyrr nodded, relieved, and Harperus reached over and turned the water off. "You may want to leave specific orders with Nob for baths," he said, as if he was continuing an existing conversation. "You know how the lights work, of course. Can you think of anything else?"

His eyebrows signalled a wider range to that question than was implied by the circumstance. T'fyrr only shook his head.

"Not really," he said truthfully, spreading his wings a little to indicate that he understood the question for what it was. "I only hope I can serve Theovere as well as you expect me to. I am, after all, less of an envoy and more of a messenger of good will."

Harperus raised his eyebrows with amusement at T'fyrr's circumspect reply. "In that case, I'll leave you to settle in by yourself," he said. "Once the boy finishes with his own gear, you should have him fetch a meal for the two of you. You'll be expected to eat in your own quarters, of course—people are likely to be uneasy dining around anyone sporting something like that meathook in the center of your face."

People will be offended if I dare to actually take my meals in public, with the rest of the courtiers and folk of rank. After all, I'm only a lowly nonhuman. I shouldn't allow myself any airs.

"Of course," T'fyrr agreed, allowing his irony to show. "I'm not at all surprised."

Harperus took his leave—and T'fyrr swallowed his own feeling of panic at being entirely alone in this situation and went to look for "his" servant. He found Nob putting away the last of his belongings in a snug little room just off the bathroom. When he suggested food, Nob was not only willing, he was eager, suggesting to T'fyrr that it was probably well past the boy's usual dinnertime.

Or else, that like small males of every species, he was always hungry.

But when Nob returned with servants bearing dinner, it was with *many* servants bearing dinner, and with three of the King's Advisors following behind. T'fyrr welcomed them, quickly covering his surprise, and invited them to take seats while the servants made one small table into a large table, set places for all of them, and vanished, leaving Nob to serve as their waiter.

"If you would arrange yourselves as is proper, my lords," he said finally, "I have no idea of precedence among you, except that you are all greatly above my rank. I would not care to offend any of you."

His three unexpected dinner guests all displayed various levels of amusement. Lord Seneschal Acreon actually chuckled; Lord Secretary Atrovel (a cocky little man who clearly possessed an enormous ego) smirked slightly. Lord Artificer Levan Pendleton only raised his eyebrows and smiled. The Seneschal, a greying man so utterly ordinary that the only things memorable about him were his silver-embroidered grey silk robes and chain of office, took charge of the situation.

"As our host, Sire T'fyrr, you must take the head of the table. As the lowest in rank, I must take the foot—"

Lord Levan and Lord Atrovel both made token protests, which the Seneschal dismissed, as they obviously expected him to.

"Lord Secretary, Lord Artificer, I leave it to you to choose left or right hand," the Seneschal concluded.

Atrovel, a short, wiry, dark-haired man robed in blue and gold, grinned. "Well, since no one has ever accused me of being *sinister,* I shall take the right," he punned. Levan Pendleton cast his eyes up to the ornately painted ceiling, but did not groan.

"Since I am often accused of just that, it does seem appropriate," he agreed, taking the seat at T'fyrr's left. "We are all here, Sire T'fyrr, in hopes of showing you that not everyone in the King's Council is—ah—distressed by your presence."

Acreon winced. "So blunt, Levan?" he chided. The Lord Artificer only shrugged.

"I can afford to be blunt, Acreon," the man replied, and turned again to T'fyrr. T'fyrr found him fascinating; the most birdlike human he had yet met. His head sported a thick crest of greying black hair; his face was sharp and his nose quite prominent. Perched on the nose was a pair of spectacles; they enlarged his eyes and made him look very owl-like. The rest of the man was hidden in his silvery-grey robe of state, but from the way it hung on him, T'fyrr suspected he was cadaverously thin.

"Why can you afford to be blunt, my lord?" T'fyrr asked, a bit boldly. The human laughed.

"Because I am in charge of those who make strange devices, Sire

T'fyrr," he replied genially. "No one knows if they are magical or not, so no one cares to discover if I can accomplish more than I claim to be able to do. That is why folk think me sinister."

"That, and the delightful little exploding toys, and the cannon you have conjured," Atrovel said with a smirk. "No one wants to retire to his room only to find one of those waiting for him, either."

"Oh, piff," Levan said, waving a dismissive hand. "They're too easy to trace. If I were going to get rid of someone, I'd choose a much subtler weapon. Poison delivered in a completely unexpected manner, for instance. In bathwater, or a bouquet of flowers. It would be a fascinating experiment, just to find out what kind of dosage would be fatal under those circumstances." And he turned toward Nob, who was offering a plate of sliced meat, his eyes wide as the plate. "Thank you, child—and I'll have some of that pudding, as well."

"There, you see?" Atrovel threw up his hands. "No wonder no one wants to dine with you! You'd poison us all just to see how we reacted!" He helped himself to the meat Nob brought him, and turned toward T'fyrr. "Levan would like to get on your good side because his worst rival is Lord Commerce Gorode; *he's* in charge of the Manufactory Guild, and they are always trying to purloin Artificers' designs without paying for them—and Lord Gorode already hates you just because you aren't human."

"Ah," T'fyrr said, nonplussed at this barrage of apparent honesty. He hoped that Harperus' little "devices" were hearing all of this.

"The Seneschal," Atrovel continued, pointing his fork at Acreon, who munched quietly on a plate of green things without saying a word, "is on your side because he actually thinks you're honest. Are you?"

"I try to be," T'fyrr managed, and both Levan and Atrovel broke into howls of laughter.

"By God, this *is* more entertaining than Court Dinner!" Levan spluttered. "T'fyrr, you must be honest, or you'd never have answered that way! What a change from all those oily, wily Guild Bards! Dare I actually ask if you are interested in *music* instead of advancing yourself?"

"Music is—is my life, my lord," T'fyrr said simply, expecting them both to break into laughter again. But they didn't; they both sobered, and the Seneschal nodded.

"You see?" Acreon said quietly. "Honest, and a true artist. Innocent as this boy, here—Sire T'fyrr, I thought you might need a friend, now I am certain of it. I hope you will consider me to be your friend, and call on me if you need something the boy cannot provide."

T'fyrr was at an utter loss of what to say, so he replied with the feeling that was uppermost at that moment. "Thank you, thank you very much,

Lord Acreon," he said, as sincerely as he could. "I am not so innocent that I do not realize that my position here is extremely delicate. The King offended many of high estate today, but I am the safer target for their wrath, and they will probably try to vent it sooner or later."

"Innocent, but not stupid," Levan said, jabbing a fork into his meat with satisfaction. "I like that. So, Atrovel, why are *you* here, anyway?"

Atrovel waved his knife airily. "Because I enjoy seeing so many of our pompous windbags—ah, excuse me, *noble Council members*—discomfited. It is no secret that I dislike most of them, and am disliked in return. The King trusts me because I amuse him; they hate that. I enjoy causing them trouble. They are boring, they have no imagination, and they don't appreciate music. That is enough for me."

"And you appreciate music?" T'fyrr asked. Although none of them really watched him eating, they weren't going out of their way to avoid watching him swallow down neat, small bites of absolutely raw meat. That was interesting. Although he could eat other things—and would dine on the cooked meat on one tray, soon—he'd deliberately chosen the raw steak as a kind of test.

Levan snorted and picked up his goblet to drink before answering. "Enjoy? Oh, my dear T'fyrr, *this* is the foremost musical critic of the Court! Or at least, *he* thinks so!"

"I know so," Atrovel replied casually, raising one eyebrow. "Your performance, by the way, was absolutely amazing. Were you simulating an instrumental accompaniment with your *voice?*"

So someone had noticed! "A very simple one," T'fyrr admitted. "A ground only. I could not have replicated a harp, for instance—"

"Oh, don't start!" Levan interrupted. "I like music as well as the next man, but having it dissected? Pah! You two wait until you're alone and let the rest of us just listen without having to know what it all breaks down to!"

"Fine words from one who spends his life breaking things into their components to find out how the universe runs," Acreon pointed out mildly. He had graduated from salad to some mild cheese and unspiced meats. T'fyrr suspected chronic indigestion; hardly surprising, considering how hard he worked.

"I prefer to leave some few things a mystery, and music is one of them," Levan replied with dignity. "However—are all your people so gifted? Or are you the equivalent of a Bard among them?"

T'fyrr passed an astonishingly pleasant hour with the three Royal Advisors, and after the Seneschal and the Artificer pled work and left, spent two more equally pleasant hours discussing the technicalities of music with Lord Atrovel. The diminutive fellow was as much of a dandy as Harperus, and just as certain of the importance of his own opinions, but he was also scathingly witty, and his observations on some of the other Council members had T'fyrr doubled up in silent laughter more than once.

When Lord Atrovel finally left, T'fyrr sent Nob off to bed (over the boy's protests that he was *supposed* to help the Haspur undress), and unwrapped himself. He let the silk wrapping fall to the floor—consciously. No more picking up after himself; no more going to fetch things.

I have to give the boy something to do, or he'll think he isn't doing his job. This was not a situation he had anticipated, to say the least.

He had thought—when he actually let himself entertain the notion of success at all—that he might possibly end up as one of the King's private musicians. He had a notion what that meant; he would have been a glorified servant himself. That would have been fine—but this was out of all expectation.

He palmed the lights off, and stayed awake awhile, cushioned in his new bed, thinking.

I have a servant, a retainer—someone who depends on me to be a good master or a bad, and has no choice but to deal with what I tell him to do. What kind of a master will I make? That was one worry on top of everything else; could he, would he become abusive? He had a temper, the winds knew; if he lost it with this boy, he could damage the child, physically. On the practical side, he had no idea of the strength or the endurance of a human fledgling; Harperus had said the boy was—what? Something like twelve years of age. What could he do? What shouldn't he do?

Perhaps it will be safest to watch him, and send him to rest at the first sign that he is tired. I wonder if he can read? If not, I shall see to it that he learns. If so, I shall find out if he enjoys reading, and make that one of his tasks. It would be a safe way to make the boy rest, even if he didn't think he should.

As for the task Harperus had assigned to *him*—

I believe I have a far wider field of opportunity than either of us thought. He would have to give this a great deal of consideration. If he was going to be the King's Chief Musician, that implied that he would be performing solo, probably quite often, possibly even on a daily basis. He would have plenty of opportunity to sing things that just might put the King in mind of some of the duties he was neglecting.

I wish that I had one of the Free Bards here; the ones that Harperus says work magic, he thought wistfully. *It would greatly help if I could use magic to reinforce that reminder. . . . If only Nightingale were here! She and I make such a good duo—and she is a powerful worker of magic, I know she must be, even though Harperus didn't mention her by name. And it would be so good to have a real friend, someone I could trust completely, to be here with me.*

As well wish for Visyr and Syri to come help him; the Free Bards were all very nearly as far away as the Fortress-City and his other two friends.

Well, it would be enough for the moment for him to keep the Deliambrens aware of developments by means of those ugly little "devices" of theirs. They must surely have gotten an earful tonight, before the talk turned to music!

And that brought him to something else he really should think about. *Lord Acreon, Lord Levan, and Lord Atrovel.*

Out of all of the King's Advisors, three—admittedly three of limited power, but still—had openly allied themselves with him. The question was, why had they done so? The reasons were without a doubt as various as the men themselves. And likely just as devious. T'fyrr was under no illusions; each of these men had agendas of their own that allying themselves with him would further. The King would certainly notice that they were openly his "friends," and that could hardly hurt them. Right now, the King was not very happy with most of his Advisors, and while he might forget that by tomorrow, he also might *remember.*

Whatever had been done to lull the King into the state he was in now, for the moment, T'fyrr had cracked it, and with that crack, some of *their* power had escaped.

Lord Acreon, the Seneschal. T'fyrr had the oddest feeling that the Seneschal had meant every word he had said; that he had sided with T'fyrr because he thought that T'fyrr was honest, a real musician, and needed a friend who understood the quagmire this Court truly was. He wasn't entirely certain if Acreon actually *liked* him, but Acreon was going to help him.

Perhaps Acreon himself is not certain if he likes me. I doubt that he has had much commerce with anything other than humans. I wonder if I frighten him a little? He does not strike me as a particularly brave man, physically, although I think he is very strong in the spirit. I also think, perhaps, he does not know how strong he is.

Could Acreon be trusted? Probably. Of the three, he was the one with the least to lose and the most to gain if T'fyrr succeeded, out of all expectation, in making the King see where his duty lay. He was already overburdened and uncredited for most of the work he did; if the High King began acting like the ruler he was supposed to be, a great deal of that burden would be lifted from the Seneschal's shoulders.

He might even be able to enjoy spiced meat again, without suffering a burning belly.

He decided that he would make use of the Seneschal in the lightest way possible—by asking advice, not on difficult things, but on the subject that the Seneschal probably knew better than any other, his fellow Advisors.

Acreon would probably tell him the truth, and if the truth were too dangerous, T'fyrr suspected he would be able to hint well enough for the Haspur to guess at the truth. Very well. Trust the Seneschal, as long as Acreon had nothing to lose by what T'fyrr was doing.

Levan Pendleton. The Lord Artificer was a puzzle. He liked music well enough. He was fascinated by the workings of things, and devoured facts the way a child devoured sweets. Those traits, T'fyrr was used to—the Deliambrens were rather like that.

He is also utterly amoral. He saw no difficulty in ridding himself of an enemy by murder; had even boasted tonight how he would do so. T'fyrr, adept at reading the nuance of voices if not of human expressions, sensed that he meant every word he said. *He might even have been warning me, obliquely. He all but said openly that he was for sale. He might have been telling me that someone might buy his services to use on me.*

There were only two things that Levan Pendleton valued—fact and truth. They were also the only things he cared about; he had said, more than once, that no matter what the cost, he would not conceal facts or distort the truth, at least when it came to his discoveries about the workings of the world. He had described, as if it were only an amusing anecdote, how his stand had already gotten him in serious conflict with the Church, and that only his rank and position had saved him from having to answer to Church authority.

T'fyrr could supply him with plenty of facts, anyway. He had traveled in lands that the Lord Artificer had never even heard of, and that meant he could enlarge Levan's knowledge of Alanda. As for things closer to home, the devices and machines that the Artificer so loved, if he could not explain the workings of Deliambren machinery, he could at least supply information on the workings of simpler things. The staged pumps that brought water up to the highest aeries, for one thing, or the odd, two-wheeled contrivance that the Velopids rode instead of horses.

I can probably entertain Levan for months, even years, and as long as I entertain him, I am too valuable for him to eliminate. I am also too valuable for him to permit anyone else to get rid of me. I can trust Levan Pendleton, but within strict limits.

And those limits would be determined mostly by what T'fyrr himself could or could not supply. An added benefit was T'fyrr's vast collection of music, much of it from strange cultures. Levan liked music, and to have someone who could not only perform it but explain the meaning or the story was something *he* had not anticipated. This could be a very good position to be in, so long as T'fyrr did not overestimate the limits of his entertainment value.

Levan Pendleton would be most useful simply as a patron. If people didn't like to go to dinner with him—they would also be disinclined to try to eliminate or disgrace one of his friends.

Lord Secretary Atrovel. Now there was a puzzle! He seemed completely shallow, a sparkling brook that was all babble and shine on the surface, but was nothing more than a lively skin of water, unable to support or hold anything of value. Yet the man was witty, and while it was possible to be witty *and* be stupid, it wasn't very likely.

Atrovel had access to everything the King did and said. That was his job. Now, it was probably not a bad idea to have a flippant fellow for a secretary, a man who really didn't care a great deal about the correspondence and documents he handled. But still—T'fyrr had the feeling that that sparkling surface was not all there was to Atrovel.

Perhaps, though, the deepest thing about him is his pride. He was certainly a man who had no doubts whatsoever about his own worth, and had no modesty about it, either. He would be the first to tell you just how important he was.

That might have been what T'fyrr sensed: beneath the flippant exterior was a man with a deep sense of pride in himself. If that was true, then the worst thing one could do to Lord Atrovel would be to harm his pride, to make *him* look foolish. He would never forgive that, and as Secretary he had access to the means to take revenge. Certain papers could fall into the hands of an enemy, perhaps . . . certain others vanish before they could be signed.

Lord Atrovel could be trusted—warily. And T'fyrr would have to be very careful of that touchy little man's feelings.

Oh, this is all too much to think about—Yet there remained one more human that T'fyrr sensed he must consider tonight, before he slept.

High King Theovere.

Now there—there was a puzzle and a question more complicated than that of Lord Atrovel.

For one thing, he is not *sane. He is not rational. He has mood changes that do not necessarily correspond to what is going on around him, and his ability to concentrate is not good. His priorities are skewed. His Advisors don't care, because his insanity gives them leeway to do anything they really want. The problem is, what caused this?* Theovere was *not* the man he once was. Harperus had been quite emphatic about that. High King Theovere had been well-respected, if not precisely beloved; he had kept every one of the Twenty Kingdoms under his careful scrutiny. So what happened? Why did he suddenly begin to lose interest in seeing things well-governed?

Was it a lack of interest? Was he ill, in some way that simply didn't show itself on the surface? There were certainly hints of that in the childishness, the petulance, the obsessive interest in music and other trivialities.

And yet—and yet there was still something of the old King there as well. King Theovere wanted T'fyrr the way a child wants a new toy, yes, but there was something else beneath that childish greed.

He is using me. Something in him is still vaguely aware that there is trouble in his Kingdoms, trouble involving nonhumans, and he is using me, he said so himself. I am to provide an example of excellence and tolerance. And I don't think the Advisors are truly aware that he is using me in that way, even though they heard him say *so. They don't believe he could still have that much interest outside his little world of Bards and Musicians.*

So, was there something there that T'fyrr could touch, perhaps even something he could awaken?

I think so. In spite of the childishness, the pettiness—there is something there. I believe that I like him, or rather, I like what he could be. There is a King inside that child, still, and the King wants out again.

At some point, King Theovere had been an admirable enough leader that his bodyguards were *still* inspired to a fanatic loyalty. A man simply did not inspire that kind of loyalty just because he happened to have a title.

I wish I could talk to one of the bodyguards, honestly, T'fyrr thought wistfully. It would never happen, though. They had absolutely no reason to trust *him*. For all they knew, he was just another toy, this one presented to the King by a foreigner instead of one of his Advisors, but a toy and a distraction, nevertheless.

I don't want to be a toy, and I especially don't want to be a distraction. I want to remind him of what he was.

Well, to that end, he had delved into Harperus' store of memory-crystals and come up with several songs *about* King Theovere. Most of them weren't very good, which didn't exactly come as a shock, since they had been composed by Guild Bards—but there were germs of good ideas in there, and decent, if not stellar, melodies. *I could improve the lyrics; even Nob could improve on some of those lyrics.* He could sing those, and literally remind the King of what he had been.

And there were other songs he had picked up himself on the way, songs that actually had some relevance to one of the situations the King had sloughed off into the Seneschal's hands.

I can certainly sing those songs that Raven and the rest wrote about Duke Arden of Kingsford—how he saved all those people during the fire, how he's beggaring himself to rebuild his city. That should get his attention where reports won't!

And if T'fyrr got his attention, he just might be moved to do something about the situation.

If I put a situation in front of him in music—ah, yes, that is a good idea.

And who better to suggest such situations than the man who would otherwise have to take care of them—Lord Seneschal Acreon? Oh, now *there* was an idea calculated to make the Seneschal happier!

He'll help. This is exactly the kind of help that he *has been looking for—I would willingly bet on it. The only problem is that if anyone besides Acreon figures out what I'm doing, they'll know I'm not just a blank-brained musician; they'll know I'm getting involved, and I might be dangerous. Which will make me even more of a target than I was already.*

Well, that couldn't be helped. He had made a promise and a commitment, and it was time to see them through. *Now I have a plan. Now I have a real means to do what Harperus wants me to. And I have a chance to redeem myself in the process, to counter the evil I have already done.*

Suddenly the tension in his back and wing muscles relaxed, as it always did when he had worried through a problem and found at least the beginnings of a solution.

That was all he needed to be able to sleep; in the next instant, all the fatigue that he'd been holding off unconsciously descended on him.

Ah . . . I didn't realize I was so . . . tired.

He was already in the most comfortable nest he'd had in ages, and in the most comfortable sleeping position he'd had since he'd begun traveling with Harperus.

This nest is very good . . . very, very good. I don't think I want to move.

It was just as well that he was settled in, for as soon as he stopped fighting off sleep, it stooped down out of the darkness upon him, and carried him away—to dreams of falling, iron manacles and screams.

Midnight. You'd think the city would be quiet.

It wasn't though; the rumble of cartwheels on cobblestones persisted right up until dawn, and a deeper rumble of the machineries turned by the swiftly moving river water permeated even one's bones.

Nightingale perched like her namesake on the roof of Freehold, staring out into the darkness at the lights across the street. No Deliambren lights, these—though they were clever enough; she'd noticed them earlier this evening, just outside the building, where two of them stood like sentinels on either side of the door. Some kind of special air—a gas—was what these lights burned. One of her customers had told her that. It was piped into them from somewhere else, and burned with a flame much brighter than candles, without the flicker of a candle.

With lights like that, you wouldn't have to wait for daylight to do your work. . . .

No, you could work all night. Or, better still, you could have someone else work all night for you.

There were similar lights burning inside that huge building, but not as many as the owner would like. He would have been happier if the whole place was lit up as brightly as full day. Only a few folk worked inside that building at night, those who cleaned the place and serviced the machines.

Nightingale leaned on the brick of the low wall around the roof, rested her chin on her hands, and brooded over those lovely, clear, cursed lights and all they meant.

She had learned more in her brief time here than she had ever anticipated, and most of it was completely unexpected.

When she had arrived here, she had been working under the assumption that the Free Bards' and the nonhumans' chiefest enemies were going to be the Church and the Bardic Guild, that if anyone was behind the recent laws being passed it would be those two powers. It made sense that way—if the High King really *was* infatuated with music and musicians, it made sense for the most influential power in his Court to be the Bardic Guild, and the Bardic Guild and the Church worked hand-in-glove back in Rayden.

Well, they have gotten a completely unprecedented level of power, that much is true. But the Bardic Guild was by no means the most important power in the Court. They weren't even as important as they thought they were!

No, the most important power in this place is across the street. In those buildings, in the hands of the men who own them.

The merchants who owned and managed the various manufactories were individually as powerful and wealthy as many nobles. But they had not stopped there; no, seeing the power that an organization could wield, they had banded together to form something they called the "Manufactory Guild." It was no Guild at all in the accepted sense; there was no passing on of skills and trade secrets, no fostering of apprentices, no protection of the old and infirm members. No, this was just a grouping of men with a single common interest.

Profit.

Not that I blame them there. Everyone wants to prosper. It's just that they don't seem to care how much misery they cause as long as they personally get their prosperity.

And the Manufactory Guild was now more powerful than the Bardic Guild and even many of the Trade Guilds. They even had their own Lord Advisor to the King!

Their agenda was pretty clear; they certainly didn't try to hide it. They tended to oppose free access to entertainment in general, simply because entertainment got in the way of working. They wanted to outlaw all public entertainment in the streets, whether it be by simple juggler, Free Bard or

Guild Bard. They had laws up for consideration to do just that, too, and some very persuasive people arguing their case, pointing out how crowds around entertainers clogged the streets and disrupted traffic, how work would stop if an entertainer set up outside a manufactory, how people were always coming in late and leaving early in order to see a particular entertainer on his corner. There was just enough truth in all of it to make it seem plausible, logical, reasonable.

Oh, yes, very reasonable.

They had another law up for consideration, as well, a law that would allow the employers at these manufactories to set working hours around the clock, seven days a week. It seemed very reasonable again—and here was the example, right across the street. There was no reason why people couldn't be working all night, not with these wonderful, clear lights available. It would be no hardship to them, not the way working by candlelight or lamplight would be. It was the Church that opposed *this* law; it was the Church that decreed the hours during which it was permissible to work in the first place, and the conditions for working. Church law mandated that Sevenday be a day for rest and religious services. Church law forbade working after sundown, except in professions such as entertainment, on the grounds that God created the darkness in order to ensure that Man had peace in which to contemplate God and to sleep—or at least, rest from his labors, so he could contemplate God with his full attention.

The Manufactory Guild wanted a law that permitted them to hire children as young as nine, on a multitude of grounds—and Nightingale had heard them all.

So that children can be a benefit to their families, instead of a burden. So that families with many children can feed all of them instead of relying on charity. So that children can learn responsibility at an early age. To keep children out of the street and out of wickedness and idleness. Oh, it all sounds very plausible.

Except, of course, that one would not have to pay a child as much as an adult. A family desperate enough to force its nine-year-old child into work would be desperate enough to take whatever wage was offered. And that child, who supposedly was learning to read and write from his Chapel Priest, would be losing that precious chance at education. There *were* Church-sanctioned exceptions to the law—children were allowed to be hired as pages or messengers, and to help their parents in a business or a farm. But all of those exceptions were hedged about with a vast web of carefully tailored precepts that kept abuse of those exceptions to a relative minimum, and all those exceptions required that the child receive his minimum education.

You can't keep a child's parents from working him to death, or from abusing him in other ways, but you can at least keep a stranger from doing so. That was basically the reasoning of the Church, which decreed the completely contradictory precepts that a child was sacred to God and that a child was the possession and property of his parents.

Then there's that lovely little item, the "job security law." That was a law that specifically forbade a worker in a manufactory from quitting one job to take another—effectively keeping him chained to the first job he ever took for the rest of his life, unless his employer chose otherwise, or got rid of him. That one had yet to be passed as well, but there was very little opposition, and the moment it was, it would mean the complete loss of freedom for anyone who went to work in a manufactory.

They say that retraining someone is costly and dangerous, since folk in a manufactory are generally operating some sort of machinery. Oh, surely. "Machinery" no more complicated than a spinning wheel! But I would think that to most people, who think a well-pump is very complicated machinery, they'd look at the manufactories and agree that having an inexperienced person "operating machinery" could be very dangerous. As if most of what I've been watching people actually do was any more complicated than digging potatoes.

But the Manufactory Guild wanted to keep that ignorance intact. And here the Church itself was divided; one group saw clearly the way this would take freedom away from anyone who worked in those places, leaving them virtual slaves to their jobs, but the other group was alarmed at the wild tales painted of accidents caused by "inexperience," and was in favor of the law.

She shifted her position, turning her back on the lights of the manufactory to stare up at the sky. You didn't see as many stars here as you could in the country; she didn't know why. Maybe it was all the smoke from the thousands of chimneys, getting in the way, like a perpetual layer of light clouds.

The nastiest piece of work she'd heard about was something that so far was only a rumor, but it was chilling enough to have been the sole topic of conversation tonight, all over Freehold.

This was—supposedly—a proposed law that had the support of not only some of the Church but the Manufactory Guild *and* the trade Guilds as well.

They called it "the Law of Degree."

Nightingale shivered, a chill settling over her that the warm breeze could not chase away. Even the name sounded ominous.

It would set a standard, a list of characteristics, which would determine just how "human" someone could be considered, based on his appearance. But the "standard" was only the beginning of the madness, for it would mandate that those who were considered to be below a certain "degree" of humanity were nothing more than animals.

In other words, property. Bad enough that such things as being indentured are allowed everywhere, and that slavery is sanctioned in at least half the Twenty Kingdoms. The Church at least has laws that govern how slaves are treated, and an indentured servant has the hope of buying himself free. But this—this would be slavery with none of the protections! After all, it wouldn't be "reasonable" to have a law stating that a man couldn't beat his dog, so why have one saying he can't beat his Mintak?

Deliambrens, for instance, would be considered human under the law —but Mintaks and Haspur, with their hides of hair and feathers, their nonhuman hands and feet, their muzzles and beaks, would be animals.

Some people were arguing that as property, these nonhumans would actually have protection they did *not* have now—protection from persecution by the Church. "Animals" by Church canon could not be evil, because they had no understanding of the difference between good and evil. It was also argued that some of the violence done to nonhumans in the past—the beatings and ambushes—would end if this law was passed, because since they would then be the property of a human, anyone harming one of them would have to pay heavy restitution to the owner.

Naturally all those nonhumans not falling within the proper degree of humanity would have their property confiscated—cattle can't own homes or businesses, of course—and both they and their property would be taken by the Crown. I'm sure that never entered the Lord Treasurer's consideration. And of course as soon as the ink was dry on the confiscation orders, the Crown would then have itself a nice little "animal" auction. More money in the King's coffers, and it wouldn't even be slavery, which is wicked and really not civilized.

Nasty, insidious, and very popular in some quarters. Yes, it would "protect" the nonhumans from the demon hunters, for a little while—until Church canon was changed to make it possible for animals to be considered possessed!

Which it would be; after all, it's in the Holy Writ. There were the demons possessing a human that were cast out, and then possessed a herd of pigs and made the pigs drown themselves.

Small wonder that the Manufactory Guild was also behind this one, at least according to the rumors. If it was passed, the owners of manufactories could neatly bypass all the Church laws on labor by acquiring a nightshift of "animals" to run the machines without wages. There was no Church law saying animals couldn't work all night—nor any Church law giving them a rest day. If it passed—

Well, most of the nonhumans would flee before they could be caught, I suspect, but there are always those who can't believe that something like that would happen to them. There would probably be just enough of those poor naive souls and their children in Lyonarie to make up a workforce large enough to work the manufactories at night.

There would be a business in hunters, too, springing up in the wake of this law. *Hunters? No, more like kidnappers.* They would be going out and trying to entrap nonhumans in whichever of the other human kingdoms existed that did *not* pass this law, and bringing them back here to sell.

Nightingale clutched her hands into fists and felt her nails biting into the palms of her hands. If she ever found out who the nasty piece of work was that first came up with this idea, she would throttle him herself.

With my bare hands. And dance on his corpse.

She told herself she had to relax; at the moment, it was no more than a rumor, and she had only heard about it *here.* No one had mentioned it in the High King's servants' kitchen this morning, nor even in the Chapels friendly to all species. It might be nothing. It might only be a distortion of one of the other laws being considered.

It might even be a rumor deliberately started by the Church in order to make some of the other things they were trying to have passed look less unappetizing.

Or to allow them to slip something else past while the nonhumans are agitating about the rumor.

She would wait until the morning, and see what was in the kitchens and on the street.

She took a deep breath—after a first, cautious sniff to make sure that the wind was not in the "wrong" direction. She let it out again, slowly, exhaling her tension with her breath. This was an old exercise, one that was second nature to her now. As always, it worked, as did her mental admonition that there was nothing she could do *now, this moment.* It would have to wait until tomorrow, so she might as well get the rest she needed to deal with it.

When she finally felt as if she *would* be able to sleep, she got to her feet and picked her way across the rooftop, avoiding the places where she knew that some of her fellow staff might be sheltering together, star-watching. Supposedly the Deliambren who owned this place was considering a rooftop dining area, but so far nothing had materialized, and the staff had it all to themselves.

And a good thing, too. The streets hereabouts aren't safe for star-watching or nighttime strolls before bed. When customers of wealth came here, they came armed, or they came with guards. Not only were there thieves in plenty, but there were people who hated those who were not human, who would sometimes lie in wait to attack customers coming in or out of

Freehold. They seldom confined their beatings to nonhumans—they were just as happy to get their hands on a "Fuzzy-lover" and teach him a lesson about the drawbacks of tolerance.

Once or twice a week, some of the staff would turn the tables on them, but that was a dangerous game, for it was difficult to prove who was the attacker and who the victim in a case like that. If the night-watch happened to hear the commotion and come to break it up instead of running the other way as they often did, the Freehold staff often found themselves cooling their heels in gaol until someone came to pay their fines. The law was just as likely to punish Freehold staff as the members of the gang that had ambushed the customers.

Nightingale was still ambivalent about joining one of those expeditions; she *could* add a good margin of safety for the group if she used Bardic magic to make gang members utterly forget who their attackers had been. But if *she* was caught doing something like that, and fell into the hands of the Church—

Flame is not my best color, she thought, trying to drive away fear with flippancy.

She reached the roof door to the staircase going down, and turned to take one last look up at the stars. And she thought, oddly enough, of T'fyrr.

I am glad he is safe with Old Owl, the Deliambren, she thought soberly. *If any of the rumors are true, he would be in grave danger. At least, with Harperus, he has protection and a quick way out of any danger that should come.*

So at least one person she cared for was safe. And with that thought to comfort her, she took the stairs down to the staff quarters, and to her empty bed.

CHAPTER FIVE

Nightingale slipped out into the early morning mist by way of a back staircase. She had learned about it from one of the waiters, the second day of her arrival at Freehold. It was mostly in use by night, rather than by day; it locked behind you as you went out, but Nightingale had learned from that waiter that she already had a key. Every staff member had a ring of keys they got when they settled in; Nightingale didn't know even yet what half of them went to, but one of them locked the door to her room, and one unlocked this back staircase door.

She had visited the used-clothing market soon after setting up her network of children, and had acquired a wardrobe there that she really didn't want too many people in Freehold to know about. It was *not* in keeping with Lyrebird, or with the sober and dignified woman she had portrayed herself as when she arrived.

In fact, she rather doubted that she would have had a hearing if she'd shown up at the door in these patched and worn clothes. They *were* clean, scrupulously clean, but they did not betoken any great degree of prosperity. That was fine; she wasn't trying to look prosperous, she was trying to look like the kind of musician who would be happy to sing in the corner of a kitchen in exchange for a basket of leftovers.

She made one concession to city life that she hoped no one would notice, for it was quite out of keeping with her costume. She wore shoes. She had no stockings, and the shoes were as patched as her skirts, but she did have them, and no one as poor as she was supposed to be would own such a thing.

But I'm not going out into a mucky street or traipse around on cobblestones all day without something to protect my feet, she thought stubbornly, as she crossed the street headed east, skipped over a puddle and skirted the edge of a heap of something best left unidentified. There was just so much she would do to protect her persona, and there was such a thing as carrying authenticity too far.

She did not carry a harp at all, only a pair of bones and a small hand-drum, the only things a musician as poor as she would be able to afford.

The mist here beneath the overhanging upper stories of the buildings chilled the skin and left clothing damp and clammy, but in an hour or so it would be horribly hot, and the one advantage this costume had was that it was the coolest clothing she had to wear, other than the Elven silks. That was mostly because the fabric was so threadbare as to be transparent in places. It was all of a light beige, impossible to tell what the original color had been now. The skirt had probably once been a sturdy hempen canvas, but now was so worn and limp that it hung in soft folds like cheesecloth, and was as cool to wear as the most finely woven linen. She didn't have a bodice; no woman this poor would own one. Nor did she have a shirt. Only a shift, which if she really *was* this impoverished, would serve as shirt, petticoat, and nightclothes, all one. It was sleeveless, darned in so many places she wondered if any of the original fabric was left, and had at one time been gathered at the neck with a ribbon. Now it was gathered at the neck with a colorless string, tied in a limp little bow.

She hurried along the streets, sometimes following in the wake of one of the water-carts that was meant to clean the streets of debris and wash it all into the gutters. In the better parts of town, that was probably what it *did* do—but the street-cleaners were paid by the number of streets they covered, and every time they had to go back to the river filling-station to get more water, they lost time. So in this neighborhood, the water sprinkling the street was the barest trickle, scarcely enough to dampen the cobbles, and certainly not enough to wash anything into the gutters. Those few businesses who *cared* about appearances, like Freehold, sent their own people out to wash the street in front of the building. And there were those who lived here who didn't particularly care for having garbage festering at the front door, who did the same. But mostly she had to pick her way carefully along the paths worn clean by carts and rag-pickers.

As the light strengthened and the mist thinned, she got into some better neighborhoods, and now she took advantage of the directions her children had given her, slipping along alleyways and between buildings, following the paths that only the children knew completely. Even the finest of estates had these little back ways, the means to get into the best homes, so long as you came by the servants' entrance where no one who mattered would see you.

Even the Palace. They can put gates across the roads and guard the streets all they like, but even the Palace has to have an alley. Even the Palace has to have a way for people to come and go—people that the lords and ladies don't want to know exist.

Rat catchers. Peddlers. Rag-and-bone men. Dung collectors. Pot scrub-

bers and floor scrubbers and the laundry women who did the lower servants' clothing. Garbage collectors. There was a small army of people
coming and going through that back entrance every day, people who
didn't live *at* the Palace, despite the huge servants' quarters, but who lived
off the Palace. Even the garbage from the Palace was valuable, and there
was an entire system of bribes and kickbacks that determined who got to
carry away what. The Church actually got the best pickings of the edible
stuff, and sent the lowest of the novices to come fetch it every day. They
carried away baskets of leftovers from the royal kitchens that fed the lords
and ladies and the King himself. Allegedly those went to feed the poor;
Nightingale hadn't seen any evidence for or against that.

None of these people were "good enough" to warrant the expense of
clothing them in uniforms and housing them in the Palace; they got their
tiny wages and whatever they could purloin, and came and went every day
at dawn and dusk. They never saw a lord or a lady—the most exalted
person they would ever see would be a page in royal livery.

But, oh, they knew what was going on in that great hive, and better than
the lords and ladies who lived there! Each of them had a friend or a
relative who *did* rate quarters above, and each of them was a veritable
wellspring of information about just what was going on. Gossip was almost
their only form of entertainment, so gossip they did, till the kitchens and
lower halls buzzed like beehives with the sounds of chattering.

Very few of them ever got to hear even a street-singer; no one was out in
the morning when they would scamper in to work, and by the time they
went home in the evening, it was generally in a fog of exhaustion.
Sevenday was the day for Church services, and if one picked the right
Chapel and began at Morningsong and stayed piously on through Vespers,
the Priest would see that piety was rewarded with three stout meals. No
street-singer could compete with all the bean-bread, onions, and bacon
grease to spread on the bread that one could eat, and a cup of real ale to
wash it down. Sometimes on Holy Days, there were even treats of a bit of
cheese, cooked whole turnips, cabbage soup, or a sweet-cake . . . all the
more reason to come early and stay late. And if one happened to doze off
during the sermon, well, Sevenday *was* a day of rest, wasn't it?

So when a poor musician like Tanager showed up, looking for a corner
to sit in, asking nothing more than the leftovers that the kitchen staff
shared, she was generally welcomed. As long as she didn't get in the way
and didn't eat too much, her singing would help pass the time and make
the work seem lighter, and one just might be able to learn a song or two to
sing the little ones to sleep with.

So in the corner Tanager sat, drumming and singing, and between songs listening to the gossip that automatically started up the moment that silence began.

Now the alley was hemmed on both sides by high walls, walls with tantalizing hints of trees and other greenery on the other side. Nightingale —or "Tanager"—joined the thin stream of other threadbare, tired-looking people all making their way up this long, dark alley, some of them rubbing their reddened eyes and yawning, all of them heading for their jobs at the Palace.

There was nothing at the end of this corridor of brickwork, open to the sky, but a gate that led to the Palace grounds.

By now, she was elbow-to-elbow with the Palace servants, none of whom were distinguished by anything like a livery. No one ever saw these people but other servants, after all. She slipped inside the back gate with the others, completely ignored by the fat, bored guard there, whose only real job was to keep things from *leaving* the Palace, not from entering it.

Now she saw the first real sunlight she'd seen this morning; the cobble-stoned courtyard and kitchen garden was open to the sky. Here, the sun had already burned away the mist, and she squinted against its glare as she stared across the courtyard to the great stone bulk of the Palace, dark against the blue sky, with the sun peeking over it.

She had no real idea just how big the Palace was; huge, that was all she knew for certain—at least the size of several Freeholds. From all she had been able to gather, this was only one building of several, all joined by glazed galleries, and all as big as this one was. It made her head swim just to think about it.

She paused just a moment to take in a breath of fresh air before she headed for the back door to the servants' kitchen.

The servants, of course, were never fed out of the same kitchen that conjured up the meals for the lords and ladies. In fact, there were *two* kitchens that fed the servants: Upper and Lower. Upper Kitchen was the one that fed the pages, the personal maids and valets, the Court Musicians, nannies and nursemaids, tutors and governesses, all those who were not *quite* "real" servants, but who were not gentry, either. Lower was for the real servants: anyone who cleaned, cooked, sewed, polished, served food and drink, washed, mended, or tended to animals or plants. Tanager would never have dared intrude on the Upper Servants' Kitchen; Lower was where she fit in, and Lower was where she went.

She needed that breath of fresh air when she got there; as usual, it was as hot as a Priest's Personal Hell in there, with all the ovens going, baking bread for afternoon and evening meals before it got too warm to keep the ovens stoked. Breakfast bread had been baking all night, of course, and Tanager's arrival was greeted right at the door by one of the under-cooks, with enthusiasm and a warm roll that had a scraping of salted lard melting inside it. Tanager got out of the doorway and ate the roll quickly, as would anyone for whom this would be a real breakfast. Then she hurried across the slate floor and took her seat out of the way, off in a corner of the kitchen that seemed to be an architectural accident; a bit of brickwork that *might* have served as a closet if it had been bigger, and *might* have served as a cupboard, if it had been smaller, and really wasn't right for either. Before she had come to sing, there had been a small table there. You could put a stack of towels there, or a few of the huge pans needed to cook the enormous meals they prepared here—or Tanager. There were other places for the towels and pans; now the wedge-shaped corner held a stool for her to sit on.

The kitchen was a huge, brick-walled room, lit by open windows and the fires of three enormous fireplaces, where soup and stew cooked in kettles as big around as a beer barrel. There were five big tables, and counters beneath the windows, where the cooks and their helpers worked. No fancy pastry cooks here; the fare dished out to the lower servants was the same, day in, day out: soup and stew made with meat left from yesterday, sent from the Upper Servants' Kitchen, bread, pease-porridge and oat-porridge. On special occasions, leftover sweets came over from the Upper Servants' Kitchen, as well—breakfast sweets came over at noon, lunch-sweets at dinner, and dinner-sweets appeared when all the cleaning up had been accomplished, by way of a treat and a reward for the extra hours. So far, Tanager hadn't seen any of those.

Tanager thought long and hard as she settled herself on her stool. This was the first time she had needed to hear about something specific. Something as odd as the "Law of Degree" was not going to come up in normal conversation.

And I'm not going to ask about it myself. That leaves only one option; I'll have to use Bardic Magic to coax it out of them.

Tanager was a simple girl; Nightingale was anything but. Easy in her power and comfortable with it, she had been using Bardic Magic for as long as she had been on her own, on the road. Often she had no choice. The use of Bardic Magic to influence the minds of those around her had sometimes been the only way she had gotten out of potentially dangerous situations. Living with the Elves had refined her techniques, since Bardic Magic was similar to one of their own magics. Now she scarcely had to think about tapping into the power; she simply stretched out her mind, and there it was.

I need a song as a vehicle; something that includes nonhumans. But nothing too jarring to start with; something they would enjoy listening to under ordinary circumstances. And it will have to be something with a strong beat as well, since I only have the drum to accompany me. Ah, I know; that song Raven wrote: "Good Duke Arden." It has several verses about Arden taking care of nonhumans in his train.

So she began with that, then moved on to other melodies, songs that dealt with nonhumans in a favorable light. And all the while she sang, she concentrated on one thing. *Talk about the nonhumans, what the lords and ladies are saying about them.*

She sat and sang and drummed until her wrist and voice tired; one of the pot scrubbers, with an empty dishpan and nothing better to do at the moment, brought her a cup of flat ale. Tanager pretended to drink it, but it really went down a crack at her feet. And while she drank, she listened.

There was nothing at all in the gossip about the "Law of Degree," but there *was* something that made her sit up straight in startlement.

"La, Delia, did ye see th' lad wi' all the snow-white hair, him an' his coach with no horses come in yestere'en?" asked one of the under-cooks. "Faith, 'tis all m'sister, her as is Chambermaid t' Lord Pelham's nannies, can talk about!"

Lad with all the hair? Coach with no horses? Dear Lady, that can't be—oh surely not—

"Coo, ye should'a seen what came w' him!" said another, one of the chief cooks. " 'Tis a great bird man, 'twas, w' wings an' all, an' a great evil beak like a hawk i' the middle'v his face! An' *claws!* I wouldn' want t' get on the wrong side uv him!"

Tanager sat frozen, her hands wrapped around her empty cup. It was! It was Harperus—and with him, T'fyrr! It must be! But why here, and why now?

"Ah, but ye haven't heard the best of it," said a third girl knowingly. "*My* second cousin is best friend t' Lord Atrovel's secretary's valet, an' this birdy-man like to set the whole Court on its ear!"

As Tanager sat in stunned silence, the girl gleefully told the entire story, while the rest of the kitchen worked and put in a word or two of commentary. According to the girl, a nonhuman who *had* to be a Deliambren from the description, and another who was either T'fyrr or another of his race, had come in yesterday afternoon to Court. They had been announced as some kind of envoy, and at that point, for a reason that the girl either didn't know or couldn't explain, the bird-man broke into song. From there, her version differed slightly from the ones offered by a few others. The others claimed that the bird-man had challenged the King's Musicians to a contest and had won it; the girl maintained that he had simply begun singing, as a sample of what he could do.

At any rate, when it was all over, the King had appointed the bird-man to be his Chief Musician (the others claimed Laurel Bard), the rest of the

Court Musicians were furious (no one differed on that), and most of the King's Advisors were beside themselves over the fact that the King had overruled them.

Ah, but if the first girl was to be believed, the King had not only appointed the Haspur—for it must be a Haspur, even if it wasn't T'fyrr—as his Chief Musician, he had appointed him directly to the Royal Household, made a Sire out of him, and installed him in a suite in the royal wing of the Palace!

I only hoped to hear something about the Law of Degree, Tanager thought dazedly, *not this—*

Could it be T'fyrr and Old Owl? She didn't know of any other Haspur and Deliambrens traveling together. But why would they come here?

Why am I here? Whoever these strangers are, it is for the same reason, surely.

Now she was very grateful that she had been so careful to keep her real identity and purpose here a secret. With *two* sets of agents blundering about, it would have been appallingly easy for them to trip each other up.

Now I need only watch for them, and avoid getting entangled in whatever scheme they have going. Oh, yes, need only. If it is Harperus, that will be like trying to avoid the garbage in the streets! He's more clever than twenty Gypsies in his own way, and encompasses everyone he meets in his grand plots in some way or another. Ah, well, at least he doesn't know I'm here; I just hope he doesn't get T'fyrr in trouble. . . .

Somehow she managed to pull herself together and continue singing and playing for the rest of the morning. That was all the time she ever spent here—and that was reasonable, for Tanager. Mornings were fairly useless for a street-musician; the afternoon meant better pickings, and Tanager would now, presumably, go on to whatever street corner she had staked out as her own. There she could expect to earn "hard currency" for her work; pins, mostly, with a sprinkling of copper coins, and some food.

As usual, she spread out a threadbare napkin, and the chief cook filled it with her "pay"—mostly leftover bread, with a bit of bacon and a scrap of cheese, some of last night's roast from the Upper Servant's Kitchen that was too tough and stringy to even go into soup today. Tanager thanked her with a little bobbing curtsey, tied it all up into a bundle, and slipped out the door just in time to avoid the lunchtime rush.

She always hurried across the cobbles to the gate, but today she had more reason to half-run than usual. She wanted to find out if anyone in the city had heard anything about the bird-man, *or* the Law of Degree, and to that end, there were two places she needed to go. First, as Nightingale, the Chapel of Saint Gurd. Second, the square just down the street from

Freehold where she generally met Maddy and the rest of her army of urchins just after lunch.

Surely, between them, Father Ruthvere or the children would have heard or seen something. And at the moment, she was not certain whether she wanted to hear more about the Law of Degree or—T'fyrr.

If that was who the feathered wonder was.

Nightingale slipped back into Freehold by the back door feeling quite frustrated. There had been nothing worth bothering about in the way of news at the Chapel; the Priest, Father Ruthvere, had heard nothing about a "Law of Degree," but he promised Nightingale fiercely that he would do his best to find out about it.

Father Ruthvere was something of an odd character, and Nightingale never would have trusted him with her true Bard-name if it had not been that *he* had recognized her Free Bard ribbons during one of her visits (not as Tanager) and had asked her how Master Wren and Lady Lark were faring. It turned out that he had some sort of connection to that cousin of Talaysen's who was also in the Church. He had been promoted to his own Chapel here, and he had promised Priest Justiciar Ardis when he was sent on to Lyonarie that he would keep an eye out for Free Bards and help them when he could.

That in itself was either an example of how small a world it truly was— or that there *was* something in the way of Fate dogging her footsteps.

The convoluted twists that this little mission of hers was taking were beginning to make her head spin.

For the meantime, however, Father Ruthvere was an ally she was only too glad to have found. He was one of the faction that followed the "we are all brothers" faith, and that made him doubly valuable to her, and vice versa. *He* knew what was going on, to a limited extent, within the Church —*she* had her information from the street and the Court. Together they found they could put together some interesting wholes out of bits and pieces.

Maddy and her crew hadn't come up with anything either, though as usual they were glad enough for her bag of leftovers and the pennies she gave them all. The only thing that one of the boys knew was that his brother had actually *seen* the horseless wagon on its way to the Palace. It had not been pulled or pushed by any beasts, and from the description, it could have been the wagon that Harperus used.

But then again, she thought to herself, as she scrambled up the staircase, *wouldn't any Deliambren wagon look like any other? I don't know for a fact that Harperus is the only one traveling about the countryside.*

But would any other Deliambren have a Haspur with him?

She slipped down the hall, making certain first that there was no one around to catch her in her Tanager disguise, then unlocked the door to her room and whisked inside.

"I don't even know that it's a Haspur," she told herself, thinking out loud. "There is more than one bird-race, and most of them would match the description that girl gave. It could be anyone. In fact, it's just not *likely* that it's Harperus and T'fyrr."

But as she changed out of her Tanager clothing and headed for the bathroom for a needed sluicing, she couldn't help but think that—given the way that things were going—the fact it wasn't likely was the very reason why it would turn out to be her friends.

She drifted down the stairs in one of her rainbow-skirts; the blue one this time. Today, Lyrebird was in a casual mood and had dressed accordingly.

Actually, today Lyrebird was ravenous and wanted to be able to eat without worrying about delicate dagging and fragile lace. She had missed her lunch in order to fit in a stop at Father Ruthvere's Chapel, and she'd given all those leftovers to the children without saving even a roll for herself.

Not that she had been hungry enough for stale rolls and stringy beef. Her stay here had spoiled her; there had been plenty of times when those leftovers would have been a feast.

Well, plenty of times in the long past, when she was between villages and her provisions had run out, maybe. Nightingale had *never* been so poor a musician that she'd *had* to sing for leftovers.

This hour was too late for lunch and a bit too early for dinner. Only a few of the eating nooks were open and operating, and all of those were on the ground floor. Lyrebird went to one of her favorites, where the cook was a merry little man with no use of his lower limbs because of an illness as a child. Not that he let it get in the way of his work; he *was* a cook, after all, and he didn't need to move much. He plied his trade very well from a stationary seat within a half-circle of round-bottomed pans, all heated on Deliambren braziers to the sizzling point. You picked out what you wanted from a series of bins of fresh vegetables, and strips of fowl, fish and meat in bowls sunk in ice, and brought it to him in your bowl; he would quick-fry it in a bit of oil, spice it according to your taste, and serve it all to you on a bed of rice, scooped out of the huge steamer behind him. If he wasn't busy, he was always happy to talk.

Nightingale was always happy to talk to him, and this time of day she was often his only customer.

"Well, Lyrebird, you're eating like a bird indeed today—twice your weight in food! You're eating like dear little Violetta!"

He winked at that; most of the staff found Violetta amusing. The name was female, and surely the little misfit dressed like a woman, but there wasn't a person on the staff who was fooled.

No matter. Freehold was full of misfits, and if "Violetta" wanted to dress in fantastic gowns and gossip like one of the serving-wenches, no one here would ever let "her" know that they had seen past the disguise.

"Skip your breakfast?" Derfan asked, eyeing the size of the bowl she had picked up at the start of the bins.

"And lunch," she confirmed, bringing him her selection and taking a seat on one of the stools nearby to watch him work. He had the most amazingly quick hands; *she* would have scorched everything, or herself, but Derfan never spoiled a meal that she had ever heard. And he never once burned himself, either.

He pursed his lips and shook his head at her. "That's very bad of you. You'll do yourself harm if you make that a habit. I should think you'd be ready to faint dead away. What was so important that you had to skip two meals?"

"That business with that new law people were so upset about last night," she replied casually. Since it had been the talk of Freehold, there was no reason why she should not have been out looking for confirmation. "I know a good Priest who keeps his ear to the ground and hears a great deal, but he's halfway across the city."

"And?" Derfan prompted, dashing in bits of seasoning and a spot of oil while he tossed her food deftly on the hot metal.

"He hadn't heard a thing," she told him. "I'm halfway convinced now that it was a rumor being spread so that our good leaders can slip something else into law while *we* are out chasing our tails over this."

"Could be, could be," Derfan agreed, nodding vigorously. "It wouldn't be the first time they've done things that way." The jovial man grinned infectiously as he ladled some juices here and there. "But we've got enough excitement right here in Freehold to keep everyone stirred up for the next few days, and never mind some maybe-so, maybe-no law out there."

She shook her head as he handed her the bowl full of rice and stir-fried morsels. "I haven't been here, remember?" she said, fanning the food to cool it, and daring a quick bite. It was too hot, and she quickly sucked in cool air to save her tongue.

"Our leader's shown up." Derfan raised both eyebrows at her.

She wrinkled her brow, unable to guess his meaning.

"Our real boss," Derfan elaborated. "The one Kyran works for." He sighed when she shook her head blankly. "Tyladen, the Deliambren, the owner of Freehold. He's here."

She stopped blowing on her food and looked up at him sharply. "No," she said. "I thought he never came here!"

Oh, this is too much! she thought as Derfan nodded and shrugged. *Not one, but* two *Deliambrens showing up in the space of a single day? What is this, a conspiracy? Is* everyone *around here involved in some kind of plot?*

"It isn't that he never comes here, it's just that he doesn't do it often," Derfan told her as she applied herself grimly to her food again. "Maybe he's decided he ought to, seeing as there's been all that law talk. Maybe it's about time he did, too—*he's* the one with all the money. Precious little you and me could do if the High King decides to make trouble for our friends, but Deliambrens have got the stuff that the high and mighty want, and that means they have money *and* a reason for the lords and ladies to listen to 'em. They've used that kind of influence before, I've heard."

"Well, if he wants to have any customers, he'd better get involved, I suppose," she agreed mildly.

Now what? What happens if he recognizes me? I didn't recognize his name, but that doesn't mean he doesn't know me. I've met a lot of Deliambrens, and I don't remember half of them. Damn! The last thing I want is some wealthy fuzzy-faced half-wit breathing down my neck right now, watching everything I do and wanting to know why I haven't found out more!

As if to confirm her worst fears, Derfan had even more news about Tyladen. "Word is," Derfan said in a confidential tone, "that Tyladen's going to make the rounds of the whole place tonight; look in on all the performers, the cooks and all, see how they're doing, see how many customers they're bringing in."

"Well, you have no worry on that score," Nightingale pointed out. Derfan blushed, but Nightingale spoke nothing but the truth. Derfan's little corner was always popular, since his customers always *knew* what was in the food he fixed for them. Some of them, like the Mintak, were herbivorous and could not digest meat. In addition, the food was ready quickly, and if you were very hungry, you didn't have to spend a lot of time waiting for someone to prepare your dinner, the way you did in some of the other little nooks.

"You don't either, from what I've heard," he countered. "You're very popular."

She shrugged. "Usually I would agree with you, but any musician can have a bad night. It would be my luck that tonight would be the one."

Derfan snorted. "I doubt it," he began. "A bad night for you is a terrific night for some other people around here and—" He interrupted himself.

"Turn around! There he is, out on the dance floor, looking up at the light-rigs on the ceiling!"

She turned quickly and got a good view of the mysterious Tyladen as he stood with his hands on his hips, peering up at the ceiling four floors above. And to her initial relief, she didn't recognize him.

He was much younger than she had thought, although age was difficult to measure in a Deliambren; the skin of his face was completely smooth and unwrinkled, even at the corners of the eyes and mouth. He was dressed quite conservatively for a Deliambren, in a one-piece garment of something that looked like black leather but probably wasn't, with a design in contrasting colors appliqued from the right shoulder to the left hip and down the right leg. His hair was relatively short, no longer than the top of his shoulders, and so were his cheek-feathers, although she could have used his eyebrows for whisk brooms.

He dropped his eyes just as she took the last of this in, and she found herself staring right into them. For one frozen moment, she thought she saw a flash of recognition there.

But if she had, in the next instant it was gone again. He waved his hand slightly in acknowledgement of the fact that he knew they were both watching him and they were his employees, then went back to staring at the ceiling, ignoring them.

But now she was so keyed up, she even read *that* as evidence that he was going to try to interfere in her careful and cautious plans.

She finished her dinner quickly, thanked Derfan, and hurried up to the Oak Grove, certain that Tyladen was going to show up there and demand an explanation.

But as the evening wore on and nothing happened—other than Violetta showing up, as if Derfan's earlier mention of "her" had conjured "her"— she began to feel a bit annoyed. Granted, she really didn't *want* some Deliambren meddling in her affairs, but she wasn't sure she liked being ignored either!

When Tyladen finally did show up, it was during the busiest part of her evening and she was in the middle of a set. She didn't even realize he was there until she looked up in time to see him nod with satisfaction, turn, and walk out the door.

Just that. That was all there was to it.

Her shift came to an end without anything more happening, and none of her customers had any more information about either the Law of Degree or the mysterious bird-man at the High King's Court. Not even Violetta, who knew or at least pretended to know something about everything, had anything to say on either subject. On her way upstairs, she stopped at a little nook that sold prebaked goods and got a couple of meat rolls and an apple tart to take up to her room, half expecting to be intercepted between her room and the Oak Grove. No one materialized, though, and no one was waiting in her room.

She ate and cleaned up, and finally went to bed, feeling decidedly odd.

She was just as happy that she wasn't going to be interfered with, but after getting herself all upset about the prospect to find that she was being ignored was a bit—annoying!

But that's a Deliambren for you, she decided, as she drifted off to sleep. *If they aren't annoying by doing something, they're bound to annoy you by not doing it!*

T'fyrr checked the tuning on his small flat-harp nervously for the fifth time. He had decided this morning what he was going to perform for this, his first private concert for the High King, and he was going to need more accompaniment than even *his* voice could produce. The flat-harp would be ideal, though, for the songs he had selected were all deceptively simple.

He had wanted to do something to remind the King of his duty; he had found, he thought, precisely the music that would. He had modified one of those songs about the King himself for his first piece—not changing any of the meaning, just perfecting the rhyme and rhythm, both of which were rather shaky. But from there, he would be singing about Duke Arden of Kingsford, a series of three songs written since the fire by a Free Bard called Raven. The first was the story of the fire itself, describing how the Duke had worked with his own bare hands in the streets, side by side with his people, to hold back the fire. While not the usual stuff of an epic, it was a story of epic proportions, and worthy of retelling.

Let him hear that, and perhaps it will remind him that a ruler's duty is to his people, and not the other way around.

If nothing else, it might remind the King of Duke Arden's straitened circumstances, better than a cold report would. *That* might pry the help out of him that the Duke had been pleading for.

That will make the Lord Seneschal happy, at any rate.

The second was a song about the first winter the city had endured, a saga as grueling, though not as dramatic, as the fire. It described the lengths to which Arden went to see that no one died of hunger or lack of shelter that season. The third and final song described not only Arden but his betrothed, the Lady Phenyx Asher, a love story wound in and around what the two of them were doing, with their own hands, to rebuild the city.

Actually, it is more about the lady than about the Duke; Raven truly admires her, and his words show it.

The next songs were all carefully chosen to do nothing more than entertain and show off T'fyrr's enormous range. A couple of them were not even from human composers at all.

And the last song was another designed to remind the King of his duties —for it had been written by another High King on his deathbed, and was called "The Burden of the Crown." Though sad, it was a hopeful song as well, for the author had clearly not found the Crown to be a burden that was intolerable, merely one that was a constant reminder of the people it represented.

If that doesn't do it, nothing will, T'fyrr thought, then sighed. *Well, I suppose I should not expect results instantly. I am not a Gypsy, with magic at my command. If he only listens to the words, it will be a start.*

He had been given nothing whatsoever to do except practice and wait for the King to send for him. He hadn't especially wanted to venture out of his suite, either; not until the King had heard him play at least once. He had spent all his time pacing, exercising his wings, and practicing. Nob had enjoyed the virtuoso vocalist's practice, but the pacing and wing-strokes clearly made him nervous. He had sought his room when T'fyrr suggested that he might want to go practice his reading and writing for his daily lessons with the pages' tutor.

Finally the summons had come this afternoon, and Nob brought T'fyrr to this little antechamber to the King's personal suite, a room with white satin walls, and furnished with a few chairs done in white satin and gilded wood. There he was to wait until the King called for him.

It seemed he had been waiting forever.

At last, when he was about to snap a string from testing them so often, the door opened and a liveried manservant beckoned. T'fyrr rose to his feet, harp under one arm, and followed him, the tension of waiting replaced by an entirely new set of worries.

As it happened, it was just as well that he had not set his expectations unrealistically high, for the King did not show that the songs affected him in any way—other than his delight and admiration in T'fyrr as a pure musician. He asked for several more songs when T'fyrr was through with his planned set, all of which T'fyrr fortunately knew. One of them gave him the opportunity to display his own scholarship, for he knew three variants, and asked which one Theovere preferred. That clearly delighted the King even further, and when at last the time came for Afternoon Court, a duty even the King could not put off, Theovere sighed and dismissed the Haspur with every sign of disappointment that the performance was over.

"You will come the same time, every day," the stone-faced manservant said expressionlessly as he led T'fyrr to the door. "This is the High King's standing order."

T'fyrr bobbed his head in acknowledgement, and privately wondered how he was going to find his way back to his own quarters in this maze. He had *no* head for indoor directions, and more than a turn or two generally had him confused. It didn't help that all these corridors looked alike—all white marble and artwork, with no way of telling even what floor you were on if you didn't already know.

To his relief, Nob was waiting for him just outside the door, passing the time of day with the guard posted outside the King's suite. This was another of those dangerous looking bodyguards, but this one seemed a bit younger than the ones actually *with* the King, and hadn't lost all his humanity yet.

"Thought you might get lost," the boy said saucily, with a wink at the guard, whose lips twitched infinitesimally.

T'fyrr shrugged. "It is possible," he admitted. "Not likely, but possible, I suppose. This is a large building."

The guard actually snickered at that little understatement, and Nob took him in charge to lead him back to their quarters. "I admit I wasn't entirely certain I knew the way," T'fyrr told the boy quietly, once they were out of the guard's earshot. "The hallways seem to be the same."

"The art's different," Nob told him, gesturing widely at the statues. "This one, the statues are all of High Kings, see? We turn *here,* and the statues are wood-nymphs."

Nude human females sprouting twigs and leaves in their hair. So that is a wood-nymph! No wonder the shepherds in my songs are so surprised; I don't imagine that it is every day that a nude female prances up to the average shepherd and invites him to dance.

"We turn again here—" Nob continued, blissfully unaware of T'fyrr's thoughts, "and the statues are all shepherd couples."

Oh, indeed, if one expects shepherds to be flinging themselves after their sheep wearing a small fortune in embroidery and lace! This is as likely as nude women frolicking about among the thistles and thorns and biting insects, I suppose.

"Then this is our corridor, and the statues are historical women." Nob stopped in front of their door. "Here we are, between Lady Virgelis the Chaste, and the Maiden Moriah—"

Between someone so sour and dried up no one would ever want to mate with her, and someone who probably didn't deserve the title of "Maiden" much past her twelfth birthday, T'fyrr interpreted, looking at the grim-visaged old harridan on his left, who was muffled from head to toe in garments that did not disguise the fact she was mostly bone, and the ripely plump, sloe-eyed young wench on his right, who wasn't wearing much more than one of the wood-nymphs. He wondered if the juxtaposition was accidental.

Probably not. He had the feeling that very little in this palace was accidental.

"So," he said, as Nob opened the door and held it open for him, "to get to the King's suite, I go—right, through the ladies to the shepherds, left, through the shepherds to the wood-nymphs, left through the nymphs to the High Kings, and right through the Kings to where the guard is."

"Perfect," Nob lauded. "You have it exactly right." The page closed the door behind them, and T'fyrr decided that he might as well ask the next question regarding directions.

"Now," he said, "if I wanted to go into the city, how would I get out?"

One of the so-called "supervisors" in charge of expelling rowdy custom-ers—who elsewhere would have been called "peace-keepers"—inter-cepted Nightingale on her way upstairs after her performance the second night after the Deliambren Tyladen arrived to take over management from Kyran.

"Tyladen wants to see you in his office," the burly Mintak said shortly, and Nightingale suppressed a start and a grimace of annoyance. "Tonight. Soon as you can."

"Right," she said shortly, and continued on up to her room to place her harp in safekeeping. *So, he recognized me after all, or someone warned him, or he got a message back to the Fortress-City with my description or even my image and they've told him I'm supposed to be doing some investigation for them*—She clenched her jaw tightly and closed the door of her room carefully behind her, making certain she heard the lock click shut. *I could deny it all, of course, and there is no way that he can* know *that I am Nightingale unless I admit it. Still, even if I deny it he'll be watching me, trying to see if I'm doing anything, likely getting underfoot or sending someone to follow me. Oh, bother! Why did I ever even consider this in the first place? I must have been mad. Every time I get involved with Deliambrens there's trouble.*

She fumed to herself all the way down the stairs, and even more as she wormed her way through the crowds on and surrounding the dance floor. That was no easy task; at this time of the night, the dance floor was a very popular place. Special lights suspended from the ceiling actually sent round, focused circles of light down on the dancers; the circles were of different colors and moved around to follow the better dancers, or pulsed in time to the music. Some folk came here just to watch the lights move in utter, bemused fascination. Many spectators watched from the balconies of the floors above. Nightingale was used to such things, but for most people, this was purest magic, and they could not for a moment imagine what was creating these "fairy lights." It was easy to see why Freehold was such a popular place; there wasn't its like outside the Fortress-City, and not one person in ten thousand of those here would ever see the fabulous Deliambren stronghold.

The lights made Nightingale's head ache, especially after a long, hard day, and she was less than amused at being summoned *now*. She wanted food, a bath, and bed in that order. She did *not* want to have to go through a long session of deception and counter-deception with some fool of a Deliambren.

Fortunately, she was tall for a woman, and hard to ignore. One or two human customers, more inebriated than most, attempted to stop her. All it took, usually, was a single long, cold stare directly into the eyes of even the most intoxicated, and they generally left her alone quickly. A touch of Bardic Magic, a hint of Elven coldness, delivered with an uncompromising glare—that was the recipe that said *leave me alone* in a way that transcended language.

She finally reached the other side of the dance floor with no sense of relief. The offices were down a short corridor between one of the eateries that catered to strict herbivores and a bar that specialized in exotic beers made from all manner of grains, from corn to rice. The corridor was brightly lit, which was the best way of ensuring that people who didn't belong there weren't tempted to investigate it. Somehow the adventurous never wanted to explore anything that was lit up like a village square at noon on midsummer day. It wasn't very inviting, anyway; just a plain, white-walled, white-tiled corridor with a couple of doors in it.

There were two doors on the corridor to be precise; the nearest was Kyran's office. She tapped once on the farthest and entered.

There wasn't much there except for a desk and a couple of chairs, although the Deliambren sitting at the desk quickly put something small, flat and dark into a desk drawer as she closed the door behind her. She guessed that whatever it was, she wasn't supposed to see it or know it existed. *More Deliambren devices, I suppose,* she thought sourly, *more Deliambren secrets. As if any of them would be useful to me!* But she schooled her face into a carefully neutral expression, and said shortly, "You wanted to see me, Tyladen?"

No "sir"; she was quite annoyed enough with him to omit any honorifics. But he didn't seem to notice the omission, or if he did, he didn't care. He smiled, nodded at the nearest chair, and put his hands back up on the empty wooden desktop.

"I did. Lyrebird, is it?" At her nod, he smiled again. "Good name.

Appropriate for a musician. Quite. Well." He laughed, and she had to wonder if he was as foolish as he seemed at this moment. Probably not. "Seems you're very popular here at Freehold."

He waited for an answer, and again she nodded, cautiously, as she dropped gracefully into the chair. It didn't look comfortable, but to her surprise it was. "I'd like to think so," she added, making a bid for an appearance of modesty.

"Oh, you are, you are—one of our most popular musicians among the nonhumans, that's a fact." He continued to smile, and she waited with growing impatience for him to get to the point. What was he after? Did he want to know *why* she, a human musician, should be so popular among those who were not of her race? Was he going to challenge her and demand that she reveal her true identity?

He just waited, and finally she came up with another short answer for him. "That's what they tell me." She shrugged again, trying to appear modest.

"Well, they tell you true." He nodded like the child's toy they called a "head-bobber," still giving her that silly smile.

I know that Deliambrens have a hard time relating to humans and their emotions, but this is ridiculous. I can see why he has Kyran acting as manager here most of the time. He doesn't know the first thing about interacting with us. I know he can't be stupid, but he certainly projects himself as a prime silly ass.

Of course, he could be trying to soften her up for the confrontation. He could be hoping to make her think he was an idiot so that she would underestimate him and let something slip.

Well, if that was what he was waiting for, he'd be here until the building fell to pieces around him.

"Yes, they tell you true," he said, head still bobbing vigorously. "So I'm going to have to move you. Oak Grove isn't big enough, and some of the customers can't get up all those stairs, anyway. I want you down here, on the ground floor. Silas wants to join the dinner-to-midnight dance group, they want to have him, and that frees up the Rainbow, and that's where I want you."

The Rainbow? her mind babbled. *The biggest performance room in Freehold? Me? Take over from Silas? Me?*

As she sat there in stunned silence, he added, as if in afterthought, "Oh —and you'll be getting what Silas was, if that's all right. Two Royals a night?"

Two—two Royals? Me? Nightingale? Has he got the right person?

"Oh, that's quite fine," she replied in a daze, and he reached his hand across the desk. "Thank you. Thank you very much!" Without thinking, she leaned forward to take it as a token of her acceptance.

"Done then. We'll see you down here tomorrow night, then, Lyrebird." He took her hand, shook it once, awkwardly, and let it go. Then he waved his hands at her as she continued to sit there blinking, shooing her playfully out the door. "You need sleep, if you're going to open in the Rainbow tomorrow, my lady. Off with you."

She rose, opened the door in a daze, and walked back out into the noise and the music.

The Rainbow? It was the biggest performance room in Freehold! The only other venue larger was the dance floor itself. Silas was another human—or so he claimed—with an inhumanly beautiful face and body, a waist-length mane of golden curls, and a voice like strong bronze, powerful and compelling. Silas liked to display that body in clothing much like Tyladen had worn that first day, except that Silas' skintight garments *were* real leather. He was extremely popular with both male and female customers, and by reputation, distributed his favors equally between both sexes. She had heard rumors that he wanted to join the dance group, and she could certainly see why; he would be able to concentrate on singing, and choose the powerful and rhythmic music he preferred instead of the ballads that a performance room demanded. His guitar playing was the weakest part of his act; now he wouldn't need to worry about it, with an entire ensemble to back him.

And the dance floor will be more crowded than ever—Silas is bound to sing fast music, which will make people thirsty, which will sell a great many drinks. It is a good bargain all around, even at continuing to pay him his current salary or above. But—me? The Rainbow? Who am I? I'm not gorgeous, like Silas. I know I'm good, but I don't have a fraction of his charisma. I'm just a Gypsy street-player, a good one, but nothing more than that. How can I ever fill the Rainbow?

She found herself on the staircase, with no clear memory of how she had crossed the intervening floor. The Rainbow Room was easily three times the size of the Oak Grove. How could she ever justify being put there? Who would come?

All those people who wait for seats now, whispered an elated little voice in the back of her mind. *All those people who stand crowded into the back wall. And all those who* want *to hear you, but can't climb three flights of stairs. You know there are plenty of those. Derfan's said as much. Lady of the Night, now Derfan can even come listen to you!*

Well, that was true. Many of the folk who crowded into Freehold of a night were the human misfits of the city; those who, like Derfan, were *not* sound of body by everyday measure. Out there, they were cripples. In any other tavern in the city, they would still be cripples. Here, they were no stranger than anyone else, and their only limitations were how far up the staircases they could get—and there were plenty of nonhumans who couldn't manage that. Kyran and Tyladen spoke vaguely of putting in some sort of lifting system to accommodate them, but apparently there was some problem with getting it to work reliably. There *were* hoists for food and drink for the various tiny kitchens, but they were all powered by the muscles of Mintaks and other strong creatures and not really practical for hauling people up and down.

Besides, the worst that happened if a hoist failed was the loss of a little food and profit. The worst that could happen if a lift full of customers failed was not to be contemplated.

That was why the most popular acts were all on the first floor, where everyone could see them that wanted to.

Can I do it? she asked herself, and forced herself to think about it dispassionately. *Yes,* she decided, on sober contemplation. *I think that I can.*

But she had to stop on the way up and bespeak a pot of very hot water from one of the tea vendors. Mingled excitement, anticipation, and stage-fright were beginning to build inside her at the prospect of facing the largest audience at the greatest rate of pay she had ever, in her life, warranted. If she was going to be able to do anything tomorrow, she was going to need to get some sleep tonight, as Tyladen had pointed out. Fortunately, she had packed a number of herbal remedies in her panniers, and one of them was for sleeplessness.

And tonight she was going to need it.

The excitement was almost enough to drive her real reason for being here out of her mind.

Almost.

As she reached her room again, shut and locked the door behind her, and began to prepare for bed, her mind went back to what Tanager had heard at the Palace today. The Haspur—and if the mysterious new Court Musician wasn't a Haspur, he was of some race so like them that it made no difference—was the sensation of the Court and had inspired some of the most envious hatred in the King's musicians she had ever heard of. Some of them were threatening to pack up and leave the King's service; others swore they would "get rid of" the interloper. Nightingale was not particularly worried about the ability of the Court Musicians as individuals to "get rid of" their rival; they were Guild Bards after all, and as a group, Guild Bards were singularly ineffectual at doing anything of a practical nature. The trouble was that they all had been placed where they were by *someone;* they must have powerful allies, and those allies might decide to

take an interest. Allies and patrons of that sort had access to all manner of
unpleasant things, from simple thugs to sophisticated poisons. They might
consider the new Court Musician to be too trivial a problem to bother with
—but in a Court ruled by a High King with an obsession for musicians,
that was not as likely as it would otherwise have been. In fact, the new
musician might be considered as deadly a potential rival as any of the
Grand Dukes and Court Barons—and one with fewer protections.

Did the Haspur know this?

I hope so, she thought, slipping into her nightshift and preparing her pot
of soporific tea. *Oh, I hope so. I hope he is finding himself some equally
powerful allies. Because if he doesn't—he's going to find himself wing-clipped
and surrounded, and that lovely position he has earned himself will be no
more than a beautifully gilded trap. . . .*

Like most of the other performance rooms in Freehold, the Rainbow
Room lived up to its name, but not in the way that anyone who had not
seen it would have expected. It was not decorated in many colors, nor
worse, festooned with painted rainbows like a child's nursery. The Rainbow Room was the plainest, simplest performance room in the building,
its walls and ceiling painted a soft white, the floor and tables some seam-
less substance of a textured, matte black, the booths and chairs uphol-
stered in black as well, something as soft and supple as black suede
leather, although Nightingale was fairly certain that was not what it was. It
would have cost a fortune to cover that much furniture in black leather,
and not even a Deliambren had that much to spare on furnishings in a
performance room.

No, it was when the lights were dimmed and the special performance
lighting lit that the Rainbow Room lived up to its name.

For there were crystal prisms hidden everywhere: in the ceiling fixtures,
in the pillars supporting the ceiling, set into the leaded glass windows that
divided the room itself from the dance floor. When the performance
lighting was illuminated, those prisms caught and refracted it into a hundred thousand tiny rainbows that flung themselves everywhere, and since
many of the prisms were free to move with air currents, the rainbows
moved as well in a gentle dance of color. With that as a backdrop, no
performer needed anything else.

Silas had shown himself to advantage here, and Nightingale hoped to
emulate him. To that end she had chosen her black Elven silks for this first
performance in the new room.

And in fact, she was beginning to think farther ahead than just the next
few days or even weeks. If she could sustain her popularity here—why go
anywhere else? Why go back on the road, once she had collected the

information that the Deliambrens, the Free Bards, and the Elves all wanted? She didn't particularly have a sense of wanderlust the way some Gypsies did; she simply had never found a place she wanted to stay for more than a few months at a time.

Why *not* stay here?

Granted, she hated cities, but she couldn't avoid them altogether, and if she was going to have to endure them, why not do so where she was guaranteed a level of comfort that she would *never* get anywhere else? Where else would she have her own room with her own bathroom, heated and cooled to perfection. Where else would she get her choice of food-stuffs, so that she could go all month and never eat the same meal twice? And where else would she find a performance venue like this one?

And to that end—if she stayed, she would need new costumes, many new costumes, all of the same quality as her silks. The Elves would owe her once she got their information back to them; she *could* send word back with her own messages that she needed new dresses, and ask for specific colors and designs. . . .

She shook herself out of her reverie as the doors of the room opened and people began to make their way in. *Concentrate on what's going on right now, foolish woman,* she scolded herself. *Deal with what you have before you. Worry about far into the future when you know you will have that kind of future.*

Outside on the dance floor, Silas and the other musicians were setting up; she saw them clearly through the window. He must have sensed her watching, for he turned toward the Rainbow Room and waved, grinning broadly, then gave her the Gypsy sign for well-wishing. She smiled back and did the same, knowing that he could see her as easily as she saw him. He looked particularly wonderful and outrageous tonight, and his tight leather costume would give most Church Priests heart failure. It was cut out in unexpected patterns that allowed his golden-tan skin to show through, and unless she was very much mistaken, he was wearing a leather codpiece with a red leather rose appliqued on the front.

Showoff. But she smiled as she thought it. It was impossible not to like Silas; he went out of his way to be kind to even the lowliest of the waiters and cleaners and encouraging to the worst of his fellow entertainers. There wasn't an unkind bone in Silas' body.

Unfortunately, there wasn't a chaste bone in there, either. "Promiscuous" did not begin to describe him, and Nightingale feared he would meet an early end, either torn to pieces among a dozen jealous lovers, each of whom was sure he or she was Silas' only true love, or worn away to nothing by the exertion of all his love affairs. Silas' one fault—and it was a bad one—was that he had a habit of telling his lovers whatever they wanted to hear. That had gotten him into trouble in the past, and he had never learned better. Perhaps Silas unconsciously feared the same early end that she suspected for him; he seemed to be trying to pack a lifetime's worth of experience into months rather than years.

But for now, at least, he's having a fine time as far as I can tell. Still, it wouldn't be my choice to burn up like a falling star for the sake of a single spectacular bout of fireworks. I would rather leave a carefully crafted and large legacy of music behind me.

This new venue was only going to give him more trouble in the popularity department; now he was free to move about the stage as he sang, instead of being pinned to a stool behind a guitar. That was only going to make him *more* attractive so far as his admirers were concerned. Up until now they'd had no reason to suspect Silas danced as well as he sang.

Well, this wasn't the time to worry about Silas and his troubles; her harps were in perfect tune, and the place was about as full as it was going to get until and unless word spread tonight that her performances were not to be missed. So—

So it's time to start creating a performance that is not to be missed, foolish wench!

She ran her hands over her harp strings, and the quiet murmur of talk died away as the lights above the stage brightened and the ones out in the room dimmed slightly. She took a deep breath, mentally ran over all of her options, and decided to begin with something she hoped would impress even the most difficult critic. She chose an Elven piece, and backed it with the appropriate Bardic Magic meant to enhance the moods called up by the song.

After that, all of her attention was bound up in her music and the reactions of her audience. It seemed to her that the listeners were impressed; they were quiet when she wanted them to be, nodded or tapped along in time when she played or sang something lively, and responded to the subtle textures she added with the Bardic Magic she wove into the fabric of her songs. In this incarnation, the magic was only meant to enhance an experience, not to manipulate anyone's thoughts. That was how the Elves generally used it among themselves. The room continued to fill as she played, until at the end of her first set, there were not too many tables or booths empty. And this was at supper—once people were finished eating, the audiences should grow larger.

The lights came back up as she signaled the end of her set; she stepped off the stage and went into the back of the room, where a cleverly concealed door led into a small closet-like affair. This was where another of the nonhumans, a fellow whose race she didn't even know, sat doing arcane things with a board of sliding bits and buttons. Xarax was a likable fellow, though he didn't speak much to anyone; he looked as human as Nightingale until you got close to him and saw that his eyes were exactly like a goat's, with an odd, sideways, kidney-shaped pupil, and his skin was covered with tiny hexagonal scales. She didn't know if he was completely hairless, but his "eyebrows" were nothing more than a darker pattern of scales, he had no sign of a beard, and he always wore a shirt with a hood and kept the hood up. He was the one in charge of the lighting here; he worked this room for Nightingale now as he had worked it for Silas before.

"That was perfect," she told him warmly. "I couldn't have asked for anything better."

His thin, lipless mouth stretched in a smile. "Excellent," he replied, with no hiss at all to his words. "You are a more subtle performer than Silas; I hoped I would match that subtlety. The audience likes you. The exquisite Violetta actually came here to listen to you *before* she went off to the dance floor. That is a *good* omen and proves that the customers like you."

"They do?" she replied, knowing she sounded pathetically eager, as eager as any green child in her first appearance, and knowing it would not matter to Xarax. "Oh, I hope so—"

"Tyladen did not choose you wrongly to take Silas' place," the nonhuman assured her, even reaching out with one three-fingered hand to pat her on the shoulder in an awkward gesture of reassurance. "He was half minded to choose another exactly like Silas, but I told him that would be a mistake, for such a choice would only invite comparison and unwelcome rivalry. I said to him to choose someone as *unlike* Silas as possible; someone whose emphasis was on the music rather than the performer—and here you are, and you prove me right. And Tyladen, who chose you."

That was the longest speech she had *ever* heard out of Xarax, and he abruptly turned back to his buttons and boards, as if embarrassed by the outpouring of words. She knew better than to be offended at his abruptness; she thanked him again and left him alone with his beloved machinery.

When her break was over, most of the people from her first performance were still in the room, sipping drinks they had ordered from waiters during the interval, and many more had arrived to fill up the rest of the seats. As the lights dimmed again, she saw the dance group had ended its first performance, and the dance floor had emptied. Silas and his group would be taking a longer break than she did—their work was physically more demanding. For a while, at least, the music in here would penetrate onto the open dance floor, and might attract more people here.

And even as she began her first song of the second set, she caught sight of someone who startled her so much that for a moment she faltered—

Then she recovered, so quickly that she doubted anyone in her audience noticed, or thought the break was more than a dramatic pause. But out there, striding across the empty dance floor, wings swept dramatically back behind his shoulders, was—

T'fyrr!

It *had* to be him! It was not just the wings, the feathered body, the raptorial head—it was the costume, the way that closely wrapped fabric fell in particular folds that she remembered, the color of the fabric itself. It was also the color of his feathers, a rich grey-brown with touches of scarlet on the edges of his primaries and tail feathers. Nightingale had a peculiarly good color memory; she was able to match even greys and beiges without having a swatch of the fabric in question with her. She knew, from all of her years as an observer of nature, that no two birds were *exactly* colored alike; there were subtle shadings of tone that enabled someone who watched them a great deal to tell them apart. Surely that was the same with the Haspur—

And yet he looked through the window of the Rainbow Room, straight into her eyes, and showed no sign of recognition. Her hands played on, a peculiar, haunting Gypsy song; it was one she was certain that T'fyrr could never have heard, and it had been a Gypsy melody that had brought him to her in their first meeting. Surely he could not have resisted a second such song—

But although he must have heard the music, he paid no attention to it or to her. He *was* looking for someone, however, and in a few moments, as Kyran brought Tyladen to him, it was obvious just who he was looking for. The two nonhumans strolled together in the direction of Tyladen's office and were soon out of sight, leaving Nightingale puzzled and a bit confused.

It can't have been T'fyrr. T'fyrr would never have gone past without at least greeting me. It must have been some other Haspur.

But how many Haspur were there? And how could another Haspur look so *exactly* like T'fyrr?

The lighting is odd out there. Maybe I mistook his coloring. I saw T'fyrr in shadowed daylight under trees; the light out on the dance floor is a lot dimmer than that, and there are all those colored lights to confuse things.

Maybe so—but in every other way, this Haspur looked enough like T'fyrr to have been his twin. . . .

And I only saw him for a day or two. I could be wrong. It feels as if his image has been branded into my memory, but I could be wrong.

All she really knew, if it came down to it, was this. There was a Haspur in this building who had come looking for a Deliambren. There was a birdman *with* a Deliambren who had arrived at the High King's Palace. These two might even be the same as that pair. In a way, she hoped so. This city was no place for someone like T'fyrr right now, and the position that Haspur held at Court was no position for T'fyrr to be in. If there had to be a Haspur in danger, she would really prefer it wasn't one she knew, one she cared for.

So why, she asked herself, as she started on her next song, *am I still so certain it is* him—*both here and there, and probably in danger in both places?*

Nob's directions were exact to the last detail, and he had not been at all surprised that T'fyrr wanted to visit the tavern called Freehold. "Pages aren't allowed to go there," he'd said wistfully. "But as soon as I'm old enough—"

"As soon as it is possible, I will take you there," T'fyrr promised, and the boy's eyes lit up. "If it is as wondrous as I have heard, it would be a crime not to let you see it."

And with that, armed only with directions and a bit of money secreted in his body-wrappings, he ventured into the city. He was not particularly worried about being attacked; not in broad daylight, at any rate. He had trodden the streets of worse neighborhoods than Freehold was in with perfect safety. Most would-be attackers took one look at his foot-talons, his hand-talons, and his beak, and realized that he was better armed than the worst bravo. He wanted to reach Freehold now, before he *needed* to go, so that he knew the way. If Nob's directions proved misleading or erroneous in any way, he wanted to know now, when he had the leisure to ask for better directions.

Still, there was always the chance that he would be followed—and he really didn't want to walk the *entire* way.

So once he was out of the Palace and onto the grounds, he did the obvious; he took to the air.

His shadow passed over the guards at the gate and they gaped up at him as he flew overhead. They had heard of him by now, of course, but hearing about him and seeing him in the air were obviously two different things. His eyesight was good enough to see that their hands tightened on their weapons as he passed them, but they did not make any kind of threatening gesture. But—probably when he returned, he should come in on foot and show them his proper safe-conduct from the King.

No point in giving them a target for arrow practice.

He was quite glad that he had decided to fly when he saw how crowded the streets below him were. It would be hot down there, too; another reason to put off landing until he had to.

On the other hand, I'm not exactly inconspicuous. Anyone who wanted to know where I'm going need only climb into the nearest Church tower and watch me to see where I land.

But if he was being followed—that might not occur to someone who didn't himself fly.

Well, what's done is done. No use closing the coop door after the pigeons have flown.

It wasn't at all difficult to follow Nob's directions from the air, and in a remarkable short period of time, he landed in a square next to a fountain about three blocks away from the building that housed Freehold. It took him longer to walk those three blocks than it had to fly the rest. Although foot traffic tended to part before him, the streets were still crowded, and there weren't too many places for other pedestrians to move in order to get out of his way.

He suspected that he was indeed being followed when he was two blocks from the place, and only then did it occur to him that it probably didn't matter if he flew or walked. This, as Harperus had pointed out, was a logical destination for him. All anyone had to do was to leave a watcher near the place, and sooner or later he was bound to show up.

If I'd had any sense, I would have sent a message to Tyladen that I was coming and would land on the roof, he told himself angrily. *But no, I have no more sense than an unfledged eyas. And this is all for no reason! I don't have anything at all to report!*

Other than to make T'fyrr the very visible symbol of his new policy of tolerance for nonhumans, the King literally had not done anything since T'fyrr's arrival. At least, he hadn't done anything that T'fyrr had witnessed. He left everything in the hands of his underlings, just as he had that very first day, and those underlings were making very certain that T'fyrr was given nothing whatsoever to do when the King wasn't requesting private performances. Other Court musicians regularly played for the humans gathered at various places during the day; not T'fyrr. Someone was being very careful to see that T'fyrr stayed out of sight. T'fyrr, on the other hand, was making very sure that he stayed visible, attending every open Court session that he could—but he really hadn't learned anything new.

Well, it was too late to do anything about followers now; he walked up to the front door of Freehold as if he hadn't a care in the world and presented himself to the doorkeeper with casual aplomb. He did enjoy the way the man's eyes widened at the sight of his wings and talons, but when he asked to see Tyladen, the man did not ask why or claim that the Deliambren was busy. Instead, he directed T'fyrr to go inside and said that he would tell Tyladen to come meet him.

T'fyrr followed the human's directions, but once inside the door, his senses were assaulted in a fashion that left him momentarily dazed by the barrage of light and sound. People—not only humans, but other peoples—

were everywhere. Music pounded at his ears from the center of the room and echoed down off the high ceiling. A space in the middle of the room was full of creatures dancing to a wild reel; above the gyrating bodies was the group responsible for the high-volume, fast-paced music itself. *They* were all humans, but they played as if they were the demons that the Church claimed T'fyrr had represented.

A moment or two later, to his relief and gratitude, the music ended; the bronze-maned human singer threw back his hair, acknowledged the applause of the dancers, and indicated that he and the group were about to take a rest. T'fyrr sighed in gratitude; it would have been impossible to cross the rapidly emptying floor with it full of dancers, and he wasn't certain he would have been able to maintain his equilibrium—literally! — with that much music pounding into his ears.

As the dance floor cleared, T'fyrr started across it, sweeping his glance across the many odd alcoves and glass-fronted rooms surrounding the open space. Harperus and Nob had both described Freehold to the best of their abilities, but both descriptions had come up rather short of reality. If he had not been so concerned about those who had followed him, he would have been happy to explore the place—

And then, as he glanced into a rainbow-laced room with a single performer upon the stage, his heart and footsteps faltered for an instant.

No.

But, yes. It was Nightingale. Not the Nightingale he remembered from that single memorable afternoon, but a more elegant and exotic version of the same woman. She wore a night-black gown that flowed about her body like a second skin of feathers, and her hair had been left to flow down her back in a single fall of darkest sable. But it was her—it was her.

And if he acknowledged her, whoever was following him and watching him would want to know *why* he had done so—would want to know how she had met him, and where, and what she was to him.

If those followers were from *any* of his enemies at Court, she would not be safe, not even here. Her only safety lay in his pretending that she was as much a stranger to him as anyone else here.

Yes, they would see him meeting with the Deliambren, Tyladen—but the Deliambren could take care of himself. Beautiful, fragile Nightingale could not.

So he allowed his eyes to brush across hers with feigned indifference and pretended not to see the shock of recognition in *her* face. Instead, he waited until he caught a glimpse of a Deliambren hurrying toward him from a nearby corridor—who could only be Tyladen, the owner of this place. He gave all of his attention to his host, and as Tyladen hurried him into a back room, he did not even spare a second glance for the musician in the room of rainbows—however much his heart yearned for a welcoming smile from her.

"I'm glad you came," the Deliambren said as he closed a reassuringly solid door behind T'fyrr and turned a chair around so that the Haspur could lean his arms on the back and have his tail and wings unencumbered. "I was hoping to be able to catch you up on news from the Fortress-City before things get to a point where they are critical. The listening devices are no replacement for regular contact. We can *hear* you just fine, but unfortunately we can't tell you what it is we'd like you to talk about."

"Something new?" T'fyrr asked.

The Deliambren shook his head. "Not exactly new—just that there is some information we need to help us fill in some holes in our knowledge. You know that we still want to map all of Alanda, of course. That hasn't changed."

"I didn't think it would," T'fyrr rumbled with a little reluctant amusement. "Once you people get a direction in your heads, you're as hard to sway from it as a migrating goose."

Tyladen smiled. "We've run into some obstacles. There are some of the human kingdoms that have decided they don't want any part of us, and in order to carry out the expedition properly, we'll *have* to cross their lands. The High King can override their objections, so now we *need* his blanket permission in order to get the expedition underway."

T'fyrr blinked, as the conversations of several of the past few Court sessions he'd sat through played in his head. He had made a point of going to every single open Court that he knew about; not only to have something to do, but to make himself visible as an act of defiance against those Advisors who were trying to make him vanish. None of them seemed to realize just how good his hearing really was; he'd overheard a lot that he wasn't supposed to, both on the dais and among the courtiers. Once you knew the factions and who belonged to what, you knew where to listen.

In addition, he had been present at several private meetings between the King and his Advisors, in his capacity as the King's Personal Musician. He'd heard quite a bit there, too. He just hadn't realized that it meant anything.

"I believe I know what you need," he said. "There are several of the King's Advisors who are against the expedition, but they have not been showing their hands openly."

"Yes!" Tyladen exclaimed. "And we couldn't tell how the King himself really feels about it."

T'fyrr coughed. "Oh, the King—well, he is very enamored with your *technology,* though he refers to it as 'Deliambren magic.' He would like to have still more of your little wonders, and as long as he has that desire, he will be swayed in favor of letting you have anything you want, within reason. However—the Advisors are not the only problem you have to deal with."

"They aren't?" Tyladen looked puzzled.

"You forget," T'fyrr said, trying *not* to sound bitter, "How much these people are herded by the opinions of their religious leaders. There are several of them who are not happy with your 'magic' and are quietly lobbying the King against it. They are not necessarily the ones who are against nonhumans, by the way."

The Deliambren's eyebrows rose sharply. "Ah! I see! Yes, the religious leaders who hate and fear nonhumans are depressingly easy to recognize, but I had not realized that there were others who might be against technology."

T'fyrr snorted. "Think about it. Your ways have the potential to *prove* some of their assertions are a pile of mutes and castings, and that would be bad for their business. Of course they fear you! Now, since I know what it is that you need, let me name you some names."

He closed his eyes and brought up faces and attitudes in his mind's eye, then began to recite all that he knew. In the background, he was vaguely aware of a faint hum that was probably one of the recording-crystal devices at work, and of a steady tapping, which might mean that Tyladen was taking notes in some other way. He was rather surprised at the sheer volume of information he had, really. It wasn't only the King's Advisors who were important, it was also the factions with whom they were involved.

All of those factions were represented by people, and all of those people had names, descriptions, attitudes—weaknesses that could be exploited, perhaps—likes and dislikes.

He had to stop, rest and enjoy some cool water more than once in the course of his recitation. It all took a very long time, even for someone like him. His people relied on oral history before they met the Deliambrens, and as a consequence they were very good at organizing their memories. Still, it took *time* to get everything out, and when he was finished, he was well aware that it was very late.

"That was fabulous," Tyladen said with admiration as he tapped a few more things into some sort of device on his desk and slipped the device itself into a drawer. "You are going to prove to be a lot more useful than you thought, I'm sure of it. This is all information none of our human agents were high enough to obtain."

"I hope you are correct," T'fyrr told him sincerely. "I was not as sanguine about this position of mine as Harperus was; I simply did not see what a simple musician could learn that would make any difference to all of us."

It was the Deliambren's turn to snort. "Well, most 'simple musicians' can't hear a mouse squeak five hundred *sdaders* away, either. You're over-hearing far more than anyone has any reason to believe. *Don't* let them know that, whatever you do."

"I won't!" T'fyrr hastened to assure him. "My safety lies in that, as I know all too well! Don't think for a moment that I am not aware of that."

"Good." Tyladen pushed himself away from his desk. "I need to go into the back and transmit all this home. Can you see yourself out? Oh—you can feel free to stay a while if you want. I left orders that whatever you ask for is no charge."

After all that—hmph. I should hope so. Then T'fyrr chided himself for the uncharitable thought and thanked his host. "Perhaps I will. Right now, I should like just a drink of something for my throat, and then I will look around a little, perhaps."

"Whatever." The Deliambren opened a door in an apparently blank wall. "Enjoy yourself." He slipped inside, and the door closed behind him, leaving, again, an apparently blank wall.

Evidently Tyladen *literally* meant for T'fyrr to show himself out. And evidently he trusted T'fyrr not to snoop around in the office, either.

Not that it was any kind of a temptation, no more than it had been a temptation to snoop in Harperus' exotic travel-wagon. If this had been a library full of music recordings, perhaps, but there was nothing likely to be in this office that would hold even a hint of interest for T'fyrr.

Not unless there is something on the personal records of the musicians here—

No. No, he would *not* try to look up Nightingale to see what had brought her here. That would be rude.

But he *could* go out and at least listen to her sing without revealing his presence. That wouldn't hurt anything or anyone.

Maybe, if the opportunity presented itself, he could find a way to con-tact her discreetly, privately. A note or a message, perhaps.

So with that thought in mind, he opened the door and walked out into the main room, which was once again crowded with dancers, preoccupied with the idea of seeing his friend again, and a little surprised at the pleasure that gave him.

CHAPTER SIX

It can't be T'fyrr. But how can it not be? It must be—but how can it be him? The thoughts circled one another in her head, mutually antagonistic. For a while, Nightingale was so taken aback by the appearance of a Haspur who could be T'fyrr's twin that she didn't pay a great deal of attention to the customers as people, only as her audience. That is, she reacted to them and paid attention to the way in which they reacted to her, but as a group, not as individuals.

And she also wasn't watching them for potential trouble. She *used* to keep a careful eye on every person in her audiences when she was on the road, because she never knew who or what was going to cause a problem for her. Sometimes trouble came from someone who just happened to be offended by the lyrics of a particular song; sometimes it came from a more obvious source, a drunk, or a person who had arrived with his own set of prejudices riding his shoulders like a pack. She had gotten out of the habit of looking for problems in her audience since she'd been here, and maybe that wasn't such a good thing. . . .

It wasn't until her second set was over that she shook herself out of her reverie and began that kind of "watching" that was normally second nature and due entirely to a Free Bard's healthy sense of self-preservation. Even when trouble erupted *around* a Free Bard, it generally came to *include* the Free Bard, even if it hadn't been intended to.

She scolded herself for neglecting that here in Freehold. Perhaps her instincts had been convinced that this was a kind of "safe" place, like a Waymeet or a Gypsy camp—after all, there *was* someone else watching out for trouble and troublemakers here. Many someone elses, actually, most of them Mintaks, or extremely large humans of the Faire-strongman variety. The "peace-keepers" generally kept the peace very effectively; their mere presence was enough to keep some types outside the doors.

But where the Haspur who was the King's Chief Musician was showing up—given that the possibility of *two* Haspur in the same city was vanish-ingly small—there might be someone following.

No. There would *be someone following. The only question would be if it was a friend or a foe.*

And the chances of the Freehold staff recognizing that sort of trouble if it walked in the door were remote. A "friend" would be fine—a guard assigned to protect the King's Musician discreetly. But a foe—well, any-one following the Haspur would be hired by someone attached to the Court, and he would not be the kind to catch the notice of one of the "peace-keepers." He would not be drunk, nor rowdy—in fact, he would take pains not to catch anyone's attention unless the Haspur showed up again.

But this was not the first time that Nightingale had needed to watch for *that* sort of trouble. Free Bards were always acquiring enemies among Bardic Guild musicians, for instance, and the Bardic Guild had plenty of coin to hire experienced ruffians. So as she took her break between sets, she got herself something to drink and began to stroll the floor, watching the customers, seeing who didn't quite fit in.

There was a general feeling about the customers at Freehold. No matter how well or poorly or oddly they dressed, they all acted pretty much the same. They were here to have a good time in a place where very few people were going to make any judgments about them; that engendered a certain relaxed air. Even those who were here for the first time generally succumbed to that all-pervasive mood after a while. This was especially true of the crowd around Silas and the dance-floor.

That was why the three men sitting at one of the tables near the en-trance struck her watchful instincts immediately.

They were not here for a good time. They had drinks, and they watched the dancers, but there was nothing relaxed about them. They weren't even paying any attention to Silas, and that in itself was unusual. She let her barriers down just a trifle, and her immediate reading was confirmed by the state of alert, slightly nervous tension she read in them, the edginess showing they were prepared to do something physical, and soon. These men were here on some kind of dirty business, and they didn't want anyone to notice them.

She also had the feeling that she had seen them before, but not in this part of town. There was a nagging something about them; their clothing was wrong somehow. They didn't match the clothing; that was it. It was just a little too new, a trifle too expensive, and they were not comfortable in it.

Still, that edginess, the *waiting* feeling, could just mean they were here to meet a lady of negotiable virtue.

Or someone else's wives.

Just because they were here and on edge, and they weren't regulars, that really didn't mean much.

Maybe.

Then again . . . *They didn't show up until after the Haspur did, and they wouldn't have gotten through the door in time to see where he went. Now they're down here, near the entrance, just off the dance floor, in a spot where anyone arriving or leaving is going to have to pass them.*

She took her own drink to a table nearby, where she could see both the corridor leading to the offices and the table holding the three men. She watched them out of the corner of her eye, feeling rather put out; this was one of Silas' better performances, and she wasn't able to give it more than a fraction of her attention. Silas always needed one set to warm up, and by the fourth or fifth of the night he was beginning to tire, making his second and third sets perfect for someone who really appreciated seeing him at his best. And tonight was his first night with the dance group, making *him* doubly eager to do his finest. Nightingale would have liked to be able to sit back a little and enjoy it. Although Silas wasn't really her type, the sensuality he radiated tonight was enough to stir a corpse, and that skintight leather outfit of his made it very clear that however else Silas indulged himself, he did *not* neglect his physical health.

What was even more annoying was the simple fact that she couldn't sit here forever; *she* had her third set to do shortly, and she would have to leave. She was debating whether or not she should ask one of the peacekeepers to keep an eye on the three for her when the Haspur finally emerged from the office corridor, and one of the three men caught sight of him and sat straight up, as if someone had stuck a pin in him.

Then he quickly slumped back down, but not before Nightingale had seen his sudden interest. And not before she saw him lean over and say something quickly to his two companions.

No more than a heartbeat later, one of his companions calmly got to his feet and reached out onto the dance floor for one of the dancers.

He just seized whoever was nearest; it happened to be a human male, dressed, as many of Silas' followers did, in a carefully crafted imitation of one of Silas' outfits.

The dancer turned toward the man who had grabbed him in bewilderment—he started to say something, and the stranger calmly slung him around toward the tables and punched him in the face hard enough to knock him backward. He knocked over two tables as he fell and landed on a third, collapsing it. Those tables overturned, and their occupants scattered, more than a few of them getting to their feet and looking for the cause of the trouble with fire in their eyes.

Another heartbeat later, and that entire corner of the room was involved in a free-for-all—which quickly spread in the Haspur's direction.

Peace-keepers converged on the brawl from every part of Freehold; Nightingale spotted them making for the stairs and pushing their way through the dancers, most of whom were not yet aware that there was anything wrong.

But more violence erupted along a line between the strangers' table and the Haspur, with fighting breaking out spontaneously and spreading like wildfire.

Soon an entire quarter of the room was involved in the brawl, and fists were flying indiscriminately.

Fights were not all that usual here, especially not one of this magnitude. It was almost as if there was someone going through the crowd provoking more violence, instigating trouble and moving on before it could touch him—

Nightingale was still outside of the fighting, though many people around her had abandoned the dancing or their tables and were peering in the direction of the altercation. She jumped up onto her chair, then stood on her table and scanned the crowd as the fight converged on the openly startled Haspur and engulfed him.

Intuition and a feeling of danger warned her that the strangers must be in there, somewhere—and if the Haspur was their target, they would be moving in on him now.

Her flash of intuition solidified into certainty as she spotted them widely separated in the crowd. *There* they were, all right, converging on the Haspur from three directions as he tried to extricate himself from the brawl without getting involved himself.

And as for the Haspur's identity—there was no glass between her and him now, and she had a good look at his head and face, at the way he moved. It *was* T'fyrr; it had to be. If it had been a stranger, she might have been tempted to let the peace-keepers handle it.

Well, it wasn't. *And damned if I am going to let these ruffians go after a friend!*

Her harp was safe in the Rainbow Room; she was no bar-brawler, but she hadn't been playing the roads for all these years without learning a few tricks. She jumped down off the table and began slithering through the crowd of struggling, fighting customers. As long as you knew what you were doing and what to watch out for, it was actually fairly easy to wade through a fight without getting involved—or at least, without suffering more than an occasional shove or stepped-on toe. She made her way to the spot in the milling mob where she'd last seen T'fyrr fairly quickly—but she actually got within sight of one of the men that were after him before she saw the Haspur.

That was when she *knew* that T'fyrr was in danger, real danger, and that these men weren't just planning on roughing him up. After all, if these people *weren't* after him, why would this one be carrying a net—why carry a net into a place like Freehold at all? Lyonarie was not a seaport—Freehold might offer a lot of entertainment, but fishing wasn't part of it—and this lad didn't look anything like a fisherman!

She looked around frantically for something to make his life difficult before he got a chance to use that net. If he caught T'fyrr in it, he could entangle the Haspur and—

No, best not think about that. Find a way to stop him!

There! She darted out of the fight long enough to seize a spiky piece of wrought-iron sculpture—or, at least, Tyladen alleged that it was sculpture—from an alcove in the wall. It wasn't heavy, but it *was* just what she needed. She slid back into the crowd nearest the fellow with the net, just in time to see him back out of the crowd a little himself and spread the net out to toss it.

She heaved her bit of statuary into the half-open folds just as he started to throw it.

He lurched backward, unbalanced for the moment by the sudden weight of iron in the net. He was quick, though; he whipped around to see if someone had stepped on the net, and when he saw how the spikes of the sculpture had tangled everything up, his mouth moved in what was probably a curse. He pulled the mess to him, since no one seemed to be paying any attention to him, and began to untangle it, moving out of the crowd completely for just a moment.

That was when Nightingale slipped up behind him and delivered an invitation to slumber with a wine bottle she'd purloined from an overturned table.

He dropped like a felled ox: net, statue, and all. Nightingale dropped the bottle beside him after giving him a second love-tap to ensure that he stayed out of the conflict for a while.

There was no longer a background of music to the brawl; Silas and the rest had probably deserted their stage before the fighting engulfed it.

She moved around the periphery of the fight, looking for T'fyrr, and finally spotted him again as his wings waved above the crowd momentarily. She worked her way in toward him.

But as she got within touching distance of him, she saw that another of the bully-boys was moving in on him, and the weapon *he* carried was like nothing Nightingale had ever seen before. In fact, she wouldn't have known he had a weapon at all if she hadn't seen the "blade" glint briefly in the light. It was needlelike, probably very sharp—and poisoned? Dear Lady, who knew? It might very well be!

She was too far away to do anything!

She opened her mouth to shout a futile warning as the man lunged toward the Haspur.

But T'fyrr was not as helpless as he looked; somehow he spotted his attacker, coming from an angle where no human would have seen him moving. He grabbed a chair, whirled with the speed of a striking goshawk, and intercepted the weapon as the man brought it down toward the point where his back had been a heartbeat before. With all the noise, there was no sound as the man drove it into the chair-back, but he staggered as he hit the unyielding wood instead of the flesh and feathers he had been aiming for.

It must have embedded too deeply in the wood of the chair to pull free, for he abandoned the weapon and leapt back, looking around for help.

But there wasn't any help to be had. The third man had either seen Nightingale fell his partner, or simply had noticed that he was down. Instead of dealing with his part of the attack, the third man was helping the semiconscious net-wielder to his feet and dragging him out of the fight toward the door. There was no doorkeeper at this point, and he was not the only person helping an injured friend out.

They're going to get away, and I can't stop them, damn it!

The man with the stiletto took another look at T'fyrr, who had tossed the chair aside, and with wings mantling in rage, was advancing on him.

He gave up. Faster than Nightingale would have believed possible, he had eeled his way into the brawl and out of T'fyrr's sight and reach. While T'fyrr looked for him, futilely, Nightingale saw him reappear at the side of his two companions, taking the unconscious man's free arm, draping it over his shoulder, and hustling both of the others toward the entrance and out before she could alert anyone to stop them.

She cursed them with the vilest Gypsy curses she could think of—but she couldn't follow them with anything more potent than that.

With the peace-keepers converging on the fight wholesale, and no one around trying to keep it going, the battle ended shortly after that. Peace-keepers didn't even try to sort out who started what; they simply separated combatants and steered them toward the entrance, suggesting that if there was still a grievance after the cool air hit them, they could resume their discussions outside. There didn't seem to be anyone with any injuries worse than a blackened eye, either, and a good three-fourths of the people involved had only been trying to keep themselves from getting hurt by the few folk actually fighting.

Nightingale had seen it all before; people who, either drunk or simply worked up over something, would take any excuse to fight with anyone who wanted to fight back. The three bravos must have known something like this would happen, too, and had counted on it.

Which, unfortunately, argued very strongly that they were professionals in the pay of someone with enough money to hire them.

While the peace-keepers dealt with the mess, Nightingale picked her way through the overturned tables and chairs toward T'fyrr. There was an uncanny silence beneath the dance lights—as she had thought, Silas and his crew had decided that discretion was better than foolhardiness and had abandoned their platform for the safety of one of the performance rooms. She saw them across the empty dance floor, with Silas in the lead, making their way cautiously back toward their stage.

But at the moment, she had someone else she wanted to talk to.

The Haspur stood so quietly that he might have been frozen in place—but there was a faint trembling of his wing feathers that told her he was locked in some kind of emotional overload.

Better break him out of it.

"Hello T'fyrr," she said calmly, touching his arm lightly, and projecting peace and a sense of security at him.

He jumped in startlement, and she saw, still floating in that strange, detached calm that exercising her power brought her, that he extended his talons for a moment before he recognized her. And he *did* recognize her; that tiny touch was all she needed to read the recognition and dismay flooding through his mind and heart.

He looked for one short moment as if he might still try to pretend that he didn't know her, but she kept her eyes fastened on his, and he finally shook his head.

"Hello, Nightingale," he replied in that deep, rumbling voice she knew so well. The tension in the arm beneath her hand told her he was still caught up in the fighting rage the attack had stirred up in him. But he spoke to her calmly enough to have fooled anyone but her, or someone like her. "I—I am sorry I did not greet you, but I was afraid that something like this might happen. I did not want anyone following me to know that I knew you."

She nodded; it would be time enough later to find out *why* he was being followed, and what in the world had brought him to Lyonarie—presumably with Old Owl, since that was the last Deliambren she had seen him with. Right now, there were other things she needed to do.

Bring him calm, for one thing, and help him convince himself that the danger is over for now.

"I saw them; there were three of them. One never got close to you, one had that stiletto knife, and one had a net."

His eyes widened at the mention of the word "net."
Well, that certainly touched a nerve.
"Whoever they are, they're gone now," she pointed out quickly. "I saw them leave—unfortunately, I wasn't in a position where I could get someone to intercept them."
He took a deep breath. "I would rather that they escaped than you got yourself involved in my troubles," he replied.
She only shook her head. "I have to start my next set," she said instead, changing the subject completely. "Why don't you join me?"
He blinked at her slowly, as if he didn't quite understand what she had just said. "Do you mean to listen," he asked, "or to participate?"
"Either," she told him. "Both. It will do you good to think about something else for a little until your thoughts get organized and you have a chance to calm yourself down. I know how good your memory is; surely we both know enough of the same music to fill a set. I also know how good *you* are—and there is no one else I would rather share a stage with. I would love to have you join me, unless you'd rather not."
But he took a deep breath and let it out slowly, as if her reply had answered some need of his own. "There is nothing I would like better," he said, his voice now a bit more relaxed. "If you would care to lead the way—?"
By the time the two of them reached her little stage, Nightingale noticed that Xarax had altered the lighting to suit both of them. She gave T'fyrr her stool and took a chair for herself; after a brief consultation to determine some mutually acceptable music, they began.
The Rainbow Room had emptied as the brawl began, now it slowly filled up again with customers who were shaken by what had just happened. While fights were not unheard of in Freehold, there had never been one of this magnitude, and the regular customers were still asking themselves how and why the violence of the outside world had intruded on this place they had considered immune to it. Nightingale could have told them, of course.
When powerful people are determined that something will happen, no place is safe that has not been warned and has not created specific defenses against the weapons that they can bring to bear. Powerful people have the means to make things happen, no matter what anyone else might want.
But that was not what these people wanted to hear, and at the moment, that was not what they needed to hear, either. They needed to be soothed, and since that need matched T'fyrr's, that was what Nightingale gave them all.
As she played and sang, and wove a web of magic to hold them all in a feeling of safety and security, she opened herself cautiously to T'fyrr.

"Reading" a nonhuman was always a matter for uncertainty, but she thought that she knew him well enough to have a solid chance at getting a little beneath his surface.

Do I? It is an intrusion. But he is in need—it's like the ache of an unhealed wound. Could I see him wounded physically and not help? No, this is something I must at least try to help with.

She closed her eyes, set part of herself to the simple task of playing, and the rest to weaving herself into the magic web, opening herself further to him, letting herself slide into his heart.

There is fear; that is the surface. Singing seemed to ease him somewhat, but beneath the obvious concerns—anxiety over being followed, remnants of fear from the moment when he had seen an attacker targeting *him*, more fear for what the attack really meant—there was some very deep emotional wounding, something that went back much farther than the past few hours, or even weeks.

She sensed that, but she did not touch it. Not yet.

We are too much alike, more than I knew. If I go deeper—he will have me. She felt that old, unhealed ache of her own, the scars from all of those *others* that she had given herself to, who had in the end only seen that she knew them too well, and fled. *If I had known he would be another—*But she had not known.

She could pull herself back and *not* give what he needed to him. There was still time to retreat.

I cannot retreat. He is my friend. He was trying to protect me by pretending he did not know me; I owe him enough to venture deeper.

So she did, slipping past the fear, the anger—

Ah. The fear and the anger are related. He fears the anger.

There was pain, dreadful pain both physical and spiritual; more fear, and with it a residue of self-hate, deep and abiding doubt, and a soul-wounding that called out to her. There was nothing to tell her *what* had caused all this, what had changed the confident, happy creature she had met in the Waymeet to the T'fyrr who doubted, even despised himself and sought some kind of redemption here in Lyonarie. She could only read the emotions, not what caused them.

But being Nightingale, now that she knew the hurt existed, now that it was a part of her, there was no choice for her, either. She had to find out what it was that troubled him, and why, and help him if she could.

The hurt was hers; the soul-pain was hers now, as she had known it would be. That was the curse that was also her gift. Once she read a person this deeply, she was committed to dealing with what she found—

Which was one of the reasons why she preferred to spend as much time in the company of those who were not human as possible. It was difficult to read nonhumans, harder still to read them to that extent; very seldom did she find those whose hearts called to hers for help. The concerns of the Elves were either only of the moment, or of the ages—she could help with neither. The Deliambrens were as shallow streams to her, for they simply did not understand human emotions. Other nonhumans either could not be read at all, or their needs were so alien to her that their pain slipped away from her and vanished into darkness before she could do more than grasp the fact that it was there.

Not so with T'fyrr. She braced herself against the pull of his needs and his hurts, but only to keep herself from being devoured by them. His aches were hers now, and would be until and unless she helped him to heal them. The bond between them might even last beyond that moment; it was too soon to tell.

And too late to call it back and say, "No, wait—"

She brought her awareness back to the here and now, her hands playing of their own will, despite the new hurts in her heart, the hurts that were not hers, and yet were now a part of her. She felt, as she always did on these occasions, as if the pain should somehow manifest itself physically, as if she should bear bleeding wounds on her hands and breast, as if she should look as bruised and broken outside as T'fyrr was within.

But of course there were no such signs, nor was it likely that T'fyrr had any notion what had just happened. He sang on, finding his momentary release in music, just as she herself often did.

Ah, Lady of the Night, we are more alike than I had thought!

With the readiness, if not the ease, of long practice, she walled as much away as she could inside herself and smoothed over the pain that she could not wall away. Eventually, it would all be dealt with. . . .

Or not. . . .

But for the moment, it was *this* moment that counted.

And there were more duties that she owed than this one. She had her duty as a musician as well as a healer, and it was as a musician that she was operating now. She sang and smiled, played and probed the needs of her audience, and answered those needs. And eventually, the set was over.

"Let's go somewhere quiet for the break," she said once they had taken their bows and left the stage. "We have a great deal of catching up to do." And as the skin around his eyes twitched, she added quickly, "Unless you have somewhere you need to go? I don't want to get in the way of anything that you are already committed to."

"No," he said after a moment's awkward silence. "No, I don't have anywhere to go, and no one is expecting me. I had hoped to get back before darkness fell, but—"

"Darkness had already fallen by the time you left Tyladen's office," she pointed out, and he sighed.

"I thought as much." He said it in a discouraged, but unsurprised tone. "I suppose I can fly in the darkness; there is enough light coming up from the streets—"

She interrupted him, feeling more than annoyed at Tyladen for not taking care of this himself. "It was Tyladen's fault that you were here longer than you wanted to be, and Tyladen's fault—or so I suspect—that you were caught here by those men. Tyladen can *damn* well arrange for you to be taken to—ah—wherever it is you need to go in some kind of protected conveyance! And I'll tell him so myself!"

She actually started in the direction of Tyladen's office, when T'fyrr, laughing self-consciously, intercepted her. "By the four winds, *now* I see the Nightingale defending the nestling!" he said, catching her arm gently. "So fierce a bird, no wonder nothing dares to steal her young! No, no, my friend, I *can* fly at night, I am not night blind like a poor hawk. And I will be far safer flying above your city at night than I will be in any kind of conveyance on the ground!"

She let herself be coaxed out of going to confront the owner of Freehold; he was right, after all. It would be difficult, if not impossible, for a marksman to make out a dark, moving shadow against the night sky. But that did not make her less wroth with Tyladen for his sake.

If I didn't dare let him know that I am working for the Deliambrens, I would give him a real piece of my mind! The wretched, stupid man! Oh, how I'd like to—

She forced herself to remain calm. Even Tyladen could not ignore this night's near-riot, and when she told him what she had seen—

Well, he just might decide to take a little better care of his agent!

She hesitated, then offered her invitation. "Then if you can stay—and want to stay—I have one more set. After it's over, we could go up on the roof; it's quiet up there, and no one will bother us. And no one will know if you leave from there if I don't tell them."

He pondered a moment, then agreed. But she sensed not only reluctance but resistance. He knew, somehow, that she was going to try to get him to talk about what had happened to him, and he was determined not to do so.

And being Nightingale, of course, this only ensured that she would be more persistent than his determination could withstand.

Just wait, my poor friend, she thought as they spoke of inconsequentials that he apparently hoped would throw her off the track. *Just wait. I have learned my patience from the Elves, who think in terms of centuries. If I am determined to prevail, you cannot hold against me.*

*   *   *

T'fyrr sat through Nightingale's last set as part of the audience, watching those who were absorbed in the beauty of her music and the power that she put into it. She held them captive, held them in the palm of her hand. There was no world for them outside of this little room, and every story she told in melody and lyric came alive for them. He saw that much in their dreaming eyes, their relaxed posture, the concentration in their faces.

Was this that mysterious Bardic Magic at work? If so, he couldn't see any reason to find fault with it. She wasn't doing anything to hurt these people and *was* doing a great deal to help them. They listened to her and became caught up in her spell, losing most of the stress that they had carried when they entered the door of her performance room. How could there be anything wrong with that?

He only wished that he could join them. He was shaken by the fight, more than he wanted to admit. The entire incident was branded with extraordinary vividness and detail in his memory, and there was no getting rid of it. If he closed his eyes, he could still see the stiletto and the man holding it, the man with the cold eyes of someone who does not care what he does so long as he is paid for it.

The eyes of High Bishop Padrik. . . . Padrik had looked that way, the one time he had really *looked* at T'fyrr. He had weighed out T'fyrr's life in terms of what it would buy him and had coldly determined the precise way to extract the maximum advantage from killing the Haspur. T'fyrr had been nothing more to him than an object; and not even an object of particular value.

As much as by the memory of his attacker, he was shaken by the memory of his first instinctive reaction.

I lost all control. No one knows it but me, but I did. I could, easily, have murdered again. Granted, this time my victim would have been someone who was attacking me directly, without provocation, but it would still have been murder.

Rage had taken him over completely. A dreadful, killing rage had engulfed him, a senseless anger that urged him to lash out and disembowel the man. Only luck had saved the man, luck and the ability to get out of sight before T'fyrr could act.

Would he have felt that same rage a year or more ago? He didn't think so.

Singing with Nightingale calmed him; simply sitting here listening to her sing alone calmed him even more, but he was still shaking inside. That was as much the reason why he had decided to stay here for a bit as was his desire to talk to Nightingale.

Lyrebird. I must remember that she is called Lyrebird here. I wonder why? In fact, paired with his desire to talk with her was his fear of resuming their interrupted friendship. *I cannot place her in jeopardy, and she will be in as much danger as I am from my enemies if they learn that we are friends. I am not certain that Tyladen will be willing to protect her even if I warn him; after all, she is nothing more than an employee to him.* And he knew, with deep certainty, that he *was* in danger from at least one enemy who was willing to hire bravos to come after him. He had known, even before Nightingale told him, that there were at least two people in that staged brawl who had been targeting him, and perhaps three or more. Being thwarted once would not stop them; they would only seek him somewhere else.

Or seek some other way to reach me than the direct route.

If he came and went via the sky, there would only be two places where they could ambush him: within the Palace grounds, or within Freehold. Both places had their own protections, and both had people who would protect him. But Nightingale had no wings; she could not travel except on the ground. He knew her kind, she was a Gypsy, and it was not natural for her to stay in one place for long; she *would* not stay here even if he warned her that it wasn't safe to leave. If his enemies knew that he valued her, they would not hesitate to use her against him.

He sighed and sipped at the iced herbal drink someone had brought him, while Nightingale sang and played one of her strange Gypsy songs. *I wish that I knew who my enemy was, and why he sent men after me. It could be one of the other Court musicians, who wishes to be rid of me. It could be one of the Advisors, or one of their allies, who thinks that I have too great an influence with the King.* He sighed. *If only I did! But that doesn't matter as long as someone believes that I do. It also could be someone who simply does not wish to see a nonhuman in a position of such importance and visibility. Or it could be for none of those reasons, for a cause I cannot even think of.*

It could also be that someone in this city, possibly with the Church, had recognized him as the "demon" who killed a Church Guard. Since that killing could not actually be *proved,* this might be their own way of seeing that justice was done.

All of those people would have ample reason to try to use Nightingale, even someone connected with the Church and High Bishop Padrik.

That might be worst of all for her. He had seen the shadowed fear in her eyes on the single occasion when they had spoken about the power of the Church—the idea of Nightingale in the hands of a sadist like Padrik left him cold and shaking.

He would not have been happy until he had forced her to confess to some awful crime, so that he could have her done away with in a way that brought him more power. He would have done it as casually as swatting an insect, and I know that there are more men like him in this human Church. I have seen them, watched them as they watch me in the Court, their eyes full of hot hatred, or worse, cold and calculating indifference. Like Padrik, others are important to them only as the means to power, or the taking of power from them.

He was so lost in his own bleak thoughts that he didn't realize Nightingale's last set was over until she came to his seat and tapped him on the shoulder. He started and stared up at her.

"Let's go up to the roof," she said, not commenting on how jumpy he was. "You'll feel better up there with open sky above you."

Now, how did she know that? Or was it simply logical deduction for a creature with wings?

Whatever the cause, it shows a sensitivity that I had not expected from a human.

He followed her up several flights of stairs, down a corridor on the fourth floor that she said was part of the staff's area, and up a short set of ladderlike stairs. She pushed open a hatchway and climbed up; he followed her to find himself once again under the open sky. But now it was quite dark, with stars winking through thin, high clouds.

She shut the hatch quietly. "There are probably a few more people up here," she said quite softly, "but they won't bother us, and I know where they are likely to be." She beckoned to him, and he followed her, a gracefully moving shadow, lightly frosted with silver from the half moon overhead. She took him to the very edge of the roof and patted the raised rim of knee-high poured stone that kept people from walking right off the edge.

"This makes a perfectly good bench if you aren't afraid of heights," she told him, laughing a little at the absurdity of the idea of a Haspur with no head for heights. He echoed her laugh—though it sounded a bit feeble to him—and joined her on the improvised seat. A warm thermal rose from the pavement below, still heated from the afternoon's sun.

"I come up here nearly every night except when I am very weary," she told him as she looked out over the city below, then up at the moon and stars above. "It's very peaceful. I'm sure Freehold is a wonderful place, but if you work here, you get very tired of it, especially if you aren't particularly used to cities. I don't like cities very much, myself. I prefer the countryside. I'd trade a hundred Freeholds for one good Faire at Kingsford."

He had more than his share of questions that he wanted to ask her about *that*. What in the world was she doing here, for one thing! Why here and why now? The last time he had seen her, she had been going in the

opposite direction of Lyonarie! There were no Free Bards ⸮
none that he knew of, and probably not many Gypsies, either. S⸜
possessed her to come here, and what had possessed her to take a ⸜
as an entertainer in *Freehold* of all places?

The trouble was, if he asked questions, she would be as free to ask
questions of him. "I was rather surprised to find you working here," he
said finally, trying to find a topic that would not lead back to the weeks he
did not want to discuss.

*Only a few weeks, really. Not very long at all to turn me into a rabid
murderer.*

"Not half as surprised as I was," she replied dryly. "I have been wondering if I should tell you this—but given what happened tonight, I think
perhaps I'd better."

*If she should tell him—*She gave him no chance to collect his thoughts.

"Our mutual friends, the Deliambrens, wanted me to come here to
ferret out information for them," she said, surprising him all over again.

Nightingale? Working as a Deliambren agent? But—

"Them, among others, that is," she added, and coughed. "I have many
friends among the nonhumans, and they seem to have a high regard for
my ability to observe things. They asked me to come here and try to
discover what I could about—oh, I know this sounds ridiculous, but there
are reasons—about the High King. He used to be a great leader, but now
it seems that there are other people making all the decisions. I was be-
sieged on all sides, when it came down to it; I had at least *three* different
people ask me to come here and simply keep my eyes and ears open."

"Why you?" T'fyrr finally asked.

She tapped her fingers on the balustrade. "To be honest, I'm not certain.
I *have* done similar things in the past, but—T'fyrr, it was never something
like this. They have more faith in my limited abilities than I do, I suppose." She shook her head. "As it happens, they are all people to whom I
owe something—loyalty, favors, respect. I did listen. I understood why
they were asking me. I knew that there were, indeed, *some* things I could
learn, even with my limited abilities. Much to their disappointment, I
refused to promise anything, and I *hope* they are not even aware that I
made it here."

He felt his beak gaping in shock at her words. Not just that the Deliambrens had tried to recruit her as an agent—but that she was going along
with it *without* any of the help she would be getting if she had agreed to aid
them!

"But why—why are you doing this alone?" he asked. "Isn't it more
dangerous, uncertain?"

"One of my friends told me that they had already sent people in who had been uncovered and had to leave. It seemed to me," she continued, idly tapping out a rhythm on the stone, "that if even one person that I didn't *personally* know and could count on became aware that I was here and working as a Deliambren agent, that was one person who might betray me, either on purpose or inadvertently. That's why I call myself 'Lyrebird' here—and I have yet another name out on the street. If I find anything of substance, I will tell those who wanted me to come here, but not before, and not until *I* am out of Lyonarie."

He reflected ruefully that it was too bad *he* could not have done the same. "It is a little more difficult to hide a pair of wings, a beak, and talons," he replied by way of acknowledgement that he was doing the same work as she.

"Ah." She listened for a moment, but he could not tell which of the street sounds or night sounds had caught her attention. "I take it that you *are* the new Court musician that everyone has been babbling about? And that our dear Deliambren friends talked you into promising what I wouldn't?"

He did not bother to ask how she knew; if the Deliambrens had tried to recruit her as an agent, she must have ways of gathering information that he had not even guessed. And here he had been under the impression that she was nothing more than a simple musician!

The more she revealed, the more mysterious she became, and the more attractive. And the more he was determined to protect her from the danger following him.

"It was Harperus' idea," he replied. "He seemed to think I might have some kind of influence for good on the High King. He was certain that I would at least be able to overhear things that would be useful."

"Hmm." He wished he could see her face so that he could tell what she was thinking. "And have you? Had influence on the High King, that is. I assume you would not have come here tonight if you hadn't already learned some things that were useful."

"Not that I have seen," he said honestly, then added, greatly daring, "but then, I have not got the magic that some of you Free Bards do. If I did, perhaps I could actually do something to influence King Theovere." *Now, let me see if that shakes loose an admission of magic from her!*

"Do we?" she retorted sharply. "Well, if I *had* magic, what do you think I would use it for, if I were in your position?"

"To get the High King to *listen* to what I am singing," he replied, feeling the pain and frustration he felt at seeing the King acting the fool building up in him yet again. "The King still has his moments when he does things that are not only wise but very, very clever. He was a good ruler, and not that long ago—yet now—"

"Now he delegates all his power to people who abuse it, and wastes his own time with musicians and Deliambren toys," she finished for him. "I know; I've heard all about it from the Palace kitchen. No one there knows why, though; or what caused the change. He hasn't been ill, he hasn't had an accident, and there's no record of this kind of—of loss of mental power running in his family. Is he being drugged, or has he simply been listening to the wrong people for so long that he no longer thinks clearly or pays heed to the warning signs about him?"

"I don't know either," he admitted, deflated. "And if anyone else knows, they haven't confided in me."

Nightingale turned toward him in the darkness and made a little sound —not quite a chuckle, but full of irony. "They wouldn't now, would they? After all, you are only a lowly musician. One of the very things that the King is frittering away his time with. Why should anyone who wants to restore Theovere to what he *was* trust you?"

He felt his talons scraping along the stone of the balustrade as he clenched his fist in frustration. He said nothing, though, and she did not press him.

"I heard—" she began again tentatively, and he sensed she was going to change the subject. "I heard that you had been traveling with Harperus all this time, that you were somewhere around Gradford last fall at around the time Robin and Kestrel were there, too."

Too near the bone! He shied away quickly. "I don't remember all the places we were," he lied, knowing the lie sounded clumsy. After all, given how precise his memory was, how *could* he forget where he had been? "Harperus' wagon travels faster than beasts can pull it, if he chooses to make it so. We have been too many places to count."

"I thought for certain I heard Harperus say the two of you were heading for Gradford when we parted company, though," she persisted, and he had the feeling that she *was* trying to probe for something. "Didn't you even tell me yourself that you were going to meet Robin and Kestrel there?"

He winced this time, and was glad that it was too dark for her to see it. "I don't recall," he lied again. "It's been a year, at least, after all."

"And a great deal has happened between then and now," she replied, but then she stopped pressing him. "Except, perhaps, to me. I didn't do very much in the time since you left me; I spent most of the time I passed among humans in very small villages where nothing much ever happens. My audiences are small, my recompense smaller, but it is enough to keep me. That is all the news that I have for you, I fear."

It took a moment for that statement to sink in, and when it did, he was astonished. *Why would she do that? Look how she fills rooms here, where there are all sorts of entertainers! Why would she choose places where they could never understand what a great musician she truly is?*

"But—" He fumbled for words that would not sound like an insult. "But you are a *superb* musician! You should be performing in places like Freehold all the time! Why do you spend your time, your talents, among people who can never appreciate them?"

"Never?" He heard the irony in her voice again. "But one of those people, not that long ago, was our own little Lady Lark. There are hidden treasures in those tiny villages, T'fyrr. Now and again I come upon one with the music-hunger in him, and I wake it up and show him that he does not have to remain where he is and let it starve to death. For that alone, it is worth the days and weeks among people who would not care how well I played, so long as I could play 'The Huntsman' twenty or thirty times running."

And from the tone of her voice, that was probably precisely what happened in those tiny villages she claimed to like so much. There must be other reasons—

"There are other reasons," she admitted, as if she had read his thoughts. "If some authority has a grudge against Free Bards or Gypsies, I generally know it the moment I set eyes on the people there, and I can keep moving. That is better than thinking that I am safe and suddenly finding an angry Mayor or Priest with a mob come to drive me out of town. And, at any rate, I try not to spend much time actually *in* those villages. There are other places where I am welcome."

Such as with the Elves, perhaps? Hadn't Harperus said something about that, at a time when he was trying to distract T'fyrr from his depression? He hadn't been paying as much attention as he wished he had now.

Something about Nightingale being considered odd, "fey," he said, even among her own people. That she spent more time among the Elves and other nonhumans than among her own kind. That sounds uncannily like—myself. Is there something that she is trying to avoid, I wonder, even as I? Is that why she spends much time among those who care little about her *and much about her music?* There was a great deal that she was not saying, and he found himself wondering what it was. She had her secrets too.

If that was the case, would she understand him and his guilt, as Harperus had not?

He was tempted to unburden himself, sorely tempted, but resisted the temptation. He really did not want to drag anyone else into his troubles or his dangers. And he did not want to burden her, of all people, with the knowledge of his guilt. She had enough to bear.

"I suppose I should go," he said finally, and glanced at her out of the corner of his eye. She nodded; reluctantly, he thought, but nodded.

"I have work tomorrow, and so do you," she said—then hesitated. "I don't suppose that you might be free tomorrow afternoon, though, would you?"

"Normally the King does not need me in the afternoon," he said cautiously. "And at the moment, I believe I have learned all that I am likely to for a while from the Afternoon Court. Why?"

"Because I'd like to guide you in the city, to give you some idea what places are safe for you," she replied unexpectedly. "And there is someone I would like you to meet. Well, more than one person, actually, but there is one person I *particularly* want you to meet, someone I think will surprise you very pleasantly. I know he would like to meet you. If you'd like to come along with me, that is."

He struggled with his misgivings for some time before answering. He was so lonely—he hadn't realized just how lonely he was until tonight, but the few hours spent with Nightingale had forced him to see just how much he needed a real friend. Not someone like the Lord Seneschal, nor like Nob. The former was using him, and T'fyrr was using the Seneschal, and both were aware and comfortable with the arrangement. The latter was a child, and no real companion or equal. But Nightingale was different, even among all of the people he had met since leaving the mountains. She was comfortable with him; when he was with her, sometimes turned to her and blinked to see that she did not have a beak and feathers. The only humans *that* comfortable among the Haspur were the ones who lived among them, sharing their mountaintop settlements and their lives. In a way, those people were as much Haspur as human.

"I—I think I would enjoy that," he said finally, letting his hunger for companionship overcome his misgivings. "Shall I meet you here, on the roof?"

"Perfect," she said. "Just after noon. Now, you'd better go, while the moon is still up."

He nodded—then, impulsively, reached out with a gentle talon and touched her cheek. She placed her own hand on the talon, and brushed her cheek and hair along the back of his hand in a caress of her own.

Then she released him—and afraid of doing or saying anything else that might release his pent-up emotions, he turned away from her abruptly.

Without stopping to make a more protracted farewell, he leapt to the top of the balustrade and flung himself over the edge of the roof, snapping his wings open and catching the rising current of warm air coming from the pavement below. In a moment, he was too far from Freehold to see if she was still there watching him.

But he sensed her, felt her eyes somehow finding him in the darkness, as he winged his way back to the Palace.

And he wished that he could turn and fly back to her.

In deference to Nightingale—

Tanager, he reminded himself. *On the street, she is Tanager.*

—in deference to Tanager they were afoot, but this section of the city was not as crowded as the streets around Freehold, and as before, crowds seemed to part before them, anyway. It was hot; he held his wings away from his body in a futile effort to cool himself, and his beak gaped a bit as he panted. Tanager looked comfortable enough, although there were beads of moisture on her brow and running down the back of her neck. She wasn't wearing much by human standards, although her costume revealed less than that of some of the humans he'd seen in the Palace.

Many of the people here were wearing similar clothing, anyway. Perhaps in deference to the heat, they had foregone some of that silly human body modesty. He would have been more comfortable doing without his body-wrapping, but Nob had advised against such a move.

"Where are we going?" he asked, dodging around a child playing in the middle of the walkway, oblivious to the foot traffic around her.

"I told you, I want you to meet someone, but first I want you to hear him speak," she said as she threaded her way along the narrow, stone-paved streets, slipping skillfully between pushcarts and around knots of playing children. "You'll understand why I want you to meet him once you've heard him."

At that moment, she darted across the street with him in tow and trotted up the worn steps of a fairly nondescript grey stone building. It wasn't until they were almost inside the door that he suddenly realized the building had a steeple—it was, in fact, a Church building, a Chapel, as they called them here.

He started to balk, but changed his mind just as abruptly as Tanager slipped inside the open door. *I have heard her express fear of Church Priests. I have seen the trouble that some of these men have caused her people as well as me. She would not bring me here if she did not have a very good reason.* Was *this* the place where she intended to have him meet that special person she had spoken of last night?

Could it—could it be her lover?

For some reason, his chest tightened at that thought, and he wanted, passionately, for that person to be anything, anyone, *but* a lover.

Be sensible. She said nothing about a lover. And why would she meet a lover in a Church building?

He followed her, noting with relief that it was much cooler inside the building than it was in the street. She seized his hand as they entered the sanctuary itself, gestured that he should be silent, and pulled him into a secluded nook at the rear of the sanctuary. They stood beneath the statue of a kind-faced, grieving man, out of the way, where his wings would be lost among the shadows.

The Chapel was relatively full for a mid-afternoon service, and the first thing that T'fyrr noticed was that not all of the people here were human. There were at least two Mintaks, and he noted a Felis, a Caniden, an entire family of Caprins—heads too oddly shaped to ever pass as human poked up among the caps, hoods and uncovered hair of the human attendees.

Nor did the humans seem to care!

He quickly turned his attention to the Priest presiding from the pulpit— for the Priest of such a congregation must be as remarkable as the congregation itself.

He was a middle-aged man, if T'fyrr was any judge. The hair of his head had thick strands of grey in it, and the hair of his beard boasted the same. He was neither short nor tall, and his build was not particularly memorable. His square face had the same kindly look to it as that of the statue they sheltered under, and his voice, though soft, was powerful, with pleasant resonances.

But it was his words that caught and held T'fyrr, just as they held everyone else here.

Perhaps not the words themselves, for it was evident that the Priest was no writer of superb speeches as Bishop Padrik had been. But the content of the sermon was something that T'fyrr had never expected to hear from the lips of a human Priest.

For this Priest, standing before humans, in a Chapel built by humans, was preaching the brotherhood of *all* beings, and citing examples of the "humanity" of nonhumans to prove his point.

T'fyrr's beak gaped open again, and not because he was overheated.

The more the Priest spoke, the more confused T'fyrr became. Bishop Padrik had used his Church's Holy Book to prove that any creature not wearing human form was evil. This Priest used the same Book—almost the same words!—to prove the very opposite.

He was sincere; T'fyrr could not doubt it. He was devout; there was no doubt of that, either. But he was saying, and clearly believed, the very opposite of what the High Bishop of Gradford swore was true.

How could this be?

He was still gaping in surprise when the Priest finished the service, and the congregation happily filed out, leaving the Chapel empty but for the Priest himself and the two of them. The Priest turned to the altar, putting away the implements of the service and cleaning it for the next service. Tanager remained where she was, and T'fyrr stayed with her.

"You can come out, now, Tanager," said the Priest over his shoulder as he folded and put away a spotless white altarcloth. "And your friend, too. I'm glad you came."

Tanager laughed—her laugh had a different sound than Nightingale's laugh; it was lighter, and somehow seemed to belong to a younger person. T'fyrr could only marvel at her ability to assume or discard a persona with a change of the costume.

"I persuaded my friend to come here to meet you, but he didn't know he was coming to a Church service, Father Ruthvere," she said banteringly. "I haven't had a chance to ask him if he was bored or not."

The Priest put the last of the implements away and turned, stepping off the dais and descending into the main body of the Chapel. "I hope he wasn't, my dear child," Father Ruthvere said, chuckling, "but I make no claims for my ability as a speaker. I never won any prizes in rhetoric."

As he moved forward, so did they; and as T'fyrr came out of the shadows, Father Ruthvere's eyes widened and then narrowed with speculation.

"There can't be more than one bird-man in this city," he began with hesitation in his voice. "But I have to wonder what this gentleman is doing *here,* rather than on the Palace grounds."

T'fyrr glanced down at Tanager, who nodded encouragingly.

"I am the only Haspur in all of this kingdom that I know of, sir," he replied gravely. "I am pleased to make your acquaintance, Father Ruthvere. I can assure you, you did not bore me."

"Coming from the High King's newly appointed Personal Musician, that is quite more praise than I deserve," Father Ruthvere responded just as gravely. "I hope you know that I meant every word, and I am not the only Priest in this city who feels this way." He held out his hand, and T'fyrr took it awkwardly. "I should be very pleased if you might consider me a friend, Sire T'fyrr," the Priest continued, then twinkled up at him. "I think, though, despite the message of my sermons, it might be a bit much for me to ask you to consider me as your brother!"

That surprised a laugh out of T'fyrr. "Perhaps," he agreed, and cocked his head to one side. He decided to try a joke. "If I were to present you as such, my people would be much distressed that you had feather-plucked yourself to such a dreadful extent."

Father Ruthvere laughed heartily. "That is a better joke than you know, Sire T'fyrr. I have a pet bird that unfortunately has that very bad habit— and my colleagues have been unkind enough to suggest that there is some resemblance between us!"

Tanager smiled; she was clearly quite pleased that T'fyrr and the Priest had hit it off so well. For that matter, so was T'fyrr.

They exchanged a few more pleasantries before T'fyrr and Tanager took their leave; the Priest hurried off to some unspecified duty, while they left the way they had arrived.

"Surprised?" Tanager asked when they reached the street again. "I was, the first time I heard him. And he's telling the truth; he's not the only Priest preaching the brotherhood of all beings. He's just the one with the Chapel nearest Freehold. It is a movement that *seems* to be gaining followers."

"I am trying to think of some ulterior motive for him, and I cannot," T'fyrr admitted. "Perhaps attendance falling off, perhaps a gain in prestige if he somehow converted nonhumans to your religion."

"Neither, and there're more problems associated with attracting nonhumans than there are rewards," Tanager told him. "As I told you, I was just as surprised, and I tried to think of some way that this could be a trick. I couldn't—and information I have assures me that Father Ruthvere truly, deeply and sincerely believes in what he was preaching."

T'fyrr picked his way carefully among the cobblestones and thought about the way that the Priest had met his own direct gaze. It was very difficult for humans to meet the eyes of a Haspur, for very long. Just as the gaze of a hawk, direct and penetrating, often seemed to startle people, the gaze of a Haspur with all of the intelligence of a Haspur behind it, seemed to intimidate them. Father Ruthvere had no such troubles.

"No, I believe you," he said finally. "And I find him as disconcerting as you humans find me."

"He is one of my sources of information," she said as they turned into a street lined with vendors of various foods and drink. "We share what we've learned; he tells me what's going on inside the Church, and I tell him the rumors I've learned in Freehold and in the Palace kitchen."

T'fyrr nodded; she had already told him about her clever ploy that got her into the Lower Servants' Kitchen every day. "Well, I can add to that what I learn," he said, "though I am afraid it will be stale news to him."

She shrugged. "Maybe; maybe not. Oh—look down that street. That might be a good place for you to go if you're caught afoot and need to get into the air—"

She pointed down a dead-end street that culminated in a bulb-shaped courtyard. Unlike the rest of the street, there were no overhanging second stories there. He nodded and made a mental note of the place.

She continued to guide him through the narrow, twisting streets, pointing out flat roofs and protruding brickwork where he could land, then climb down to the street—finding places where he could get enough of a running start that he could take off again. And all the while she was showing him these things, she was also questioning him. . . .

She was so subtle and so good at it that he didn't really notice what she was doing until he found himself clamping his beak down on a confession of what had happened to him in Gradford. It was only the fact that he made a habit of reticence that saved him. The words tried to escape from him; he put a curb on his tongue, and still his heart wanted to unburden all of his troubles to her.

So he distracted both her and himself with a description of what the High King had done that day. Or, more accurately, what the High King had *not* done, and how troubled he was by it all.

"There is something fundamentally wrong with the way Theovere is acting," he said finally. "My people have no equivalent to his office, but— if you allow yourself to take advantage of great privilege and great power, should you not feel guilty if you do not also accept what obligations come with it? Should that not be *required,* in order to enjoy the privilege?"

Tanager sighed. "You'd think so, wouldn't you?" she replied. "I know that I would feel that way."

"The King's Advisors do not," he told her. "They continue to tell him that the most important thing that a King must learn is how to delegate responsibility. They praise him for shirking his most important tasks, for ignoring the pleas of those who have nowhere else to take their grievances and concerns. I do not understand."

Tanager looked very thoughtful at that—and more like Nightingale than she had since they had begun their tour of the streets. "I think that perhaps I do," she finally said. "Let's go back to Freehold. I want to talk about this somewhere I know is safe from extra ears."

That place—*somewhere safe from extra ears*—turned out to be her own room in Freehold, supplied as part of her wages. T'fyrr examined it while she took a change of outfit into the bathroom and turned from Tanager to Lyrebird.

There probably had not been much supplied with the room other than the furniture—and it was, unmistakably, the Deliambren notion of "spare." But Nightingale had put her own touches on the place: the bench and bed were covered with dozens of delicately embroidered and fringed shawls, and there were extra cushions on both. The walls had been draped with more shawls, and she had hung a small collection of jewelry on hooks fastened there, as well. Her harps sat in one corner, out of the way, and a hand-drum hung on the wall above them.

"I'd begun to wonder about something lately," Nightingale told him, her voice muffled a little by the closed door. "And what you just told me confirmed it."

She emerged, gowned in the dark green dress she had taken in with her, and settled herself on the chest, leaving the bed to him. "Humans are odd creatures," she said finally. "We often go out of our way to justify things that we *want* to do, and do it so successfully that we come to believe the justifications ourselves."

He nodded, waiting to hear more.

"Take King Theovere," she said after a pause. "He was working hard, *very* hard. He was certainly one of the best High Kings that Alanda has seen for a while. And he solved four of the most terrible problems the Twenty Kingdoms have seen, all in a very short period of time." She held up a finger. "The Bayden-Anders border dispute." A second finger. "The Grain Smut and the resulting famine." A third finger. "The Kindgode incursion." And the fourth and final finger. "The Black Baron's Revolt. All four of those took place within a single decade. Any one of them would have been enough for a single High King to fail at or solve."

T'fyrr nodded, although he hadn't heard anything about three out of the four problems she mentioned—but then again, he had just begun to scrape the top of the Palace archives, and he didn't imagine there was much about a grain smut that would make a good ballad. "Your point?" he asked.

"Theovere would have every reason to be tired, *bone* tired, by the end of that time. And when his Advisors began to tell him that he had done enough, that he should rest, that he *deserved* to take a rest, he listened to them." She tilted her head to one side and stared up into his eyes, waiting for him to think about what she had said.

"But he did deserve to take a rest—" T'fyrr pointed out. "At least, he deserved *some* rest, if those problems were as weighty to solve as you say."

"Of course he did!" she exclaimed. "I'm not saying that he didn't—but the point wasn't that he didn't deserve to rest, the point is that he *couldn't* rest." She licked her lips, clearly searching for an explanation. "He is the High King; he *could* and probably *should* have reorganized his duties so that he had some time to recuperate, but he *could not* abandon his duties! Do you see what I'm saying?"

"I think so—" T'fyrr said hesitantly. "There really isn't anyone who can do what he can, who can be *the* ultimate authority. So when his Advisors started telling him to rest, to delegate important business to someone else—"

"They were telling him what he wanted to hear, but not the truth," she finished for him, when he groped for words. "He *could* arrange to take more time in solving those problems that won't get worse with time. He *can* ask for help from any of the Twenty Kings. He can look to his allies for some help. He *cannot* tell someone else to solve them for him."

T'fyrr shook his head. "It is easy to feel sorry for him," he said, thinking back to Theovere and realizing that he had seen signs of strain that he had not noticed at the time. Perhaps even those temper tantrums were a sign of that strain. "It seems like too much of a burden for one man. No one should be expected to bear that much."

Nightingale spread her hands in a gesture of bafflement. "There's no good answer," she admitted. "There is a reason why the High King has the privileges that he has; why he lives in a place that is second only to the Fortress-City in luxury, why virtually anything he wants is given to him. Since his duties can't be made easier, his life is made easier. But do you see what our answer might be?"

T'fyrr thought it all through before he answered. "Theovere was tired; his Advisors told him what he wanted to hear—that he needed to stop working so hard, he needed to rest, he needed to give over some of his responsibility to others. So he followed their advice and found that he liked the new life—and his Advisors only reinforced his feelings when they told him that he was doing the right thing. It probably began with very little things, but by now—by now it has built up to the point that Theovere is actually doing very little in the way of his duty, and the Advisors are still telling him what a wonderful leader he is."

Nightingale nodded emphatically as she put her hair up into a complicated twist. "Furthermore, since they are not letting anyone in to speak to him who is likely to tell him something that contradicts what they are saying, he believes that everything is exactly as it was when he was in his prime. He *wants* to believe that, and the sycophants are only too happy to tell him so."

T'fyrr fanned his wings a little in the breath of moving air from the ventilator grille. "It will be difficult to turn that trend around," he offered diffidently. "I have been trying—I have been inserting songs with a particular theme, that great power demands the acceptance of responsibility, into the performances that the King has asked me to give. But as I told you, I have not seen any evidence that he has paid any more attention to them than to the story ballads or the love songs."

Nightingale's hands stopped moving for a moment. Her eyes took on the expression of someone who is looking deep into her own spirit, and T'fyrr wondered what she was thinking.

Then, with an abrupt motion, as if she had suddenly made up her mind about something, she put the last twist into her hair and folded her hands on her lap. "T'fyrr, who told you that some of the Free Bards have—magic?" she asked.

"Harperus," he replied promptly. "Harperus told me that *you* have it, in fact. Well, not *magic,* as such—he told me that many of you have some sort of power that he and his people could not weigh or measure, but that observation would prove existed. He said that you could influence people's minds, among other things. He suspected that you could—well, see into the future. He said that some Deliambrens believe that you can influence events as well as minds, provided that the influence need only be very small. He has real evidence that you can heal people in ways that have nothing to do with medicine as he knows it."

She bit her lower lip and looked away from him for the first time. "I am not really supposed to admit to this," she said finally. "Especially not to someone connected with the Deliambrens." She looked back at him with a wan smile. "Harperus and his kind are driven mad by things they cannot measure, and if they knew we really *did* have abilities such as you describe, they would be plaguing us constantly to find out what it is we do and how we do it."

T'fyrr nodded but said nothing, only waited quietly for her to continue.

"There is—there is a power in music properly performed," she said after another long moment of silence, broken only by the sound of the air in the ventilators and the distant murmur of all the sounds of Freehold below them. "You might call it 'magic.' Certainly the Gypsies and the Elves do, and so does the Church, although the Churchmen have no idea how great or little that power really is. I'll put it to you briefly: some Bards are mages, and—among other things—we can influence the thoughts of others through our music. Some of us can do the other things you described as well, but it is that one particular power that pertains to our situation now. *Sometimes,* not often, we are powerful enough to make others act against their will. Most of us confine ourselves to very minor acts of—well, it *is* manipulation, and as such, it could be considered improper. Most of the time, all we do is to enhance our audiences' ability to appreciate the music."

"But you can do more," T'fyrr stated. He had no doubt that she, personally, could do much more.

She nodded reluctantly. "This might be a case where doing more is justified. Would you care to add me, and my magic, to your performances for the King? All you need do is bring me in as your accompanist, and I can do the rest. Between the two of us, we may be able to reawaken his sleeping conscience and rouse his slumbering sense of duty. But I won't lie to you; this is interference in someone's mind, his thoughts. Before you take me up on this, you need to think about that—and if you would appreciate having something like this done to you, if your situation and his were reversed."

Now that she had put it baldly and *offered* her services, and now that she had admitted that this "magic" was as much a form of manipulation as the overt form that Theovere's Advisors were doing, the idea wasn't as attractive as it had been. In point of fact, the notion made him feel rather—shaken up inside.

Did he want to do this? If he were the King—if he were in Theovere's place—

If he were thinking clearly, thinking as his old self, he might. But doesn't this preclude his thinking clearly? Wouldn't we be clouding his mind as much as all that bad advice?

"It is a great power," Nightingale said softly. "This is why we so seldom use it. It is far too tempting to misuse it."

He took a deep breath. "It is also too great an issue to decide on impulse," he told her firmly. "I need to think about this at length."

And I wish there was someone, anyone, who I could ask for advice!

He was afraid that Nightingale would be annoyed with him for prevaricating after she had taken the great step of not only admitting she had this power, but offering to help him with it. But she only nodded, as if she had expected him to say something like that.

"You should see what you can do on your own," she told him. "You haven't been doing this for very long; you may be able to stir the King's conscience without any outside influence. That would be better—for him, and for you, I think."

She *did* understand. "I promise, I will think about this, the morality of it," he told her, and grimaced. "It may well be that the morality of manipulating one person's mind to rid him of bad influences is of less moment than the welfare of all the people, human and otherwise, in the Twenty Kingdoms."

"There is that," she agreed. "But I am not the one in the position to make the decision; you are. And I will not make your decisions for you."

"But what would you do if you were in my place?" he asked—no, begged.

She sighed and shook her head. "If I were in your place—I have traveled the roads of several of the kingdoms, and seen some of the worst places in this one. I can see what I think are unpleasant trends that are only going to continue if the High King remains neglectful. I am prejudiced; the people most immediately affected are friends of mine, my own people, and the Free Bards. There *are* other people who will prosper if things go as I believe they will, and they would certainly not thank us for interfering." She smiled a little. "This is a long explanation for a short answer, so that you can see why I feel the way I do. In your place, having weighed all the options and outcomes, I would use the magic and see what happened. You may not come to the same conclusion. If you do not, I cannot and will not fault you for it."

Silence hung between them for a long time. She broke it first.

"It may be that by using the magic this way, we are making ourselves into worse monsters than even the Church believes us to be. The next time we are tempted, we might not resist. And the time after that, for something purely selfish? We might be able to justify it to ourselves as easily as the King justifies his current neglect. That is the danger."

He could see that. Oh, how easily he could see that! "I understand," he said very softly.

She rose. "And I must go, to the *legitimate* uses of my magic," she said, lightly, although he thought she was covering a heavy heart with her light tone. "You know the way to the roof?"

"I do," he replied, and then formed his beak into something like a human smile. "But I have time enough to let you work some of that magic on me, before I go."

He thought for a moment that he had startled her, but it might only have been a sudden shadow as she moved. In the next breath, she looked as serene as always.

"Well, then, shall we go down?" she asked. "I should be happy to include you in the spell."

"Perhaps one day, I shall ask you to weave a magic for me alone," he said playfully, opening the door for her as she picked up her harp to carry it down the stairs.

Once again, that startled look came over her face, but this time, when she turned to look at him, her expression was not as serene. There was a shadow there, and a hint of speculation.

"Perhaps you shall," was all she said. "And—perhaps I shall oblige you."

T'fyrr looked up from his reading as someone rapped on the door to the suite, but he did not rise to answer it. He knew better, now, after several sharp lectures from Nob about the propriety of the King's Chief Musician answering his own door. Nob answered the summons instead; he spoke briefly with someone there and came back to T'fyrr with a message in his hand.

"There's someone to see you, T'fyrr," he said with a grin. "That Deliambren who dresses like a tailor's worst nightmare." He handed the small piece of paper to T'fyrr, who found it was simply a note from Harperus asking if he was free. "Shall I tell the page to bring him up?"

"Certainly!" T'fyrr replied. "Absolutely!" At the moment he couldn't think of anyone he wanted to see more.

Except Nightingale, perhaps—

He shook the thought away. The one person he *dared* not think about was Nightingale, not now, not with Harperus around. While she hadn't exactly sworn him to secrecy about her magic, she had certainly told him in no uncertain terms that she did not want the Deliambrens to know she was in the city. If he thought about Nightingale, he might let that fact slip.

And she would be justifiably angry with me.

It was a pity, since Harperus, for all his faults, was the one person he wished he could discuss this "morality of magic" business with. But he couldn't do that without revealing who would actually be working the magic.

Well, I will just have to deal with this on my own.

It had occurred to him, more than once, that this just might be the chance he had hoped for, the act that would expiate his crime of murder. The only question was—*which* act would be his redemption? The act of using the magic? Or the act of *not* using the magic?

The choice was almost as difficult to deal with as the aftermath of the crime. . . .

"T'fyrr!" Harperus exclaimed, breaking into T'fyrr's thoughts as Nob let him into the room. "You're looking well!"

"Let us say, the High King does not stint his servants," T'fyrr replied, rising to his feet and clasping Harperus' hand in his claws. "And you? What mischief have you been up to, Old Owl?"

"A great deal of mischief," Harperus replied, but soberly, and switched to Deliambren. "Actually, I am now, officially, and with absolute truth, the appointed Envoy to the High King from the Fortress-City. I am here with a direct request from the Deliambrens for Theovere; we absolutely need his blanket permission for the mapping expedition."

So the last attempt at local negotiations broke down. T'fyrr nodded and replied in the same language. "And you need from me?"

"Advice," Harperus told him. "We know more about the Advisors than we did—" he glanced at one of the "sculptures" to make his point "—but we still need to know the best time and place to approach Theovere on this."

T'fyrr closed his eyes and thought hard. Technically, this was *not* a problem that the King needed to call a Council about; he knew that much now, from all of his listening. It was also not something that needed to be brought up at official Court. It was, in fact, in the nature of a personal favor, and well within the High King's purview.

If, of course, Theovere chose to see it that way.

"Everyone except the Seneschal is going into Lyonarie in two days, in the afternoon," he said slowly, returning to the human tongue. "There is some sort of processional—religious, I think. It is apparently important for them to be seen attending, and many of them have made some elaborate arrangements for viewing stands and the distribution of alms and largesse."

"In the King's name, of course," Harperus said smoothly.

T'fyrr's nares twitched. "Of course," he agreed. "Theovere himself has been advised not to go—it is going to be very hot, and it would require standing in the direct sun for many hours. It has been deemed inadvisable for health reasons. So he, and the Seneschal, will remain at the Palace. I have been asked to perform for him then—but there will be an informal sort of Court at the same time."

Harperus' eyes narrowed. "What sort of Court?" he asked sharply.

T'fyrr shrugged with elaborate casualness. "Very minor. The presentation of some gifts, the requesting of personal favors, that sort of thing. I would not be performing if it were anything important, but it strikes me that you just might have a gift with you that you meant to present to Theovere."

"I just might." Harperus smiled and stroked the hair on his cheekbones. "I know how much he enjoys our little gifts."

Too much, T'fyrr thought a little sourly, but he didn't say that aloud. "He does indeed, and that would be a good time to give him such a gift, without disturbing those members of his Court who don't approve of Deliambren craftwork."

"True enough." Harperus suddenly stretched, and all of the tension ran out of him like water from a broken jug. He glanced around, looking for a piece of purely human furniture, and threw himself into a chair with casual abandon.

"So, old bird," he said cheerfully. "What *have* you been up to?"

"More than you would guess," T'fyrr replied with perfect truth. "For one thing, I have visited that fabulous Freehold place that you recommended. . . ."

Two days later, T'fyrr was unsurprised to hear Harperus' name announced during his performance at the informal Court. Theovere had been playing a game of Sires and Barons with the Lord Seneschal, but he readily abandoned it as Harperus came into the Lesser Throne Room, holding a small package in his hand. T'fyrr brought the song he was singing to a polite close, so that the King would not be distracted by the music.

And if Nightingale were here, we would be singing instead of staying silent.

"Harperus!" Theovere said. "What brings you back here so soon?" His delight at seeing the Deliambren was obvious—in fact, T'fyrr didn't think he even noticed that Harperus was carrying a package.

"Two things, Theovere," Harperus said genially. "This, for one." He handed the package to one of the bodyguards to open. "One of my people came up with a rather delightful little star-projector—ah, you simply put it in a dark room, and it will mimic the patterns of the night stars on the ceiling and walls. Very soothing to look at; orient it to the north and it will follow the stars in all the changes of the seasons. Build a room shaped like a dome, and it will mimic the sky perfectly."

"Really?" Theovere took the lumpy little device from the guard and examined it with interest. "Why, you wouldn't have to go outside to cast a horoscope, would you?"

Harperus had the grace not to wince; the Deliambrens were usually very vocal in their scorn for astrology and astrologers. "No," he agreed. "You wouldn't. The purpose is mainly entertainment, though."

"Well, it's a delightful gift," Theovere told him with a real smile. "Now, what is the other reason? I have to assume that since you brought a gift, you're going to ask a favor. Everyone else does it that way."

T'fyrr winced. That was a little too cynical, even for Theovere.

But Harperus only laughed. "Now who am I to go against the trend? Yes, we do need a favor, but it's a minor one. It won't cost you or anyone else a clipped copper, and it's mainly just to take care of some rather stubborn folk who think we're demon-spawn."

Theovere sat back in his chair, wearing a widening grin. "Oh, I know the type you're talking about. So what *is* this favor?"

"We need your blanket permission to cross the Twenty Kingdoms with a rather large vehicle," Harperus told him. "We're going to map all of this continent of Alanda. *Accurately.* We'll supply you and any other government with maps of your own territories, of course—they'll be detailed down to the nearest furlong. We *can* do maps more detailed than that, but they'd fill a room this size if we gave you maps of all of the kingdoms."

Theovere looked thoughtful at that. "We might need something that detailed," he said finally. "You ought to have some copies made up for the archives here if nothing else." Then he grinned again. "Oh, I know why those old goats don't want you crossing their kingdoms, and it has nothing to do with what you Deliambrens and your machines are or are not."

"It doesn't?" Harperus raised both his eyebrows in feigned surprise.

As if you didn't know the reason, too, Old Owl. It occurred to T'fyrr that Theovere's cynicism was contagious.

"Of course not!" Theovere glanced at his Seneschal for confirmation. "They know that once I have *accurate* maps, I'm likely to find out they've been adding to their territory an inch or two at a time for years! And, of course, once I have maps like that, I *have* to send my personal surveyors out to make certain that the borders are marked *correctly*. Don't I?"

The Lord Seneschal nodded, his lips compressed into a thin line, though whether from tension or because he was trying not to say something he shouldn't, T'fyrr wasn't certain.

"I believe you ought to give the Deliambrens that blanket permission, Your Majesty," the Lord Seneschal said, after a moment's pause. "You really don't have to call a Council on it, any more than you *had* to call a Council to add Sire T'fyrr to your personal household. It *is* in the nature of a favor from you to Lord Harperus, after all."

T'fyrr held his tongue, though it was difficult. It was very clever of the Seneschal to have brought up the stormy Council session that ended with his own appointment to the King's personal household. Theovere was still steaming over that one—and the reminder of how recalcitrant most of his Advisors had been was exactly what Harperus needed.

Theovere would see this as a multiple opportunity now. He could do Harperus, who he liked, a favor. He could do the Deliambrens a favor that might earn him more little toys like the star-projector. He could thwart the Council, taking revenge for the way they had tried to block his appointment of T'fyrr.

He could obtain maps that would help him to solve disputes between the Kings, between the Barons, between the Sires. He could enforce decisions on the strength of those maps.

And he can prove that he is still the High King. Perhaps my music is working?

"This will harm no one, Your Majesty," the Seneschal urged. "And it will be of great benefit to many."

Theovere did not think it over for more than a heartbeat after that. "Fine," he said, and gestured to three of the Royal Scribes. "Consider it done." He leaned his head back for a moment and rattled off the appropriate language for the official document; the scribes took it all down as fast as Theovere recited.

Feeble-minded? I don't think so, T'fyrr remarked to himself. *Not when he can do that, without even blinking.*

When they finished, they presented all three copies to the Seneschal, who made certain that they were identical, then handed them on to Theovere to sign and seal.

One of the three he presented to Harperus on the spot. "There you are, Lord Harperus," he said with a smile. "Signed, sealed and official. No one will argue with your little expedition now." He turned to the Chief Scribe and handed him the remaining two copies. "See that the usual duplicates are made, and so on," he told the man, "but—send them along to the

Councilors with, oh, the household documents. This certainly doesn't have any more importance than an inventory of linen."

The scribe bowed, face expressionless, and took himself out. The Lord Seneschal's mouth twitched. T'fyrr knew why.

They'll take those household accountings and give them to some flunky to file and never look at them. They'll never know about this declaration unless Harperus has to use it in some way that draws attention to it, and by then it will be too late, of course. Oh, clever! Feeble-minded? No, no, not Theovere.

"Now," the High King said, turning toward T'fyrr, who was *very* glad that he did not have a face that was as easy to read as a human's. "I'd really like you to hear more of your friend's magnificent singing, if you have the time for it."

Harperus smiled and took a seat when the King indicated he could. "I always have time for T'fyrr, Your Majesty," he said smoothly. "And I am glad that you have learned that my friend is far more talented than he seems."

T'fyrr only bowed without blinking an eye—but in subtle revenge, he began a Deliambren courting song, full of double and triple dealings, and such vivid descriptions of who did what to whom that a human Priest would have had it banned on the spot as the vilest of pornography.

And watching Harperus' face as he struggled to remain polite was revenge enough for all Harperus had thus far inflicted on him.

CHAPTER SEVEN

Nightingale waited for T'fyrr, perched on a metal balcony on the exterior of Freehold; streetlamps gave all the light she needed to see what lay below her, although it wasn't much cooler now than it had been this afternoon. T'fyrr had told her three nights ago that he wanted to arrive at Freehold openly tonight. She hadn't been all that sure it was a good idea, but apparently Harperus and Tyladen thought it was best if he were actually *seen* coming and going now and again.

But for him to be seen by the maximum number of people, he would have to arrive afoot just after sunset, and not come flying in to the roof long after dark.

No one has tried to attack him since the first attempt, she reminded herself. *No one has even dared to enter Freehold and so much as look at him crossly. We have walked the streets of Lyonarie during the day together, and no one has tried to ambush us. He believes the danger is over.*

So why did she still have misgivings? Why did she expect trouble, when there had been no sign of trouble?

She sighed, and rested her chin on her hand, peering between the bars of the railing. *Because I am always seeing danger,* she admitted to herself, *even where there might not be any danger. Isn't that why I am waiting here, above the street, watching for him? I'm going to extremes because there could be trouble.*

At least she had the night off; those who were featured performers got one night in seven to rest. Silas was playing, though, and she was looking forward to listening to him with T'fyrr.

The exterior of Freehold was festooned in several places with metal balconies, staircases and walkways, some of which connected the building with others on the block, none of which could actually be reached from the ground outside, only from special window exits above the second floor, or from the roof itself. That made them good places to watch the street below. Many of the staff did just that in their off hours, especially in the balmier months.

This was not a balmy month; the heat rising from the street below was enough to bake bread on the balcony, and Nightingale's hair was damp with sweat. *I'm going to feel the right fool if nothing happens,* she thought ironically. *Getting baked for nothing but a stupid feeling that things have been too quiet. Ah well, it won't be the first time that I've made a fool of myself.*

At least there was no one here to see her, and from below, it was very difficult to tell that there was anyone at all on this second-floor walkway. She had made it even harder, since she was sitting cross-legged below the railing and had taken care to wear one of her nondescript "Tanager" outfits.

Nothing clever about that, though. I just didn't want to get anything nice all sweaty and dirty.

Freehold faced a much newer block of buildings across the narrow street; it was one of those blocks with second floors that overhung the street below. Just about everyone took shelter in the shadowed area under the overhang even at night. For one thing, people had a bad habit of tossing noxious things out of the second-floor windows at night, even though it was supposed to be against the law. For another, it was marginally cooler there; the pavement hadn't been baked all day long by the sun.

It wasn't hard to identify people, even from this walkway, and she amused herself by trying to recognize some of her regulars coming toward Freehold. Movement of something larger than a pedestrian coming up the street caught her eye, and she turned to see what was coming. *Odd. I haven't seen that many horsemen here in a long time. At least, not all together.* But she dismissed them from her mind as soon as she saw them, for she spotted T'fyrr turning the corner at the other end of the block, approaching Freehold from the shelter of the overhang like everyone else.

He looked relaxed; his wings were not held tightly to his body as they were whenever he was nervous. She smiled to see that tiny sign; something must have gone well for him today.

But her smile vanished—for the horsemen suddenly spurred their beasts into a lurching run, scattering the other pedestrians before them, and converged on him. The horses were quick, nimble-footed and used to the city streets, cutting T'fyrr off before he even knew they were there!

Her heart started up into her throat, and her chest constricted with sudden fear. There were seven of them; whoever his attackers were, they weren't taking any chances on him getting away.

They had closed in on him and surrounded him, trapping him under the overhang where he couldn't take to the air. His talons were of limited use in a situation like this one. No one was going to come to his aid, not in this neighborhood—there were a few of her army of children loitering about the street, but children could do nothing against horsemen, even unarmed horsemen. One of the boys rushed toward the door of Freehold and began to pound on it frantically, but there was no way that enough help would arrive in time from inside. In a few moments, they could subdue him, haul him onto a horse, and carry him away!

But she was a Gypsy, and a Gypsy is never unarmed.

She pulled the sash from around her waist and dove into her pocket for the pennies left over from her distribution of largesse to the children this afternoon. *Those aren't battle-trained cavalry beasts, those are only common riding horses*—Even as the first of the riders moved to pull something from his belt, she had fitted a penny into the pocket of her sash, whirled it three times over her head, and let it fly.

She had kept herself fed, many a time, with the sling. Her aim did not fail her this time, either, with a much larger target than the tiny head of a squirrel. Her penny hit the rump of the horse with a satisfying *smack,* and more satisfying was the horse's natural reaction to the stinging missile. It was, as she had hoped, *much* worse than the worst biting fly.

As the first horse reared and neighed wildly, completely unseating his rider, she lobbed another two pennies at two more of the hapless mounts. As the first man landed—badly—on the pavement, the next two horses reacted the same way the first one had. Only instead of simply throwing their riders and dancing around like beasts possessed, these two reared, bucking their riders off and bolted, lumbering into the rest of the horses, scattering them for the moment.

That was enough to give T'fyrr the opening he needed. He dashed into the gap left when the first horse ran off and launched himself into the air, wings beating powerfully, further panicking the horses.

The street was full of neighing, dancing horses, or so it seemed. Their riders had their hands full for the moment.

She didn't wait to see what would happen next; if anyone down there suspected that they had been attacked from one of the balconies and happened to look up, she could be in serious trouble. She ducked inside the nearest window exit, getting into hiding quickly, before any of T'fyrr's assailants had a chance to calm his beast, look up, and spot her.

Then she ran for the inside stairs, heading for the roof. That, surely, would be where he would go. Freehold meant the nearest point of safety, and the roof was the best place for him to land.

He'll be in a panic, and once he gets out of the street-lights, his eyes won't have time to adjust and he'll be flying half-blind. He may land hard—

She burst out onto the roof at the same time he landed as hard and clumsily as she had expected, and as he heard her footfall behind him, he whirled to face her, hands fanned, talons extended in an attack stance. His eyes were wild, black pupils fully dilated. His beak parted, and his tongue extended as he hissed at her.

"T'fyrr!" she cried, "it's me! It's all right, Joyee is getting the Freehold peace-keepers at the door—no one is going to get past them—"

She expected him to relax then, but he didn't so much relax as collapse, going to his knees, his wings drooping around him. One moment, he was ready to slash her to ribbons; the next, he was falling to pieces himself.

Dear Lady! She ran to him in alarm; he moved to reach for her feebly, and when she touched his arm, his emotional turmoil boiled up to engulf her, making her own breath come short and her throat fill with bile.

Quickly she shunted it away; helped him to his feet, and led him as quickly as she could to the staircase. *My room. I have to get him somewhere quiet. If he panics more—*

She didn't want to speculate. He was armed with five long talons on each hand, and four longer talons on each foot, not to mention that cruel beak. This collapse might only be momentary. If he thought he was in danger again, and lost control of himself—

Well, she had seen hawks in a panic; they could and did put talons right through a man's hand. T'fyrr was at least ten times the size of a hawk.

Somehow she got him into her room and shut the door; she lowered the bed and put him down on it, dimming the lights. He seemed to be in a state of shock now; he shook, every feather trembling, and he didn't seem to know she was there.

All right. I can work with that. I don't need him to notice me.

Of course not. All she needed was to touch him—and open up every shield she had on herself.

But there was no choice, and no hesitation. She sat down beside him, laid one hand on his arm, and released her shielding walls.

It was worse, much worse, than she had ever dreamed.

After a time, she realized that he was speaking, brokenly. Some of it was in her tongue, some in his own, but she finally pieced together what he was saying, aided by the flood of emotions that racked him. He could not weep, of course; it seemed horribly cruel to her that he did not have that release. If ever anyone needed to be able to weep, it was T'fyrr.

He *had* gone to Gradford, on behalf of Harperus, and he had been captured and held as a demon by agents of the Church. They had bound him, imprisoned him in a cage so small he could not even spread his wings, which had driven him half mad.

She tried to imagine it, and failed. Take all the worst nightmares, the most terrible of fears, then make them all come true. The Haspur needed space, freedom, needed these things the way a human needed air and light. Take those away—and *then* take away air, and light as well—

How did he endure it? Only by descent into madness. . . .

But that had not been enough for them. Then they had starved him— which had sent him past madness altogether, turned him from a thinking being into a being ruled only by fear, pain and instinct.

As familiar as she was with hawks, she knew only too well what they were like when they hungered. Their entire being centered on finding prey and eating it—and woe betide anything that got in the way. But T'fyrr had never been so overwhelmed by his own instincts before; he had not known such a thing could happen. He retained just enough of his reasoning ability to take advantage of an opportunity to escape provided by the Free Bards.

He did *not* have enough left to do more than react instinctively when one of the Church Guards tried to stop him.

He did not realize what he had done until after—after he had killed and eaten a sheep on the mountainside, and remembered, with a Haspur's extraordinary memory, what had happened as he escaped. He could not even soften the blow to himself by forgetting. . . .

He killed. He had never killed before, other than the animals that were his food. Certainly he had never even hurt another thinking being before. For all their fearsome appearance, the Haspur were surprisingly gentle, and they had not engaged in any kind of conflict for centuries. It was inconceivable for the average Haspur to take a sentient life with his own talons. Oh, there were Haspur who retained some of the savage nature of their ances- tors, enough that they served as guards to warn off would-be invaders, or destroy them if they must. But the average Haspur looked on the guards the same way the average farmer looked on the professional mercenary captain; with a touch of awe, a touch of queasiness, and the surety that *he* could not do such a thing.

To discover that he could had undone T'fyrr.

To learn, twice now, that his battle-madness had been no momentary aberration was just as devastating.

Gradually, he allowed her to hold him, as he shook and rocked back and forth, his spirit in agony. He had come close, so close, to killing again tonight, that the experience had reopened all his soul-wounds. The man who had been nearest him had been reaching for a hand-crossbow at his belt—and that was how he had been captured the first time, with a drugged dart shot by a man who caught him on the ground. The horror of that experience was such that he would rather die—

—or kill again—

—than endure it a second time.

And with her spirit open to his, she endured all the horror of it with him, and the horror of knowing that he could and would kill as well.

His throat ached and clenched; his breath came in hard-won gasps, harsh and unmusical, and every muscle in his body was as tight as it could be. If he had been a human, he would have been sobbing uncontrollably.

He could not—so she wept for him.

She *understood,* with every fiber of her spirit, just how his heart cried out with revulsion at the simple fact that he had taken a life, that if forced to he would do so again. There was no room in his vision of the world for *self-defense,* only for those who killed and those who did not. She *knew,* deep inside her bones, why he hated himself for it.

He had not stopped; had not tried to subdue rather than kill. Never mind that he was mad with fear, pain, hunger. Never mind that the man who had tried to stop his escape would probably have killed him to prevent it. The man himself was *not* his enemy; the man was only doing the job he'd been set. T'fyrr had not even paused for a heartbeat to consider what he was doing. He had struck to kill and fled with the man's heart-blood on his talons.

And she told him so, over and over, between her sobs of grief for him, just how and why she understood. She would have felt the same, precisely the same, even though there were plenty of people she considered her friends and Clansfolk who would never agree with her. Her personal rule —which she did not impose on anyone else—forbade killing. She knew that she *might* find herself in the position one day of having to kill or die herself. She did not know how she would meet that. She tried to make certain to avoid situations where that was the only way out.

Which was why, of course, she avoided cities. Death was cheap in cities; the more people, the cheaper it was. At least out in the countryside, life was held at a dearer cost than here, where there were people living just around the corner who would probably strangle their own children for a few coins.

All of that flitted through her thoughts as a background to T'fyrr's terrible pain, and to the tears that scalded her own cheeks. But there was a further cost to this ahead for her. She had thought that she had opened herself to him completely before; but now, as she held him and sensed that *this* would bring him little or no ease, she realized that she had still held something of herself in reserve. Nothing less than all of herself would do at this moment—because of what *he* was.

The Haspur had an odd, sometimes symbiotic relationship with the humans who shared their aeries and villages. Most of the time, it never went any deeper than simple friendship, the kind she herself shared with the Elves who had gifted her with her bracelets.

But sometimes, it went deeper, much deeper, than that.

She had always known, intellectually, that she was not the only human to have her peculiar gift—or curse—of feeling the needs and the emotions of others. She had never met anyone else with the gift to the extent that she had it, though. She had never encountered another human who found him- or herself pulled into another's soul by his pain or his joy; never found one who was in danger of losing himself when bombarded by the emotions of others.

But it seemed that there were many more of the humans who lived among the Haspur with that curse—or gift. Their gifts were—at least from what she gleaned from T'fyrr—as formidable as her own. And for those who bore that burden, a relationship with a Haspur could never be "simple" anything.

They felt, and felt deeply, but had no outlet for their extreme emotions. At the ragged edge of pain, or sorrow, or that dreadful agony of the soul, the Haspur could only try to endure, dumbly, as their emotions tore them up from within, a raging beast that could not break free from the cage of their spirits.

But humans did have that outlet—at least, the humans he called "Spirit-Brothers" could provide it, by becoming unhesitatingly one, without reservations, with their friends, and sharing the pain.

Becoming one, without reservations. Giving all, and taking all, halving the pain by enduring it themselves.

She had one lover in all her life—one *real* lover, as opposed to friends who shared their bodies with her. She had not known; she was so young, she had not known that when she gave all of herself, the one she gave to might not be able to give in return—that he might not even realize what she had done. She had not thought she was the only one with this curse—or gift—and had supposed that her lover would surely feel all that she felt.

He didn't, of course. He hadn't a clue; he'd thought she was the same as all the other ladies he'd dallied with, and she lacked the words, the skill, the heart to tell him.

When Raven had left her the first time, it had felt as if something that was a part of her had been ripped away from her soul. She smiled and bled, and he smiled and sauntered off with a song on his lips.

And he had never understood. He still didn't; not to this day.

She had learned to accept that, and had forgiven him for not knowing and herself for her own ignorance. But she had vowed it would not happen again and had never opened herself to another creature that deeply, never under any other circumstances, until this moment. But nothing less would do now, but to give everything of herself, for nothing less would begin the healing T'fyrr needed so desperately.

She did not know, could not know, what would come of this. Perhaps an ending like the end of her love affair with Raven, and pain that would live in her forever, a place inside her spirit wounded and scarred and never the same again.

But she could bear the pain, and she could heal herself again, over time. She had done it once, and she could again. T'fyrr could not, not without her help, for he did not truly understand the emotions festering inside his soul.

Great power demands that the user consider the repercussions of actions. She had the power; she had long ago accepted the responsibility, or so she had thought.

I was fooling myself. I should have known that the Lady would put this on me.

But this was no time to have second thoughts; really, she had made all her choices long before she met T'fyrr, and this was only the ultimate test of those choices. What was it that Peregrine had said to her a few months ago? She had known at the time that he was trying to warn her of an ordeal to come—

You cannot speak truly of the path without walking it.

And she could not. Not without repudiating everything that she said, that she thought, that she was.

So she opened the last of her heart to him, opened her soul's arms to him and gathered him up inside the place where her own deepest secrets and darkest fears lay—she brought him inside, and she gave him all that she was, and all the comfort that she had.

T'fyrr did not know how he had gotten to Nightingale's room; he did not even realize that he was talking to her until he heard his own voice, hoarse and cracking, telling her things he had never intended to share with anyone.

Especially not with her.

She was too fragile, too gentle—how could she hear these horrible things and not hate him? He knew she was one of the kind who *felt* things; he had sensed that the first time he met her.

The same as the Spirit-Brothers, perhaps.

But not the same, not with the training or the knowledge, surely. The idea of *murder*—it would surely send her fleeing him in utter revulsion.

Only Harperus knew he had killed. Harperus had told him that it was an accident, something he could not have helped.

Harperus had not even begun to understand.

The Spirit-Brothers of the Haspur would have been able to help him bear the guilt, although it would have meant that he and the Brother who chose to help him would have been in debt to one another for all their lives, bonded in soul and perhaps in body as well. The latter happened, sometimes, though not often. But the Spirit-Brothers, male and female, were far away and out of reach, and he had no hope of reaching them for years, even decades. . . .

At some point in his babbling, it began to dawn on him that Nightingale not only understood, she *felt* as he felt. She wept for him as a Spirit-Brother would have wept, gave him her tears in an outpouring of release for both of them.

Something in him turned to her as a flower turns toward the sun, as a drowning creature seizes upon a floating branch. Something in her answered that need, granted him light, kept him afloat. He was beyond thinking at that point, or he would never have let her do what she did. It wasn't fair, it wasn't right, not for her! She was a Gypsy, a Free Bard, who should be as free as the bird that was her namesake, and not bound as a Spirit-Brother!

But it was already done, before thoughts even began to form in the back of his terror-clouded mind.

She stayed awake with him until his internal sense told him that the sun was rising, comforting and holding him, and even preening his feathers as another Haspur would—

—a Haspur, or a Spirit-Brother.

He did not understand how she knew to do this; he did not understand why he accepted it. He was beyond understanding now, beyond anything except feeling. It was feeling that held him here, weak as a newborn eyas, simply accepting the comfort and the understanding as an unthinking eyas would accept them.

Finally, he slept, exhausted.

When he woke again, she was there beside him, stroking his wings with a hand so gentle it had not even disturbed his sleep, although he had felt it and it had soothed him out of the nightmares he had suffered for so long. He blinked up at her, astonished that she was still there.

Silence stretched between them; he felt as if he must be the one to break it. Finally, he said the only thing that was in his mind.

"You should hate me—" And he waited to see that hate and contempt in her eyes for what he had done.

Her expression did not change, not by the slightest bit.

"How could I hate you?" she asked, softly. "You hate yourself more than enough for both of us. I want to help you, T'fyrr. I hope you will let me."

He blinked at her again, and slowly sat up. She shook her hair back out of her face, and rubbed her eyes with her hand as she sat up too.

"I think that there is something that you believe you need to do, to make up for what you did," she said then. "I will help you, if that is what you want. I will come with you to the King, and stand beside you in your task. I will give you my music, and I will give you my magic; you can have one or both, they are freely given."

"And when the King sees again the things that he does not want to see?" T'fyrr asked, very slowly. "Will that—"

She nodded, deliberately. "I believe that will be what you need, as your duty and your penance. It will not be easy, and it will not be pleasant."

He sighed, and yet it was not because of a heaviness of spirit. Somehow, in truly accepting this burden, his spirit felt *lighter* rather than crushed further down. "No penance is," he replied somberly. Somehow, in the dark despair of last night, he had come to a decision—hopefully, it was one of wisdom and not of weakness and expediency. Theovere was too far down the road of irresponsibility to be recalled by ordinary means. "I will need your magic, if you will give it," he said, feeling as if he were making a formal request or performing a solemn ceremony with those simple words.

She nodded, and bowed her head a little. "Since you will have it, I will give it," she said, making her words a pledge as well as an answer.

Then she raised her lovely, weary eyes to his again and smiled tiredly. "And you should eat—for that matter, so should I. We can do nothing half-starved."

Those words, which would have made him wince away less than a day ago, only made him aware that he was ravenous. "And after we eat?" he asked. "Will you come with me to the Palace?"

"Yes." She brushed her hair back over her shoulders. "It is time that I accepted my responsibilities as well, and stopped hiding in corners behind the name of 'Tanager.' But I will *not,*" she added, with a warning look in her eyes, "be Nightingale. Not here, and not now. I do not trust Tyladen's friends, nor Harperus' associates. They speak too lightly and too often to too many people. They can afford to; they have many protections. I am only a Gypsy, and far from the wagons of my Clan. What few magics I have will not protect me if powerful men come hunting."

"As you are far from your people, I am far from the aeries of mine," he said impulsively, laying his hand over hers. "So perhaps we should fly our pattern together, from now on?"

"And we should begin now." She rose at that, and stretched, lithe and graceful. "Let me get clean, first, then Lyrebird and T'fyrr will eat together, and he will take her to the Palace to present her as his accompanist. Or should you go and make some formal request for an accompanist? Should this be an official, perhaps a royal, appointment?"

He actually managed a smile at that. "It would be easiest simply to *do* so," he pointed out. "Just as Harperus did with me. If the King hears you once, he will see to it that the appointment simply happens. He is not about to put up with interference from his Council a second time over so 'trivial' a matter as his personal musicians. *They* believe it is trivial, and it is both unfortunate and our good luck that he does not. This one time, his obsession can work for us."

She paused for a moment, one hand on the door to the bathroom, then nodded. "I think I see that. It is a risk, but so is everything we are doing."

She closed the door behind her, and there came the sound of running water from beyond it. He lay back down on her bed, closing his eyes for a moment, intending to plan out the next few hours in detail. He would have to get her past the guards, first, of course. . . .

But his body had other ideas, and he dozed off, to awaken again with her hand on his arm. She was dressed in one of her most impressive costumes, and he had little doubt that the Ladies of the Court would attempt to emulate her dress before too long. He also had a shrewd notion that they would not succeed.

He got up, finding himself less stiff than he would have expected, given that he had spent the night in a human bed. She sent the bed back up into the wall with a touch of her hand; slipped the carrying case over her larger harp, and slung it across her back. It did not look as incongruous as he would have thought.

"Shall we?" she asked, gesturing to the door. He led the way; she locked the door after them both.

She disappeared into Tyladen's office for a moment, presumably to tell him where they were going and how long they expected to be gone. *She is one of their chief attractions; she owes her putative employer that much, I suppose.* After a hearty meal in the single eating nook open at this early hour, they went out into the street together. There was no sign of last night's altercation, but the moment they crossed the threshold of Freehold, his hackles went up, and he moved into the center of the street, away from dangerous overhangs.

It did not escape his notice that she made no objection to this, that, in fact, her eyes scanned the mostly-deserted street with as much wariness as his.

They stepped out together onto the cobble-stones of the street, both of them dreadfully out of place in this part of the city. Between his appearance and her costume, anyone looking for them was likely to find them immediately.

Well, there was no help for it.

Nightingale walked beside him as serenely as if the previous night had never happened, as if she did not look like an invitation to theft. He tried to imitate her and actually succeeded to a certain extent.

But there was one thing, at least, that he *was* going to do. He had coins in his garment, plenty of them, and he was *not* going to appear at the gate to the Palace with her, walking afoot like a pair of vagabonds. As soon as they reached one of the more respectable sections of the city, he hailed a horse-drawn conveyance, an open carriage with two seats that faced each other, and gestured her up into it.

She raised an eyebrow at him, but said nothing. He took his place beside her, although it was dreadfully uncomfortable and he had to hold his wings and tail at odd angles to get them to fit inside.

Now, how am I going to get her inside the gate? The guards aren't going to want to let her pass, she hasn't a safe-conduct or an invitation. . . . He worried at the problem without coming to a satisfactory solution as the streets grew progressively busier, and stares more covert. This was not the only conveyance on the street, but many of the others were private vehicles, whose occupants gazed at them with surprise. He ignored them, trying to think what he could do with Nightingale. Perhaps he could leave her at the gate, go in, find the Seneschal and get a safe-conduct for her—

But that would leave her alone at the gate, and anyone who spotted her with me on the way here could—do whatever they wanted. She is with me, which makes her presumably valuable to me.

Would anyone dare to try anything under the noses of the guards?

Oh yes, they could and would. Especially if my unknown adversary is highly placed in the Court. A little thing like a kidnapping at the gate would hardly bother him. He could make it a private arrest, for instance.

There was reasonable foot traffic at this hour, and the conveyance made excellent time; not as good as he would have flying, of course, but still quite respectable. The two horses drawing it were able to trot most of the way.

They reached the gate long before he had come to any satisfactory solution to his problem. But, as it happened, the solution was waiting for him, standing beside the guards with a smaller and far more elaborate and elegant, gilded version of the conveyance waiting beside him. The Palace grounds were extensive enough that there was an entire fleet of conveyances and their drivers available for those who lived here, just to ferry them around within the walls.

Nob? What's he doing here?

"Is that someone you know?" Nightingale asked, as his eyes widened in surprise.

"Yes, it's my servant—but *how* did he know I was coming in this morning, and why did he order a conveyance?" T'fyrr asked, more as a rhetorical question than because he expected an answer.

But Nightingale shrugged. "I told Tyladen where I was going. Tyladen probably foresaw the difficulty of getting me inside without waiting around at the gate and sent word to Harperus. Old Owl must have exercised some of his diplomatic persuasion and got me an invitation or a safe-conduct. I expect that's why your lad is here; to bring the pass and to get us to the Palace in the manner suitable to your rank."

T'fyrr nodded; it made sense. But Nightingale added, "The one thing I *don't* want is to run into Harperus. He knows me on sight, and I don't want *any* of the Deliambrens aware that I'm here."

He grimaced; at this point, that was a very difficult request to satisfy. "I don't know how—"

But she interrupted him. "I can keep him from noticing me as long as I stay in the background. If Old Owl shows up at all, T'fyrr, *you* keep him busy, please? Don't let him think about talking to me. Tell him I'm shy, whatever it takes to get him to leave me alone. Make up something—or better yet, tell him about the attack last night. That should get his mind off me."

He wasn't at all sure he could do that, but he nodded again. "I can try," he said truthfully, and then the conveyance stopped in front of the gate, and it was too late to discuss anything more.

Nob had indeed brought "Lyrebird's" safe-conduct, although from here on she would have to come and go through a lesser gate elsewhere; she was only a lowly accompanist, after all, and not a Sire dubbed by the High King's own hand. Nob chattered excitedly at a high rate of speed, which kept T'fyrr from having to say much and Nightingale from having to say anything. The safe-conduct was from Theovere himself; Old Owl had gone straight to the highest authority available. He must have described Lyrebird in the most glowing terms; the King was most anxious to hear this remarkable player from the infamous Freehold.

"The Bardic Guild found out, too. I don't know how, but they had a Guildmaster protesting to the High King before I even got the safe-conduct," Nob continued, after describing how Harperus had come to get him early this morning. "They tried to get this lady banned from the Court because she's a Gypsy, then they tried to get her barred because she plays at Freehold and they have some kind of arrangement about the musicians at Freehold. The High King just ignored them. They were even going to make a fuss so you couldn't be heard, but Theovere got word of that before it ever happened and told them if they did *anything* he'd have them all discharged, so they gave up, I guess. The High King made her your Second, do you know what that means?"

T'fyrr shook his head. Nob was only too happy to explain. "She's more than a servant, like me, but she's not the High King's musician, she's yours. So nobody but you can discharge her, you see, not even Theovere if the Guild pressures the High King to do it, but she doesn't have the immunity you do if she offends somebody at Court. She can only be arrested by Theovere's personal guards, though, if she's accused of something."

"Then I'll just have to be certain I don't offend anyone," Nightingale said in a low, amused voice. Nob giggled.

"The Guild people are all pretty disgusted, but Harperus says not to worry, they can't do anything, and as long as you're real careful and never let any of them get you someplace without witnesses so they can claim you offended them, it'll be all right," Nob finished in a rush. He kept glancing over at Lyrebird with a certain awe and speculation in his eyes.

"When is Theovere expecting us to perform for him?" T'fyrr asked. That was the question of the most moment.

"As soon as you get there—I mean, after you get cleaned up and all," Nob replied, correcting himself with a blush. "You can't go before the King with dust on your feathers!"

Nightingale gave T'fyrr an amused look that he read only too easily— she had warned him something like this might happen, which was why *she* had made her own careful preparations before they left Freehold.

Nob hurried them both inside and, while Nightingale waited in the outer room, rushed him through his usual preparations.

Still harried by the energetic Nob, like a pair of hawks being chivvied on by a wren, they hurried up the hallways to the King's private quarters.

This time will be different. This time there will be magic. Elation and worry mingled in him in a confusing storm of emotion, leaving him feeling unbalanced. The least little things were unbalancing him, after last night. . . .

After last night. . . .

What exactly had happened? *Something* had passed between them, as ephemeral as a moon shadow and strong as spider silk. A whisper more potent than any shout, that was what it felt like; a stillness at the center of a whirlwind. As if every feather had been stripped from his body, leaving him bare to the winds.

Perhaps it was just as well that they had work to do immediately, so that he had no time to think about it. He did not want to think about it, not now, perhaps not ever.

But you will, his conscience told him. *You will have to, eventually.*
He didn't want to think about that, either.

Nightingale was too weary to be impressed by the Palace, the High
King, or anything else for that matter. There wasn't much left of her this
morning, except the magic and the music; she had saved enough of her
energy for that, and had very little more. She felt as if she was so insub-
stantial she would blow away in a breeze, and so tired she could hardly
walk.

It was not the physical weariness, although that was a part of it, certainly. She had stayed up to play for revels all night long and traveled with
the dawn a thousand times. But this morning was very different.

But part of me dwells within him, now, and part of him in me. Strange and
yet familiar, a breath of mountain air across her deep and secret forest; a
hint of music strange and wild, a brush of feathers across her breast.

No time to think about it now; time only to enforce her *don't look at me*
glamorie, spun with a touch of Bardic power and sealed with a hummed,
near-inaudible tune. Time only to take her place behind T'fyrr in the
King's chamber, set up her harp, tune it with swift fingers, and wait for his
cues.

He would have to be the one to choose the tunes; she could only follow
his lead, and try to set the magic to suit. They'd had no chance to discuss
this, to pick specific songs. "If it is something you don't know, I'll sing the
first verse alone," he whispered. "If we do that enough, it will seem done
on purpose."

She nodded, and then they began.

With no time to set what they were to perform, with only their past
performances together to use as patterns, he was not able to choose many
songs suited to their intent. She was not particularly worried about that,
not for this first attempt. She was far more concerned with setting so good
an impression of her ability on the King that he would continue to support
T'fyrr and, indirectly, her. It would take more than one session of magic to
undo all the harm that had been wrought with years of clever advice and
insidious whispers. It might be just as well that they were not too heavy-
handed with the message for the first performance; better that they had
more songs merely meant to entertain than to carry the extra burden. *She*
must impress the King as well as convey the magic, after all.

She knew that she had done that much when the King ceased to play his
game of Sires and Barons with one of his lords, and ignored everything
else in the room, as well, closing his eyes and listening intently to the
music they made. She knew that there was something more than herself at
work when the bodyguards' faces took on an unexpected stillness, as if

they, too, were caught up in the spell of harp and voice, when even the lord who had been playing at the game with the High King folded his hands in his lap and simply listened.

There is something of me in T'fyrr, as there is part of him in me. Has he learned to touch the magic through me? It could have been; Raven had his own touch of the magic, and she would never have noticed one way or another if he had acquired a little more of it from her after their bitter-sweet joining. So much of her soul was bound up in the magic, could she have ever spun it out to wrap T'fyrr's if the magic didn't come with it?

She sensed a terrible weariness in that second man, and as sensitive as she was this morning, she could not help but move to ease it. So when the music chosen did not particularly suit their purposes with the High King, she turned her attention and her magic to that weary lord, sending him such peace as she could. He was not a man who would ever feel much peace; his concerns were too deep, his worries never-ending. But what he would take in the way of ease, she would give him gladly. No one with such weariness on his heart could ever be one of the lot who were advising the King to neglect his duty. This could only be a man who was doing his best to make up for the King's neglect.

The King made no requests; T'fyrr simply picked songs as he thought of them, so far as Nightingale could tell. Finally, at some signal she could not see, he stopped, and it was a long, long moment before the King opened his eyes again and set his gaze on the two of them.

It was another long moment before he spoke.

"I do not ever wish to hear your musical judgment called into question again, T'fyrr," he said quietly, but with a certain deadly quality to his words. "You may bring whosoever you wish to accompany you from henceforth—but it will be my request that it be this gentle lady. Her safe-conduct to this Palace is extended for as long as she *wishes* to come."

The High King turned to the lord that had sat at play with him. "What think you of my Nightingales, Lord Seneschal?" he asked, but with a tone full of wry amusement, as if he expected some kind of noncommittal answer. Nightingale suppressed a smile at the unintended irony.

But the Lord Seneschal turned toward Theovere with an expression of vague surprise and a touch of wonder. "You know that I am not the expert in music that you are, Your Majesty," he said with no hint that he was trying to flatter. "I enjoy it, certainly, but it has never touched me—until today." He closed his eyes briefly, and opened them again, still wearing that expression of surprise. "But today, I felt such peace for a moment, that if I were a religious man, I would have suspected something supernat-ural . . . I thought of things that I had forgotten, of days long ago, of places and people. . . ."

Then he shook himself and lost that expression of wonderment. "Memories of—old times. At any rate, Your Majesty," he continued briskly, "if I were not so certain of the honor of the Guildmasters, I would have been tempted to say that they were opposed to this lady's performance because she would provide an unwelcome contrast to the performance of the Guild musicians."

Nightingale bowed her head to hide her smile. The Lord Seneschal's tone of irony was just enough to be clear, without being so blatant as to be an accusation against the Guild musicians. For all that the King had supported her against them, he had a long history of supporting them as well. At any moment, he could spring again to their defense, so it was wise of the Lord Seneschal to be subtle in his criticism.

Nor was that lost upon Theovere, who answered the sally with a lifted eyebrow.

"Let us discuss that, shall we?" he said, and T'fyrr, taking that as the dismissal that it was, bowed them both out.

Nightingale parted company from him quickly after that, since Nob brought word that Harperus wanted to speak with him, and she most certainly did not want to be there when he showed up. She returned unaccompanied to Freehold, resolving to make her journeys hereafter in something less conspicuous in the way of a costume. The Elven silks would pack down readily enough, and she could change in T'fyrr's rooms, even if that would scandalize young Nob. With the safe-conduct in her hand, the quiet and respectable clothing would do very well for her to pass the gate reserved for those who were higher than servants but less than noble.

But she should think about spending some of her rapidly-accumulating monies on other clothing, as well. Granted, she could not lay her hands on more Elven silk, but there were perfectly good seamstresses in the city who would not scorn to sew to her design. She needed something appropriate but less flamboyant than Elven-made clothing. She was a commoner, an outsider, and it would not do to excite the jealousy of the ladies of the Court in the matter of dress. Every time she stepped onto the Palace grounds, she went completely out of her element, a songbird trying to swim like a fish. There was no point in making herself more problems than she already had.

She was uncomfortably aware of speculative eyes on her as she made her way to Freehold, and she was grateful that, although the hour tended toward noon, it was still too early for any of the more dangerous types to be wandering the streets. Pickpockets were easy enough to foil; she could leave broken fingers in her wake without seeming to do more than brush her hand across her belt-pouch. But in this particular outfit, she was fair game for ransom-kidnappers who could legitimately assume she had money or had family with money. And she was even more vulnerable to those looking to kidnap for other purposes.

So she set the *don't look at me* spell again, all too aware that it would only work on those near enough to hear the melody she hummed under her breath. If she were less tired, she could have included anyone within sight of her—

But she had just spent all night and part of the morning working the magics of music and the heart, and she had scant resources to spend on herself. She sighed with relief when Freehold loomed into view, and she had seldom been so glad to see a place as she was to see that deceptively plain door.

She took herself straight upstairs; fortunately, word had not yet spread of her Royal Command Performance, and she did not have to fend off any questioners. Only one of the Mintak peace-keepers appeared, silent as a shadow, to take her harp from her—and one of the little errand boys, with a tray of food and drink beside him. Neither asked any questions; they simply followed her to her room, put their burdens down, and left her.

She ate and drank quickly, without tasting any of it; she stripped off her gown and lay down in her bed, still rumpled and bearing the impression of her body and T'fyrr's, and the faint, spicy scent of his feathers. And then, she fell asleep, and slept like one dead until an hour before her first set of the evening.

She woke with the feeling that she had dreamed, but with no memory of what her dreams had been about. She woke, in fact, a little confused about where she was, until her mind began to function again. Then she lay staring up at the ceiling, trying to sort herself out.

There was a difference, a profound and yet subtle difference, in the way everything felt, but she had known that there would be.

Some of the magic—had not precisely left her, but it had changed. If she sang alone, she would still command the same power—but if she performed with T'fyrr, it was another story altogether. Together they would command more than the magic of two people; their abilities would work together as warp and weft, and the magic they wove would be stronger and firmer than anything she had ever dreamed of. *So T'fyrr shares the Bardic Magic now—or else, I have awakened the magic that was already there.* Not entirely unexpected, but certainly welcome, for as long as the two of them remained partnered.

She shoved that last niggling thought away, with a hint of desperation. She would not think of that. The pain would come soon enough, she did not need to worry at it until it *did* come, and T'fyrr went on his way again without her.

Or until she was forced by circumstance to leave him. The road traveled in both directions, after all.

The other changes within her were precisely as she had expected—except for the depth to which they ran. She did not particularly want to think about that, either.

But she wouldn't have to; there was a performance to give. T'fyrr would probably not be able to come—he could seldom manage two nights in a row. A brief stab of loneliness touched her, but she had expected it, and absorbed it.

I have been lonely for most of my life; I do not expect this to change. That was what she told herself, anyway. *Being lonely has never killed anyone yet, no matter what the foolish ballads say.*

And with that thought to fortify her, she finally rose from her bed and prepared to face another night of audiences.

She made her way across the city with far less of a stir this morning than she and T'fyrr had caused yesterday. No one would look twice at her, in fact, in her sober and honest clothing. The bundle at her back could be anything; unless you knew what a harp case looked like, there was no reason even to think she was a musician.

She presented herself and her safe-conduct at the Bronze Gate; the guard there scarcely glanced at it or her, except to note the size and shape of the bundle she carried and to order her to show what it was she had. When he saw it was only a musical instrument and a small bundle of cloth, he became bored again and passed her through.

She found a page to show her to T'fyrr's rooms, in plenty of time to use his bathroom and change into the gown she had brought with her. He was pacing the floor when she arrived, and turned to greet her with relief and disappointment.

Another sign of how we are bound, now; I know his feelings without needing to try to interpret his expression. The relief was because she was early; the disappointment he made clear enough.

"Theovere hasn't changed," he said as she asked him how they had been received yesterday. "He still hasn't done anything any differently. I don't understand—"

Before he could say anything any further, she seized his hand and drew him into the bedroom, away from the odd devices she recognized as Deliambren listening devices. She did *not* want the Deliambrens to know about the Bardic magic—at least, she did not want them to know that she was exercising it. They already knew there was something like it, of course, and they knew, from the results she got, that she used it. They might put "magic" and "harpist" together and come up with "Nightingale."

"Don't be impatient," she told him as his tail-feathers twitched a little from side to side and he shook his wings out. "Even with the magic, this is going to take *time*. For one thing, we didn't have the chance to select songs that would channel his mind in the direction we wanted it to go. For another, we are trying to change something that took several years to establish; we aren't going to do that overnight."

He opened his beak, then shut it abruptly, as if he had suddenly seen what she was talking about.

"Besides, you aren't in the special Council sessions," she continued. "You have no access to the one place where he actually gets things done and issues real orders. You have no idea how he is speaking or acting within them. If I were the King—"

She let the nebulous thought take a more concrete form, then spoke. "If I were the King, and I began to take up the reins of my duty again—I would know that I would have to be careful about it. The Advisors aren't going to like the changes we're trying to bring about in him, and they are powerful people. He can oppose them in small things successfully, but—" She shook her head. "He was a very clever man, and I don't think that cleverness is gone. He was also a very observant man, and he must realize what has been going on. If I were the King, with my sense of duty reawakened, I would start working my will in very small things, taking back my power gradually, and hopefully by the time they realized what I was doing, it would be too late. And I would be very, very careful that I didn't *seem* to act any differently."

T'fyrr nodded then. "In a way, since he has let the power slip from his hands, Theovere has less power than any of them. Is that what you are saying?"

"More or less." She moved back into the other room with its insidious little listening devices. "Well, more to the point, what are we performing today? If you have anything that I don't know, I can probably pick it up with a little rehearsal."

"Which you have cleverly provided time for by arriving early." His beak opened in that Haspur equivalent of a smile, and she warmed with his pleasure in her company and *her* cleverness. "Well, here is the list I had thought we might perform."

He brought out a written list, which was thoughtful of him, and was what she would have done in his place. Armed with that, she was able to suggest alternatives to several of the songs she did not yet know, which left them enough time for her to pick up the melodies to the most important of the rest.

This time, she was no longer so tired that the white marble corridors blurred, one into the other, like the halls in a nightmare. She had a chance to make some mental notes as she walked beside him, his talons clicking oddly on the marble floor.

Did I have a nightmare involving these halls last night? Something about looking for T'fyrr in an endless series of corridors, all alike, all filled with strangers? Yes, and I kept finding single feathers, broken or pulled out at the roots—could you actually do that with feathers that long and strong? But I never found him, only rooms full of more strangers staring at me and saying nothing.

She didn't care much for the statuary, though. It all had a remarkable sameness to it, mannered and smug, beautifully carved and lifeless.

Rather like the Guild versions of our ballads, actually.

Was there a sculptor's version of a Bardic Guild? From the looks of these statues, she suspected there must be.

Theovere wasn't responsible for this, though; she had seen his suite and knew for a fact that he had better taste than to order anything like this statuary.

Huh. A Deliambren has better taste than this.

Some other High King—or more likely, some other servants of some other High King were responsible. The King had probably waved his hand and ordered that the austere corridors be decorated, and lo—

There were statues by the gross.

He might even have done it for the simplest of all reasons; to keep people from becoming lost. Certainly Nob and probably everyone else navigated the endless hallways by the statuary. If that was the case, the statues didn't need to be inspired, just all of the same theme. They could have been ordered like so many decorated cakes.

Let's see, we'll have a dozen each—High Kings, nymphs, shepherds, famous women, famous men, famous generals, famous warriors, famous animals, dancers, musicians, saints—what did they do when they ran out of obvious subjects? She amused herself, thinking that somewhere there was a corridor decked out in the theme of Famous Village Idiots, or Famous Swinekeepers.

*Each with his favorite piggy at his feet—*She smiled to herself, holding back a giggle, as they reached the door of the King's suite.

Well, once more into the fray. That was enough to sober her.

There was another potential problem, as if they did not have troubles enough. She had not told T'fyrr about a thought that had disturbed her own dreams last night. She did not *know* that there were people other than the Bards and Elves who could detect Bardic Magic at work, but there might be. After all, those who used Bardic Magic could detect other magics than their own. She did not know if the High King had someone with him or watching over him with the intention of catching anyone working magic on the King in the act. But it was a real possibility, and it was not likely that anyone would bother to ask *why* they were weaving spells if she and T'fyrr were caught at it.

As they waited for the guards to open the doors now, there was the chance that she had been detected yesterday, and that they were not going in to a performance but a trap.

But in all the years she had practiced her art, no one had ever accused her in a way that made her think they had proof she used magic. Nor had anyone else among the Gypsies. Churchmen, village heads, and Guildsmen told wild tales, but never with any foundation.

And never with any truth—that was the odd and interesting part. In all the times that Free Bards and Gypsies *had* worked magic, there had been no hint that anyone, even their worst enemies, had a notion that anything of the sort had been done. It was only the unbelievable stories that were spread, of how impressionable youngsters were turned to demon-worship, immorality, or suicide by one or another particular song. They accused the *song*, and not the singer, as if it were the song that held the power.

What nonsense. These are stories created by people who want to find something else to blame than themselves for their children's acts.

How could words and music, lifeless without the life given to them by the performer, ever influence anyone against his will or better judgment? Books could suggest new possibilities to an open mind, yes, so music could, too—but people were not mindless and they had their own wills, and it was the mind and the will that implemented decisions. The mind that made the decision was ultimately the responsible party.

She had to assume that would hold true now; had to, or she would be too apprehensive to perform the task she had sworn herself to.

She had sworn herself, knowing that this might take years, that it might cost her not only her freedom but her life if she were caught at it. She would not take back her pledge now.

T'fyrr sensed I was making a formal pledge, even though I didn't make a ceremony about it. Interesting.

The doors opened, and the King was waiting, and it was time to make good on that pledge; now, and for as many days as it took to bring the bud to flower. *If* it could be done.

T'fyrr watched Nightingale leaving the Palace from the balcony at the end of his corridor. It was a good vantage point, with the formal fore-gardens spread out beneath him in neat and geometric squares of color divided by walkways of white paving-stone, and was even better as a place from which to take to the air. He was at least four stories up—apparently, the higher you were in rank, the higher your rooms within the Palace. He could see all the way to the Bronze Gate from here, and he made a point of watching to see that Nightingale got that far. She always turned, just before she went through the Gate, and waved at him, knowing that he would see her clearly even though she was nearly a mile away.

She could not see him, though, so he didn't bother to wave back. Instead, he waited until that distant figure passed between the open leaves of the gate, then launched himself into the air, wings beating strongly, gaining altitude. The air above the Palace grounds was sweeter than that above the city, and cooler, yet another example of the difference between those who dwelled *here* and *there*.

They had been at this for two weeks now, and although he still had not seen any change in Theovere's behavior, his Advisors were increasingly unhappy with the High King. In Court, Theovere continued to act as if he were supremely bored with his duties, but the Lord Seneschal frowned a bit less these days, and the rest of the Advisors frowned a bit more, which argued that in private Theovere might be flexing his royal muscles discreetly.

Harperus showed no signs of disappearing the way he had right after he had gotten T'fyrr installed as Royal Musician. That *should* have been comforting, having at least one real ally with power and a great many tricks up his capacious and frothy sleeves, but it wasn't as comforting as it could have been. For one thing, the Deliambren clearly had his attention and his mind on other things than T'fyrr. The Haspur actually saw the Lords Seneschal, Artificer, and Secretary more than he saw Harperus.

They often arrived to share T'fyrr's otherwise solitary dinners. The Lord Seneschal Acreon was more relaxed these days, though he was very disappointed to discover that Nightingale did not reside with T'fyrr in his rooms. She had impressed Acreon profoundly, it seemed.

I think she must have done something for him specifically with that magic of hers. I shall have to propose a special concert for him—perhaps a dinner concert on Nightingale's night off? We could do worse than have him on our side.

Lord Secretary Atrovel was his usual acerbic, witty, flippant self; whatever was going on in the private Council sessions didn't seem to be affecting him in the least. He continued to amuse T'fyrr with his imitations of the other Advisors, and his opinions on everything under the sun.

Lord Artificer Levan Pendleton came less often, as he was involved in some complicated project, but he was the only one of the three who actually *said* anything about changes in Theovere, and only a single comment. "He's up to mischief," the Lord Artificer had said briefly but with ironic approval, as if Theovere was a very clever, but very naughty, boy.

Atrovel was there last night with Pendleton, both of them flinging insults at each other and enjoying it tremendously. I wish Nightingale could have been there, too. I wish she would move into my suite. . . .

T'fyrr suppressed the rest of that thought and used his deepest wingbeats to get himself high into the sky, to a carefully calculated point where *he* would be able to make out Nightingale in the street below, but *she* would not see anything but a bird-form above if she looked up. He was worried about her. She told him not to worry, but he did anyway.

They tried to capture me, maybe even kill me. They haven't been successful, and it is going to cost them to find someone willing to make a third try. At least, that is the way Tyladen says things are done here. He thinks that makes me safe.

Well, maybe it made *him* safe, but it did nothing to protect Nightingale. An idiot could tell that he not only "hired" her, he cared for her. She was a single unarmed female; much easier to capture than a Haspur. She was, therefore, as much a target as he, and a much cheaper target at that.

She had to travel the dangerous streets between Freehold and the Palace twice a day, every day. *He* had volunteered to escort her, in spite of the fact that the crowds made him queasy and the streets brought on that fear of closed-in places all Haspur shared.

She had refused. He had offered to pay for a conveyance, and she had refused that, as well. Tyladen seemed unconcerned, saying only that "Gypsies can take care of themselves."

All very well and good, but there was only *one* Gypsy in this city, and she would have a difficult time standing up to six armed horsemen, for instance!

So he had started following her himself; not only from the air, but in the places where the streets were too narrow to make out where she was, by descending to use the metal walkways that connected buildings together above the second stories.

So far, nothing whatsoever had happened, but that did not make him less worried, it made him more worried. His unknown enemy could be waiting to see just how high a value T'fyrr placed on her before moving in to kidnap her. His enemy could also be trying to figure out just where she figured in Theovere's altering personality. Anyone who wanted to ask the bodyguards could find out what they were singing for the High King, and at least half of the songs were of a specific kind. You wouldn't even need magic to get a particular message across to Theovere, *if* he was listening. Their choice of music alone would alert that enemy to what they hoped to accomplish.

He looked down, spotting her from above by the misshapen bundle of the harpcase on her back. She was out of the better districts and down into the lower-class areas of the city; the streets narrowed, and it was getting harder to watch her from this high. On the other hand, she was jostled along by the crowd, and it would be a bad idea for her to look up now that she was in this part of the city.

He descended. It wasn't time to take to a walkway, yet; just the point where he should skim just above the roof level. People doing their wash or tending their little potted gardens would gawk at him as he flew past, but he was used to that now. He moved fast enough that their interest didn't alert anyone in the street below.

And speaking of the street below—

He fanned his wings open, grabbing for a now-familiar roost. He came to rest on a steeple, clinging with all four sets of talons, and watched her as she turned the corner into another narrow street. He particularly didn't like this one. There were a dozen little covered alleys off it, places where you could hide people for an ambush. This was one of the worst districts she had to cross to get back to Freehold, too. There had been murders committed here in broad daylight with a dozen witnesses present, none of whom, of course, could identify the murderer.

She was nervous here, too; he sensed that as his neck hackles rose. His beak clenched tight, and the talons on his hands etched little lines into the shingles on the steeple. She felt that something was wrong—

And it was.

Three men stepped out of an alley in front of her just as three more stepped out of one behind her. They were armed with sticks and clubs—and as everyone else sandwiched in between their ranks fled the immediate area without being stopped, it was obvious who they were after.

One of them stepped forward and gestured with his club as Nightingale shrank away, putting her back up against a building.

T'fyrr shoved himself away from the steeple, plunging toward them in a closed-wing stoop.

Nightingale knew she was being followed; she'd known it the moment that her tailer picked her up just outside of Leather Street. He had been following her for the past five days, in fact, always picking up her trail at Leather Street and leaving it just before she got to Freehold. He was good, but not good enough to evade someone who could sense a tracker's nerves behind her.

That was why she had paid all of her army of street-urchins an extra penny to follow her, as well, from the Palace gate to Freehold. They might be children, but they weren't helpless; you couldn't live in and on the street around here if you were helpless. They had their own weapons; tiny fists as hard as rocks, the stones of the street, slings like her own, even a knife or two. They had their orders: if someone tried to hurt Nightingale, they were to swarm him, give her a chance to escape, then run off themselves.

But she had not expected to be attacked by more than one or two at the most.

The three stepping out in front of her made her freeze in shock; the three closing in from behind brought a cold wave of fear rushing over her.

Quickly, as the normal denizens of the street vanished into their own little hiding places, she put her back to a wall and reached inside her skirt for her own knife. This was no time or place for magic—

Although a nice Elven lightning bolt would be welcome right now!

At that moment, the bolt from above *did* come in, wings half furled, talons outstretched, screaming like all the demons of the Church put together.

T'fyrr!

He raked the scalp of one with his foreclaws as he plunged in, striking to hurt and disable, not to kill. *That* man was down, blood pouring over his face so that he couldn't see; he screamed as loudly as T'fyrr. The pain of his wounds probably convinced him that T'fyrr had taken the top of his skull off and not just his scalp.

With a thunder of wings that sent debris flying, and a wind that whipped the ends of her hair into her face, he landed beside her and turned to face the rest of her enemies.

He didn't speak; he just opened his beak for another of those ear-shattering screams.

But any hope that he might simply frighten them into giving it up as a bad job died when three more appeared behind the five that remained standing.

Nightingale's fighting knife was out and ready in one hand, a nasty little bit of chain in the other. Good enough in the ordinary run of street fighting—

None of those men seemed at all impressed as they closed in.

She had never been in this kind of a fight before; she spent most of her time ducking, and the rest of it trying to fend off grasping hands with her knife. Fear choked her and made it hard to breathe; T'fyrr panted harshly through his open beak. Every fiber of her wanted to run, but there was nowhere to run to, no opening to seize. Bile rose in her throat; she tasted blood where she had bitten her lip. One of them kicked at her legs, expertly, trying to bring her down. She ducked head blows, but not always with complete success. Her breath burned in her throat, and sweat ran into her eyes and coldly down her back.

Nightingale fought like a cornered alleycat and T'fyrr like a grounded hawk, but neither of them were willing to strike to kill, and that actually worked against them. There were too many times when the only option open would have meant killing one of their assailants. . . .

A glancing blow to her shoulder made her drop her bit of chain as her arm and hand went numb; she slashed feverishly at the man who'd struck her, but he only stepped out of the way and came in again, swinging his lead-weighted club. With the chain, she might have been able to get the club away from him—

We're not going to get away—She swallowed bile again, and backed away from the man with the club, her stomach lurching with fear.

Suddenly, the street erupted in screams.

The children swarmed fearlessly into the fight, screaming their lungs out, kicking, biting, throwing stones, hitting, and most of all getting underfoot. They were too small and agile for the startled attackers to stop them, and there were too many of them to catch; when one of the bullies actually managed to grab an urchin, three or four more would mob him, kicking and biting, until he let go.

Nightingale spotted an opening at the same time T'fyrr did; they seized each other's hands, and T'fyrr charged through first, knocking one man aside with a wing, Nightingale hauled along in his wake.

They ran until their sides ached; ran until they could hardly breathe, ran until they were staggering blindly with exhaustion—and did not stop running until they came to Freehold.

CHAPTER EIGHT

"I can't believe you didn't break anything," Nightingale said as she carefully checked every bone in T'fyrr's fragile-appearing wings. She had already checked every inch of his body, from feet to sheath to keel, knowing from her experience with birds that the feathers could hide a number of serious to life-threatening injuries, and that seemingly insignificant tears in the skin could spread under sudden pressure to an unbelievable extent, especially across the breast muscles. Fortunately his skin proved to be much tougher than the average bird's.

She ached, not only from her own injuries, but from his. *I know every bruise, every sprain, every torn muscle. I feel as if I am inside his body. This never happened with Raven!*

He sighed, and rubbed one elbow. Bruises didn't show on the scaly skin of his lower arms and legs, but there was so little muscle there that the bruises went to the bone. "It feels as if I have broken a hundred bones, but I know that I have not. It will be days before I can fly again."

He did not voice the fear that put into him; the fear of the winged creature left helpless on the ground. He did not have to voice that fear, for she felt it as well.

I was an idiot. I should have taken him seriously. I should have confronted Harperus and demanded some kind of damned Deliambren protection! I should have confronted Harperus and Tyladen and moved into the damned Palace. I was enjoying the anonymity that kept them from manipulating me, and enjoying my notoriety as Lyrebird too much. I was enjoying all the adulation and success I had here in Freehold, too. Now he's grounded and it's all my fault. Guilt made her avoid his eyes, but she could not avoid the emotions coming from him.

She sat back on the bed for a moment, once she had assured herself that he truly did not have any broken bones. She had injuries of her own, of course—a badly bruised shoulder, bruised shins, lumps on her head—but his injuries were far more numerous than hers. He had shielded both of them with his wings, used the wings as weapons to buffet their attackers, and interposed himself between her and a blow she had not seen aimed at her any number of times.

Well, at least there is a solution to his injuries, if he'll take it. He might be grounded, but not for long.

"T'fyrr, I can—I can heal some of this, if you like," she offered tentatively. "It will still hurt, but I can sing it half-healed today, and do the rest tomorrow." Then she frowned. "I *think* I can," she amended. "I'm not sure if the magic will work on a Haspur, or if it will work the same. It should. I have not healed a nonhuman before, but my teacher Nighthawk has, and she never said anything about the magic working differently for them."

His feathers twitched, and she felt his relief at the idea that she *might* be able to give him enough freedom from pain and damage that he need not be caught on the ground. "Please!" he begged with voice and eyes and clenched talon-hands. "Half-healed will let me fly again!"

"You know how the magic works," she said, and smiled when he shook his head.

He'll find out in a moment.

"No, I don't—" he began, then his eyes widened in wonder. "Oh. Yes, I do. . . ." His voice trailed off, as his eyes sought hers, seeking answers.

They were answers she was not prepared to give him yet—perhaps never. Better that he should never know where that touch of magic and the knowledge of it came from, if there was to be nothing more between them than there had been between her and Raven. "Simply listen for the music and give yourself to it," she said, and placed both her hands atop his hard, sinewy talons. It no longer felt strange to reach for a hand and find something all bone and sinew and covered with the tough, scaly skin of a raptor's feet. Did it still seem strange for him to touch her, and find soft skin over muscle, with five stubby little scales instead of talons?

She gave him no chance to ask all the questions she felt bubbling up inside of him; she did not want to face those questions herself.

The answers, in all probability, would hurt far too much.

Instead, she plunged into the magic that Nighthawk had taught her— the combination of Bardic Magic and Gypsy healing, all bound up in the tonal chanting that suited Nighthawk's strong, harsh voice better than any song. But the Bardic song lay behind the chanting, and for Nightingale the chant turned into something far more musical than Nighthawk ever produced.

The results were the same, though; as she had when she had tried to ease T'fyrr's soul-wounds, she became one with him and his hurts and felt them as clearly as if they were hers. She came between him and the pain, in fact, shielding him from it as he had shielded her from the blows that had injured him.

If I had wings, and I could fly. . . . That was the refrain in many of the songs she and her kind sang to their audiences; now she spread wings of power rather than feathers and muscle, spread them over him and sheltered him beneath them, as he had sheltered her beneath his own. She was once again aware of the spicy scent of his feathers, and the bitter scent beneath it of sheer exhaustion.

With her song and the power in the song, she drove into each injury, speeding the healing that had already begun, strengthening the torn muscles, weaving reinforcement into the sprains, soothing the bruises. In the back of her mind, she reflected that it was too bad in a way that his skin was covered with feathers; nothing she had done would be visible. *On the other hand, injuries will not be obvious, either. He will appear up to full strength, which might mislead other would-be attackers.* She sensed him relaxing as the pain eased, sensed his surprise in the lessening of the pain, sensed him finding the song she chanted under her breath.

But then—

Instead of simply opening himself up to the song as she had asked, *he* began to sing, too.

And the power no longer flowed only from her to him, but came from his hands into hers, as if two great, rushing streams ran side by side, but in opposing directions.

Her shoulder stopped aching and throbbing, as he touched *her* with that brush of power as warm as the caress of a feather and as light. The many points of pain in her skull ebbed, as he brushed the power over them as well.

The quality of the chant changed a little, becoming more musical, with odd tonal qualities, but she was able to follow it effortlessly.

But she almost lost the thread of the chant in her own astonishment when she realized consciously what he had just done, and she felt his amusement and wonder—amusement at *her* surprise, and wonder at the thing that had been born between them.

In the past, anytime she had done this, when she had opened herself to someone, it had been entirely one-sided, as she had learned to her sorrow with handsome Raven. Even when she limited her openness to the minimum required to heal, she had still been open enough to feel the mental anguish that all too often came with injury, and always she had felt the pain itself. Never, ever, had someone *else* returned the gift. Never had someone joined her in the chant, to heal her.

And never had anyone ever opened himself to her heart as she had opened herself to his.

Until T'fyrr.

She *knew* that he read her soul as she had read his, felt the long loneliness, and the resignation deeper than despair and just as sorrowful. Her heart had no more secrets from his, for every wound, every scar, every bruise was laid bare to his raptorial eyes.

She was so surprised that she could not even react by closing herself off again.

She could not read thoughts—but she could read the feelings that came with the thoughts: feelings so mixed she could not have said where his wonder began and his own long loneliness ended. He began to speak aloud, giving her the images, the memories, that were calling up those feelings—and clearly he *knew* what she sensed.

"There are humans who live among the Haspur," he said, softly, as she continued to sing her healing chant, so lost in it now that she could not have stopped if she tried. He fitted the words to the music, and sang them to her as he sang healing into her body as well. "Most of them are as ordinary as bread, but some are granted a rare gift, that of seeing into the Spirit. That is why we call them Haspur Spirit-Brothers, for as often as they use that gift with their fellow humans they also use it with the Haspur, who are their friends and fellow-defenders. Mostly, they provide the simpler gifts: healing of the body as you are doing, ease of the heart in time of trouble. But sometimes, once in a very, very long time, there is need and a compatibility of spirits that binds healer and healed more closely than that. That is when the Spirit-Gift of the Haspur is awakened, and the two become a greater whole than two Spirit-Brothers are singly. They are—"

He sang a long, fluting whistle that somehow melded itself into the healing chant without disturbing it.

"There are no words in the human tongue for this. They are partner-healers, they are wisdom-keepers, they are two souls in two bodies still, but bound together in ways that neither time nor distance can change or sever. Sometimes they are lovers. They are the great treasures of the Haspur. I had not thought to find that potential in myself, though every Haspur at one time aspires to and dreams of such a thing. I would never have dreamed to have found it with you, O Bird of the Night, wild winged singer, dreamer of beauty and gentle healer of hearts—"

There was more, but half of it was in his own language, and at any rate, Nightingale would have lost half of it in her own daze at a single phrase.

Sometimes they are lovers.

How could—well, she knew *how,* physically they were as compatible as many unlikely human pairings. Now that she had tended his hurts, she knew what was beneath that modesty-wrap he wore, and if he *said* that his people and humans sometimes became lovers, then of course it was possible. But how—

With care, of course, an impudent mental voice chided her. *Those talons could cause a bit of trouble, but on the other hand, you probably weigh more than he does, so—*

Oh, it was a very good thing that neither he nor she could read *thoughts.*

With her mind and body whirling, all unbalanced and giddy, she realized that the chant was nearing its end. She brought it to a close, rounding it in on itself, curling it into repose. And she opened her eyes to find herself curled in his arms, and he in hers, her head pillowed on the soft breast feathers, his on her unbound hair.

Nor did either of them care to move, for a very long time.

The immediate effect of the healing chant was two-fold: both healer and healed were ravenous afterwards, and exhausted, so weary that even had she been ready to deal with the consequences of what had just happened between them, neither of them would have had the strength.

She had more strength than he for she had more experience at the healing than he. It was not the power itself that came from the healer, only the direction—but as riding a fractious, galloping horse takes strength, so did guiding the power. She had just enough reserves left to go down the stairs, leave a message for Tyladen saying that she was indisposed—which was *no* lie—and order some food brought up. He was asleep when she returned, and only came half-awake when the food arrived, just enough to eat and fall back into sleep. She was not in much better shape; she really didn't remember what she had ordered and hardly recognized it when it arrived. Her head spun in dizzy circles as she got up to put the tray outside the door; she lay back down again beside him and dimmed the light, and that was all she remembered.

But her dreams were wonderful, full of colors she had no names for, sensations of wind against her skin and a feeling of unbearable lightness and joy. She'd had dreams of flying before, every Free Bard did, it seemed, but never like this. This was real flight; the sensation of powerful chest muscles straining great wings against the air to gain height until the earth was little more than a tapestry of green and brown and grey below, then the plummeting dive with wind hard against the face and tearing at the close-folded wings, and the exaltation of the freedom, the freedom. . . .

She woke to find him already awake and watching her, a bemused expression in his eyes.

"Not now—" he said, before she could speak. "Not now. You have never known this was possible. You must think, you must meditate, or you will regret any decision you make in haste."

She nodded; he knew her as well as she knew herself.

Of course he does, said that little, amused voice. *And he knows that the outcome is perfectly certain. He can afford to wait, he knows what you will do, eventually, and he is patient enough to wait for that "eventually" however long it takes.*

"I want to talk to Tyladen," she said, finally. "This—I only have two choices that I can see, after this last attack. I either move to the Palace with you, or I reveal who I really am and get some of that protection these damn Deliambrens were so free in offering."

"My suggestion would be the latter," he replied. "As long as you are openly still Lyrebird, you have an ear in the city that I do not, that no one who is not human would have. You would not be able to discuss things with our friend Father Ruthvere, for instance. But it is your choice."

She nodded thoughtfully, agreeing with him. *He's right. We need that ear inside the Church that Father Ruthvere provides, and* he *needs the knowledge of the Court that we can give him. Church and Court are wound in an incestuous dance these days, and if anyone is to break the pattern, it will be Father Ruthvere and those who are with him. Moving into his suite would have forced me to make certain decisions anyway, and I'm not sure I want to even think about them much less make them.*

Things were already complicated enough.

It was something of a relief to close herself into the privacy of the bathroom and let the hot water from the wall nozzle run over her, washing away fatigue and letting her empty her mind, as well. She didn't have to guess that he might be feeling as uncertain as she; that was another complication to this situation. It was one thing to imagine finding someone for herself as she sang those love songs of longing and loneliness. It was quite another to find herself presented with a resolution.

And yet, hadn't she wanted someone exactly like this? Well, the old Gypsy proverb advised, "Be careful what you wish for, you might get it." She could not have designed a better partner than T'fyrr, for they were alike enough for joy and different enough for exploration.

And, oh, doesn't that open up a number of possibilities? One can just imagine. . . .

She fiercely shoved that little voice back into its corner. *One thing at a time,* she told it. *We'll take one thing at a time, and the most important comes first. We must deal with the High King and finish the task we have begun, assuming it can be finished.*

T'fyrr was all ready when she emerged, and he had cleaned up the room and put the bed into the wall, too. Perhaps he felt as uncomfortable with that particular piece of furniture so blatantly on display as she was.

Of course he is. He's feeling what I'm feeling, which will ensure that he feels the same! Oh, what a bother! No more polite and discreet lies just to salve his feelings! If we disagree on something, one of us will have to find a way to persuade the other, or the bad feelings will chafe between us until we are half-distracted!

They went downstairs together, to find that they were so early this morning that they were, by the standards of Freehold, still up late. The sun was just rising and the last-shift dance group performing its final number. So Tyladen would still be awake, not a bad thing, since she wanted first to speak with him. She was quite prepared to wake him, if she needed to.

Not that she was sure when he ever slept. The Deliambrens didn't seem to have the same sleep needs as humans did; she thought, perhaps, that he slept in the mid-morning hours, perhaps a little in the afternoon, but never for more than two or three hours at a time.

Of course they don't need to sleep the way we do. They don't have to sleep deeply enough for dreaming. They express their dreams and nightmares in their clothing.

Tyladen *was* still awake, but looked a bit surprised to have both of them strolling into his office together, and at that early hour. Nightingale shut the door firmly and put her back to it as T'fyrr leaned against the wall, giving him the advantage of looking *down* at the Deliambren.

"First of all, Lyrebird was attacked yesterday. She was hurt, and so was I, in trying to help her." His face was without expression, but Nightingale knew that every word was carefully chosen. "You might take note of the bruises, if you should happen to doubt my word."

Nightingale had sent word down at the same time that she had ordered the food that she was indisposed; presumably, Tyladen had found a substitute singer for last night. He just nodded, mobile face solemn for a change. Then again, there wasn't much he could respond to, yet.

And he didn't know that they were together, in more than one sense.

"We have reason to believe that the attack was more of an attempt to gain control over *me* than because she got in the way of some gang or other," T'fyrr continued. "In fact, we believe that the same person who was behind the other two attacks on me here was behind the one on her."

"That makes sense," Tyladen said cautiously, looking from Nightingale's face to T'fyrr's, as if he was trying to put a number of disparate bits of information together and not coming up with much. "Perhaps she ought to quit her position here, then, and move to the Palace? She doesn't precisely need to work here anymore, and surely you have—"

T'fyrr deliberately leaned over and placed both taloned hands on Tyladen's desk, scoring the surface. "Enough of the nonsense, Tyladen! We both know *why* I come here! It's not because I'm savoring the nightlife, nor because I happen to enjoy this lady's playing! We both know that I would *still* have to come here even if the lady moved into my suite at the Palace, so that I could continue to report to you! I'm your little Palace spy, Tyladen, an unpaid spy at that, and it's about time you and Harperus began giving me a bit more protection! And you might as well start offering that same protection—no, *more* protection—to Lyrebird!"

Tyladen didn't bat an eye; he simply put on a skeptical expression and said, "I can't see any good reason why—"

"Because," Nightingale interrupted him, "my name isn't Lyrebird. It's Nightingale—Nightingale of the Free Bards and the *Getan* Gypsies. And I've been working here on behalf of the Deliambrens *without* any support since I arrived."

For the first time in her life, Nightingale actually saw expressions of shock, dismay and surprise pass across a Deliambren face. And for the first time in her life, she saw one caught at a loss for words. Tyladen sat in his chair with his mouth half open; his lips twitched, but he couldn't seem to get any words out.

It would be funny, if the situation weren't so serious. He looked exactly like a stunned catfish.

Nightingale sat down gracefully. "Now," she said sweetly. "About that protection?"

T'fyrr smiled. "For both of us," he added, coming to stand behind her and putting both his taloned hands on her shoulders.

Tyladen just sat and stared at them both.

They returned to the Palace with a double Mintak guard; twins, or so it was said. They certainly looked like twins, insofar as a human could tell. Since this pair had been known to break up fights with their bare hands and now were armed with very impressive axes in their belts, Nightingale doubted that there would be any more ambushes today.

In fact, their path was remarkably clear of interference. Even peddlers found reasons to take their pushcarts out of the way.

As they walked steadily toward the Palace, her street-children slipped up to her one and two at a time, pretending to beg, but in actuality making certain that *she* was all right and gleefully recounting their own parts in the melee. It made her a little sick to realize that they had seen it as normal, quite in keeping with life on the streets. Perhaps a bit more fun than most of the violent situations they witnessed or were a part of in the course of a month or so. She slipped each of them an extra couple of pennies for diligence and quick thinking; she would have given them more, but that would leave all of them open to robbery or worse. No street-urchin dared carry more than a couple of pennies on his person, and very few of them had a safe place to cache money.

I can give them more, later. I can double their "wages." I can see to it that they can come to the kitchen door of Freehold and be fed, and have it taken out of my wages.

When they neared the Palace, T'fyrr took off into the air, much to the astonishment of the passers-by, leaving Nightingale to go on to the Bronze Gate with her double Mintak guard flanking her. Their presence raised an eyebrow from the gate guard, but one of the Mintaks grunted and said to him, "Been some trouble for Freeholders. People roughing up folks as works for us, callin' em Fuzzy-lovers. Boss wants his investment protected."

The gate guard nodded at that and waved her through; the inexplicable had been explained in terms he could understand. Nightingale passed inside and the two Mintaks went back across the street, took up a station in a nearby cafe that catered to the servants of those who came and went through the Bronze Gate, and set out a tiny portable Sires and Barons game between them. They would be there when she came out again, and they *might* even hear or be told something useful while they were there.

Now all she had to worry about were the dangers *inside* the Palace. *About which I can do nothing. Hopefully Tyladen or Harperus have something that can protect me.*

T'fyrr landed beside her in a flurry of wing feathers, as she traversed the stone-paved path between two regimented beds of fragrant flowers. With her practiced eye, she knew by his careful landing that he was still in some pain; his wingbeats were not as deep, and he landed on both feet, rather than one.

The flowers in these formal gardens weren't anything she recognized, but then, the High King's gardeners had access to flowers found nowhere else inside the Twenty Kingdoms, and their breeding programs could make even familiar blooms unrecognizable. She allowed herself to be distracted from her concerns for a moment by their beauty and their perfume, but she couldn't be distracted for long.

Among the major concerns, there were some minor ones. Nothing that really mattered in either the long or the short run, but somehow they nagged at her.

One was strictly personal, and a cause for some embarrassment. Would there be gossip about them? It was certainly possible. It would be the second time that T'fyrr had remained out of the Palace all night, and both times (if anyone was keeping track) he had been at Freehold, in her room. She found herself blushing at the notion of what people might be thinking, which rather surprised her. After all, hadn't she been willing to move into his suite and live there?

But that was different. . . .

Oh, certainly. With a preadolescent boy to act as chaperon, it was different. Indeed. She blushed even more.

This is ridiculous! I'm a Gypsy, a Free Bard; people have been saying things about me for as long as I've been alive, and I didn't care! I laughed at them! She managed to get her blushes under control before they reached their goal, by dint of much self-scolding. Which, in itself, was ridiculous. . . .

But when they arrived at the Palace itself and entered the huge, self-opening doors, they found the place as chaotic as an overturned beehive.

The great hall at the main doors was full of courtiers and servants and everyone in between, all of them chattering, and all of them upset. People of all stations were standing together in tight little groups, rigid with apprehension, or rushing about—apparently with no clear destination in mind. Pages ran hither and yon on urgent errands, their eyes wide and faces pale. All that Nightingale could pick up was fear; fear and excitement, and all that those emotions engendered.

What's been happening? She and T'fyrr stood just inside the door, and no one noticed them, which in itself was nothing short of astonishing.

T'fyrr solved the entire question by reaching out and intercepting one of the page boys as he ran past. The boy felt the talons close on his shoulder and stopped dead, with a little squeak of surprise.

"*What* is going on here?" T'fyrr rumbled down at his captive. "What has happened since yesterday? Why is there all this commotion?"

The page stared at him with wide blue eyes and stuffed his fist into his mouth as he blinked up at them. He wasn't very old, no more than seven or eight—and very sheltered. One of Nightingale's street-urchins would have replied already and been well on his way. T'fyrr waited patiently. Finally the boy got up enough courage to speak.

"It's the D-deliambren, S-sire!" he stammered, then seemed to get stuck, staring up into the Haspur's raptorial eyes exactly like a mouse waiting for the hawk to strike.

"What about the Deliambren?" T'fyrr asked with a little less patience. "I haven't been here, I've just come in. What *about* the Deliambren?"

"H-he's—he's been attacked!" the boy blurted. "He's hurt, they say badly, they say someone tried to kill him!" Then as T'fyrr's grip loosened with shock, the page pulled away and ran off again.

T'fyrr's shock didn't last past that moment; he knew where Harperus' suite was, and may the Lady help anyone who got between him and his destination. He headed off in that direction with a purposeful stride that Nightingale had to match by running. Her mind flitted from thought to thought, infected a little by all the fear around her. *Attacked? By who? Is he really hurt badly? Is he—oh dear Lady, not dead, surely!* The idea of Old Owl dead—no, it was not to be thought of, surely not he, not with all of his

Deliambren devices to protect him? He had outlived her grandfather with no sign of old age, how *could* he be dead?

But how could he have been attacked? How could anyone have gotten in to him, past his devices, to attack him?

They ran past rank after rank of statuary, taking the quickest path to the Deliambren suite. Past animals, past famous generals, past mermaids—up the stairs to the fourth floor and past guildsmen, past famous Bards, past farmers—*oh dear, there* is *one with his favorite piggy at his feet!* she thought distractedly—past the Allies of the Twenty Kingdoms—

And there was the door to Harperus' suite, *now* guarded by a pair of the King's personal bodyguards, who let T'fyrr and herself past without so much as a challenge. T'fyrr flung himself inside immediately. But she stopped at the door and caught the attention of one of the guards, one she thought she recognized from the King's suite. "What happened?" she asked shortly.

He looked down into her eyes, his own as flat and expressionless as blued steel. Finally he opened his thin, grim lips and answered.

"Someone broke in here last night while Envoy Harperus was with the High King. They—there was more than one—were ransacking the suite when the Envoy came in and found them still there. His devices had stunned and captured one of them, and the others were trying to get him free. When the Envoy surprised them, they clubbed him and fled. The Envoy is still unconscious. The High King has put his own personal servants in place here, since the Envoy's assigned servants have disappeared and might even have been in collusion with his attackers."

"We have the one the device caught in custody," the other guard said at last. "The Envoy regained consciousness long enough to tell us what had happened, how to free the man, and to ask for Sire T'fyrr, and then collapsed again."

She might have thought she was imagining a faint tone of disapproval that T'fyrr had not been here when Harperus asked for him, except that she sensed the disapproval as well as heard it. She simply nodded with dignity, and said, "Sire T'fyrr and I were attacked by nine armed men in the city last night. We were some time in being tended to and unable to send word to the Palace. It seems that someone would like to harm the High King's foreign allies."

Then she passed on through the doors into the Deliambren suite, knowing that the Bodyguards were far more than mere soldiers, and knowing that what she had just said would be recounted, with exact tone and inflection, to the High King's Spymaster. And whether that mysterious gentleman served Theovere only, or served some of the Advisors as well, there would be no doubt that she and T'fyrr were well aware of *what* their attackers were, if not who.

It was a risk to reveal that, but it was an equal risk to seem unaware of their situation. Perhaps this would make their enemy a bit more wary.

But for right now, she was grimly certain that Harperus had better have someone at his side who was his friend, guarding him. The King's body-guards might help so long as whoever was after Harperus tried to pass the doors, but they wouldn't be of much help if an attacker were one of the King's servants, or came in by some other means.

The suite didn't look a great deal different from theirs, except in one small detail. Harperus had none of the "Deliambren sculptures" around the suite. That might explain why Tyladen didn't know about the attack.

Yet.

Nightingale passed through the reception room and into Harperus' bed-room, where there were two more guards at the door. T'fyrr had already settled at Harperus' bedside, displacing a servant; Nightingale bit her lip, then reached out to touch the Deliambren's bruised brow and hummed a fragment of the healing chant under her breath.

But she emerged almost immediately from her brief trance with a feel-ing of profound relief. "He'll be all right," she told T'fyrr, whose tense shoulders and twitching tail signaled his own worry and fear. "He's healing himself; he doesn't even need me to do anything. That is why he went unconscious again. He has a concussion, but when he wakes it will have been taken care of. I'm going to your suite to get something; I'll be right back."

T'fyrr started up at that, and she knew what must be in his mind. "If anyone got into your suite last night, it won't matter," she pointed out. "Whoever was behind this was probably behind the attack on us, and he *knows* where we were. After Harperus was attacked, the King's men prob-ably checked all the suites to make sure no one else was hurt, so even if the attackers got into yours, Nob is surely all right."

He sank back down on his stool, and nodded. "Nob is all that I care about," he said, a bit hoarsely. "Anything else can be replaced, and most of it is not mine, anyway. Things can be restored; people cannot."

She hurried out, running as soon as she reached the hallways, picking up her skirts like a child so that she could run the faster.

Despite what she had told him to reassure him—*thank the Lady we can't read thoughts!*—she was by no means sure that she would find either the suite or Nob intact. In the excitement, the guards might *not* have thought to check. Nob could be lying with his skull cracked in the bathroom of the suite or in his own room even now.

But as she pushed the door open, Nob came flying out of the bedroom with a cry of relief to see her, and the room seemed intact.

"T'fyrr is all right," she said, and gave him the short version of the attack in the streets—and then, for the benefit of Tyladen's listening devices, a short story of the attack on Harperus. Nob had known that there had been an attack on *someone,* for guards had come checking the other suites as she had suspected they might, but he had known nothing more than that one of the envoys had been hurt. He hadn't known which one, and he'd been afraid to leave the suite to find out. He hadn't known what to do; his training in etiquette hadn't covered this sort of situation, and he was afraid to act without orders.

But now that T'fyrr was back he had someone to give him orders, which put *his* world back in place again. Nightingale gave him the first of those orders, on behalf of his master.

"Have someone bring T'fyrr his breakfast in Harperus' suite," she said, "then you bring him fresh clothing. He'll want you to stand guard over Harperus while he uses the envoy's bathroom. He still hasn't had much of a chance to get completely clean after those bravos attacked us."

Nob nodded; his eyes were full of questions, but he was too well-trained to ask them. Nightingale was not going to say anything; it wasn't her place. Whatever T'fyrr wanted him to know, T'fyrr would tell him.

"I will perform for the High King, as usual," she told the boy. "We will hope he will find me a satisfactory substitute. I'll be going there as soon as I get my harp in tune."

As soon as Nob was out of the room, she locked the door and gave a much more detailed accounting of everything for the sake of the listening devices. "That is all we know now," she said. "I presume we will find out more when Harperus awakens. In the meantime—"

She stopped herself; after all, what could she suggest that was of any real value? "In the meantime, I will substitute for T'fyrr with the High King, unless I receive orders from the King to the contrary. I will not be back to Freehold for the next day or so."

As she took her harp in its case off her back—she was so used to the weight that she hadn't really noticed it, even when she'd run to the suite—she tried to calm herself. She would not be able to call the magic if she was too tense to hear its melody above her own.

The trouble was that this second attack pointed all too clearly to an enemy within the highest ranks, an enemy who had at least some inkling that she, Harperus, and T'fyrr were all working together, presumably to bring about changes in the King that this enemy did not want to see occur.

And depending on *how* high that enemy was—

We are already marked. We could be doomed.

And with that cheerful thought in mind, she passed out of the doors and into the hall, walking swiftly on her way to entertain the King.

She and T'fyrr sat beside Harperus turn and turn about; sometimes they practiced their music, softly, but without the addition of the magic. Their only connection to the world outside the suite was Nob. She worried, briefly, about the Mintaks she had left. Presumably someone from Freehold would send for the twins—

But in case Tyladen didn't think of it, she finally sent Nob down to the Bronze Gate with a note for them, letting them know what had happened and that she would not be coming out today. If they were thorough, they would probably wait to see if this was a ruse, and when she didn't show up, return to Freehold on their own. Tyladen could confirm her note to them then. At any rate, they would have passed a fairly pleasant morning and afternoon in congenial surroundings paid for by Tyladen.

There were other things she would *like* to see him pay for, but she was unlikely to see *that* happen in her lifetime.

Damned Deliambrens, interfering in our lives and playing at games with us, never thinking there might be any real danger involved—after all, we're all backward barbarians, and how could we be a danger to anyone. . . .

Then the two of them watched over their friend with care and concern, thinking no more of the outside world, until the outside world intruded on them, in the form of the King's Physician.

He did not deign to explain himself to them, nor did he pay any particular attention to them. He simply breezed past the guards and into Harperus' bedchamber, ignoring them both. While this was rude, it was not entirely unexpected, at least to Nightingale. While T'fyrr theoretically outranked a mere physician, it was only in theory, and there wasn't much T'fyrr could do if this man chose to ignore his rank and even his presence just because he was not human.

But the moment he ceased doing a simple physical examination and opened up the bag of instruments he brought, he found T'fyrr's talons clamped around his wrist.

He had reached out so quickly that Nightingale did not even see him move, only that his talons were suddenly locked around the physician's wrist.

He told me once that a Haspur can kill a deer with his hands, and a buffalo with his feet. I hope this physician cooperates. He will find it difficult to practice medicine with a broken wrist.

"What do you think you are doing?" the Haspur snarled, his beak parted in threat.

Startled, the human glanced around for help from the guards. But the guards were not disposed to interfere, at least not yet. T'fyrr hadn't done anything contrary to their orders, and Nightingale doubted that they had any idea just how much pressure those hand-claws could exert.

And if they did, they still might not interfere.

The man made an abortive move to free his wrist and discovered just how strong a Haspur's grip was. Nightingale stayed out of the way and in the background. The less she drew attention to herself, the better. Too many people already had her marked as it was; she didn't need to add the physician to the list.

Finally the man decided that answering was better than standing there with his wrist in the grip of a giant predator—although he tried to look as important as possible. That was a bit difficult, given that he was also wincing from the pain of T'fyrr's grip.

"I am going to wake him," the physician said arrogantly.

Oh, truly? Then he is more of a fool than I took him for! Nightingale thought in surprise. If Harperus' trance had not been self-induced, it *would* have been very serious indeed. It might have been dangerous to Harperus to wake him—and it might have been impossible.

And even though the trance *was* self-induced, and therefore it was unlikely the physician could break down the wall of Harperus' will, trying to wake him could easily interfere with the self-healing process.

"And just how much do you know about the Deliambren?" T'fyrr all but purred, dangerously. "Have you studied Deliambren head injuries? Have you ever had a Deliambren patient before?"

"Well, no, but—" the man stuttered, surprised into telling the truth. He had probably never had anyone challenge his expertise before.

"Have you ever had *any* nonhuman as a patient?" T'fyrr persisted, his eyes narrowing, his voice dropping another half-octave so that the purr became a growl. "Have you even studied nonhuman injuries?"

The man blanched and tried to bluff. "No, but that hardly matters whe —*ouch!*" T'fyrr had tightened his talons on the man's wrist. Nightingale winced. Surely the bones were grinding together by now.

"Why then is it so imperative that Lord Harperus be wakened," T'fyrr asked, "when you know that you know nothing of how his body functions, and in waking him you might kill him? Is this on the orders of the King?" He pulled the man a little closer to him, effortlessly, and looked down at him with his beak no more than a few inches from the physician's face.

"It—no—*ow!*—it's because of the escape, you fool!" The physician was dead-white now, with anger as much as with fear, although fear was swiftly gaining the upper hand.

After all, there is a beak fully capable of biting through his spine less than a hand's-breadth from his nose.

T'fyrr shook the wrist he held, ever so slightly. "What escape?" he asked urgently, and Nightingale felt the hair on the back of her neck rise, both in reaction to his dangerously icy tone and in premonition. Her stomach knotted with T'fyrr's, both of them with chills of fear running down their backs.

"The man—the man who was caught here," the physician stammered, unable to look away from T'fyrr's eyes. "He escaped early this evening. We need to talk to the Envoy to discover if there was anyone he recognized among the rest of his attackers. We need to find more of the perpetrators before they have a chance to get away."

"*What?*" T'fyrr dropped the man's wrist; the physician did not even stop to gather up his instruments. He fled the suite, leaving only T'fyrr and the guards. T'fyrr turned toward the guard nearest him, who shrugged.

"I hadn't heard anything, Sire," the man said. "We've been here as long as you have. I can send to find out, though."

"Do that," T'fyrr ordered brusquely. "If the man really did escape, there are now at least three people who need to see that Lord Harperus does not get a chance to identify them, all loose in this Palace. Now we don't know who any of them are; they could be among the very servants sent here to serve Lord Harperus. You might consider that when you send your message."

The guard's grim face grew a bit grimmer, and he himself disappeared for a moment or two, leaving his fellow twice as vigilant. When he returned, it was with his own Captain striding by his side. Nightingale recognized the Captain from the High King's suite; he was one of the ones usually close at Theovere's side.

"I understand you have not heard the latest of our incidents, Sire T'fyrr," the Captain said with careful courtesy. "I can tell it to you in brief: the Palace does not normally hold prisoners. Normally we send them elsewhere, within the city, which has better gaols than we. This time, however, it was deemed better to keep the man here, in one of the storage rooms in the cellars, with a guard on his door. Not," he added, with a wry lift of an eyebrow, "one of *us*. This was merely a Palace guard, not one of the Elite."

T'fyrr nodded, and the Captain went on. "I am told that at about dinner time, according to the guard left on duty, a woman appeared with whom several of the guards were familiar, he among them. She is ostensibly a maid here, and yet no one will admit now to having her in their service. At any rate, there was supposedly a good reason for her to be in the storage area, and when she saw the guard who knew her, she flirted with him as she has often done in the past. He allowed his caution to slip; she was only a woman after all, and alone."

"She then incapacitated the guard and let the prisoner escape," T'fyrr concluded, seeing the obvious direction the tale was heading.

"She didn't bloody incapacitate him; she knocked him cold with a single punch!" the Captain corrected bitterly. "A single woman, no taller than his chin! It's unnatural! I've never seen nor heard of the like, for a woman half a man's size to take him down with one blow, even if he didn't expect it!"

Nightingale had, of course, but she kept her peace. There was no point in getting suspicion pointed in her own direction. The regular guards by now were smarting with the disgrace; they would be looking for an easy suspect, and she was in no mood to provide them with one. It would be all too easy for someone to claim that *she* had somehow slipped down to the cellar, perhaps during one of the brief times she had gone to fetch something for T'fyrr from his suite.

Especially since she *had* been seen in the Lower Kitchen and could have been mistaken for a maid, with a long stretch of the imagination. There were cooks and the like who would be perfectly able to identify her as "Tanager," and for a noble, there wasn't a great deal of difference between a "maid" and a "street-musician."

"So the man is gone, and we have no suspects whatsoever." T'fyrr clacked his beak with anger. "This is not cheerful news, Captain."

"Do tell," the man retorted heatedly. "At the moment our best hope is that Lord Harperus regains consciousness and can tell us what he saw. That is probably why the physician was sent—I expect it was by the Captain of the Watch." The Captain's tone turned condescending. "I'm afraid that he hasn't had much experience with injuries. I am certain he thought a head injury was no more serious than a drunken stupor and could be dealt with in much the same way."

His tone implied that the Watch Captain had no combat experience, which was probably true—and the scars on his own face and hands spoke volumes for *his* expertise.

"So your best hope is to keep him *safe.*" T'fyrr turned the full force of his gaze on the Captain. "I am the nearest you have to an expert on Deliambren medicine—although, if you want a real expert, there is a Deliambren running a tavern in the city, a place called Freehold. His name is Tyladen. He probably has a great deal more knowledge than I."

"I know the place," the captain replied. "Many of my men have been there, now and again, and they speak highly of the place. I've been there myself."

For entertainment? Not primarily, I warrant. Probably to see if it was a hotbed of Fuzzy subversion. But it wasn't, and so he permits his men to visit it recreationally.

"Tyladen of Freehold might be persuaded to come attend to his fellow countryman's needs," T'fyrr said, and Nightingale sensed his fragment of ironic pleasure at the notion that Tyladen just might be forced to *do* something besides sit in his office like a spider in a web, collecting information at no cost or danger to himself. She was beginning to have a very poor opinion of Tyladen's courage, and she knew T'fyrr shared it. "Other than Tyladen, I am your nearest source, and I assure you, it would be *much* better to wait until Lord Harperus wakes of his own accord. It could be dangerous to try to bring him to consciousness at this point."

The Captain acknowledged T'fyrr's expertise with an unwilling nod. "I'll have that noted, Sire T'fyrr," he added politely. "Now, by your leave, I'll take mine."

T'fyrr bowed slightly, and the Captain walked out, at a slightly faster pace than he'd arrived. T'fyrr had impressed him with a level head and good sense, at any rate.

They both returned to their seats beside Harperus' bed. Nob had long since closed the curtains against the night and lit a lamp or two, turning them low. Most of the room was in shadow; the rest in half-light. Curtains pulled halfway around the bed to keep the light from disturbing the occupant left the bed itself in deep shadows, in which Harperus' white hair gleamed softly against the pillow.

The Haspur turned to Nightingale and touched her hand, as lightly as a puff of down, with the talon that had just come close to crushing the wrist of the interfering physician. She smiled tremulously at him.

"When do you think he'll wake?" he asked her in a tense whisper.

She closed her eyes and again dropped briefly into the healing-spell with three key notes of the chant. The song Harperus wove about himself was coming to a close, winding in and around itself the way that all Deliambren music ended, in a reprise of the beginning, a serpent swallowing its own tail. "Soon, very soon," she said, opening her eyes again. "Within an hour or two at the very most, I suspect."

T'fyrr sighed with relief. "It cannot be too soon for me."

"Nor for me," she replied. "I still need to invoke healing on you again—"

"And I on you," he interrupted, and a gentle warmth washed over her as he touched the back of her hand again. "But we may be sitting here guarding Harperus until—"

"Until what?" came a weak voice from the shadows. "Until the moon turns blue? Until the Second Cataclysm?"

"Until you wake, old fool!" T'fyrr said, turning quickly toward the head of the bed. "By the winds, you had us worried!"

"Not half so much as I worried myself," Harperus replied with a groan and a sigh as he tried to sit up. "I'm too old to be practicing self-healing. It is a bad habit to get into, relying on self-healing too much."

"It is a worse habit to put yourself in situations where you *need* to practice it," Nightingale scolded. By now the guards just outside the bed-chamber had heard the third voice, and one had come to investigate. He had come in at least twice so far today, fooled by T'fyrr's mimicking ability while they were practicing their music.

"Lord Harperus is awake and ready to speak," T'fyrr told him, as the man opened his mouth to ask what was going on. "While you are notifying those in authority, you ought to send a servant to bring some food for Lord Harperus—"

"Light food," Nightingale interrupted. "Suitable for an invalid. *And make sure it is tested before you serve it to him.* Remember, we do not know who attacked him, or what positions his attackers hold. They *could* work in the kitchen."

"Oh, not tea and toast!" Harperus complained, but subsided at her glare, sinking into the shadows of the bed. "Well, all right. I suppose you know best, Nightingale, you *are* healer-trained. What *are* you doing here, anyway? I thought you wouldn't promise to come here!"

"I wouldn't," she said, tartly, in the Gypsy tongue. "And *this* is the reason why! I've been here all along; I'm T'fyrr's accompanist. I just didn't want you delightful people to endanger my safety by telling everyone on the planet that I was your agent. None of you Deliambrens have an ounce of sense among you when it comes to keeping secrets."

The Deliambren sighed and lifted a hand to rub his head. He replied to her in the same language. "For once, I have to agree that you were probably right. But in our own defense, Nightingale, we never thought that anyone would resort to a direct attack."

"*A* direct attack?" T'fyrr said sharply. "There have been *three* thus far, *old friend,* one on me alone and one on Nightingale yesterday that I became involved in! That is why we were not here last night!"

"What? What?" Harperus sat up abruptly—too abruptly, for he sank back down again, holding his hand to his head. "Does Tyladen—"

"Tyladen knows all about it, since we confronted him about it this morning," Nightingale replied, glad that they had all switched to the Gypsy language, though she had not been aware that T'fyrr knew it. *Then again, with all the Gypsy songs he learned and has been learning, I suppose he would have had to. And I know Harperus has some sort of machine that puts languages into one's head.* "And since I spent the better part of an hour reciting what happened to *you* at those listening devices in T'fyrr's room, he knows about what happened to you, too."

"Whether or not he can be persuaded to come out of the safety of

Freehold to do anything to help you is another question altogether," T'fyrr added, and clacked his beak. "And this open chattering is another reason why Nightingale and I have been reluctant to work with you—you may *hope* that there is no listening post in the walls, and that no one else here knows this language, but I would not hope for it very hard! This is the Palace after all, and I would wager that the King's Spymaster has a man in every room, and an expert in every tongue on Alanda!"

Oh, well said, my love! she applauded mentally. *It isn't likely that anyone within listening distance actually does know the Gypsy tongue, but they could very easily find someone to listen, now that they know we're likely to use it among ourselves. Since I am a Gypsy, it is logical to assume that we are using that language.*

Harperus shrank down into his pillows. "I am rebuked," he said in a small voice. "Justly rebuked. And I apologize for all that has happened so far."

"Cease apologizing and start thinking how you can protect us," Nightingale replied, switching back to the common tongue. "That will be apology enough."

At that moment, both Harperus' food and the Captain of the Elite Bodyguards arrived, and Nightingale and T'fyrr got out of the way.

"Do you think we need to spend the night here?" she asked him in an undertone.

He shook his head. "There is no point in trying to silence him now," the Haspur replied. "What would be the point? If he saw anyone he knows, he'll tell the Captain. I think we can return to the suite and get some rest of our own."

She licked her lips nervously. "I wonder," she said, tentatively, "if we might leave Nob here to take care of him? They've replaced all his servants, and I'd like someone here tonight we can trust."

He blinked at her, and she sensed his speculation and growing excitement as he realized that they would be alone in the suite if they left Nob here. He was probably wondering if she meant what he thought she did. *Well, I'm wondering if I really mean what I think I do. . . .*

"I believe that would be a good idea," he replied. He beckoned to Nob, who was sitting in a chair in the corner, pretending to read.

"I'd like you to stay here with Lord Harperus tonight until we can bring him a body-servant that we know can be trusted tomorrow," T'fyrr told the boy soberly.

Nob glowed with pleasure at the implied trust. "Yes, Sire!" he said eagerly. "I'd be happy to, Sire!"

"We're relying on you, Nob," T'fyrr added. "There isn't anyone else in the Palace I trust as much as you. We're leaving his safety in your hands. I must count on you to be clever and cautious. Test his food before he eats it —watch anyone who comes in that is not one of the Royal Elite Body- guards. And if anything seems amiss, do *not* confront the person yourself, go get the Bodyguards."

The boy sobered, but continued to glow. "You can count on me, Sire T'fyrr," he replied fervently. "I won't fail your trust."

T'fyrr parted his beak in a smile. "Thank you, Nob." He waited until the Captain had finished questioning the Deliambren, then brought the boy over to Harperus' bedside.

"Well, that was a bit of bad news and good," Harperus said as the Captain left. The bed-curtains had been drawn back, and the bruise on Harperus' forehead stood out in vivid ugliness. "The bad news being that my prisoner escaped, the good that I knew one of the others by name—he was a common guard I'd had to complain about to his superior. He's likely still on duty, or at least in the Palace garrison; probably doesn't know I have a damned good memory for names and faces. They'll have him in a *real* gaol within the hour."

"We're leaving Nob with you for the night," T'fyrr told him, resting one hand on the boy's shoulder as Nob stood straight and tried desperately to look older than his years. "He's the only one we trust to see to you until we can get Tyladen to send someone from Freehold that we can rely on."

"Whatever you need, my lord, I'll take care of," the boy replied ear- nestly. "Just ask! I can do whatever you need to have done."

Harperus looked sharply from T'fyrr to Nightingale and back again, but said nothing except, "That will be welcome indeed; I know what a good body-servant Nob is. I have seen his work in your suite, T'fyrr. I appreciate it very much, both that you, T'fyrr, are willing to do without his service for one night, and that you, Nob, are willing to put in the extra hours and the effort to help me."

Now the boy blushed and dropped his gaze, nearly bursting with pride.

"We'll leave you for now," T'fyrr said gravely, his voice giving no hint of anything but weariness and concern for Harperus. "Don't overwork Nob, Old Owl."

Harperus smiled, winked, and waved them both off, then turned to Nob with instructions for drawing him a bath. T'fyrr took Nightingale's hand in his own, and the two of them left the suite together.

He didn't seem inclined to drop her hand when they entered the hall, and she didn't withdraw hers. In spite of worry, the reminders of yester- day's attack in the form of distant aches, and the deeply lurking fear the attack on Harperus had left with her, she was happier than she had been since she was a child.

In fact, the only other time she recalled being this happy was when she had first learned to invoke the Bardic Magic. *That was—oh, too many weary years ago, when the world was all new and shining, all music was a delight, and every day brought only new adventures. The world is new again, all music is pleasure, and there are more possibilities in each new day than I can count. . . .*

She knew what she was doing—

Oh, do I?

Well, she knew what she was doing, but the consequences? Did she know that as well? Could she even *guess* at the consequences?

They passed through the statue-lined hallways in silence and met no one. It was the dinner hour; most of those who lived on this floor were in the Great Hall, dining in the presence of the High King and his Advisors. Perhaps by now the word that Harperus had identified another of his attackers had made its way to the Hall. Perhaps it had not. No one would know until tomorrow that she had stayed in T'fyrr's suite.

But once again, she blushed. She did not want his name and hers in the mouths of these idle courtiers, who would speculate and gossip maliciously just out of sheer boredom. Some would use the gossip to further damage their cause with the High King. Others would use it to create whatever damage they could elsewhere.

There were Church laws about the congress of humans and those who were not—based on Holy Writ forbidding the congress of humans and demons.

Only now was she recalling those strictures; only now that there was a moment of leisure was she able to think of them. Her earlier embarrassment had probably been because, in the back of her mind, she knew that there could be trouble over this.

Oh, it was just because I knew there would be gossip, hurtful gossip. And that someone in this vast hulk would use that gossip to cause trouble for us.

"I doubt that anyone will believe that you and I are partnering," he murmured quietly, for her ears alone. Once again, he had guessed what she was thinking from the emotions her thoughts engendered. "Most of these folk hawk for game in the game preserve, you know. Most have falcons and other raptors, and know something about them. How do you tell a male raptor from a female?"

"By the size, usually," she replied vaguely, unable to guess what his meaning was. Then it occurred to her, and she bit her lips to cover a giggle. "Oh—oh of course! You *can't* tell a male from a female by sight, unless they have different feather-colorations. They don't have—what you have!"

"Precisely," T'fyrr said, dryly humorous. "Only Nob knows that I am not like a hawk in that respect, and he will take that secret to his grave if I ask it of him. The rest assume I am as externally sexless as a saint's statue. I have heard as much, through Nob. He is very good at listening and reporting what he has heard, and no one pays any attention to the pages."

So, he had discovered that for himself, had he? It was an echo of her own observation, that no one ever paid any attention to the children. Once again, their minds ran on parallel tracks!

She squeezed his hand by way of reply, and he squeezed hers in return, just as they reached the door of his suite—which now also had a pair of the Royal Bodyguards standing watch outside. T'fyrr bid them both a grave goodnight, and they returned his salutation.

When they closed the door of the suite behind them and locked it, T'fyrr paused and looked around the room. Someone had already been here, leaving the lamps lit and food in covered dishes on the sideboard. That was probably standing orders, since he had mentioned more than once that he was not welcome to dine in the Great Hall. She wondered for a moment what he was frowning at, until she saw his eyes resting on each of the "sculptures" in turn.

"Have you any idea how sensitive those are?" he asked her quietly. "Could they hear into the next room, do you think?"

She had to shake her head. "I haven't a clue," she admitted.

"Well, then since I do not believe that Tyladen is entitled to *any* vestige of my private life, and since I believe him to be as enthusiastic a voyeur as he is a coward, I think that for one night there will be *no* listening." He took each of the "sculptures" in turn and buried it under a pile of pillows and cushions thieved from the furniture.

"There," he said with satisfaction. "That should take care of that!"

He turned to her and held out his hand again. She took it, the dry, hard skin feeling warmer than usual beneath her hand. "I would like a bath," he said. "Would you?"

She nodded, unable to actually say anything.

"I do warn you," he continued, "I look altogether miserable when wet. If your romantic inclinations survive the sight of me with my feathers plastered to my skin, they will survive anything."

She smiled, suddenly shy. "I suspect they will survive," she said in a low voice. "Yours may not survive seeing me without a beautiful costume to make up for my otherwise—"

He put a talon across her lips and led her into the bathroom, where they discovered that romance survives a great many trials, and thrives on laughter.

CHAPTER NINE

Harperus was still bedridden, many days later; T'fyrr had come to make one of his morning visits.

He had not been the only visitor, but Harperus' second guest had come as the bearer of bad tidings.

The Captain of the Bodyguards left them after delivering his unwelcome news, and if a man's retreating back could signal chagrin, profound embarrassment, and disgust with a situation, his did.

It well should have.

"I cannot *believe* this!" T'fyrr exploded, once the Captain was out of the suite and out of earshot. Harperus shrugged, philosophically, from the shelter of his huge bed. The bruise on his forehead had faded to an unpleasant pale green and brown, and on the whole he was doing well. But the effects of the self-healing trance—and the exhaustion of handling what had probably been a cracked skull as well as a concussion—were longer-lasting than either of them had anticipated.

"I had actually expected something like this," the Deliambren said with a sigh. "I didn't want to say anything, lest I be seen to imply that Theovere's people are less than competent, but I was holding my breath over it. If a man can be spirited away from a locked and guarded room in the Palace, surely the city gaols are no more secure."

T'fyrr only snarled, and his talons scraped across the floor as he flexed his feet angrily.

No sooner had the man Harperus identified been arrested, taken into custody, and turned over to a city gaol, than he was free again. This time it was nothing so obvious as a guard being seduced. No, the man escaped from a locked and barred cell, and a lace handkerchief had been left in his place.

It seemed that their mysterious female adversary was not above taunting them.

Damn her. Whoever she is. She *had* to be someone either in high Court circles herself, or with connections there. There was no other way that she could have known that the man had been arrested, much less that he had been taken to a particular city gaol. There were *three* main gaols, after all, and a dozen lesser ones, never mind the many Church gaols; he could have been in any of them.

"And the King has not called for you once since my attack." Harperus pursed his lips unhappily. "He was displeased by Nightingale? Or is he displeased with your performances?"

"Not at all," T'fyrr replied bitterly. "He made a point of thanking her for coming the day after you were attacked. No, the reason is that he has a new toy to intrigue him; I am no longer a novelty. I have been subverted, it seems, by my good friend Lord Atrovel."

Harperus raised an eyebrow. "I had heard nothing of this," he said. "What new toy? And I thought Lord Atrovel liked you!"

T'fyrr sighed and flexed his feet again. "He does—but he cannot resist a challenge, and the head of the Manufactory Guild set him one. Do you recall that box of yours that plays music? The one that Theovere has hinted he would like?"

"The one that we will not give him because taking it apart would give these people too many secrets we do not want them to have?" Harperus responded. "Only too well. Why? What of it?"

"That is what Lord Atrovel was challenged to reproduce," T'fyrr told his friend sourly. "And he did it, too."

As Harperus' eyebrows shot toward his hairline, T'fyrr amended the statement. "It is *not* a recording device, nor is it small enough to sit on a table. It would fill—oh, a quarter of the room here. It is entirely mechanical, mostly of clock-work so far as I can tell, entirely human-made, and requires a page to push pedals with his feet, around and around, to power it." He brooded on his mechanical rival. "I suppose it is a kind of superior music-box. It has more than one instrument though, and three puppets to simulate playing them. There is an enameled bird—*much* prettier than I— that 'sings' the tunes, accompanied by a puppet harpist, flute player, and a puppet that plays an instrument made of tuned bells. It is all instrumental, of course—which means no awkward lyrics to remind Theovere of much of anything."

"You've seen it, then?" Harperus asked.

"How not? It was presented in open Court two days after your injury, with more ceremony than you made with me." T'fyrr stopped flexing his feet; he was cutting gouges in the floor. "It plays exactly one hundred of Theovere's favorite songs, which he can select at will."

Harperus looked impressed in spite of himself. "I had not thought they had that much ability."

T'fyrr only ground his beak. "It was pointedly said during the presentation that the device will always play exactly whatever song is desired, and play it in precisely the same way, every single time. This, I suppose, to contrast it with me, who may not cooperate in the choice of music, who sometimes sings things that make Theovere uncomfortable, and who never sings the same song in the same way twice in a row."

Harperus pondered the implications of that. "Theovere may be tiring of the novelty of working against his Advisors; he may be recalling that responsibility is work."

"And he may be weary of hearing me sing about those who take their responsibilities seriously." T'fyrr sighed. "I did not want to tell you about this, but since Theovere still seems enamored with his toy, I am afraid that I have been supplanted for the foreseeable future. I have not precisely been demoted from my rank, but I am no longer a novelty even with Nightingale to accompany me. I have not been called for in more than a week."

Harperus rubbed his temple for a moment, his face creased with worry. "I am not certain that I care for the timing of all this. Within a day of the attacks on both of us, the Manufactory Guild presents Theovere with a new toy? Does that indicate anything rather nasty to you?"

"That they thought either one or both of us might be removed from play and had their own distraction ready?" T'fyrr countered. "Of course it occurred to me. It *could* simply be good timing on their part, however—or they could have been holding this toy back, waiting for the best opportunity to present it. There is no point in assuming a conspiracy—but there is no point in discounting one, either. I wish that *you* were in place to collect Court gossip. It would be nice to know one way or another."

Harperus picked fretfully at the comforter covering his body. "And here I am, incapacitated. Trust me, Tyladen is doing all he can; he has responsibilities you are not aware of. He is not a coward, he simply cannot do his job and mine as well."

"I will believe it if you say it," T'fyrr told him finally. "Though I doubt you would get Nightingale to believe it; she is not terribly fond of Tyladen and has called him a spider sitting snug in a safe web more than once. I am not sure she cares for Deliambrens at all, right now; Tyladen hasn't done much about the troubles in Lyonarie, either. I have more bad news from outside the Palace, I am afraid. There is more unrest in the city. The situation is deteriorating for nonhumans: more beatings, slogans written on the walls of nonhuman homes and businesses, vandalism, gang ambushes outside Freehold."

"More attacks?" Harperus started to get up, and fell back against his

pillows again, turning a stark white. *"Damn!"* he swore, with uncharacter-
istic vehemence. "Why must I be confined to my bed at a time like this?"

T'fyrr only shook his head. "I have been spending more and more time
in Freehold with Nightingale. We have been trying to do what we can with
the tools at our disposal. At least there we can do some good; our music is
heard, and the message in it."

"You are preaching to the choir," Harperus reminded him. "No one
goes into Freehold that is not on the side of the nonhumans."

T'fyrr could not reply to that; he knew only too well that it was true. But
the message he and Nightingale were placing in their music was a complicated one, and one he thought would have some effect on those who might
otherwise not take a stand but would rather stand aside. He hoped, anyway. There were plenty of those, visitors to Freehold out of curiosity, or
those who only came occasionally.

*It may be that what they need is a leader, and one has not stepped forward
thus far. I had hoped Tyladen would be that leader, but I fear he is a weak
branch to land that eyas on. Harperus would, but he is not physically able.
Which leaves—us. I could do with a better prospect.*

"I must go," he said finally. "I'll probably be staying there tonight again.
It's safer than flying back, even after dark. I'll tell Nob to come here and
help you, as usual."

At least Nob would be safer with Harperus than alone in T'fyrr's suite,
especially now that Harperus had raided his traveling-wagon for more
protective devices. Tyladen had actually ventured out of Freehold to fetch
the mechanisms and to set them up in Harperus' room—while Old Owl
was well enough in mind and spirit after his ordeal, he needed someone to
look after him. So Nob could be useful *and* protected by staying with the
Deliambren. Right now, T'fyrr would be much happier if he were working
alone—but since that was impossible, better to get those who were not
flying the attack under cover of the trees.

"Thank you," Harperus said with real gratitude. "The boy is an endless
help. I'm thinking of checking where he came from and offering to purchase his services if he hasn't any parents about. We can use young humans like him in the Fortress-City."

"What, in your—ah, what did you call it? The 'exchange program'?"
T'fyrr asked, getting up from his stool. "He'd be good there; he has an
open mind, and a clever one, and I have to keep restraining him from
taking apart your devices to see how they work."

Harperus held up a hand just as T'fyrr began to walk toward the door.
"Wait a moment, please. You and Nightingale—" he began.

What? Is he going to try to interfere there *now? I think not!*

T'fyrr shook his head and began an annoyed retort, but Harperus waved his hand before he could begin to form it.

"No, no, I don't mean to tell you to leave her alone—dear Stars, that's the last thing I'd want for either of you!" T'fyrr relaxed a little at that, and Harperus continued, with an expression of concern on his face. "I just want to know if—if you are weathering these stresses as a couple. I want to know that the two of you are still together and not being torn apart by the situation."

"Better than we would alone," T'fyrr said softly. "Much, much better than we would alone. She is the one unreservedly good thing that has happened to me since I came here. I tell her so, at least twice a day."

Harperus smiled, his odd eyes warming with the smile. "Good. Good. I feel rather paternal about both of you, you know. I have known her for most of her life—and if it were not for me, you would not be in the Twenty Kingdoms at all." He hesitated a moment, as if deciding whether or not to say something, then continued. "I want you to know that whatever I can do for both of you, I will. You have both been involved in situations you would never have had to deal with if it were not for me. I am very, very pleased that the two of you have found happiness in each other."

T'fyrr looked down on the Deliambren, sensing nothing there but sincerity. "I think I knew that," he said finally. "But thank you anyway." He shook himself, rousing all his feathers, and bits of fluff and feather sheath flew through the air. "Now I *must* go. Nightingale is waiting, and we have work in the city, even if I have none here."

Harperus nodded, and T'fyrr took himself out, via Harperus' balcony. It was safer that way; he no longer trusted even the corridors and hallways of the Palace.

He no longer made a target of himself by flying low over the city; he gained altitude while he was still over the Palace grounds, taking himself quickly out of the range of conventional weaponry. He would drop down out of the sky in a stoop, once he was directly over Freehold, landing on the roof, though never twice in exactly the same place. He hoped that this made him less of a target for projectiles from the other roofs, although a skilled hunter could probably track him in and hit him—

He tried not to think about that. He was no longer the only target in this city. He had not wanted to worry Harperus further by giving him details of the troubles in Lyonarie, but it was no longer safe for most nonhumans to walk alone in certain districts even by day—and by night, they must not only go in large groups, but they must go armed with such weapons as the laws permitted them. Some of them had gotten immensely clever with weighted clubs, tough leather jackets, and things that could legitimately be considered their "tools."

They were harassed and attacked by pairs and large gangs of bravos armed with clubs. There had been no deaths—yet—but at least a hundred males, two dozen females, and a handful of children of various nonhuman races had wound up with broken bones or concussions. That was not even detailing the beatings that left only bruises, or simple harassment or vandalism.

Nor was Harperus' attacker the only escapee from justice in the King's gaols; even when attackers and vandals were identified and brought to justice, the very next day they would no longer be in the gaol. Some were released "by accident," some released when other parties posted bonds, and some simply slipped away.

There were ugly rumors in the streets, making even ordinary folk look angry whenever nonhumans were mentioned. One of those rumors claimed that the Manufactory Guild planned to release all of the human workers and import nonhumans, since they were not subject to the laws of the Church. As miserable as working conditions were inside those buildings, apparently having any job was better than being out of work, and the folk who filled those mills and tended the machinery were looking blackly at any nonhuman who crossed their paths.

Other rumors were wilder, less believable, yet some people believed them: that the nonhumans had a new religion that required each new initiate to sacrifice a human child and eat it: that they were spreading diseases deliberately among the humans to weaken or kill them, softening up Lyonarie for future conquest; that the Deliambrens were going to bring in a huge, invulnerable, flying ship and from it lay waste to the Twenty Kingdoms, turning each of the kingdoms over to a specific nonhuman race and making the humans into slaves.

As if we'd want humans as slaves. They'd make poor slaves; not as strong as a Mintak, not as versatile as a Jrrad, not as obedient as a Fenboi. They are too self-determined, strong-willed and clever to be slaves. The spirit that makes them poor slaves is what makes them good friends.

T'fyrr reached the top of his arc, turned, and plunged downward again, his goal a tiny speck among the rest of the rooftops below him. Wind rushed past his face, tore at his feathers, thundered in his ears; he brought the nictating membranes over his eyes to protect them. At this speed, striking a gnat or a speck of dust could bring much pain and temporary blindness.

That last rumor was interesting, since it had just enough truth to supply a seed for the falsehood. The Deliambrens *were* bringing in a huge flying ship; the platform from which they were doing their intensive survey. It wasn't armed, couldn't be armed, in fact, nor was it invulnerable. It leaked air like a sieve, and couldn't go much higher than treetop level. But it did exist, and to the ignorant, it must look frightening enough. It was certainly larger than most villages and many small towns, and the vast array of nonhumans swarming over it might be taken for an army. The strange surveying instruments often looked like weapons, and the engines that bore it up in the air did sometimes flatten things below. That was one of the reasons for getting the High King's blanket permission to mount the expedition; to keep people from panicking at the sight of it, thinking it was a military operation.

As for turning humans into nonhuman slaves, now *that* was a clever twisting of the truth, since that was precisely what some of the humans were trying to do to the nonhumans in their midst.

The Law of Degree would do that very nicely.

The rooftop of Freehold rushed up toward him, filling his vision; he flared his wings at the last possible moment, and the air wrenched them open as if they'd been grabbed by a giant and pulled apart. He flipped forward in midair, extending his legs toward the rooftop as he flared his tail as an additional brake. His feet touched the surface; he collapsed his wings and dropped down into a protective crouch, glaring all around him for possible enemies.

As usual, there weren't any. As usual, he was not willing to take the chance that there might be some.

Neither was Nightingale. She slipped out of the shelter of one of the cowlings covering some of Freehold's enormous machines, but stayed within reach of other such machinery as she joined him.

But for one transcendent moment, all caution and fear was cast aside as they embraced.

As always.

Ah, my bright love, my singing bird, my winged heart—She could not hear the endearments he whispered to her in his mind, but he knew she certainly felt the emotion that came with them. Whatever happened, they had this between them—a joy he had never expected to find. If tomorrow a hunter's arrow found him, he would go to the winds with a prayer of thanks for having had this much.

"Anything new?" he asked into the sweet darkness of her hair.

"More of the same," she replied into his breast feathers. "I'll tell you inside."

They sprinted for the door to the roof, hand in hand, but ducking to remain out of the line of sight of possible snipers. Once they were safely on the staircase, she sighed and gave him the news.

"Outright sabotage, this time," she said. "Three incidents, all uncovered this morning. Someone burned down a Lashan-owned bakery; the printing presses at Kalian Bindery were smashed, the page proofs and manuscripts there were burned, and the type cases overturned all over the floor. And the furnaces at the new Ursi glassworks were—just blown up. They say that no more than two bricks out of every five will be salvageable."

"How?" T'fyrr asked astonished. "That doesn't sound like anything a human could do!"

She shrugged. "Tyladen has some theory about pouring water into the furnaces while they were hot; I don't know. But do you see a pattern there?"

He nodded; living at the Palace as he was, he would be the first to see it. "The glassworks was in the process of making a special telescope for Theovere as a presentation piece on behalf of the Deliambren expedition. Kalian Bindery was putting together a library of nonhuman songs in translation—as a presentation piece for Theovere. And the bakery makes those honey-spice cakes he likes so much, that his own cooks at the Palace can't seem to duplicate."

"All three, places with projects on behalf of Theovere or meant to impress him and gain his favor," she agreed as they wound their way down the stairs toward the ground floor, his talons clicking on the stair steps. "And only someone at Court would know that, just as you have been saying."

He ground his beak, thinking. "The man Harperus identified escaped last night as well. And everyone who has escaped has done so from the *High King's* city prisons. Not the Church prisons, or the city gaols."

She turned to look at him with her eyes wide. "Why—that's right! The few criminals we *have* managed to hold onto were all in the city gaols!"

"That argues for more than an informant," he said, his eyes narrowing with concentration. "That argues for cooperation, at the very least, from an official. Probably a high official. Likely an Advisor."

She didn't groan, but he sensed her spirits plummeting. "How can we possibly counteract someone with that much power?" she asked in a small voice. He felt her fear; she was not used to opposition at so high a level. She had always been the one to run when opposition grew too intense. He understood that, and in the past it had made sense for her to do that. She was a Gypsy; she could go anywhere, so why remain someplace where an authority wanted to make trouble for her?

But she could not do that now—and more importantly, neither could all the nonhuman citizens, not only of Lyonarie, but of the Twenty Kingdoms.

If they were going to do what he had decided *must* be done—to give the nonhumans here the leader they so urgently, desperately, needed—he had to put some heart in her.

He stopped, seized her by the shoulders, and looked deeply into her eyes. "Think, Nightingale! Think of how much damage has been done in the past few days—as if our enemy was desperately trying to do as much damage as he can before he is caught or rendered ineffective! I think he *is* desperate, that although Theovere may be wrapped up in his new toy, the novelty of it can't last forever. Sooner or later he will grow tired of the same songs, played the same way, and look for us again. What is more, I think the magic we set in motion is still working, and Theovere is coming back to himself, whether or not he *likes* the fact. And I think our enemy knows that, too. I believe he *is* at the end of his resources, and he's hoping to overwhelm us now, before Theovere recovers."

"She," Nightingale said. "Our enemy may be a female. Remember the lace handkerchiefs left in cells, the woman who seduced the guard? A woman's been seen in other places as well, just before things happened."

"She, then. He or she, or they, it doesn't matter much. There may be two, working in collusion—whoever it is, I sense the desperation of a hunter-turned-hunted." He waited for Nightingale's reaction; it was slow in coming, but gradually the fear within her ebbed, and she nodded.

"Now, let's get down to the street, collect Tyladen's friends, and go about our business," T'fyrr continued, after first embracing her. "Father Ruthvere is waiting for us. It is time for us to act, instead of waiting for something to happen to us and reacting to that."

"What are you thinking of?" she asked sharply.

"We need to provide these people with more than a message," he told her slowly, thinking things out as he spoke. "We need to give them something more than words. Tyladen won't do it, and Harperus can't."

"You're saying they need a leader," she said, and to his relief she did not seem as upset at that as he had feared she would be. "I had a feeling you were finally going to decide that—and I was afraid you would decide it should be us." She shivered a little, then shook herself. "I'm also afraid that you're right. If no one has come forward yet, no one is going to. It will have to be us, or no one."

She looked up into his eyes, standing quite still; making no secret of the fact that she was afraid, but also making it very clear that she was with him.

He embraced her impulsively. "Great power—" he reminded her.

"Yes, is great responsibility." She sighed. "I think I would prefer being a simple musician—but on the other hand, this may be the payback for all those times I charmed my way out of trouble." She leaned into his breast feathers for a moment, then pushed herself gently away. "Well, if we are going to do it, let's get it over with."

He smiled, and took her hand. "Leadership, once assumed, cannot always be released. Are you willing to accept that as well, lover?"

Nightingale nodded again, eyes suddenly clear of worry. "As readily as I accepted you into my heart and soul."

Three days later, T'fyrr stood in a most unfamiliar place—the pulpit of Father Ruthvere's Chapel—and surveyed the closely packed faces below him. There was no room to stand in the Chapel; people were crowded in right to the doors. Roughly half of those faces were not human, but it was the human faces among the rest that gave him hope that this might work.

He cleared his throat, and the quiet murmur of voices below him ceased. Behind him, Nightingale sent a wordless wave of encouragement to him, which held him in an embrace that did not need arms or wings. They were going to try something different today: Bardic magic without a melody, a spell of courage and hope, meant to reinforce his message and give them the strength to take advantage of the leadership he promised them. With luck, it would work.

With none, we will fall flat on our faces.

"I asked Father Ruthvere to call some of you here on my behalf," he said slowly, allowing his eyes to travel over the entire group assembled below. "Some of you are friends or patrons of Freehold. Some are simply merchants and workers; all of you are people of good will and open minds. I ask you all to open your minds a little further, for I have a message that may shock you. There is an enemy of *all* of us, human and nonhuman, working in this city, and he is working to enslave us."

He waited for a moment for them to take that in, then continued. "Our enemy is skilled, cunning and devious; our enemy's weapons are clever. The chief of them is fear. He spreads rumors to increase that fear and divide us, each rumor carefully calculated to prey upon the things that we all fear most."

He looked directly into the eyes of a clutch of human manufactory workers. "Fear of poverty," he said to them. "Fear of failure. Fear of a future full of uncertainty." And he knew that he had struck home when he saw their eyes widen.

He turned toward a group of families, human and not, who lived near the Chapel. "The terrible fears that all parents of whatever race have for their children." This bolt too struck the heart, as the hands of fathers tightened on their children's shoulders—mothers' arms closed protectively around their babies.

He swept his gaze over them all. "These fears divide us, each from the other," he told them. "They make us fear each other and keep us from talking to each other. Let me tell you who are human what rumors have been circulating among *our* homes and workplaces."

He told them about the Law of Degree, about the other rumors flying wildly among the nonhuman communities. He added some he had heard elsewhere—how a demon-worshiping *human* sect had sprung up, whose initiates must murder and eat a *nonhuman* child, and how the humans were planning to descend on the homes and workplaces of nonhumans on a particular night to burn and pillage them, killing adults and making children into pets and slaves. He added the rumors of drugs in the water supply that would kill or incapacitate nonhumans but were harmless to humans, and the stories that there were those within the Church who planned to declare all nonhumans to be demons or descended of demons.

He saw by the startled looks among the humans that they had heard nothing of these tales—and as he and Nightingale wove their web of courage and clarity, he saw that they were all beginning to *think,* comparing the rumors and finding them suspiciously similar.

"Do you see what is happening?" he asked them. "Can you see the hand of *one* source behind all of this? How could these tales be so similar, and yet so cleverly tailored to match our darkest nightmares? And how else could someone keep all of us from even speaking to one another, except by making us fear one another?" Then he challenged them. "Can you think *why* someone would do this? What would he have to gain? Ask yourself that—for there is gain to be had here, in making us fear each other, in keeping us hiding in the darkness of our homes and listening only to rumors and wild tales."

He chose his next words with care. "For all that I am strange to you who are human, I am a student of your history. I have seen this pattern repeated before—in your history, and in our own, for we are not as different from you as you may think. *We* have had our tyrants, our exploiters, our would-be dictators. Here is what I have seen, over and over again. When people are divided against one another, there is *always* a third party standing ready and waiting to profit when both sides have preyed so much upon each other that they cannot withstand the third. Sometimes it is another land, another people, but I do not think that is the case here." He took a deep breath, and made the plunge. "I think that the third party here is a single person; a person who would see both humans and nonhumans enslaved to his purposes. First he drives fear enough into the humans that they grant him the power he needs to make slaves of the nonhumans. *Then* he turns that power upon those who gave it to him, and enslaves everyone."

There were a few nods out there; only a few, but that much was encouraging. The rest would need time to think about what he was saying.

"Ponder this, if you will," he finished. "How soon would it be before something like a Law of Degree was applied, not only to those who do not *look* human, but to those who do not meet some other standard? When have any of you ever seen a law that took away the freedom of one group used *only* against that group? How about if our unknown enemy convinced you all that it should be applied to the indigent—street trash, beggars, and the like? It sounds reasonable, does it not? And who would really choose to have beggars and slackards sleeping in doorways, if they could be out doing useful work—and at least, as slaves, they would not be drinking, robbing, causing trouble in the street. But how if, after a delay of time to make it comfortable, it was then applied to those who—say—do not own property? After all, if you do not own your home, are you not indigent? What if it were applied to those who did not have a business, were not in a Guild, or happened not to have a job at a particular moment? After all, if you have lost your job, are you not indigent?"

Startled looks all around the room showed him that he had not only caught their attention, he had brought up something they had never in their wildest dreams thought of. Very probably the majority of the humans here only rented their tiny living-quarters from someone else—and every manufactory worker lived in fear of losing his job.

"Before you dismiss these truths as fantasy, remember that every one of you who has been robbed, cheated or raped—or knows someone who has, human or nonhuman—knows that there are those in our world who are capable of such evils. Remember that it is *fear* that makes all this possible," he concluded. "Fear which keeps us from organizing, from questioning to find out the truth, which keeps us divided, human from nonhuman, men from women, those who are prosperous from those who are not. Remember that, go and think and talk and ask questions; and then, if you will, come back to Father Ruthvere. He is a man of caring and courage, and he has tasks that need doing to make certain that this enemy does *not* take all our freedom away from us."

He stepped down from the pulpit then, in an aura of stunned silence, and Father Ruthvere stepped back up into it.

Then the talk broke out, an avalanche of words, as those of the Chapel and those who were not cast questions up to Father Ruthvere, and he answered them as best he could.

His best was fairly accurate, since he, Nightingale and T'fyrr had been talking about this for the past three days, gathering all the information they could and putting this little meeting together. They had decided that Father Ruthvere, and not T'fyrr, should be the putative leader of this group; he was human and would be trusted by the humans—he was a man of the Church, and presumably honorable and above reproach. Not that the real leader would not be T'fyrr—

Or rather, the real target. I am the obvious target, leaving Father Ruthvere to do his work.

Fortunately, the Father *was* honorable and above reproach, and he was trained to be a leader of his flock. He had the skills T'fyrr did not; T'fyrr had the skills of rhetoric that he did not.

Perhaps, rather than the leader, I should style myself as a figurehead. Or perhaps an organizer? Oh, no, I believe I like Nightingale's term better: "rabble-rouser."

But standing behind the pulpit and filling the choir loft was another group that T'fyrr and Nightingale turned to face—as many of Father Ruthvere's fellow Churchmen as could be gathered together here at such short notice. T'fyrr had not had a chance to look them over before he stepped up to make his speech, but now he saw that among the grey, black, and brown robes, there were two men dressed in the red robes of Justiciars, two men and a woman in the deeper burgundy of Justiciar Mages, and one iron-faced individual in the white and purple robes of a Bishop.

His hackles rose for just a moment at that—but a heartbeat later, he smoothed them down. While the face of this man might be implacable, his eyes were warm and full of approval. He had heard T'fyrr out, and he seemed to like what he heard.

He knows the truth when he hears it. He is hard and cannot be shaken, but he is no fanatic. He knows reason; he does not let fear blind him. And he is no one's tool or fool.

It was this man who approached them first, while Nightingale swallowed and groped for T'fyrr's hand. He clasped it, reassuringly. The Bishop's eyes flickered down to their joined hands as the motion caught his attention, then they returned to T'fyrr's face with no less warmth in them than before.

And he sees nothing wrong with a human and one who is not being together. That alone shows more of an open mind than I had dared to hope for.

"You are a remarkable speaker, musician," the old man said in a surprisingly powerful and musical voice. "Your command of rhetoric is astounding."

T'fyrr bowed a little, acknowledging the compliment. "It is not just rhetoric, my Lord Bishop," he said in reply. "Every word I spoke was the truth, all of it information gathered not only across this city, but across the Twenty Kingdoms."

"That is what makes it astounding," the Bishop said with a hint of a smile. "Rhetoric and the truth seldom walk side-by-side, much less hand-in-hand. And that was what I wished to ask you, for some of those rumors I had not heard in this city. So the poison spreads elsewhere?"

T'fyrr nodded, and the Bishop pursed his lips thoughtfully. "That seems to match some things that I have observed within the Church," he mused.

"And—I believe I agree with you and your friends. There is a force moving to destroy our freedoms, a secular force, but one with fingers into all aspects of life, including the Church. Would you not agree, Ardis?" he called over his shoulder.

The woman in the robes of the Justiciar Mages stepped forward, regarding T'fyrr with eyes that were remarkably like that of a Haspur—clear, direct and uncompromising. "I would agree, my Lord Bishop," she said in a challenging voice as remarkable as the Bishop's. "That, in fact, was why I was visiting my friend Ruthvere. His letters indicated to me that there were some of the same elements moving in Lyonarie as had been at work in Kingsford just before the fire that destroyed our city. I wanted to see if that was the case and do something to prevent a similar tragedy if I could."

A thread of excitement traced its way down T'fyrr's back, but it did not come from him but from Nightingale. She knew something about this woman—something important. He would have to ask her later—

But then the woman turned her eyes toward Nightingale and said, in a tone as gentle as her voice had been challenging before, "Please tell my good cousin Talaysen that I miss his company—and far more than his company, his wisdom and his gentle wit, and if his King can spare him for a month or two, I have need of both in Kingsford. It need not be soon, but it should be within a year or so."

Nightingale bowed her head in deepest respect—something T'fyrr had never seen her do before to anyone. "I shall, my Lady Priest," she replied. "I believe that I can send him word that will reach him before the month is out. I will tell him to direct his reply to you with all speed."

The Justiciar Mage smiled. "I had thought as much," she said, and turned back to the Bishop. "My noble lord, are you satisfied now that Ruthvere and I told you nothing less than the truth?"

"More than satisfied—I am in fact convinced that there is more amiss than even you guessed." He extended his hand to T'fyrr, who took it—a little confused, since he was not certain if he was to shake it or bow over it. The Bishop solved his quandary by simply clasping it firmly, with no sign that the alien feel of the talon disturbed him. "Sire T'fyrr, I thank you for your courage and your integrity—and your dedication. Rest assured that there are enough men and women of God in the Church to take the reins of the situation there and bring it under control. I wish that I could promise you help in the secular world as well, but I fear it will be all our forces can muster to cleanse our own house. At least you need not look for attack on one front."

He let go of T'fyrr's hand then, and turned toward the rest of the Priests. "My brothers and sisters—it is now our task to go and do just that. Let us be off."

With that, he strode through the group, which parted before him and formed up behind him, and led the way to the Priest's door at the rear of the choir loft. They were remarkably well organized and regimented; within moments they were all gone, with no milling about or confusion.

He glanced over at Nightingale. "What was that business with the woman all about?" he asked.

Nightingale shivered, but not from any sense of fear, more of a sense of awe, a reaction he had not expected a Priest to invoke in her.

"Lady Ardis is Master Wren's cousin," she said quietly. "Talaysen trusts her more than anyone else in the world, I think. I knew she was a Priest, but I *didn't* know she was a Justiciar Mage! They may be the strongest mages in the Twenty Kingdoms—and I know that they are the best schooled. Could you hear the power in her?"

Now that he thought about it, there *had* been a deep and resonant melody about her, though not of the kind he associated with Bardic Magic. Not precisely droning—more like the kind of chant that he recalled from Nightingale's healing magic. But stronger, richer, with multiple voices. He nodded.

"I've never heard anyone like that," Nightingale continued. "Never! With power like that, she doesn't *need* rank; in fact, high rank would only get in her way." Exultation crept into her voice. "And she's on *our* side! Oh, T'fyrr, this is the best thing that could have happened to us!"

Father Ruthvere turned his head toward them for a moment. "Between Ardis and the Lord Bishop, we do not need to worry about the Church aiding our enemy, I think," he said, his voice sounding more relaxed and confident than in the past several days. "As the Bishop said, this means one less front to guard; it means that I have leave to do whatever I can to help you, including offering you the sanctuary of the Church if you need it."

"And it means one less ally for our enemy," T'fyrr added. But Father Ruthvere was not finished.

"I do have another concern that Lady Ardis' presence reminded me of. There is one other thing I believe you have not made accounting for," he said, and worry entered his voice again. "Magic. Our enemy has not been able to silence you by direct attack, or by indirect. That leaves magic. Ardis and her companions cannot stay for they will be needed in Kingsford, and there are no Justiciar Mages in Lyonarie who can devote themselves to your protection."

Magic! That *was* one thing he had not counted on! He had witnessed so little magic in his life, and most of it was of the subtler sort, the kind that Nightingale used. "But what can they do?" he asked, puzzled. "Surely anything magical can be countered."

But Nightingale's hand had tightened on his own spasmodically. "They can do quite a bit, T'fyrr," she said hesitantly, "if they have a powerful enough mage. I have seen real magic, the kind that the Deliambrens do not believe exists. If I told you some of what I have witnessed, you would not believe it either. I think perhaps I had better call in someone I had not intended to ask favors of—"

He shrugged, unconvinced. "If you will," he said. "You know more about this than I do. But in the meantime, I will not be stopped. We have momentum now, and we must keep it going! Any hesitation at this moment will bring everything to a standstill!"

Father Ruthvere nodded agreement, and turned his attention back to the assembled group below. The crowd had thinned somewhat, but those remaining were the leaders of their own little coteries. And all of them, human and nonhuman, seemed inspired to work together.

"We need to get back to Freehold," T'fyrr said in an aside to Nightingale, as the bells in the tower overhead chimed the hour. "We still have the meeting there this afternoon. *That* will be as much your meeting as mine."

She knew the folk of Freehold, the customers, the staff. She knew them the way he never could, for she had been reading their feelings for the past several weeks. He might be able to make a fine speech to rouse those who were unaware of what was going on around them, but for those of Freehold who knew only too well the rumors circulating, the harassment, and the sabotage, it would take another skill to rouse their courage and show them that they must work together—that they literally *dared* not stand aside at this moment.

She squeezed his hand. "I think Father Ruthvere has this end well in hand," she agreed. "Let's go."

Perhaps T'fyrr didn't realize it, but Nightingale knew only too well how much of a target he had made himself. *He* was the obvious focal point of this new organization; *he* was the King's Personal Musician, the one who came and went from the Palace, who presumably had the King's ear at least part of the time. On his own, he had no more power or wealth than any of the denizens of the neighborhoods around Freehold, but *they* didn't know that. The folk of the streets saw only that here was a powerful courtier, a Sire, no less, who was urging them to stand up for their freedom and their rights against the nobles, the fearful or uneducated, and this unknown enemy.

And Ruthvere had been absolutely right. Their enemy had tried every other way to eliminate T'fyrr's influence, and that had been *before* he went on his campaign to organize the nonhumans and their human supporters and friends. Now he was not only an influence, he was a danger. He reminded them all that the Twenty Kings, the Court, and the High King himself ruled only as long as the people permitted it.

Those were frightening words to someone whose ultimate goal was surely more power.

If there was one thing that the powerful feared, it was that those they sought to rule discovered that ultimately the real power lay only in their own acquiescence to be ruled.

Lions can only be convinced that they are sheep as long as no one holds up a mirror to show them their true faces.

All attempts to silence T'fyrr, open and covert had failed. But their foe had not yet tried magic. If ever there was a time when he—

Or she, Nightingale reminded herself, yet again.

—or she, would use magic, it was now.

They had a little time before the Freehold meeting, and Nightingale used it.

T'fyrr was in the bathroom, and he was a most enthusiastic bather. He would be in there for some time, giving her a space all to herself.

She settled herself cross-legged on her bed as T'fyrr splashed water all over her bathroom, and laid her right wrist in her lap. The thin band of Elven silver gleamed beneath the lights of her room, a circlet of starlight or moonlight made solid.

She had been given a gift, she had thought; could it be that it was not a gift after all, but a promise? The Elves had a flexible view of time; sometimes their vision slipped ahead of human vision—seeing not what *would* be, but all of the possibilities of what *might* be. And sometimes, when one was markedly better than the rest, they would move to see that it came to pass.

No one with ambition for ruling all the Twenty Kingdoms could afford to let the Elves live in peace, she thought soberly. *They are too random an element: unpredictable and unreliable, and most of all, ungovernable. Whoever this person is, he cannot allow the Elves to remain within human borders. So perhaps that is why the second bracelet came to me.*

She laid her left hand over the warm circle of silver and closed her eyes. As she held her mind in stillness, listening, she caught the distant melody of Elven Magic, so utterly unlike any other music except that of the Gypsies.

She added her own to it, brought it in, and strengthened it. It must carry her message for her, and it had a long, long way to travel.

She sang to it, deep within her mind, weaving her words into the melody, to be read by every Elf that encountered it. The more that knew, the better.

First, her name, which was more than just a name; it was the signature of her own power, her history, and her place among her Elven allies. *Bird of song, and bird of night,* she sang, *Healing Hands and Eyeless Sight. Bird of passage, Elven friend, walks the road without an end. Pass the wall that has no door, sail the sea that has no shore—*

No one but the Elves would know what three-fourths of that meant; it was all in riddles and allusions, and if there was anything that the Elves loved, it was the indirect. There was more of it, and she sang it all. One did not scant on ceremony with the Elves, especially not with *their* High King. He might have been her lover, once—but that had been a long time ago, before he became their High King. It had been nothing more than a moment's recreation for him, and scarcely more for her. He had been the ease after Raven—a physical release. She had been—amusement. Later she became more than that, once he learned of her power and heard her play; *that* was what had made her an Elven friend, not the idyll amid the pillows of his most private bower.

But that was part of her history with them, and she could not leave it out without insulting him.

When she came to the end of her Name, she began the message; first, a condensation of everything she had learned here, beginning with the fact that it was the Elves who had asked her to come here in the first place.

And lastly, her request, a simple one. It was couched in complicated rhyme, but the essence was not at all complicated. *I may need you and your magic, and if I do, my need will be a desperate one. You know me, you know that I would not ask this frivolously; if I call, will you come?*

She had not expected an answer immediately. She had no idea, after all, how far this message would have to travel, or how many times it would be debated in the Elven councils before a reply was vouchsafed her.

She had most definitely not expected a *simple* answer. She had never gotten a simple answer more than a handful of times in all the years she had known them.

So when she sent the message out, and sat for a moment with her mind empty and her hand still clasping her bracelet, it was not with any expectation of something more than a moment of respite before T'fyrr emerged from his bath.

But she got far more than she had reckoned on.

The spell of music and message she had sent out had been a delicate, braided band of silver and shadow. The reply caught her unawares and wrapped her in a rushing wind, spun her around in a dizzying spiral of steel-strong starlight, surrounded her with bared blades of ice and moon-beams, and sang serenely into her heart in a voice of trumpets and the pounding sea.

And all of it, a simple, single word.

YES.

When T'fyrr emerged from the bathroom, he found her still shaking with reaction and the certainty that if their reply had been so ready and so simple, there must be a reason. So she sat, and trembled, and she could not even tell him why. She could only smile and tell him it was nothing to worry about.

She moved through the day holding onto each moment, savoring every scrap of time with him—but trying her best to act as if nothing had changed between them. He knew there was something wrong, of course, but she was able to convince him that it was only her own fears getting the best of her. She told him that she would be all right; and she bound herself up in the rags of her courage and went on with all their plans.

But when the blow came, as she had known it would, it still came as a shock.

He had spent the night at the Palace, hoping for a summons from the High King, but not really expecting one. She was expecting him in mid-morning, as always; she sensed his wild surge of delight as he took to the air, and went to the roof to await his arrival.

She shaded her eyes with her hand and peered upwards into the blue and cloudless sky, even though she knew she would never see him up there. It would take the eyes of an eagle to pick out the tiny dot up there; if she'd had a hawk on her wrist, it *might* have looked up and hunched down on her fist, feathers slicked down in fear, all of its instincts telling it that a huge eagle flew up there. Nothing less than a hawk's keen senses would find T'fyrr in the hot blue sky, until the moment he flattened out his dive into a landing.

But she always looked, anyway.

She was looking up when the blow struck her heart, and she collapsed onto the baked surface of the roof, breath caught in her throat, mouth opened in a soundless cry of anguish.

It was pain, the mingling of a hundred fears, a wash of dizziness and a wave of darkness. She could not breathe—could not see—

She blacked out for a moment, but fought herself free of the tangling shroud of unconsciousness, and dragged herself back to reality with the sure knowledge that her worst nightmare had come to pass.

They had taken T'fyrr, snatched him out of the sky by magic.

And there was nothing that anyone could have done to prevent it, for the sky was the one place where they had thought he was safe.

T'fyrr was gone.

* * *

"You're sure?" Tyladen said for the tenth time. She bit her lip, and said nothing. She'd already told him everything there was to say, at least three times over.

But Harperus, who had a listening device of his own, growled at both of them from his room in the Palace, his voice coming through a box on Tyladen's desk. "Of course she is sure, you fool! Didn't I just tell you that he left here an hour ago? He went straight from my balcony—and he was going directly to Freehold! If Nightingale says he was kidnapped, then you can take it as fact!"

"B-but magic—" Tyladen stuttered. "How can you kidnap someone with something that doesn't—"

"These people believe that what we do is magic, child," Harperus interrupted. "If you must, assume it's a different technology; for all *we* know, that's exactly what it is! Just accept it and have done! Nightingale, what can we do, if anything?"

She had thought this out as best she could, given that her stomach was in knots, her throat sore from the sobs she would not give way to, and her heart ready to burst with grief and fear. "I don't know yet," she said honestly. "I'm not certain how you can combat magic. I have to do something myself—I was promised help from the Elves, and I'm going to get that help when I am through talking to you. I think that I can find T'fyrr myself, or at least find the general area where he's being held. After that— I may need some of your devices, if there are any that could find exactly where he is in a limited area." She had some vague notion there were devices that could probably do that, some Deliambren equivalent of a bloodhound, but that those devices probably had a limited range. They couldn't scour the whole city for her, but if she could give them a small area, they might be able to narrow down the search to a specific building. "I do need someone to watch the High King and the Advisors around him. Father Ruthvere will provide sanctuary if we are being hunted from the Palace, or by someone connected with the Palace, but I need to be warned if someone comes up with a charge against us. If you can think of anything—"

"I will take care of it," Harperus promised. "Now—you go do what you can."

"I will—" Then her voice did break on a sob as she told him the one thing she *did* know. "Old Owl, wherever he is, he's hurt. He's hurt badly. I don't know *how* badly, but all I can feel from him is pain—"

Harperus swore in his own language, a snarl of pure rage. She had never heard him so angry in her life.

"Go—" he urged. "This youngster and I will work together."

She rubbed at her burning eyes with the back of her hand, got up from her seat, pushed open the office door half-blinded with tears, and fled up the stairs to her room. She had not yet called in her promise from the Elves, and she needed to prepare the room before she could do that.

The Elves did not care for the human cities and did not like to walk among the artificial buildings, but it seemed that for her sake, they would put their dislikes aside. She put the bed up into the wall, and pushed all the furniture out of the way. She put her harps in the bathroom. She swept every vestige of dust and dirt from the floor so that it was as white and shiny as the day the surface was laid. Only then did she lay ready the circle with a thin trickle of blue sand on the white floor, inscribing a pattern that the Elven mage she had been pledged service from would be able to use as a target.

Then she stood outside the circle, clasped her hand around her bracelet, and let her heart cry out a wordless wail of anguish and a plea for help.

The air in her room vibrated with a single, deep tone, like the groaning of the earth in an earthquake; the floor sang a harmonic note to the air, the walls a second, the ceiling a third, the whole room humming with a four-part chord of dreadful power.

Then the blue sand exploded upward in a puff of displaced air.

She did not recognize the Elven mage who stood where the circle had been, blinking slowly at her with his amber eyes slitted against the light. His hair was as amber as his eyes; his clothing of deep black silk, a simple tunic and trews without ornamentation or embroidery of any kind. By that, she knew he was more powerful than any Elven mage she had ever yet met; only a mage of great power would be confident enough to do without the trappings of power.

"Tell me, Bird of Night," he said as calmly as if he had not appeared out of thin air in her room, so alien to his kind; as serenely as if he had not heard the tears of her heart calling. "Tell me what you need of me."

She told him in the same words that she had told Tyladen and Harperus, and it did not get any easier to bear for the retelling. He nodded and waited for her to answer his second question.

"From you, my lord, I need protection," she said. "Protection from the spells of human mages, for myself, and for the one who once wore this—"

She handed the Elf a feather, shed only yesterday from T'fyrr's wing. He took it and smoothed it between his fingers.

"A mage-musician, with wings in truth," he said, as his eyes took on the appearance of one who is gazing into the far distance. "But he is in a place that is dark to me; I cannot find him."

"I can find him," she said promptly. "But I cannot protect myself from the magics that stole him, nor can I protect him from the spells of our enemy, once I find him."

"I can," the Elven mage replied, with a lifted brow. "There is no mortal born who can set a spell that can break my protections, if those protections are set with consent."

She nodded, understanding his meaning. With consent, the mage was not limited to his own power in setting a protection; he could draw upon the strength of the spirit of the one he protected as well.

"You have mine," she promised him instantly, "and you will have his, once I reach him."

"Then I will be away," the mage replied, and as she widened her eyes in alarm, he smiled thinly. "Fear not, I do not desert you, nor shall I travel far, but I must go to a place more congenial to my kind. Your walls and metals interfere with my working. I have his feather, you have your Silver. That will be enough. When you need the protections, clasp your hand about the band of Silver, and call me." He regarded her with an unwinking gaze, and then added, "I am Fioreth."

She bowed slightly, acknowledging the fact that he had given her part of his Name, enough to call him with. It was a tremendous act of trust on the part of an Elf. He bowed in return, then the room hummed a four-fold chord of power once more, and he was gone.

Now there was only one thing left to do.

Find him.

The pain in her heart had a direction: north, and a little east. She needed to follow that—

Someone pounded at her door, and before she could answer it, the door flew open.

"Lady!" gasped one of the younger serving boys, panting with the effort of running up four flights of stairs. "Lady, there are guards at the door, and they want *you!* They say they have a warrant—"

"What colors are they wearing?" she asked instantly.

The boy blinked at her for a moment, obviously thinking that she was crazy. "Green and blue, but—"

"Then they *aren't* the High King's men; they're someone's private guards," she replied. "They can't have a warrant; they probably just have a piece of paper to wave, counting on the rest of us not to know it has to be signed and sealed. Since I'm T'fyrr's Second, they would *have* to have a warrant signed by Theovere directly, and he would have sent his own bodyguards. Tell Tyladen to demand the warrant and if it isn't signed and sealed with Theovere's seal, it isn't valid. That should delay them. And tell him to tell Harperus!"

Before the boy's scandalized eyes, she stripped off her skirts. "Give me your breeches!" she ordered.

"What?" he gasped.

"Your breeches! I can't climb in skirts! *Now!*" She put enough of the power in her order that he obeyed her, blushing to the roots of his hair, and she pulled his breeches on, leaving him to look frantically for something to cover himself with.

Which is ridiculous; he's wearing more now than some of the male dancers wear on stage.

"Go!" she snapped at him, running for the stairs to the roof. "Tell Tyladen what I just told you!"

She didn't wait to see how he solved his embarrassing quandary; time was not on her side.

The King can't know about this; that means that this arrest is on a trumped-up charge at worst. That means I won't have to dodge every guard in the city, only the ones in blue-and-green livery.

They would probably bully their way inside, and might even get as far as her room before Tyladen called in enough help to throw them out again.

And I left my harps!

But T'fyrr was worth all the harps in the world. The Elves could make her a new pair of harps; all the universe could not make her a new T'fyrr.

She scampered across the roof in a bent-over crouch, in case someone was watching from one of the other rooftops. When she got to the edge, she scanned the area for a lookout.

There was one, but he wasn't very good; she spotted him before he saw her, and commotion down on the street caught his attention long enough for her to get over the side away from him and down onto one of the walkways. She paused just long enough to coil up her hair and knot it on top of her head—then, from a distance, she was just a gangly boy, not a woman at all.

She stood up and shoved her hands in her pockets, and strolled in a leisurely manner along the walkway until she got to the building across the street. No shouts followed her, and she did not sense any eyes on her for more than a disinterested few heartbeats.

She took care not to seem to be in any hurry; she even stopped once to look down with interest at the milling knot of guards at the side door of Freehold. One or two of them looked up, then ignored her.

Then she reached the haven of the next building and threw her leg over the side of the roof there, climbing up onto it, rather than going down to street level. Just as if she had been sent on an errand over to Freehold and was returning.

When she was reasonably certain that no one was watching her, she sprinted across to the other side of the roof. There was another walkway down the side of the building there, and this one went all the way to the ground if you knew how to release the catch on the last staircase.

All Freeholders, of course, did.

She careened down the metal staircase, knocking painfully into the handrails and slipping on the steps in her hurry. She tumbled down to the drop-steps, hit the catch, and let her weight take the steps down into the noisome alley below.

Then, at last, she was in the street, and it would take a better tracker than a noble's guard to find her.

CHAPTER TEN

I had not known it was possible to hurt so much. T'fyrr had always thought that when you were injured, you lost track of the lesser pains in the face of the greater. *Evidently, I was mistaken,* he thought, far back in the fog of pain and background fear. Odd how it was possible to think rationally in the midst of the most irrational circumstances. Probably that ironic little mental voice would go right on commenting up until the moment he died, since it seemed more likely that he would die of his many wounds rather than maddening hunger.

So T'fyrr cataloged every pain, every injury, working inch by inch over his abused flesh in his mind. He had to; it was the only way he could keep himself sane. As long as he had something to concentrate on in the face of darkness, fear and the absolute certainty that not only did he not know where he was, no one else did either, he could stay marginally sane.

Whoever had plucked him out of the sky at the height of his climb had known exactly what they were doing. They were ready for him the moment he tumbled, sick and disoriented, onto the floor of the room they had brought him to. He had not been able to raise so much as a single talon in his own defense.

Magic. They caught me in a magic net and dragged me down to their hiding place. And to think I was laughing in my heart at Nightingale's "irrational" fear. Magic could do nothing to me, of course. It has no power over the physical world. I wonder if I will get a chance to apologize to her?

Before he could move, four burly men had swarmed over him, trussing him up like a dinner-fowl. But they had more surprises in store for him.

They hooded me. They hooded me like an unruly falcon! The hood *had* to have been made to order, as well; there were no hunting birds out there with heads as large as T'fyrr's. Maybe they were willing to kidnap him by magic, but they weren't counting on magic to keep him docile.

And someone, somewhere, made them a hood to fit a Haspur. Not them, I think. They do not strike me as the sort to be falconers, or they would know that hooding a raptor does not make him deaf or unconscious. So someone, somewhere, probably in this city, made them a hood. That someone will know who they are. If I can get free. If I can pursue justice against them. . . .

Then to add insult to injury, they had put some sort of contraption over his beak that kept him from opening or closing it completely. *A bit,* he thought, *combined with a muzzle.* It was somewhat difficult to be sure, since they had put it on him after they hooded him.

Padrik's people only starved and beat me. At least they didn't torture me like this. . . .

They had already pulled all of his primaries; the feather sockets ached any time he moved his wings. They were working on the secondaries. They'd clipped his talons until blood flowed in order to collect that as well. This in addition to bruises and aching bones.

Correction. They weren't exactly *torturing* him, technically, since that wasn't their intention.

Whoever they are.

In fact, he wasn't supposed to be alive at all. The mages hired to steal him from the sky had been ordered to kill him on the spot. They'd had a little argument about it while he lay there bound and hooded and helpless. One of them had been in favor of carrying out their orders as stated, but the rest had overruled him.

Thank the winds for temptation, and those unable to resist it.

He had heard them talking, every word; they might have been under the impression that he couldn't understand them, rather than thinking that he was like a falcon and would "go to sleep" when deprived of light. It seemed he was very useful to these mages, and a source of much profit. *My blood and feathers—and the talon bits too, I suppose—are valuable, but only when taken from a living creature; and therefore I am more valuable alive than dead. I doubt their employer knows of this little trade on the side.*

Why bits of *him* should be useful to a mage, he had no notion—but then again, this situation was frighteningly similar to a rumor circulating about human mages who were capturing nonhumans and "sacrificing" them. What if there *were* human mages who were capturing nonhumans, but using bits of them for magic? The idea would have made him sick, if he'd had the leisure to be sick.

Do they do this to their own kind, I wonder? Or is this reserved for "lower creatures"? They were so indifferent to the amount of pain and damage they inflicted as they collected their trophies that he could well imagine they were not above kidnapping fellow humans and treating them the same way.

Which might account for the rumors of nonhumans who captured *hu-*

mans and sacrificed them . . . and would certainly account for the expertise with which he'd been trussed up.

Why was it that humans were inclined to spawn both the best "saints" and the worst villains among their numbers? Was it just that humans were inclined to the extremes?

His mind was wandering, ignoring his urgent need to find a way out of his bindings and escape, and meandering down philosophical paths that had nothing to do with what he wanted it to think about.

How long have I been here? He wasn't certain. They never took off the hood, and although they hadn't been feeding him, he had "heard" the music of magic near him several times, as if they were nourishing him that way instead of by conventional means. He wasn't thirsty or hungry, at any rate, which was different from his captivity at the hands of Padrik's men.

But closed inside the hood, with his body racked with pain, there was no way of telling how much time had passed. It could have been hours . . . or days.

There was an escape open to him; a realm of illusion and hallucination that would at least take him out of his pain and current fear. All he had to do would be to give in to the beckoning, grinning specter of madness, as he had when the Church had held him, and—

I will not go mad. I will not lose heart.

Nightingale was out there, somewhere; he sensed her, a tugging in his soul that actually had a physical direction. She was as racked with grief for his loss as he was with pain, but she had not given up to despair. Yet. He could not tell what she was doing, but he knew that much at least.

She is trying to find me, trying to find a way to free me. I must believe that. She has those damned Deliambrens to help her, and maybe more help than that. She must come; she will *come.* But it was hard to hold on to hope when his strength drained away steadily.

I have made some difference in the world, he told himself defiantly. *I have redeemed myself—and I have had love. Even if I die—*

No, that was the way of despair! He shied away from the thought with violence. *I will not die!* he shouted against the darkness. *I will not! I will fight every step of the way, with everything at my command!*

Which at the moment was not a great deal. . . .

Voices, muffled by a wall, grew nearer. They were coming again. He waited, wild with rage at his own helplessness, as a door opened and two men entered, still talking.

"—probably another week or so," one was saying. "I don't know how these creatures replace blood loss, but we're draining him fairly quickly."

He felt hands fumbling at his restraints. This time they didn't seem to have brought any of their bravos with them. Could he—?

He tried to lash out at them as they freed his arms, tried to leap to his feet. *If I can injure one, the other will run and I can hold the injured one and make him take off the hood—*

Visions of escape flashed across his mind.

He flung out his taloned hands with a strength only slightly less than that of an unfledged eyas; he got as far as his knees before he threw himself off balance and tumbled in an ungainly sprawl across some hard surface.

The men both laughed, as he sought for a reservoir of strength and found it empty. "I see what you mean," said the other. "Still—we can't keep him around for too long, or our client is going to hear about the new artifacts in the market and is going to wonder where all those vials of blood and feathers are coming from."

"He gave us permission to take what we wanted—" the first man argued.

"But you don't get fresh blood from a week-old corpse," the other reminded him.

Artifacts, T'fyrr thought miserably, as the two men threw him on his stomach, pinned his wing and arms effortlessly, and plucked another handful of secondary feathers. *I am nothing to them but an object, to be used at their pleasure. They harvest me as if I were a berry patch.*

Each feather, as it was pulled, invoked a stab of exquisite pain; he squawked involuntarily as his tormenters extracted them. Finally they left him alone.

They were only after feathers this time, not blood. Just as well, every talon ached where they had cut each one to the quick to collect blood. *Now I know how human victims must feel; why they deem having nails pulled out to be such a torment.* If he got free, he would not be able to walk comfortably for weeks. *And I will not fly for months until the feathers grow again.*

"Shall we truss it back up again?" the first man asked when they finally left him alone for a moment, and he decided that they were done with him for the nonce. "We'll be gone all evening, with no one here to watch him."

The second one prodded him with a toe, and all T'fyrr could do was groan. "I don't think so," he said. "He isn't going anywhere. All those bindings were breaking feathers anyway; we need to get as many perfect feathers from him as we can. Only the perfect feathers are any good, magically. Now that makes me wonder, though—we need to do some research and see if the down and body feathers could be used for anything."

The sounds of their feet receded. "Considering what we're getting for feathers and blood, can you imagine what the heart and bones will be worth?" the first one said, greed and awe in his voice. "Not to mention the skull and the talons?"

"We will be able to purchase mansions and titles, at the very least," the second chuckled over the sound of a door opening. "And as many—"

The door closed, cutting off the end of the sentence.

The heart. The skull. His people did not have much in the way of ceremony to mark one's passing, but the idea that he would be parceled out in bits to the highest bidder made him so sick to his stomach that he started to gag.

And that was when the despair he had been holding off finally swooped down on him and took him.

I am going to die here, alone, in the dark, half-mad and utterly forgotten! Nightingale will never find me; I will never see her again—

He couldn't sit up, he was too weak and dizzy; he could only curl into a shivering ball and clutch his legs to his chest, shaking with despair. No one would ever find him. There was no rescue at hand. Probably no one had even bothered to make the attempt.

No one cared.

No! I can feel her out there; I know she hasn't forgotten me! If no one else tries, she will! She will come to me by herself if she must!

But it was hopeless. How could one woman, however resourceful, find him hidden away in this hive of a city? How could anyone find him, even with all the resources of the King? Lyonarie was too big, too impersonal, for anyone to search successfully.

Even clever Nightingale. There were too many places even she could not go.

He could not weep, but his beak gaped as much as the muzzle would permit, and he keened his despair into the uncaring darkness.

Oh, I would rather that Tyladen were doing this.

The moon shone down on rooftops encrusted with ornamental false towers and crenellations, on chimney pots shaped like toadstools, flowers, trees, tiny castles—anything *but* a chimney-pot. Nightingale crouched in the lee of a chimney, bracing herself on the slanted slate roof, and took Harperus' device off her belt, holding it before her like a hand-crossbow. She braced herself a little more, then cupped her hand around it to shield it, as she would have shielded a lantern, and felt for the little raised bump near where her thumb fell.

Magical guards above and physical guards below. If this was *not* where T'fyrr was being held, then there was something very peculiar going on in the old mansion upon whose roof she now perched, less like the bird she was named for than a chimney swift.

A square area lit up inside her shielding hand, giving off a dim, red light.
It represented a square space, twenty feet on a side, with herself in the
middle.

The little bright dot that was supposed to represent T'fyrr was just a
little to the left of center—a dot that had *not* appeared on this "screen"
the other times she had used the device.

She smiled tightly; he *was* here. Getting him out—well, she would save
the rejoicing for the moment that happened. She pressed the thumb-point
again, and a set of numbers appeared.

Roughly fifteen feet below her; that would put him in the top floor, just
below the attics. That made sense; they were probably thinking of him as a
big bird. They wouldn't want to put him in a basement where he might
catch a chill and die of shock. In these town mansions, unlike those in the
country, the master and mistress had their private rooms at the top of the
house, where you might get a breath of a breeze in the summer, and where
all the heat rose in the winter. In a town mansion like this, the rooms at
street level, next to the kitchens, were ovens themselves in the summer,
and in winter, no amount of fuel kept them warm.

Her heart had led her here; it had once been a wealthy district, with
huge homes showcasing the wealth of their owners. Now the area was
shabby-genteel at best, and whoever lived here was usually out of favor,
the tag-end of a once-prosperous family now running out of money, or the
last of a long line dying out. As the homes were lost to their original
owners, they were bought by other, less "genteel" folk. She knew of at
least three brothels here, and more ominously, one of the houses was
rumored to belong to a dealer in illegal goods—very illegal, because someone had to die in order for those particular "goods" to come on the
market.

She had hoped she had the right district when she realized that mages
tended to need buildings with a great deal of space to practice their art.
She *knew* she had the right district when her street-urchins traced the
blood and feathers showing up on the mage-market to this very area.
People really *didn't* pay any attention to what children overheard.

*If we survive this, perhaps I shall set up an information service and live off
the results of that.*

That was when she sent Maddy to Tyladen for one of the devices she
had asked for. She herself had not gone back to Freehold since the guards
arrived. Freehold would be watched—but she had a secure hiding place in
Father Ruthvere's steeple, and others scattered elsewhere across the city.
She had money sewn into the money belt she never took off except to
sleep, and then kept beneath her pillow. She could look like whatever kind
of woman she chose, and she was familiar with the "bad" parts of Ly-

onarie. No guard or militia from the Palace could find her here if she did not want to be found.

The child returned with this, a set of closely written instructions, and the other child that Nightingale had asked her to find.

That was all she had been waiting for. She had waited until dark, then began scaling the walls and getting onto the rooftops of every likely building in the area—with help. She was *not* a thief, and she could not have done this alone, but she had the help of someone who was more at home on the rooftops of Lyonarie than beneath them. It was safer to operate this thing from above than from below. There was less chance of being seen, for one, and she really didn't want to be caught loitering out in the street with *this* bizarre-looking thing in her hands.

I don't believe I can claim it is a musical instrument.

Thanks to the fact that even here there was very little space between the buildings, and to the fact that her accomplice had some quite remarkable climbing and bridging devices at his disposal, she had mostly been able to scramble from roof to roof. That further limited her time on the ground; a good thing, even if it was hair-raisingly risky to pick her way across strange rooftops in the middle of the night.

She put the device away, and considered her options.

He is in the middle of the building, probably in a closet, as far as possible from a window. Now, how do I tell what room that closet belongs to?

A scrabbling of tiny hands and feet across the slates signaled the arrival of her partner in crime and guide across these heights. " 'E 'ere?" whispered Tam, the chimney-sweep, a boy about thirteen years old, but as thin as one of his brushes and with the stature of a nine-year-old.

"Right below me, just about," she whispered back. "I'm certain they're keeping him in a closet, but how do I tell which room it's in?"

He chuckled. "Easy, mum. By chimbleys. This 'un like drops down inter th' room ye want." He patted it fondly, the way a driver would pat the neck of his horse. "These big ol' 'ouses, they got fireplaces fer ever' room. Wants I should go look?"

Before she could stop him, he had clambered nimbly up the side of the chimney, and slid down inside it.

She waited, numb with shock, expecting at any moment to hear the commotion from below that meant he'd been spotted and seized.

Nothing.

Then, off to the side, a faint whistle, the song of a nightingale.

She eased her way over to the edge of the roof where the whistle had come from, and looked cautiously down.

Tam's sooty face looked up at her impudently, his teeth and the whites of his eyes startlingly bright in the moonlight. "Empty room, lots uv scratches on the floor. Got a locked closet 'ere, mum. Be a mort uv them scratches there, goes to 'tother side uv door. Mebbe some blood, too."

She didn't hesitate a moment longer; she lowered herself down over the edge of the roof, feeling for the window ledge with her feet as her arms screamed with outraged pain. Tam caught her ankles deftly and guided her feet to secure places; she caught hold of decorative woodwork and eased herself down to the window itself. She wanted to fling herself inside, but she didn't dare make that much noise—but she nearly wept with relief when she was safe on the floor inside.

I am not a thief. I am not a hero. I am only a musician; I am not supposed to be crawling about on rooftops! And we are leaving this place by the stairs, and no other way!

The room itself was completely empty; not even a single stick of furniture, just as Tam said. The moonlight coming in the windows revealed that there were traces of painted diagrams on the wooden floor, though, and she guessed that it was sometimes used for magical ceremonies.

All the more reason to get him out of here!

She went straight to the closet door that Tam pointed to, and saw that what he had mistaken for blood was nothing of the sort. It was only spilled paint. The scratches could have come from anything—dragging a heavy piece of furniture to the closet for storage.

For a moment, her heart sank; then she heard the faint scraping of talons beyond the door, and the whimpering keen of a bird of prey, exhausted and near death.

"I'm gone, mum," Tam declared, and slipped back up the chimney. That was fine; she'd already paid him for his help, and she had told him that she didn't want him around if things began to get dangerous. Since that had suited the boy just perfectly, the bargain had been easy to strike.

It had been much harder to persuade Maddy and her little army of partisans to stay behind. The loyalty of children ran deep, and somehow she had earned it. Only promising them that they could stand guard over the Chapel when she and T'fyrr were safely inside had kept most of them from following her and Tam over the rooftops.

She turned back toward the door, expecting a complicated lock—perhaps even a mage-made lock—and strained her senses for the music that magic-touched things held within them.

Silence.

Nor was there any other sign of a lock, complicated or otherwise.

In stunned surprise, she tried the doorknob automatically.

It turned easily, and swung open without so much as a creak.

There wasn't much light, but there was enough for her to see the crumpled, feather-covered figure lying on the floor of the closet, head enveloped in a giant, scuffed hood.

A surge of grief and rage enveloped her, and she flung herself down on her knees beside him, fearing she was too late.

The head turned blindly toward her as she reached for him. "I-ale?" came a whisper, a mangled version of her name as spoken from around the cruel device they had clamped on his beak. "I—a—oo?"

"It's me; I've come to get you out of here." The fastenings on the gag and the hood weren't even complicated; she had the former off and flung into a corner. The hood followed it, and she gathered him into her arms with her throat constricted with tears. He was so weak! He had no primaries at all, and few secondaries; he wouldn't have been able to fly out of here even if he'd had the strength.

I'll worry about how to get him out of here after I get him under protection. And to do that, she needed his permission. "T'fyrr," she said urgently, "I need to put barriers against any more magical attacks on you. May I?"

He wrapped his own arms weakly around her and nodded, too spent to even ask her what in the world she thought she was doing. She reached both arms around behind his back and clasped her silver bracelet with her free hand under cover of the embrace, and concentrated hard for a moment.

With a silvery glissando, the Elven protections she wore slithered over him as well, wrapping him in a cocoon of power, identical to hers.

Now, just let the mages try something! They'd waste their time trying to crack *this* shell, and if she knew Elves, that mage would take malicious pleasure in tracking the attack to its source and—dealing—with it.

Hopefully those same mages hadn't sensed the power she'd brought here. That *was* supposed to be one of the protections, but who knew? It was Elven-work, and chancy at best, constrained only by what this particular mage felt like doing at the time.

"Can you stand?" she asked in an urgent whisper, glad that she could not clearly see all the damage that had been done to him. "We have to get out of here, before—"

"The mages—are gone," he interrupted her, breathing as hard as if he had been flying for miles at top speed. "I heard them say—they were leaving—for the night."

Well! That put another complexion on it entirely! They were as secure here as they would be anywhere, and as likely to remain undisturbed. With only the guards below—who, with the absence of their masters, would be slackening their vigilance at the least, and with luck would be getting drunk on the masters' wine—there was no one to disturb them.

"I can heal you again, T'fyrr, enough to get us both out, over the rooftops. You can still climb, can't you?"

A feeble chuckle. "Only if you can heal my talon-tips, beloved. I would not be very silent, otherwise."

"I can do that," she replied, her heart swelling. *He said it! He called me "beloved"!* There had been times in the dark of the lonely nights, waiting for word of him, that she had been certain when he came to his senses, he would be revolted by her love for him. She could have misinterpreted what he'd said about the Spirit-Brothers; he could have mistranslated. But—

But he would not use those words so casually unless—

Unless they were so real to him that he *could* use them casually, as casually as flying.

"Then let me work the magic on you, beloved," she said, with a joy so great it eclipsed fear. "And this time—*don't* try and help me!"

He only chuckled again, a mere wheeze in the darkness, and let her work her will on him.

The trip back over the rooftops had been nightmarish, but not such a nightmare as trying to get out past the guards would have been. She had been able to give him strength enough to climb, and had been able to heal the tips of his talons so that they didn't bleed every time he moved a hand or a foot, but there hadn't been enough time to do more than that. Every time she thought she heard a door slam below, or footsteps in the hall, she had been jolted out of the trance.

The return trip was easier than it might have been—she didn't have to make side trips over every roof in the district to check her device for his presence. Some of those charming, ornamental rooftops had been the purest hell to get across the first time.

Why do people pitch their roofs that steeply? Doesn't it ever occur to them that someday, someone is going to have to climb all over it, replacing slates and cleaning chimneys?

Evidently not. Perhaps that was why this district had deteriorated; the charming manses were impossible to keep in repair.

She was able to pick out a path that, while not precisely *easy* or *gentle,* at least avoided the worst of the obstacles. But it was a long time before they came to one particular abandoned house at the edge of the district and were able to slip down through the holes in the roof that had let her and her accomplice have access to the roof-highway in the first place.

They felt their way along staircases that shook and groaned alarmingly with every step they took, and down halls that must have been ankle-deep in dust by the amount they kicked up. But they reached the street level without mishap, and just inside the front door, Nightingale stooped in the darkness and felt for the bundle she had left there.

It wasn't anything anyone would be likely to steal; this neighborhood hadn't deteriorated so far that a bundle of rags was worth anything: a tattered skirt for her, to go over her black trews and black shirt, a bedraggled cloak, and an equally tattered great-cloak for him, big enough to completely envelop him. It was as threadbare as the skirt and wouldn't have done a thing to protect him from the wind or weather, but that wasn't the point.

"Here," she said, and sneezed, handing him the cloak. She pulled the skirt on over her head and wiped the roof-soot from her face and hands with the tail of it. He fumbled the cloak on after a moment of hesitation.

"Won't I look just as odd in this?" he asked as he tied the two strings that held it closed at the throat.

"Yes and no," she told him. "There are plenty of people who go cloaked at night, even in the worst heat of summer—and anyone who does is probably so dangerous that most people deliberately avoid him. Someone who doesn't want you to notice him is someone you likely don't want to notice *you.*"

She picked up the second, equally tattered cloak, flinging it on and pulling up the hood. Better to broil in this thing than to have her face seen —and she could not rely on her own magic to work properly inside this Elven protection.

And two people, together, cloaked in this heat—they are twice as unlikely to be bothered.

They waited until the street was empty of traffic, and stepped out as if they belonged in the house they had just left, on the chance that someone might be looking out a window. Thieves and escaped prisoners were not supposed to stroll out like a pair of down-at-the-heels gentry.

It was a long, weary walk to the Chapel, and they had to stop often, so that T'fyrr could rest. But when they got within a few blocks of the Chapel, they were swarmed.

But not by guards looking for them, nor by the mages' men, but by Nightingale's pack of children. Tam had taken word ahead, which Nightingale had *not* expected him to do, and the children must have been waiting, watching, along every possible route to the Chapel.

A wheelbarrow appeared as if conjured; the children coaxed the Haspur into it—he had no tail and very little in the way of wing feathers to get in the way of sitting, now—and a team of a dozen rushed him along the street faster than Nightingale could run. She caught up with them at the entrance to the Chapel, her side aching, but her heart lighter than she'd had any reason to expect when she had set out a few hours ago.

Father Ruthvere was waiting for them; he opened the door to the Chapel just enough to let them inside, and shut it again quickly.

"They've been here looking for you," he told Nightingale. "They have warrants for you and T'fyrr both."

His thin face was creased with worry and exhaustion, and her heart sank. Warrants? Already? How could they have gotten legal warrants past the King?

"A warrant for *T'fyrr?*" she said incredulously. "But he's in the King's household, how could they get a warrant out on him?"

"It's part of the original warrant for the men who attacked the Deliambren," the Priest told them, his mouth twisting into a grimace as he led them into the sanctuary. "The King already signed it; they've altered it to read 'humans or nonhumans' and they're claiming that T'fyrr set up the attack in the first place—that the Deliambren Envoy recognized him, and that was why he kept asking for T'fyrr."

When T'fyrr made a growl of disgust, Nightingale only shrugged fatalistically. *It figures. I shouldn't have been so surprised.* "It doesn't have to be *logical,*" she pointed out, "it only has to be legal, and since the King has already signed it and probably initialed the change, it's legal. And me?"

"You're supposed to be the mysterious female who freed the attacker the Deliambren caught." Father Ruthvere sighed and shook his head. "I haven't a clue how they're managing to get past the fact that you'd have had to be two places at the same time—"

"If they have their way, it would never get to a trial where they'd have to produce proof," she pointed out bitterly, feeling a surge of anger at High King Theovere, who had probably just signed the warrants without ever *reading* them once he was told what they were—vaguely—about. "When criminals can escape from locked dungeons or walk away legally, it doesn't take any stretch of the imagination to see that two more 'criminals' could be murdered during an 'escape attempt.' And we don't have any friends in high places or awkward relatives who might ask questions."

T'fyrr drooped despondently. "I had hoped that we had awakened Theovere to his sense of duty enough so that things like this, at least, could not happen. I thought he—"

She took his arm, hoping to give him comfort. To have gone through all he had, only to be hit with more bad news, seemed grossly unfair.

"Never mind," Father Ruthvere said firmly. "You have sanctuary here, for as long as you like, and no one can pry you out of it since the Bishop is behind you. You can stay until you're stronger, or your feathers have grown back, and fly out."

"But what about Nightingale?" T'fyrr asked instantly.

She actually had an answer to that one, although she wouldn't bring it up in front of Father Ruthvere. *Well, an Elf who can appear in my room and disappear as well, can certainly manage to take me with him.* She knew how he was doing it, of course; opening up Doors into Underhill wherever he chose. It took a tremendous amount of magical power, but—

But they might do it, just to tweak the noses of the human leaders and prove that the human mages are no match for them.

"I can find a way to safety, love, trust me," she said, and patted his arm reassuringly. "I found you, didn't I?"

T'fyrr still looked stricken, and she felt his despair enveloping him like a great black net. She tried to think of something, anything, to say—and swayed with sudden exhaustion, catching herself with one hand on a pillar just before she fell.

Father Ruthvere took over, his expression mirroring his relief at having something immediate he could do. "Never mind all that now," he said soothingly. "Tomorrow everything may change. Before anything can happen, you both need to rest, recover your strength." He made shooing motions with his hands in the direction of the belltower. "Go!" he said. "The Bishop will be sending his own guards to make sure you aren't taken from sanctuary by force. You won't need to stay awake to avoid arrest. All you need to do is get your strength back."

Nightingale sighed with relief and let down her guard. Weariness came over her then, so potent it left her dizzy.

Fortunately they were *not* supposed to go up to the top of the belltower —for one thing, when the bells rang they would have risked deafness or even death up there. No, there was a well-insulated tiring room at the base of the tower that they would be living in for the next few days at the very least. It had a staircase that led directly up to the top of the tower, so that once T'fyrr grew his feathers back—a matter of two or three weeks, at a guess—he would have free access to one of the better take-off points in this district. If he had to fly out, and he left at night, no one would ever know.

The two of them staggered into the tiring room to find that Father Ruthvere had been there before them, laying out bedding, wash water and a basin, even food. *One* set of bedding.

But by the time they reached the doorway, they were so tired that all they cared about was the bedding. They literally collapsed into it, Nightingale only a fraction of a heartbeat behind T'fyrr, and curled up together in a comforting tangle of limbs. She pulled the blankets up over them both, as much to hide the sad state of his feathers as for warmth.

He was asleep first; she listened to his regular breathing and allowed herself to weep, very quietly, with relief and joy. Not many tears, but enough that she had to wipe her face with a corner of a blanket before she was through. That released the last of her tension; she had only two thoughts before slumber caught her.

We are as surely in prison here as in the gaol. We cannot leave without being taken by our enemies. We have been caged at last.

It doesn't matter as long as we are together.

T'fyrr would never have known how long he slept if Father Ruthvere hadn't told him.

"Three days?" he said incredulously. "Three *days?*"

The Priest nodded, and T'fyrr shook his head. "I believe you, but—"

"Well, you woke up long enough to eat and—ahem," Father Ruthvere said, blushing. "But other than that, you slept. Nightingale, too," he added as an afterthought. "Though she stayed awake a bit longer than you did."

Probably healing me. That would account for how well I feel and the memories of music in my dreams.

T'fyrr sighed and roused his feathers. "Well, what has been happening? Are we still under siege?" he asked. "Or are our enemies satisfied to have us bottled up and out of the way?"

Father Ruthvere played with his prayer beads. "The latter, I suspect," he said after a moment. "You obviously cannot press charges against your captors since you are a fugitive yourself, and as for Nightingale—" He shrugged. "The nonhumans are in an uproar, but there is no one to lead them and Theovere—"

"And Theovere is near death."

They all turned as one, T'fyrr feeling the blood draining from his skin and leaving him cold everywhere there were no feathers.

Harperus stood in the door to the tiring room, face drawn and as pale as his hair, his costume little more than a pair of plain trews and an embroidered shirt. "Thank the Stars you're awake at last," he said without preamble, as both Nightingale and T'fyrr stared at him, trying to make some sort of sense out of his first statement. "Theovere was attacked and is in a coma, his physicians are baffled—" He held up his hands as T'fyrr mantled what was left of his wings in anger. "Wait, let me tell this from the beginning."

T'fyrr subsided. "Make it short, Old Owl," he rumbled. "None of your damned Deliambren meanderings!"

Harperus nodded. "Shortly, then. The marvelous music box broke down completely this morning, and no amount of fiddling by Lord Levan would get it working again. The High King sent pages looking for you, and found me instead, and *I* gave him an earful."

The Deliambren crossed his arms over his chest, his dour expression reflecting a smoldering anger beneath the stoic surface. "I told him about your vanishing, the warrants that *he* had signed, the attacks and the kidnapping. I told him that now that the warrants had been signed, by his hand, neither you nor Nightingale had any protection *or rights* under the law. He was very—stunned."

T'fyrr only growled; he had lost all patience with the once-great High King about the time his captors had pulled out his third primary. *I am not entirely certain I even want to help him now. . . .*

"I told him the Church had you in sanctuary," Harperus continued, "convinced that both of you were innocent of any wrongdoing. And I *showed* him how all those things that you had been hinting at were true, all the abuses of nonhumans, all the things that had been happening to human and nonhumans alike. I guessed that he might have been so thoroughly shaken up that he might actually *listen* instead of dismissing it all."

"Well, was he?" T'fyrr asked. *It would take a miracle—*

But evidently that miracle had occurred. "Enough to issue orders immediately revoking the warrants on you two, and to take the Seneschal and a gaggle of secretaries into a corner and start drafting interkingdom edicts granting basic rights to all peoples of all species," Harperus said with a note of triumph. But his triumph faded immediately. "That was when, according to the Seneschal, that mysterious woman struck. He called for breakfast; it arrived, and with it a lace handkerchief and a message. Theovere picked it up, opened it, and read it before any of the bodyguards even thought to look at it first—and he collapsed on the spot." Harperus shook his head. "I looked at him, and I'm baffled. There's no contact poison I know of that would work that way, and he shows no other signs of poisoning other than being in a coma no one can wake him from."

T'fyrr looked aghast at Nightingale, who only nodded, her lips compressed into a thin line. "If our enemy can hire mages to pluck T'fyrr from the sky, she can certainly hire a mage to write a note-spell to try to disable or kill Theovere. There was nothing on the note when they looked at it, right?"

"Right," Harperus replied, looking at Nightingale with respect and a little awe. "But it didn't kill him—"

"It doesn't have to," she pointed out. "If he is in a coma, he could stay that way indefinitely. The Advisors can reign as joint Regents on the pretense that someday he *might* wake up. This could go on for years. Come to think of it, that's better than killing him for their purposes. If a new High King was selected, they'd all be out of their positions."

"But what can we do?" T'fyrr asked, puzzlement overlaid with despair. *Now—we have no choice. Nightingale and I may have a day or so to escape while our enemies obtain new warrants for us, but what of all the nonhumans in the Twenty Kingdoms? What is there left for them but to gather what they can and flee?* "We are not physicians, and even if we were, surely the King's own doctors know best what is good for him."

"The King's doctors are as baffled as I am," Harperus replied. "And *I* am baffled by the message I received less than an hour ago." He raised his eyebrows and looked straight at Nightingale as if he suspected her of some duplicity. "The messenger seemed human or Deliambren, but had—unusual eyes and ears. And he spoke in riddles."

The corner of Nightingale's mouth twitched. "Go on," she said. "That sounds like an Elf to me. I happen to know there's one—ah—in the area."

In answer, Harperus handed her a piece of paper. She took it, and read it aloud for the benefit of T'fyrr and Father Ruthvere.

" 'Tell the Bird of Night and the Bird of the King that the High King can be sung back from the darkness in which he wanders, if the guard-dog is released to return to his home. Half of the futures hold Theovere high, half of them hold him fallen. If the two Birds should sing to him as one, hearts bound, wrongs remembered but not cherished, their enemies may be confounded. No Elf, nor human mage, nor brightly-conceited artificer can command the power to accomplish this, for this is the magic of the heart and the Sight.' "

"I'm not certain I care for that 'brightly conceited,' part," Harperus muttered under his breath. Nightingale must have heard him anyway, for she treated him to an upraised eyebrow.

"Does this mean that Nightingale and I have—the ability to *sing* him out of this?" T'fyrr said incredulously. "But how?"

"It was accomplished by magic," Nightingale pointed out. "It's possible that magic can undo it. There might even be a mage somewhere inside his mind, holding Theovere unconscious; if that's the case, Bardic Magic could reach Theovere in a way no other magic could duplicate—or block."

T'fyrr thought about that for a moment, and nodded. "I believe that I see," he said, and roused what was left of his feathers with a hearty shake before straightening up and holding his head high. "Those in a coma are said to understand what happens around them. We must go, of course—"

"Wait a moment!" Harperus objected, blocking the door. "I haven't told you the rest of it. If you flee now, you'll be outrunning warrants that won't ever have a chance to catch up with you before you cross a nonhuman border. If you stay, try, and *don't* succeed—the Advisors are spreading the rumor that Nightingale is the female assassin and in the hire of T'fyrr. They're saying as proof of this that there was no trouble until T'fyrr arrived at Court. If Theovere dies, you'll die—and if he simply remains in a coma, you'll die anyway. *Someone* has decided that you two are the obstacles that need to be removed for the Advisors to have a free hand again."

Nightingale dropped the paper at her feet. "That doesn't matter," she said steadily, and glanced over at T'fyrr.

I was wrong to discount Theovere. He can be reached; he was nearly his old self before they struck him down. We must help him, for his own sake, and for the sake of all those who are depending on us.

His heart swelled with pride and love for her. "She is right," he agreed. "It does not matter. Our enemies are counting on our cowardice. We must teach them better. And—" He hesitated for a moment, as the last of his anger with Theovere washed away. "And the High King needs us," he concluded. "If we desert him—we are no better than they. Perhaps, we are worse. We will try, for nonhumans and humans alike."

Harperus wordlessly stood aside, and the two of them walked out of the tiring room, through the Chapel and out into the street.

High King Theovere needs us, and he is *the Twenty Kingdoms, for better or worse. With luck on our side—*

—perhaps we can make it, "for better."

Nightingale settled at the High King's side, next to T'fyrr. The Haspur looked very odd, with patches of down-feathers showing where coverts had been taken, with his wings denuded, with reddened, visible scars and with not even a stump of a tail.

No one could deny his dignity, however, a dignity that transcended such imperfections.

That dignity had gotten them past the Bodyguards to the Captain, and from there to the one person T'fyrr thought might still back them: the Seneschal. The Captain and the Lord Seneschal had been skeptical of their claims to be able to reach Theovere by music—but they were also no friends of the King's Physician. The Seneschal simply didn't trust someone who was often in and out of the suites of the other Advisors. The Captain just didn't trust him, period. It was his opinion that there had been too much talk of purgings and bleedings, and not enough of things that would strengthen rather than weaken a patient.

So the Captain of the King's Bodyguard chose a time when the Advisors were all huddled together in Council, threw out the Physician and smuggled them in.

"Now what?" T'fyrr asked her as she surveyed Theovere's bed. Theovere *was* in it, somewhere in the middle, hardly visible for all the pillows and feather comforters piled atop him, and lost in the vast expanse of it. The bed itself was big enough to sleep three Gypsy families and still have room for the dogs. "Do we need to have physical contact with him?"

"I don't think so," she replied as the Captain moved a little in silent protest to that suggestion. He might not trust the Physician, but he also made no bones about the fact that his trust for them was very limited. "No, there's nothing we can do with a physical contact that we can't do without it."

She turned to the Captain, then, as something occurred to her. "You were there when he collapsed, weren't you?"

The beefy man nodded, face red with chagrin and anger at himself. "And why I didn't think—"

"You're not at fault," she interrupted gently. "There should have been no way for a note to get to the King that hadn't been checked for problems first. Unless—"

He looked sharply at her. "Unless?"

"Unless that note was put on the tray by one of the King's Advisors and had the seal of the Council on it," she said, and got the satisfaction of seeing his eyes narrow with speculation. "Now, I know if *I* were an Advisor to the High King, knowing that the King wasn't getting any younger, and suspecting that a successor might be named soon who would want his own Advisors in place . . ." She let her voice trail off and raised an eyebrow significantly.

The Captain nodded, his face as impassive as a stone wall, but his eyes bright with anger. "I take your meaning, and it's one I hadn't thought of."

Nightingale shrugged, pleased that she had planted her seed in fertile ground. But the Captain was not yet finished.

"Lady, I—" She sensed him groping for words through a fog of grief, though there was no outward sign of that grief on his features. "I served Theovere all my life. I've seen him at his best, and at his worst, and—"

He stopped and shook his head, unable to articulate his own feelings. She held her hands tightly together in her lap, holding herself tightly braced against the wash of his emotions, as strong as the tide at its full. Now she knew why every man in the Bodyguards was so fanatically devoted to the King.

He could inspire that devotion once. Lady grant we make it possible for him to do so again.

She caught his eyes and nodded gravely, once, then turned back to the enormous bed and its quiet occupant. "If we succeed, Captain, it will be for the good of all—and if we fail, then at least we will have been able to give Theovere a parting gift of the music he loved so much."

"Nightingale," T'fyrr said suddenly, in the Gypsy tongue, "didn't you tell me that there might be a—a spirit of some kind, holding Theovere away? *Look over there.*"

He pointed with his beak rather than draw the attention of the Captain, and Nightingale stared in the direction he pointed.

There is a shadow there, where a shadow has no business being!

It hovered just above Theovere's head, but it did not *feel* like Theovere. It felt hungry, cruel, petty—

What is it? Whatever it was, she knew at that moment that they would have to deal with it before they could bring Theovere back to himself.

"I think it's occupied," T'fyrr whispered, his voice shaking a little. "I think—I think it might be tormenting Theovere."

Odd. That sounded familiar. A little like—

Like the Ghost that Rune fiddled for, that Robin and Kestrel helped to free! It had been bound to a pass by a malicious magician, and had taken out its rage on those who tried to cross the pass by night. *If you had something like that—a lesser spirit, perhaps—and bound it to your service—*

Then you might have something that you could set on a man simply by sending him a note to which it had been attached—something that could drive the soul from his body and keep it there. You *would* have something that would become more and more bitter and malicious the longer it stayed bound.

Which meant it was half in this world and half in the next; and wasn't that the definition of those with the Sight? She had it—she just hadn't used it much, not when her greater power lay with the heart rather than the soul.

And the Elven message had clearly said, "this is magic of the heart and the Sight." Elves simply didn't get any clearer than that. *Well, the first thing to do is get its attention. I haven't invoked the Sight in a long time. . . .*

She put her hands on the strings of her harp, and began to play quietly, humming the melody under her breath as she slowly sharpened her focus out of this world and into the next. She sensed T'fyrr following her lead, and wondered if he would *share* her Sight, or if he had a touch of it himself.

The room grew grey and dim, and faded away at the edges as she moved her vision into that other world where shadows were solid and restless spirits dwelled. She could still see Theovere, but now—

Now there were two of him.

One was in the bed, the other standing at the foot of the bed, an expression of fear and frustration on his face. And hovering above the Theovere in the bed was—something.

It wasn't human, not precisely. There was a certain odd cast to the face, as if the structure of the skull was subtly different from a human's. The red eyes were slanted obliquely toward the temples. The fingers were too long and there were seven of them; the limbs looked oddly jointless. It had the pointed ears of an Elf, but it wasn't an Elf, either. At the moment, it was watching Theovere, and it was enjoying his plight.

"Can you See anything?" she whispered to T'fyrr, and she described with she Saw. Out of the corner of her eye she saw him shake his head.

"Only the shadow," he replied. "I will trust you to know what to do."

I only wish I did! she thought; but they were in it now, and there was no turning back. Whatever It was, It didn't seem to be paying any attention to her or her music. It also wasn't *doing* much—except to keep Theovere from reentering his own body. Which meant—what?

That It's probably not all that powerful. That I'm not reaching It. But I'm not really trying. Think, Nightingale! What do you do when you have to reach an audience and you don't know what they want?

You try something so beautiful they can't ignore it.

She heard It speaking now, faintly; It taunted Theovere with his plight and his helplessness, playing with the symbols of his power that It conjured up into Its own hands. It didn't have the *real* crown, rod, or sword, of course—but Theovere didn't know that.

Her hands moved of themselves on the strings, plucking out the first chords of "The Waterfall," one of the most transcendently beautiful songs she knew. She didn't do it often, because she didn't have the range to do it justice.

But T'fyrr did.

She poured her heart into the harping, and he his soul into the music—and It snapped Its narrow head around, affixing them with its poppy-red eyes, as the ephemeral Objects of State vanished into the nothingness from which they had been conjured.

It said nothing, though, until after they had finished the song.

"What are you doing here?" It asked in a voice like wet glue.

She started to answer—then stopped herself just in time. To answer It *might* put herself in Its power; Its primary ability must be to drive a spirit from the body, then keep that spirit from reentering. It might be able to do that to more than one person at a time. But the Laws of Magic were that It could not do so if It did not know her; It must have been fed what It needed to take Theovere, but she was a stranger to It. It needed a connection with her to find out what tormented *her.*

So instead, she started a new song hard on the heels of "The Waterfall," and followed that one with a third, and a fourth.

I have to make It go away, and I can't do that by driving *It away. It's already here by coercion.* The longer It stayed silent, listening to her, the more she sensed those shadow-bindings, deeper into the shadow-world than It was, that kept It blocking Theovere's return. But the bindings were light ones; It could break them if It chose.

So It was here because It liked being here. It enjoyed tormenting people.

Well, so had the Skull Hill Ghost, but Rune and then Robin had tamed the thing, showing it—what?

All the good things of the human spirit! All the things that give life joy instead of pain!

And her hands moved into the melody of "Theovere and the Forty-Four," one of the songs that she and T'fyrr had used to try and wake the High King up to his former self.

It was a moving tale of courage and selflessness, all the more moving this time because the Theovere-spirit listened, too, and wept with heart-break for what he had been and no longer was. He was in a place and a position now where he could no longer lie to himself—and very likely, that was one of the things his captor had been tormenting him with. The truth, bare and unadorned, and equally inescapable.

He has looked into the mirror and seen a fool.

She sensed T'fyrr pouring his own high courage into the song, the courage that had sustained him while captive, the courage that made him go out and try to *do* something to remedy the ills he saw around him. And while she did not think that courage was particularly her strong suit, she added her own heart, twined around his.

She saw Its eyes widen; saw the maliciousness in them fade, just a little, and moved immediately to "Good Duke Arden." The Theovere-spirit continued to weep, bent over with its face in both its ephemeral hands, and the Shadow softened a little more.

But she sensed just a hint of impatience.

Change the mood. It's getting bored.

She moved through the entire gamut of human emotions: laughter, courage, self-sacrifice, simple kindness, sorrow and loss. Always she came back to two: love, and courage. And with each song they sang, she and T'fyrr, with their spirits so closely in harmony that they might have been a single person with two voices, It softened a little more, lost some of Its malicious evil, until finally there was nothing of evil in It anymore. Just a weariness, a lack of hope that was not *quite* despair, and a vast and empty loneliness.

That was when she thought she knew something of Its nature. It was a mirror that reflected whatever was before It—or a vessel, holding what-ever was poured into It. It was as changeable as a chameleon, but deep inside It did have a mind and heart of Its own, and she seemed to be touching It.

Her hands were weary, and her voice had taken on that edge of hoarse-ness that warned her it was about to deteriorate. And under T'fyrr's brave front, she felt bone-tiredness.

If ever we can drive this thing away—no, lead it away!—it must be now!

So she changed the tune, right in the middle of "Aerie," to one of the simplest songs she had ever learned:

"The Briars of Home."

It was the lullaby of an exile to her child, singing of all the small things she missed, all of them in her garden. The smell of certain flowers in the spring; the way that the grass looked after the rain. The taste of herbs that would not grow where she was now. The leaves falling in autumn; the snow covering the sleeping plants in winter. The songs of birds that would not fly in her new garden. The feel of the soil beneath her hands, and the joy of seeing the first sprouting plants. And the homesickness, the bitter-sweet knowledge that she would never experience any of those tiny plea-sures again, for all that she was happy enough in the new land. And last of all—how she would give all of the wealth she possessed in the new place for one short walk in her own garden at home.

And as the last notes fell into silence, It spoke to her for the second and last time.

"I have a garden."

And with those four words, It snapped the coercions binding It, and vanished.

But Theovere did not return to his body; instead, he stood there staring at it, empty-eyed and hollow. He looked old, terribly old; he stood with hanging hands, stooped-over and defeated.

What's wrong? Why won't he wake?

She stretched out her already thin resources to him, trying to sense what was wrong. But she had nothing left; she could not touch him, and her own spirit cried out in frustration—

T'fyrr began to sing. Softly at first, a song she did not recognize initially, until she realized that he was singing it in a translation so that Theovere would understand it. It was not from any of the Twenty Kingdoms, and she doubted that anyone here had ever heard it but herself before this mo-ment. It was a song T'fyrr had told her had been written by and for the Spirit-Brothers.

"What is courage?" its chorus asked—and the song answered, "It is to give when hope is gone, when there is no chance that men may call you a hero, when you have tried and failed and rise to try again." It asked the same of friendship, answering that "the friend stands beside you when you are right and all others despise you for it—and corrects you when you are wrong and all others praise you for it." There was more, much more, and the more T'fyrr sang, the more the Theovere-spirit took heart. In a strange way, these definitions, intended to guide the Spirit-Brothers of the Haspur as they endeavored to help their own kind and their adopted brothers, were equally applicable to—say—a High King.

With the words, came the *feelings*. Not only the ones called up by the definitions, but the pain-filled emotions, the things that both of them had endured over the past several years at the hands of those who hated and feared anything that did not fit their own narrow definitions of "appropriate." The Theovere-spirit took those in, too, wincing more than a little as he was forced to acknowledge that this was due to his own neglect, but accepting that as well.

He is looking into the mirror again—but this time, he is seeing not only what is, *but what was, and what may be again!*

She simply followed the music with her harpsong, as her heart, this time, followed his.

When it was over, the Theovere-spirit stood up straight and tall, looking many years younger than his true age, his eyes bright again with light and life. A sword appeared from nowhere in his hand; he swept it, silvery and bright, and used it to salute both of them.

And then he faded away into a bright mist.

Oh—NO!

Nightingale dropped back into the outer world with a violent shock.

She stared at the bed, certain that the figure in it was no longer alive. Her eyes blurred with exhaustion, as what seemed to be a hundred people suddenly poured into the room.

She shrank away, waiting for them to seize her, seize T'fyrr, haul them both off into the gaols never to be seen again.

And Theovere slowly sat up with a firm, determined smile set on his face.

The Bodyguards shoved the interlopers rudely away from the bed, and she realized that there weren't a hundred people; there weren't even twenty. Only the Advisors, and who had told *them* what was going on? Most of them seemed to be shouting at the Captain and the Seneschal, both of whom were shouting back.

Her eyes blurred again, and she slid a little sideways, into the comforting embrace of T'fyrr. "What happened?" she asked.

"I'm not sure." He held her closely, his own arms trembling with fatigue. "You did something, and made the shadow go away, then we sang Theovere back, like the Elves said to do—he woke up and spoke, and then all the Advisors began pouring in. I'm not sure how they found out that we were doing anything here."

"It's a good thing they didn't get in until we were done," she said, a bit grimly, as Theovere gained enough strength from somewhere to outshout all of them.

"Silence!" he bellowed. *"Enough!"*

The babble ceased, and he glared at all of them. "We have," he said, clearly and succinctly, his eyes shining with dangerous anger, "a traitor among us. The note that held the—call it a curse—that felled me was sealed with the Council Seal."

Out of the corner of her eye, Nightingale saw the Captain of the Bodyguards go momentarily limp with relief.

But she saw something else as well.

Heading up a contingent of his own private guards and standing at the back of the room was someone who looked oddly familiar to her.

"Who is that?" she whispered to T'fyrr, under the sound of the King's furious but controlled questioning of his guards and his Advisors. "He looks familiar somehow."

He glanced in the direction she was looking. "That's Lord Atrovel," he said. "But you can't have seen him before; he never leaves the Palace, and you never encountered any of the other Advisors except the Lord Seneschal."

Just at that moment, the odd little man moved into a wash of shadow that darkened his hair. She saved herself from gaping at him only by a strong effort of will.

She *had* seen this "Lord Atrovel" before—but not here.

In *Freehold.* And "he" had been—

Violetta. That's Violetta—one of the Great Lords of State—and the biggest gossip in Freehold. Someone who was in a position to know everything that was going on in the King's Chambers, in his private correspondence and *in Freehold—*

And who had the knowledge and the means to sabotage all of it.

And I'll bet he wasn't leading those guards here to protect us if we failed to bring back the King!

"T'fyrr—" she whispered, clutching his hand and turning her head into his feathers to make certain her voice didn't go any further. "Put long black hair on Lord Atrovel and tell me what you get."

She knew by the tension in his muscles that he had seen the same thing that she had. "Violetta—" he whispered.

Then he stood up abruptly, and she scrambled out of his way. She had never seen him like this before—but she *had* seen a hawk about to attack an enemy.

"Violetta!" he roared.

Lord Atrovel started—but so did all the other Great Lords. But none of the others had that look of panic in their eyes—and none of the others had been making his leisurely way toward the door as the King continued to question his Advisors.

T'fyrr launched himself at Lord Atrovel in a fury, and Nightingale was only a second or so behind him. Lord Atrovel's guards scattered, but the

King's Bodyguards came pouring in from the room beyond, alerted by T'fyrr's scream of anger.

T'fyrr reached the traitor first.

He seized the little man in his talons and picked him up bodily. His beak was parted in fury, his eyes dilated, and all Nightingale felt from him was a flood of red rage—

Oh, Lady, no—if he kills the man—

He'll never forgive himself.

No one moved; no one *could.*

T'fyrr held the man for a moment longer, then flexed the muscles of his arms—

And gently set Lord Atrovel down, right into the "welcoming" arms of the Elite Bodyguards.

"I believe that this is the man you have been looking for," T'fyrr said, so gently that he might have been soothing a child. "He frequented Freehold under the name and disguise of 'Violetta,' and likely other places as well. I believe he owns a house in the Firemare quarter, where you will find two or three mages in his employ who held me captive and maimed me—one of them probably set the spell that nearly slew His Majesty. Hunt through his private papers, his suite, and question his servants, and you will probably find a trail of sabotage and evil as vile as the man himself. And you will likely find lace handkerchiefs that match those left by the mysterious gaol-raider. As well as a—" he coughed "—remarkable selection of female garments made in his size, which should explain the missing 'maid' who freed that first captive."

The Captain took custody of Lord Atrovel himself and fired off a burst of orders as the rest of the Lord Advisors scattered like so many frightened quail. T'fyrr ignored them all, turning back to Nightingale.

The terrible rage inside him was gone.

She went weak-kneed with relief as she saw his face, and sensed the calm that now lay within him. *He doesn't need revenge—*

"I don't need revenge," he said softly, echoing her own thoughts, taking her hands in his. "I have you, and I have love. Vengeance is a waste of valuable time."

She smiled up at him tremulously. "It is, isn't it?"

He touched her cheek with one gentle talon. "I know that you don't like cities," he said wistfully, "but—could you consider making your home in one?"

"A home is where the people you care for are," she told him, impossible joy beginning to bubble up inside her. "And if the people I care for live in a city—or the High King's Palace—then that is where my home will be. I think I will survive living in this one."

He laughed, then, and gathered her to him for a long embrace. To-gether, they turned and walked back to the side of High King Theovere, who watched them with a truer smile than any he had worn in Nightingale's memory.

Theovere clasped the hand of the Captain of the Elite Bodyguards, and the stalwart soldier smiled as broadly as his King, with the glint of a tear in one eye.

"Welcome back, my King," was all he said, and then he turned to face T'fyrr and Nightingale. He nodded, still smiling. And as he walked away to tend to his duties, Nightingale heard with some surprise that he was whistling a Gypsy melody, of how all was right with the world.